To / Jerry, and Daisy

WITHOUT RULES

Joseph Mead

Book 2 of the *Aleera* series

Published in 2010 by YouWriteOn.com
Copyright © Joseph Mead
First Edition
The author asserts the moral right under the Copyright, Designs and Patents Act 1988 to be identified as
the author of this work.
All Rights reserved. No part of this publication may be reproduced, stored in a retrieval system, or
transmitted, in any form or by any means without the prior written consent of the author, nor be
otherwise circulated in any form of binding or cover other than that in which it is published and without a
similar condition being imposed on the subsequent purchaser.
Published by YouWriteOn.com

Also in the *Aleera* series:

Tainted Blood

For Grandad

'I do not believe in the immortality of the individual, and I consider ethics to be an exclusively human concern without any superhuman authority behind it.'

Albert Einstein

PREVIOUSLY

In a parallel evolution to that of human beings, draconics- beings with mystical capabilities descend from dragons- exist as a secret society within the human world, along with various offshoots including demons and succubae, with their laws enforced by the Guild of Guardians.

Ten years ago, a murderous demon warlord named Kudra attempted to overthrow the Dragon High Council. After a seven year campaign, Kudra died under as-yet-unknown circumstances; it was only then that the Guild discovered that he had sired a daughter, Aleera, with a succubus named Aysha. After her older half-sister Lilith left New York, Aleera was closely monitored by the Guild for fear of any influence from her father, and came to the attention of Jake Connolly, a roguish and enigmatic freelancer suspected to be far, far older and more powerful than he appears. Damning psychiatric reports attest to the deep psychological damage Aleera has suffered during her life, and she has been left unbalanced and with borderline-psychotic tendencies.

Three years after Kudra's death, Aleera finds herself targeted by Azrael, a psychotic "demon slayer" who belongs to a murderous cult that the Guild originally wiped out centuries earlier. Jake, through subtle "goading" by Guild Sergeant Khazahn, discovers that Chara, the head of the local division of the Guild, has been backing Sword of Heaven's revival as a countermeasure should Aleera ever follow in her father's footsteps, but has now lost what little control he had.

Meanwhile, Jake appears to know more about Aleera than he is letting on, suggesting to his familiar, Katya, that Aleera is part of something greater than she imagines.

Azrael's repeated attacks threaten to worsen Aleera's mental condition. Eventually, he kills two of the people she cares for most deeply, Michael Prince and Sara Lammb, and kidnaps a ten-year-old half-demon girl, losing his mind and wiping out the rest of the cult. Aleera finally tracks down Azrael and kills him with a reserve of powerful dark magic that she has so far remained unaware of. Jake, apparently having been fearing this very event, conceals the evidence from the Guild. Chara and all others associated with the conspiracy, including forensic analyst Harry Drake- until then a trusted ally of Jake and Aleera- are arrested by the High Council.

With her apartment destroyed by Azrael, Aleera moves in with Lilith when her half-sister returns to New York. Jake learns that Khazahn has not only escaped any penalty for his involvement with the events, but also intends to draft Aleera into the Guild by force when she turns eighteen years of age. The partnership between them is soured and Jake's faith in his old "friend" is shaken. He is also aware that whatever power stirred within Aleera is the beginning of something far greater.

Finally, it remains to be seen what damage these events may have done to Aleera's already-worrisome mental state.

1

The first death came during a cool, crisp autumn night in Brooklyn. The first of the three who would die that night was never Mikhail Withnall. He was not, by some measures, a man who deserved to die. He had made… mistakes. Taken wrong turns.

Those turns had led him here, keeping watch outside a crackhouse. In another life, he might never have been there. In another life, he might have looked up in time to see the thing that descended the wall. He might at least have had time to alert the others before the monsters took them as well.

And, in another life, the first mistake, the one that unleashed the horror, might never have been made. A good man would not have done a terrible thing, and many fates would have changed for the better.

In another life, Mikhail Withnall, and the other dead who followed, might have been spared.

But that was another life.

Well, well. No call, no text message, apparently Jake wasn't going to cancel on her for once.

Something taught to every draconic under the age of eighteen under the current ruling High Council was the basics of magic. Magic in itself wasn't actually too hard when the process was understood: as per the law of conservation of energy, energy cannot be created or destroyed; only transferred from one state or location to another. The same applied to magical energy, life force, chi or whatever name was given to it in a given culture.

If one took the opportunity to keep learning after age eighteen, however, the really impressive things could be learned. Jake, being Aleera's appointed tutor by his own interest, had taught her two of these already: one was a basic healing spell, and one was her personal favourite, invisibility. It meant she could get some practice with those retractable wings of hers without attracting any undue attention. Aleera had for all intents and purposes mastered basic offensive and defensive magic years back, but Jake didn't see the harm in teaching her some more advanced tricks. It would be nice if the High Council had the same view, but being the daughter of Kudra quite understandably soured their opinion.

The first knock on Jake's door went unanswered. A few seconds passed, and then it opened.

'Aleera?' Jake blinked, 'what brings you here?'

So, Aleera realised immediately, that was why he hadn't cancelled this lesson. She had a mind that made these connections fairly swiftly. Not for the first time, there was something nagging at her; it was like having a father who'd forgotten to take her to a baseball game.

'The lesson,' she said, knowing already that it wasn't going to happen.

Jake slapped his forehead. 'Oh. God. Sorry. Come in,' he stood back. Well, that was unexpected. She tried to stop herself feeling a little surge of hope as she followed him inside.

The apartment looked the same as ever; for one thing, bigger than she'd have expected. All she'd ever managed to gleam was that Jake had been experimenting with some kind of spell when he "furnished" the place. The living room's most notable feature was still that it seemed full of clutter and strewn papers; Jake, as she knew, practiced the storage system called NCS, or Nearest Clear Surface.

'Sorry I forgot you were coming,' Jake said as he put some papers away, 'just got started on a case yesterday.'

There was a sudden rustling, and Aleera found herself ambushed by a pair of skinny arms that wrapped around her in a bone-crushing hug from behind.

'Hey, kid,' Katya beamed as she let go; apparently ambush-hugs were her favourite use for the stealth that came hand-in-hand with being part-cat. 'Long time no see,' she said, somehow smiling at Katya and glaring at Jake at the same time.

'Ok,' Jake said hastily, 'come on up to the study and we'll get started.'

'Have fun,' Katya smiled as she flipped herself onto the sofa. 'Oh, Jake, can we talk for a second?'

Jake appeared to tense slightly. 'Sure,' he finally said. 'I'll be up in a second,' he said to Aleera. Knowing that it wouldn't be politic to eavesdrop, Aleera followed the familiar path to the study.

'Are you telling her?' Katya whispered. Jake didn't reply. 'For God's sakes, Jake, it's in two fucking months!'

'I know,' Jake hissed.

'How long have you put this off?'

'I'll tell her,' Jake said harshly. 'I'll be down in an hour.' With that, he left and ascended the stairs.

When he arrived in the study, Aleera was there waiting for him. The study was both lined and filled with bookcases, some of which contained beakers, vials and things that even Jake wasn't quite sure how to describe. 'Alright,' Jake said, 'let's get started. We've got some catching up to do, huh?'

'Before we start,' Aleera asked, 'can I ask something?'

'Shoot.'

Aleera found herself biting her bottom lip. Oh lord, this was awkward.

'You've been avoiding me lately,' she finally said. She couldn't think of another way to broach the topic.

'How do you mean?' Jake asked as he tried to feign innocence by taking out an old scripture.

'This is the first time we've spoken in a month,' Aleera said anxiously, 'and you've barely said two words since I got here. You don't want to talk to me, and I can see it.'

Jake appeared to freeze. He turned to her.

'I've been busy,' he said quietly, but he already knew that Aleera wouldn't believe it. Aleera was anything but stupid, and they both knew it.

What Aleera could not be certain of, was why.

'The Azrael thing?' she hazarded.

'No,' Jake said. 'Actually, no. Honest. It… it's something else.'

'What?' Aleera asked.

Jake made to reply, then shook his head. 'Maybe we should do this another time.'

Without a word, Aleera pulled out one of the chairs that sat at Jake's desk, sat down, folded her arms and crossed her legs, not breaking eye contact the entire time.

Jake sighed. 'No,' he said, 'no, we can't do this another time. I should…' he stopped himself in mid-sentence, pulled out a chair and sat down.

'Ok,' Aleera said, 'let's hear it.'

Jake, as he always did, pulled out an old, bronze coin from his pocket and started to turn it over in his fingers. 'Before I say this, he said hesitantly, 'I just want to say that I'm sorry, and the only reason, I swear to God, that I didn't tell you about this sooner was because I care about you, and I didn't want you to have this weighing on you.'

'So it's bad, then.' Aleera didn't bat an eyelid. 'About me.'

Jake nodded slowly.

'The Council?'

'No.'

'Khazahn?'

'Yes.'

Aleera pursed her lips. Jake looked down at the floor.

'Alright: what about Khazahn?'

Jake took a deep breath. He carried on turning the coin over until he held it between two fingers.

'About a month ago,' Jake said slowly, 'the day of Sara's funeral… Khazahn told me something. He said that, because the High Council considers you to be a- a potential risk-'

'I know.' Aleera said bitterly.

'-Khazahn is planning…' Jake exhaled slowly and turned the coin over again.

'Jake?'

'I'm sorry,' Jake said quietly and with as much regret as Aleera had ever seen in him, 'I'm sorry, Aleera, but it's this or a prison cell.'

Aleera felt her stomach starting to gnaw on itself.

'Khazahn,' Jake said, almost in a whisper, 'is planning to draft you when you turn eighteen.'

The room became heavy with silence as the sentence sank in until it was overflowing. Aleera felt a heavy, black pit start to open up in her stomach.

'What?' It seemed like a profoundly stupid thing to say, even at the time. She knew perfectly well what Jake had said, and what it meant.

Jake nodded remorsefully.

'I'm sorry, Aleera.'

Aleera felt her heartbeat. It was like a banging, echoing, infinitely final drum. Her stomach twisted. Her throat tightened.

'Right.'

Maybe she should have reacted… differently. More strongly, perhaps. But the fact of the matter was that she had seen this coming from quite a while back. She was Kudra's daughter. She was a tremendous risk to have walking around purely by genetic whim. They were never just going to let her go free, not from the moment she was legally an adult. No, she couldn't be allowed to make her own decisions, certainly. Oh no, not with her blood. Not because of that thing that she couldn't even help…

She felt powerless. Low. Like a piece of meat.

In a moment, she felt her future slip away. There were things she'd wanted to do; things she'd always… dreamed?... of. Maybe go to college. Graduate, preferably. Maybe work in a restaurant. When she was small, she'd always wanted to open one of her own. That would have been nice.

Oh, God, it was all gone. Her life. All of it. They'd taken her life away from her with the stroke of a pen.

She felt her eyes turn red. She felt her fingernails start to lengthen and darken. The wings tried to push their way out of her back.

She wanted to cry. Maybe she should. She didn't often, not since she was a child. When Michael had died, and Sara. Maybe a normal person would have cried.

Instead, she just felt the anger. How dare they!

And the idiots! Those unbelievable idiots! Take a barely-stable person, take their future from them with a signature and force them into a stressful job for people they hated. Oh, very clever, those absolute…

God, they were taking her damn life away!

With a screaming howl, she grabbed the back of her chair, swung round and threw it into the side of one of the bookshelves. The feeble wooden structure broke as the back of her shirt shredded before spreading black wings.

With another shout, she slammed her claws onto the desk, feeling the wood splinter as she voiced her pouring rage.

Then, as quickly as it had awakened, the screaming thing that had awoken inside her quietened, reason returned, and she was suddenly standing cold, drained and oddly embarrassed. She slumped to the floor, burying her head in her hands. Jake knelt down next to her and slipped his jacket over her exposed form.

Ok, by now she really should have cried. Her eyes should have at least dampened. But Aleera was a practical young lady, and her decision was made soon enough.

'Jake,' she said after a short while, 'please tell me you can fix this, because if you don't then I'm going to kill someone inside of a week.'

Jake shivered slightly. He could tell that this was not an idle remark. 'I'll do something about this,' he promised. 'I'll talk to Khazahn.'

'You haven't done?' Aleera demanded with not-unjustified anger.

'We haven't talked since... well, since he told me. And things at the office got a little nuts yesterday. I'll try and... I'll talk to him.'

'And if he doesn't listen?'

'If he doesn't listen,' Jake promised quietly, putting an arm around her, 'then he'll have both of us to answer to.'

Aleera took a deep, calming breath. She felt more reassured than she probably should have. 'Ok.'

'I'm sorry, Aleera,' Jake said quietly, 'I'll fix this. I promise you.'

Jake closed the door into the office behind him. On the other side of the desk, the Indian man with the dark beard turned his piercing eyes up to him and set down the papers he'd been studying.

'You're on time,' Daeiol said as if this were a great surprise. 'Take a seat.'

Jake sat down and rested his arms against the desk. He didn't bother with indiscretion when he was talking to the head of the entire Guild. The only issue was that he knew how busy someone with that job would have to be, which meant that this would have to be quick and effective.

Daeiol studied him for a moment. 'Khazahn isn't going to be happy about you going behind his back like this.'

Jake shrugged, very deliberately communicating how little he cared about what Khazahn was going to think.

'So,' Daeiol began, 'what can I do for you?'

'Aleera Maheste.'

Daeiol paused. 'That decision was made some time ago.'

'Without me being told,' Jake said coldly.

Daeiol leaned back in his chair. 'Mister Connolly, you are a freelancer,' he said.

'And dealing with Aleera was left in my hands, am I right?' That shut Daeiol up. 'Then a month ago I found out that this decision was made entirely without me.'

'This was the plan from day one,' Daeiol said simply. 'She's Kudra's daughter. She's a liability at best.'

'And you want Kudra's daughter in your organisation?'

'Don't try and call my bluff on this. That girl needs to be where we can keep an eye on her, especially since somebody destroyed all the bugs in her home.' He tented his fingers and gave Jake a knowing look. 'You've become emotionally invested in this case,' he said without emotion.'

'Bullshit.' Daeiol glared at Jake before allowing him to continue. 'You've been happy to let me take care of that situation for the last three years.'

'Yes. And then a serial killer targeted her and killed eight people.'

'You don't get to do this,' Jake pushed the door back open, 'I don't care whose daughter she is; she has rights. You can't just march up to her and say "you work for us now".'

'Why did you come here, Connolly?' Daeiol asked.

'I am asking you,' Jake insisted, 'to leave this with me.'

'And I am telling you that it's too late for that. If you'd come to me a month ago-'

'I did,' Jake interrupted him. 'You told me to come back in a month.'

Daeiol nodded slowly.

'Leave her with me,' Jake said.

'It's already in motion. In two months, Aleera Maheste becomes a Guild employee.'

Jake sat up straight. 'How much does your Guild owe me?' he asked quietly.

'As I understand it, you get a substantial paycheque for every case you're involved in,' Daeiol stated mechanically.

'Not that. How many times have I stopped this whole thing from going under? I didn't go public after the Sword of Heaven mess that one of your people created. I never told a soul that it wasn't your boys that did Kudra in.'

'Your point?'

'Do what I'm asking,' Jake insisted, 'and I call it even. I never call in another favour. I never bother you or your organisation again.'

'I think you're overestimating how large a role you play here,' Daeiol answered, unflinching.

Jake nodded.

'Alright,' he said, 'how about this instead?'

Daeiol listened. Jake made his case. And, after some deliberation, he actually called the High Chancellor herself into the room. They agreed.

Especially when Jake went so far as to mention that other thing they'd inadvertently armed him with.

At the final bell, Aleera quickly made her way there and felt a little rush of excitement. Jake definitely wouldn't be there unless it was for something important; even though she'd always thought that he could probably call. He did seem to have a certain fondness for these cloak-and-dagger routines.

Jake, as ever, was under the bleachers by the football field, leaning against a support beam arms crossed and idly whistling to himself.

'I suppose I'd better get used to seeing you again,' Aleera said to get his attention. 'What's news?'

'Oh, there's news,' Jake grinned like Aleera had never seen before. 'You want the good news or the bad news?'

'You have both,' Aleera noted, 'welcome change.'

'Well the bad news is that you're still going to end up working for the Guild. The good news: it's part-time.'

The world seemed to freeze.

'It's what?' Aleera stared.

'When you start,' Jake said with a grin, 'you're officially my assistant. You help out on my cases and I check on you twice a week. Which also means you'll be out of school, but like I said, only when they want me around.'

Part-time. Aleera actually felt herself smile. Nobody in the Guild was there part-time.

'Pleased?' Jake asked, noticing the grin that was rapidly forming on her face. Then Aleera did something she had never, ever expected herself to, and gave Jake a hug that would most likely lead to severe back problems in a few years.

'Thought so,' Jake laughed into her shoulder, hugging her back and lifting her up off the ground.

'How'd you do it?' Aleera beamed, moving aside some hair that had wound up in her face in the moment of excitement.

'Just had a word with Daeiol and the High Chancellor,' Jake shrugged.

'The High Chancellor?' Aleera repeated. He'd gone that far? The excitement of the moment was all that tempered the surge of anger.

'Yep, and since I'm much-less-strictly bound by all their regulations, I could threaten to do one thing,' Jake explained proudly,

'I threatened to quit. Of course, they wouldn't be that sad to lose me,' he added hastily, 'but it would have allowed me to go public with this and quite a few other things. A human (approximately) rights violation like this gets out, and they come crashing down.'

'You blackmailed the High Council?' Aleera grinned. She felt so giddy that she'd barely listened, but that had managed to get through.

'Blackmail, Aleera, is an ugly word,' Jake mock-lectured. 'Fun, though. I think Daeiol was about ready to eat my head.'

Aleera squeaked. She actually squeaked. In her defence, this had come as a surprise and a very great relief.

'I did try and get you out of it,' Jake brought up awkwardly, 'but it was a little late for that.

'Don't worry,' Aleera said quickly. She'd probably wish it hadn't been too late by the end of the day, but that morning she'd been fully expecting her life to be snatched away from her the moment it really began.

'You start on the twenty-seventh, so it's the Monday after your birthday,' Jake told her. 'Are you celebrating?'

'What do you think?' Aleera said. She hugged him again.

Considering the last three months and what had happened before, it was a genuine thrill to finally get some good news.

Two months passed quickly. The summer was long, dull and dry, and soon chilled into the dreary fall months. Things changed, and other things remained the same.

And somewhere, hidden and unknown, events were set in motion.

One dull September morning found Khazahn at his desk when the phone rang beside him.

'Commander Khazahn's office,' he said, and listened to the voice on the other end of the line. 'We have a what?'

His eyes widened. Some cold, unknown fear washed over him.

'Are you sure? ...Of course. I'll send someone right away.'

He set the phone down. He paled slightly.

This couldn't be what it sounded like. It was impossible. Unthinkable. But if it was true... he forced himself to repress a shudder, picked up the phone again and dialled.

'Get me Jake Connolly,' he said. 'Tell him we've got a job for him.'

2

'Hmm.' Dr. Insley closed the file and adjusted his glasses speculatively. 'Interesting… is she here yet?'

'Just arrived,' Rivers replied from the coffee machine. 'Sad, really. I read the file on her; probably be certified by the time she finishes college.'

'Fascinating case, though,' Insley thought out loud. 'Let's face it; one like this comes along once in a blue moon.' That was true; it was the first opportunity of its kind that he'd encountered in all his years as a Guild psychiatrist. It was just a shame he never got the chance to examine Kudra, or one of that anti-demon cult that was alleged to have surfaced right in the middle of New York. Hopefully he soon would, but even they were more-or-less straightforward cases. That kind of mental state was disgusting, but not complicated. This girl was something of a whole different sort. 'Well, better start, then. Room six, isn't it?' Rivers nodded.

Insley left the break room and proceeded down the hall to Room six. The heavy wooden door rustled against the carpet as he pushed it open.

She was sitting in front of the desk, legs crossed and arms folded. She was certainly a good-looking girl; sleek, black hair that ran down to her hips and contrasted sharply with her pale skin, and her curvy, well-proportioned figure was perfectly flattered by a black blouse and matching jeans. The first thing Insley noticed, though, were her eyes; shimmering chocolate-brown pools that seemed to melt seamlessly into the deep, inky blackness of her pupils. Indeed, she was an attractive- if not stunning- young woman, but more than that, she was a well of potential and a guaranteed placement at Yale after years of dealing with the kind of lunatics the Guild brought him.

'Ms. Maheste,' he said with practiced cheer- but never too much. 'May I call you Aleera?'

Her dark eyes studied him for a second. They flashed cold. Insley felt himself growing uncomfortable. 'If you like,' she finally said levelly.

'Ok. Now, Aleera, do you know why you're here?'

She regarded him again. 'Because the Guild wants to know if I've finally snapped?'

Insley was slightly taken aback. His eyes drifted down to the reports he'd been poring over all morning.

The dark- dark, *dark*- little beauty on the opposite side of the desk was primarily, to him, a once-in-a-lifetime case study, but more than that, the Guild considered her a potential risk, mainly because her father had been the worst mass-murderer in demon history. Indeed, the purpose of the examination was to see if she had, in layman's terms, "snapped". From the sound of it, she would be well within her rights to do so. Her childhood had been one of continuous verbal, physical and sexual abuse, by, as he was rather surprised to learn, both parents. God only knew exactly what had happened to her, but existing reports from when she was fourteen had deemed her as being borderline-psychotic.

Insley felt compelled to believe the report. It wasn't that she was threatening him, not really, just... she was looking right at him, giving him her full attention and staring right into his eyes. He immediately felt as though he was laid bare in front of her, and she disapproved of what she saw.

She was *authoritative*, he realised. Not in a bossy way, but she could make people cower without even trying.

Get a grip, he chided himself. She's a seventeen-year-old, for God's sake!

'Well, not in so many words,' he stammered. 'It's just that we, ah...'

'There are reports saying that I might lose my mind one day.'

Insley gulped. Lord, she'd seen right through him. Obviously, patients did that all the time, but she saw him for what he was, all that he was.

'We just need to determine whether... the recent events...' good, good. Don't name what happened. '...had any sort of impact.'

Eyes like chocolate swimming pools turned to fix his own. Insley suddenly felt like he was staring into a pair of black holes that swallowed every bit of light in the room. Something dark almost seemed to stir inside them. By the time the girl broke eye contact, Insley had forgotten the question, but had thoroughly gleamed that it was an incredibly stupid one that should not be repeated.

'So,' Insley stuttered, 'how does... what happened... make you feel?'

She stared at him again. If anything, it was even darker than the last one.

'Ahem. I see.' Maybe some discretion. Yes, that would do it. He wasn't afraid. Not at all.

'Now,' he asked, hoping that the girl would consider this a little more acceptable, 'what about your discussion a few months ago with Jake Connolly?'

Aleera seemed to become a little tenser, but nothing approaching fear. More like the look one receives after being reminded of an itch they'd just managed to stop thinking about.

'Do you ever feel angry?' Insley pressed on.

Aleera appeared to bite her tongue.

'I haven't turned into a serial killer. I'd like to leave now.' It wasn't a request any more than it was an instruction. It was quite simply a statement.

'Well, it may be in your best interests if-'

'Can I leave?' It was one of those questions to which Insley would reply "yes", whether he wanted to or not.

'I'm sorry,' he found the courage to say, 'but we really need to learn the extent of the... the effects of what happened. I understand from your teachers that you've been somewhat withdrawn lately. More so than usual. Do you have any idea why that might be?'

Aleera fixed his gaze again. 'Because my best friend and my boyfriend were both murdered.'

'I understand that this isn't easy to talk about-'

'Do you now?' Aleera leaned back. Insley hadn't even noticed her move forward.

'Excuse me?'

'I'd like to go now,' Aleera repeated.

'Are you sure you don't think you should talk about this?'

'Maybe I just don't want to talk about it because it's only been three months since the last time I saw my closest friend's body, and you want me to discuss it like a school counsellor after I got into a fight.'

'You need to understand; because of the nature of your previous psyche reports, the Guild feels it necessary to review the effect of what happened.'

'You've already said that, and I do understand.'

'Then why-'

'I'm going.' Aleera made no threat. She didn't raise her voice. She didn't even alter her tone. And yet, Insley knew that if he tried to stop her, his arm would probably cease to remain attached to his shoulder. He didn't say a word as Aleera walked calmly out of his office.

Maybe she'd been hard on him. Oh well. She could talk about what happened and fill in papers when she wasn't seeing burned faces and lifeless eyes every time she slept.

The girl seated with her legs crossed put the magazine down from in front of her face and stood up with a gentle smile. 'How'd it go?'

Aleera had been back living with her sister ever since what, to the best of her knowledge, the Guild was calling "the Azrael killings". Somehow it didn't do the event justice, though this was somewhat biased coming from the person who now couldn't seem to sleep half as much. The way she'd lost Michael and Sara gave her an entirely new reason to wake up screaming in the middle of the night. Lilith had always been good at being there for times like that, even if she was still clearly a little annoyed that her "baby sister" had, over several phone conversations, neglected to mention that she'd been targeted by a psychotic self-proclaimed demon slayer.

And all those humans out there thought demons were bad. They should try being one.

'The same as the last psychiatrist,' Aleera replied as Lilith stood up to leave with her, 'and the one before that.'

'Bad, then. C'mon, let's go. Somebody's got school tomorrow.' As they left, Aleera noticed Lilith cast a saucy stare back at the young man behind the desk.

'You don't stop, do you?' she sighed as they left.

'What? He's cute.'

'The Guild's been sending me here for a week. He's taken.'

'Girlfriend?'

'Boyfriend, actually.'

Lilith thought on this for a moment, and then said 'I can work with that.'

Aleera shook her head and sighed. Three months clearly wasn't long enough to teach a full-blooded succubus that monosexuality is not a myth.

Still, it was nice having Lilith around again; in fact, Aleera would probably have settled for just having someone around. The nightmares had been getting worse lately, even if that did make her sound like a lunatic; which, as she recalled, wasn't that far from the truth. She hadn't slept through the night since she was eleven years old. It wasn't something she should be able to get used to. Lately, she'd been getting worse, and she had a fairly good idea as to why.

She followed Lilith out to her car and got in beside her. As she fastened her seatbelt, Lilith rested both hands on the steering wheel and seemed to stare into space for a moment.

'Have you been to see Leon yet?' she asked.

'I'll see him at work tomorrow,' Aleera replied simply. This hadn't become a favourable topic of conversation for her. Then again, arrangements needed to be made.

One week and counting.

The car, which hadn't exactly been deafening when they got in, seemed to suddenly become even quieter.

'So,' Lilith said with forced brightness as she started the car up, 'what are we doing about dinner?'

Twilight seeped its way into the alleys and the cracks in the pavement. A dull haze seemed to descend on the soul. The city quietened.

Most of it.

She wouldn't refuse him. He knew it. Not tonight. Not while she was walking alone. Even if she said no, he knew what she meant.

She'd scream and she'd cry, but she'd love every second of it. He could feel his breath quickening already. Just wait, just wait…

There she was, just out of work, all long black hair and legs that went on forever. She wanted it. Of course she did. When she dressed like that, how could she not?

'Hey, baby,' he called from his position against the wall, 'you alone tonight, huh? Look at little lost.'

She kept walking. He felt himself well up with anger. That fucking little tease!

'Come on, you wanna maybe come back to my place?'

She started walking faster. He grabbed her arm.

'Let go,' she said. She didn't even raise her voice.

'No, you don't want me to do that,' he said, almost shaking, 'you don't want that, because it's not what I want.' He tugged at her arm. He pulled the gun from his pocket and pointed to the alley. 'In there. Now.'

The girl didn't move.

'I said move!' he roared. She was trying to fight him. Oh, now she'd pay. When he was done with her, oh she'd…

Then, without another word, she walked calmly into the alley. He felt his pulse surge. Yes, tonight was the night…

Except…

Something wasn't right. Why was he scared? Why did everything suddenly seem so quiet?

He pushed her against the wall. She grinned, not even slightly amorous.

'You,' she purred, 'are going to give me such a workout…'

He felt himself grin. Oh, yes… whatever that spark of fear had been, it was forgotten as he started to tug at her top, pushing one hand back and pressing the fingers to the wall with his forearm.

'So,' he breathed, still reeling inside, 'what's your name?'

The girl grinned.

'Aleera.'

There was a sick, wet tearing noise. His arm cried out in pain. He pulled it back and felt the sliced skin. He screamed.

She was actually fighting? His face contorted in fury. That… that stupid little skank! He wrapped his fingers tighter around the gun.

The girl grabbed it and pointed it to the floor. It fired off harmlessly at the same time as her elbow smashed into his face. His nose crumpled. He howled like an animal as she pulled the gun from his grip.

And *then* he knew fear.

He could see it in her face that she wasn't going to shoot him. That wouldn't satisfy her. That little bit of similarity; that was how she knew him for what he was. And from here on, he was *her* plaything.

The gun smacked around his face once, twice, three times. Teeth fell out. Bones broke. Swelling started immediately.

He looked up and screamed. He saw it, unfolding its leathery wings and brandishing its dripping claws. The red eyes held everything. The devil was come, to take him to hell.

His head struck the brick wall. His ribs cracked as she kicked him. Finally, the lid of the trashcan struck his head, and everything was dark.

Aleera dropped the lid and looked down at the bloodied mess in front of her. It was still whining pitifully. Oh, well; it'd serve him right if she killed him.

Oh, now there was an idea.

The claws twitched. Do it, they begged.

Could do.

He had it coming.

That he did.

No sense keeping herself as pent-up as she'd been.

True.

Nobody would ever know.

Again, true.

It would be a public service.

The world would certainly be a better place without murderers and rapists.

He'd have done it to her.

Only fair.

She'd enjoy it.

Oh, how she would.

The claws moved without her permission.

But she shouldn't. *He* would want her to. That dark little thing inside her was what had wanted to, and right now she was in the driver's seat.

That trumped everything.

Aleera retracted the claws and felt the wings slip into her back, not touching the low back of the top. Nice and practical, like a good little sociopath.

'Just remember,' she hissed, leaning down, 'I could have.'

She left the wretch to his swollen face, slashed arm, broken ribs and pathetic sobs.

It was night by the time Aleera got home and climbed as surreptitiously as possible through her bedroom window. This could only be considered an impressive way of sneaking in and out if, as in her case, her bedroom was on the fifth floor. She allowed the bat-like leathery wings to recede, slipping painlessly into the skin of her back and feeling them fold away neatly between her shoulder blades.

She slipped off the halter top she'd gone out in and stepped into the shower. She'd worked up a sweat, and didn't much feel like spending the night that way. A top with a low back, of course, was always good to have when she was going to get the wings out; no sense in letting a perfectly good piece of apparel get shredded to little bits.

Once she was in the shower, she sighed and allowed the cool water to wash over her body, hoping in vain that it might be able to wash away a few other things for the night.

One week to go, and tomorrow she'd been quitting the job that she'd previously have killed for. She didn't even want to think about why. She was in the shower to relieve stress, not make herself even angrier.

Still, she reminded herself, it could have been worse. She still owed Jake a hell of a lot, even if Lilith wasn't about to see it that way.

A week to go. Seven days. One hundred and sixty-eight hours. Ten thousand and eighty minutes. Six hundred and four thousand eight hundred seconds.

That was how long she'd have to wait. Even if she was hardly eager, it was the waiting that she couldn't stand. The sheer slow, dragging frustration of it all.

It was un-damn-bearable, especially to someone like her. She remembered reading that sociopaths had a very low tolerance for frustration, and she should probably have been slightly concerned that she was venting said frustrations by beating a rapist to a pulp in some dank back alley.

But the fire had risen in her chest, and she'd needed to let it out on something, *anything*. Maybe she should start taking karate again.

She finished showering, dried herself and climbed into bed. After resting her head down on the pillow, she settled in and spent the next few hours staring at the ceiling.

A pair of golden eyes turned towards the staircase. The lithe young woman turned over gracefully, with dark catlike ears twitching. 'Morning, sleepyhead,' she sang.

'Mrning,' Jake groaned as he pushed back his messy hair. He still had bags under his eyes and was still arranging a dusty gown. 'Whattimeisit?'

Katya checked her watch. 'About twelve.'

'Twelve?' Jake squinted, starting to wake up. 'You let me sleep until twelve?'

'It's the first time you actually slept through the night in five weeks. Do I even want to know what you've been doing in that study?'

'Research,' Jake answered as he slumped down onto the sofa.

'Which is your way of saying "stop asking, Katya" without actually having to say "stop asking, Katya". Fine,' she flipped herself over the back of the sofa with practiced fluidity, 'you want some breakfast?'

'Just some toast,' Jake said, now fully alert, 'I'll get it.'

'The hell you will. I cook, you clean, and you are not worming your way out of cleaning this dump,' Katya scolded from the kitchen. 'See? Perfect example.' A piece of ancient parchment covered in ancient writing landed on the seat next to Jake. 'Next time, I'm keeping it.'

There was a brisk knock at the door. 'I'll get it,' Jake called, standing up and wondering who it was. "Not Khazahn" was his favourite possibility. They hadn't spoken since the incident and Jake was fine with keeping it that way.

'Hey, boss,' it was Makian who greeted him on the other side of the door. The young Indian man's black hair was still gelled into spikes, but oddly enough he looked more… composed. It was the suit, Jake realised. The suit that was standard public disguise for any active Guild soldier.

'Hey,' Jake greeted as they bumped fists, 'you're back on duty?'

'Yeah, got reassigned two months ago; you wouldn't believe how much the Council's been shaking the place up. Long time no see, man, you look-' he glanced up and down, 'Ok, I'm not gonna lie, you look like crap, but I was sent to pick you up.'

'Without calling?' Jake asked levelly.

'It's not my fault you don't know where your phone is,' Katya shouted from the kitchen.

'Well that explains that,' Makian shrugged.

'So who sent you?'

'Khazahn.'

Jake scowled. 'What does *he* want?'

'Last time I checked, you're still a freelancer. So my guess is he wants you to do some freelancering.'

Jake groaned and leaned against the doorway. 'And I should do a damn thing for him because…?'

'…Because you get paid for it?'

Jake sighed. 'Let me get dressed,' he said achingly as he stepped back.

'No problem, I'll wait,' Makian nodded as he turned around. Before he could even blink, Jake stepped past him, fully dressed in jeans, a T-shirt and a jacket. He blinked, pulling his head back for a moment.

'Ok, seriously, you need to stop doing that; one day you're just gonna end up flashing a crime scene.'

'You should've been here the first time he tried it,' Katya said shrewdly as she followed them out. With a quiet utterance of *ThraioPhouxSola*,' her catlike ears vanished from view and her eyes turned to a more passable shade of green, while she placed a slice of buttered toast in Jake's hand so as to leave no doubt that he wasn't going anywhere without breakfast.

'Any idea what this is about?' Jake asked as they set off. The old, dingy corridor that led to his apartment, filled with cracked walls and dripping pipes, hardly conjured the image of the spacious apartment that Jake had half-bought, half-rented and half-conjured out of thin air. The three stepped into the elevator, lurching slightly as it shuddered down past the closed, rusted gates.

'All I got was that it was nasty, and Khazahn's shitting bricks, not least because one more clusterfuck like the Azrael mess and the council's ready to tear through the whole division.'

'So there's the chance of that happening?' Jake discerned, 'how bad is this?' The elevator chimed to a stop, and the doors grated open.

In the street, Makian's car sat by an old fire hydrant. 'Wow,' Katya observed, 'Audi. Nice.'

Jake nodded, glancing over the sleek black body of the car. 'That's the one thing teleporting makes me miss,' he breathed. 'How much did they shuffle things round?'

'You're looking at *Lieutenant* Makian,' Makian beamed, 'who's been saving up his pay for the last nine months and got compensation since a now struck-off Commander nearly cost him his job.'

'So where's the party?' Katya asked as she and Jake climbed into the back of the car, admiring the leather seats.

'Some shithole in Brooklyn,' Makian shrugged. 'And like I said, Khazahn sounds pretty worried, so… yeah. You've been warned.'

The drive took about an hour thanks to some exceptionally heavy New York City traffic. When they finally arrived, the old apartment building was exactly as Makian had so coarsely described it. The entire place was a peeling, dry, dark husk of a building that looked like it had been through at least three fires.

In one of the empty shells that served as rooms, what looked to the naked eye like white-clad forensic specialists were huddled around three white tarps at random positions around the room. Jake could easily guess what was under each one.

'Two seconds,' Makian waved them back as he stepped over to a far too familiar man with dark hair greying at the temples.

'Is it just me,' Katya said discreetly after noticing the way Jake was glaring at Khazahn, 'or does Makian seem a little…'

'More professional?' Jake hazarded.

'I was gonna say more bearable.'

Khazahn looked up to them. The look in his eyes wasn't friendly. 'Jake,' he said curtly, 'welcome back.' He said something quietly to a nearby soldier and then walked over. 'It's been a while since your last pay check, hasn't it?'

'Let's just get to work,' Jake said icily. 'I'm counting three of these guys.'

'One more upstairs. The Council's going to tear us apart if we don't deal with this one properly.'

'They're direct these days,' Jake noted. 'Who's running the division now?' he asked, noting how long he'd been out of the loop.

Khazahn looked up from some papers that Jake hadn't seen him pick up. 'Makian didn't tell you?'

'Hey, you're his Guild contact,' Makian raised his hands defensively.

'Which means?' Katya arched an eyebrow.

'Which means Khazahn gets to tell him the big news, and I get to keep my head attached to my neck where I like it.'

'What news?' Jake asked darkly, before the realisation dawned on him. 'Please don't tell me…' he buried his forehead in his palm.

'They needed someone to replace Chara,' Khazahn replied emotionlessly.

'They didn't have someone better?' Jake seethed.

'What do you mean by that?' Khazahn glared.

'I mean "someone who wasn't involved in the deaths of eight-"'

'*So*,' Katya wisely cut in, gently tugging Jake away from Khazahn, 'the, uh, the case, or whatever we're here for?'

Jake stepped back slowly, giving Khazahn a stare that said "I am not going to forget this. Ever."

'Just cool it,' Katya whispered as Khazahn led them over to the bodies.

'Eight people died, Katya,' Jake said hoarsely, 'a young woman was nearly murdered in front of us, this division got torn apart and a ten-year-old girl is still in therapy. And he just rides the whole thing to a big, fat promotion,' he spat disgustedly.

'Jake just- just- forget it.'

'"Forget it"?'

'For now, Ok? Just let it be while we deal with this.'

Jake took a deep, resentful breath. 'Fine.'

'Well hello, smiler.' Jake spun round to a much more welcome face.

'Dr. Tomoko Shinju,' he let himself smile. 'How's life in lab-coats?'

'Slow, until this. Makes me wish they'd assign someone else to forensics.'

'It's just you?'

'For now. It's amazing how hard it is to find a qualified draconic in this city, and don't get me started on demons in the department. The Azrael mess set that back a good ten years.'

'I turn my back on you kids for one second,' Jake quipped quietly as they knelt down. 'You're in a good mood, I notice.'

'Just trying to get some levity in,' Tomoko replied as she gripped the sheet with a gloved hand, 'because things are about to get very serious, very fast.'

She pulled back the sheet.

Jake paled. Katya gagged. Makian grimaced. Three agonisingly long seconds drifted by.

'Shit.'

The remains that lay frozen, features twisted into a nightmarish, cavernous scream, arms still raised in desperate defence, were less of a body than a husk. The skin was dark and ashen, but a shade of dark that had been pale and simply come back out another way, withered to nothing but a dry, hard shell clinging to the bone. But the face was still the worst, still screaming madly, dead, dry eyes still frozen in a last nightmare that could only have come from the most awful death.

Now if only the nature of the body was the problem.

'This is a joke, man,' Makian finally said. 'This is all just some ass thinking this is a sweet joke, right? I mean, this… this is… *fuck*.'

'Jake,' Katya whispered anxiously, 'is this what it looks like?'

Jake nodded slowly. 'Any I.D.?' he asked, somehow without emotion yet with desperation clawing at his chest at the same time.

'Three demons and a draconic,' Makian answered, 'small-timers. It looks like someone was peddling something through here. Poor dumb bastards.'

'Time of death?'

'About two this morning.'

Jake stood up and held out his hand. Quietly, he whispered *'PhoaLiah.'*

The air remained still. The spell Jake had just employed should have pulled in any ambient magic; the kind that remains after the death of a draconic. A long moment passed, and nothing happened.

'Not a trace,' Jake finally said. 'That settles it: it has to be.' He looked gravely down at the husk's frozen, screaming face.

'Wraiths'.

3

History has a way of repeating itself. As the old saying goes, "those who do not learn from history are doomed to repeat it", and as Aleera had observed a number of times, something that people were not, on the whole, good at was learning. They learned the basics, although for some of them even that was a struggle, but when it came to the really important things... well, not so much.

Sometimes it repeats itself in the big ways; the terrible ways. The ways that make the soul feel like a curse. Those who don't learn from one act of evil carried out their own, and cruelty was one of those things that really was blind. But it also repeated itself in the small ways.

Christians in Ancient Rome could not publicly show their faith; well, they were physically capable of doing so, and more-or-less all of morality is about differentiating between what you *can* do and what you *should* do. Ancient Christians *could* show their faith, but knew they *shouldn't* because if they did, the Romans would round them up and feed them to the lions. So they developed a secret call sign: a way of recognising one another. One Christian would draw an arc in the sand in his toe, and the other would complete it, creating the image of a fish, for Jesus said to his disciples: "I will make you fishers of men".

Then, of course, Jesus was crucified. Someone came along and told them to be nice to each other for a change, and they didn't listen. A few centuries down the line, they were still pretending they had done, that they didn't judge, etcetera, etcetera, and then they decided that, in the name of their victim who had encouraged them not to judge, they'd decided to have some Crusades.

If they really had learned their lesson, there would be no need for that part of history to repeat itself.

Draconics, crafty little hidden beings of the supernatural, knew that they shouldn't publicly show what they were capable of it. Around a species that shot each other in the head over the pigmentation of skin cells, it just didn't sound like a sensible idea. So they had a secret call sign; one that wasn't learned, but evolved. They could not only use magic, but feel it, taste it in the air.

So when Aleera walked into school one brisk Monday morning and tasted that burning-copper taste in the air, she knew something very personal about the new student the second they met.

The important thing to remember about draconics, demons, etcetera, and the main reason they'd never been discovered, was that there was outwardly nothing overly spectacular about them. That didn't mean there was nothing interesting about any of them; Aleera herself, being half-succubus, had, like most members of that species, less of a body and more of a work of art, and of course her eyes did that irritating turning-red thing whenever she was stressed. There was also that tiny scar on her forehead and two more on her right shoulder and hip that she'd required during a… difficult time about three months back.

Then again, while *mostly* not externally amazing, there were a few, including Aleera herself, who had one very special talent. While most of what humans believed about magic didn't so much miss its mark as leave the arrow stuck in a barn five miles away, there was something to the whole wings thing.

The new arrival was of Aleera's age and, as no half-succubus could avoid noticing, rather pretty, with tanned skin and light-brown hair tied back, a few strands framing a pair of blue eyes. While of course no draconic or demon went around in an "I'm-a-magical-being" t-shirt, the girl's attire was rather distinctive in its own way; a sky-blue spaghetti-string top and matching shorts with a bubblegum-pink belt and sneakers, all of which seemed to give off an air of childlike innocence that was universally an alien concept to succubae.

The time and place of their first meeting was apparently to be the school cafeteria, where Aleera was finishing a typically stale macaroni and cheese. As someone who'd always held a vested interest in cooking, Aleera was quite confident that she could do better; but then again, so could a monkey with a ladle in its teeth and severe learning disabilities. Hmm; she'd been back at school for about two weeks and she was already comparing the staff to animals. She'd lasted longer this year.

'Mind if I sit here?' the newcomer asked. Aleera had been eating alone and hadn't actually heard her arrive.

'It's a free lunch room,' she said before she returned to her food and idly watched the girl take a seat. She turned curiously to Aleera and appeared to examine her for a moment.

'Wow. I was actually starting to think I was the only one here.'

'I know the feeling,' Aleera replied.

'Well, I'm Jasmine. Jasmine Taylor. Just started here.'

'Give it a week,' Aleera shook her head in mock dismay, 'you'll wish you hadn't.'

'Nah. Can't be that bad.'

'Oh, believe me, it can.'

'Well, you know how to make a girl feel welcome,' Jasmine observed. 'So can I stay or will you just suck my blood?' Aleera looked up at her with a "don't-repeat-that" expression. 'Ok, never mind, I'll go.'

Manners, Aleera reminded herself. People skills had never been her best ones.

'No, I'm sorry,' she sighed, 'bad day. I'm-'

'Aleera Maheste?'

Unexpected. 'Yes.'

'Your reputation precedes you.'

'And yet you're still sitting next to me,' Aleera commented. 'Brave of you.'

'Well, it's always nice to meet another draconic. Makes for better conversation.'

'I suppose,' Aleera shrugged. 'Can't exactly discuss magic here; well, I suppose you *can*.'

'Actually, I tried once,' Jasmine recalled.

'Seriously?'

'Yup. He just thought I was a Goth. Some guy in white makeup tried a bad pickup line two weeks later. I love humans,' she giggled inwardly. So did Aleera, truth be told. They made her feel better about herself.

Offhand, she glanced at Jasmine's outfit. It hardly looked gothic.

'Mind if I steal some of that?' Jasmine asked. Aleera nodded, and she helped herself to a forkful of macaroni. 'Yech.'

'I know.'

'No worse then my last school,' Jasmine shrugged. 'Love the waistcoat, by the way.'

Aleera glanced down at herself, having quite honestly forgotten what she had on. The black waistcoat was her favourite piece of attire; she'd had it tailored to be low at the back so as to allow her wings out when necessary, but it still covered the front nicely. Hardly expecting a fight of the supernatural persuasion today, she'd worn it over an ordinary blouse.

'Thanks,' she said, admittedly taken aback somewhat by a genuine compliment. 'I like the…' she fished for a word to describe Jasmine's ensemble.

'Thanks,' Jasmine smiled, 'made it myself.'

'You made it?' Aleera looked over the clothing again. She'd never have known it was home made.

'Kind of a hobby. So what's this place like?' Jasmine asked idly.

'School,' was Aleera's all-encompassing answer. 'Boring, tedious, and we're the only two draconic students here; well, I say "draconic"…'

'Demon?' Jasmine hazarded.

'Half.' Aleera always left out exactly what the other half was. Oddly enough, "hello, I'm a sex demon" was not considered the best of introductions.

'Cool. So do you ever, y'know, any magic?' Some part of Aleera noticed that Jasmine showed positively no reaction to finding out she was talking to a demon. Even though they weren't the hellfire-and-brimstone nether-monsters that humans tended to think of, they still didn't get the best press.

'A little. You?' Wow. This was probably Aleera's first conversation in a month that hadn't been with Lilith or a psychiatrist.

'Meh, lame stuff.' What had been a surprisingly pleasant conversation for Aleera- who tended more often to send people heading for the hills- was interrupted by the ringing of the bell. 'Well, gotta go. Do we have any classes together?' Jasmine pulled out a timetable.

Aleera checked. Math, English, Biology and History, as it turned out. They parted for the moment, and then Aleera saw something flying through the air.

She caught the fork expertly between two fingers. With her kind of upbringing, a thorough knowledge of self-defence was a necessity. Less fortunately, she immediately felt the hot flush of anger towards the excuse for a creature that thought he could take a shot at her whenever he wanted, that filthy…

No. Stop it. Control yourself.

The tide of anger rose further. Aleera pushed it back down.

Without making a show of it, she threw the fork into a trashcan and turned her dark eyes to the source.

'You Ok?' Jasmine asked from the doorway.

'Yeah, just some idiot,' Aleera said.

It was still scowling at her from across the room, its face contorted in outraged fury. Well, well: Jamie Shane, the brother of that little wretch that had given her so much trouble towards the end of the last school year. They'd actually let him back in, and it seemed he hadn't learned.

Aleera could have made a mocking gesture, just a nice smirk would do. Instead, she did the one thing that always angered people even more, and left without a second look.

It was amazing how little people could change, Aleera thought, over three months.

Then again, one's circumstances could change enough in that timeframe. She ought to know, after all.

One week to go, she reminded herself, and she'd be a fully grown-up, eighteen-year-old Guild soldier.

She made a brief detour to the bathroom and splashed two handfuls of cold water over her face. She could see the bags under her eyes; hardly surprising, since she had not at all been sleeping well. It had been just about two months now since that conversation, and her eighteenth- lucky her- was exactly one week from today.

After getting herself ready the previous night, it had been straight to work; she'd been lucky, she reflected, in managing to get a job she rather enjoyed. While officially she was still employed just to do the dishes in the kitchen of a café owned by Leon, an Italian man who was surprisingly pleasant once you got past the gut and the body odour, on one occasion when the head chef had been off sick, Aleera had helped fill in. Leon had tasted her cooking and swiftly started paying her extra to help with the dish of the day at weekends. Last night, he'd noticed as Aleera had barely stopped herself from pouring salad cream into a pizza mix.

She seemed distracted, he'd said, and asked if something was wrong. She evaded the question by saying she was just tired. She was going to have to quit the job, she'd realised some weeks ago, and probably school as well. The saving grace in that respect, of course, had come later. Still, in light of what was looming over her, she had more than enough reason to be stressed.

Frankly, a small part of herself that had no sense of perspective was starting to miss Azrael.

4

Rule Number One of the Guild of Guardians was, above all else, to keep the secret. To that end, everything was geared toward secrecy: every investigation, every action, was hidden from the human beings that could never know they existed. Most importantly, their headquarters were hidden expertly, as the best-kept secrets are maintained: just as with every draconic and every demon, the Guild hid itself in plain sight. The headquarters of the Eighth Division, the intricate, dragon-carved labyrinth of chambers, was situated immediately below Times Square, under the Flat Iron Building itself, right in the middle of New York City.

Jake Connolly was now wandering around the place on a late Monday night grudgingly spent in the office.

It was a good place to think, Jake thought as he wandered through the carved pillars of the cavernous central hall that branched off into all other areas.

This Aleera thing had been weighing on his mind lately, and would take some getting used to for both of them. Whether Aleera was still angry at him, he didn't care to guess.

A stone door grated open behind him. 'Hey, boss,' Makian called, 'how's life in the fast lane?'

'I'll let you know when I find the on-ramp,' Jake shrugged. 'I miss anything?'

'Ah.' Makian winced. 'Um… Tomoko wants to talk to you. She's dug something up on the- ahem- the Wraith killing.'

'Already? What did she find?'

'She can tell you,' Makian nodded back into the autopsy room. Jake shrugged and followed.

When people thought of a supernatural society, it probably conjured images of great stone altars, dribbling candles, pentagrams, dusty old texts and bubbling cauldrons. Not so much the modern, pristine autopsy lab with the short, white-coated Japanese woman checking her findings for the hundredth time.

'We've got something?' Jake asked as he entered from one side of the room.

'Actually, Makian found it,' Tomoko said. 'Right, Makian?' She sounded a little too ready for him to say it instead of her.

'Uh…' Makian bit his tongue, 'you can tell him.'

'Why not you?'

'Because I'm calling "not it",' Makian wiped the air with his palms. 'Dude talked to Aleera. I'm not telling him a thing. You tell him.'

'So this is something that I won't like,' Jake said.

'I'm not telling him,' Katya spoke up, sitting sideways on a chair, 'I have to live with him.'

Tomoko sighed. 'You are all five years old,' she muttered before addressing Jake. 'We managed to identify our small-timers and, more importantly, who they worked for.'

'Alright,' Jake said hesitantly, 'that doesn't sound bad.'

'Because she hasn't finished,' Makian spoke up. 'You see, Jake, you're not gonna like this however it's said, so Tomoko's just going to come right out and say it.'

Tomoko glared daggers at Makian and finally turned back to Jake.

'The dealers were part of a drug racket being run by a demon crime lord.'

Jake made an immediate connection between two parts of that sentence. His eyes narrowed.

'Kheron,' Tomoko confirmed.

Jake stood still for a moment. 'Ah.'

'Turns out that the basement of the place was stuffed with uncut dust,' Makian began, 'looks like your old buddy's been making some bad deals or something, because what wraiths want with that, we couldn't say. So now we just need to get the warrants from-' he paused. 'Did you meet the new boss yet?'

'Nope,' Katya shook her head to match the quick reply.

'Oh, right,' Makian groaned, 'you're gonna love this one. C'mon.'

Katya stood up to follow Jake and Makian out of the autopsy room and into the massive stone corridor. Makian suddenly stopped and indicated to the approaching figure.

'Daeiol put him in charge of D-Unit,' he whispered, 'transferred him from Detroit; he was in charge there.'

Jake froze. He turned slowly to Makian.

'Daniel Cassidy?' he hissed.

'The same.'

'Anyone gonna tell me who Daniel Cassidy is, or should I just go along with the whole blind-panic thing?' Katya cut in.

'I'll tell you later,' Jake said quickly.

The man clearly was at least as snappy a dresser as Khazahn; a navy-blue sweater under a long, black leather jacket and matching flares. Dirty-blonde hair was worn un-styled and he pulled a pair of dark glasses down from a pair of piercing, faded blue eyes.

'Jake Connolly,' he said, casting a scalpel of an eye over the freelancer, 'your reputation precedes you.'

'And yours,' Jake said as he shook his hand. 'Daniel Cassidy, right?'

'Pleasure.' Cassidy's eye turned to Katya. 'And this is…?'

'Katya,' she introduced herself. 'Jake's familiar.'

Cassidy looked disapprovingly from her to Jake. He appeared about to say something, but clearly managed to restrain himself. 'I see,' he said flatly. 'This is my first contact with you since I took over here, I believe.'

'Been a hell of a three months,' Jake said. An odd heaviness seemed to have settled into the air.

'Well, this is certainly an investigation that calls for it,' Cassidy said, 'four dead demons and wraiths running around the city. Let's hope this lead of yours turns something up,' he said, turning to Makian- the first time Jake had seen him do so- and handing him a few papers. 'And this Kheron character I've heard so much about?'

'Don't remind me,' Jake said icily.

Something dark crossed Daniel Cassidy's face. 'Right,' he said quickly, 'yes. Well, time's of the essence. I'm sure you've heard, but the word of the day around here is "by the book". No more incidents like the last one, yes?'

The new Sergeant walked away without a sideways glance.

'And that was…?' Katya probed.

'*Sergeant* Daniel Cassidy,' Makian muttered. 'London man by birth, then special-ops in Detroit. Brought down a drug cartel run by one of Kudra's old guys; practically sent the whole thing crashing down himself. Dude's like a rock star. Just got assigned.'

'Assigned,' Katya repeated with pretend thought. 'Close to the word I was thinking of.'

'Tell me about it,' Makian sighed, 'half the place can't breathe. Word is, he's not in love with the idea of demons in the department either. Lieutenant last week got the axe and all she did was fill out a warrant wrong.'

'So "prick",' Katya surmised. 'And we're working for this guy now?'

'Until we get someone new,' Makian shrugged. 'Fingers crossed.'

Jake nodded and fished his old coin out of his pocket, turning it over in his fingers. He was already getting a distinct feeling that, by the time this case was over, he was going to wish he hadn't been involved in it.

Besides, if the Guild had called him in, then the other half of the arrangement meant one thing: Aleera was to be onboard as well.

5

For the hundred-thousandth time, Aleera woke up screaming.

After a moment, the dark room came into view, and the wave of fear subsided.

Michael and Sara again, dying in front of her while *he* laughed and scorned her.

Ok. Calm down now. Get a grip, she ordered herself. She did this often enough. It was over. Just a dream. Nothing to fear. Just relax, take a deep breath, it was just…

Calm down, Goddamnit!

It should have been working. It always worked, as long as she could remember. Now, not so much. Calm down, she told herself. It was over.

She'd never really known grief since Michael and Sara, considering that the only other person connected to her who'd ever died was the man she still spent every waking minute hating.

The memories of those psyche evaluations came drifting back to her. "Psychologically unstable". "Antisocial tendencies". "Borderline-psychotic possibilities." That last one had always been a personal favourite. She was just unstable enough to be some kind of lunatic murderer, and just stable enough not to be. It was nice to feel special sometimes.

Detached, as well. The detached thing always helped. It was useful to make decisions and, more than anything else, unnerve annoying psychiatrists. But then came the worst two weeks of her life, and during that time she'd just begun to realise what she really was, and what, to one of them, she could have been.

After spending her whole life not feeling much of anything except blind rage, all that love and grief came as quite a shock.

And just to point out, a nagging train of thought piped up, you're describing the deaths of two people you loved as "quite a shock".

Slowly, she became aware of the cold dampness of the T-shirt she'd worn to bed and the smell coming from her body. Her forehead trickled with cold sweat.

Her wings folded instinctively around her. Mercifully, since she'd started using a duvet instead of thin sheets during the colder months, the wings didn't rip her bedspread to pieces when they came out anymore. Sighing irritably, she felt them slip painlessly back into the skin of her back as she pulled off the remains of the shirt.

'Aleera?' Lilith called, knocking gently, 'are you Ok?'

'Yeah,' Aleera replied, climbing out of bed, 'just a dream.'

Aleera was long-since used to not sleeping through the night; having not done so since the age of eleven, she'd more-or-less accepted it as the norm.

It was close to five a.m., so there would be no point in trying to sleep again. She had a long day of school to put up with and a lesson with Jake after that; provided he wasn't going to cancel *again*. It would be, she recalled, the first time they'd met in a month. She couldn't really blame him if he was avoiding her.

Once dressed, she "treated" herself to a breakfast consisting of a few slices of toast coated in her single greatest vice: lashings of honey, the perfect comfort food. No, drink, no drugs, but she allowed herself this one vice: honey was the perfect mood-elevator to keep a barely-stable young demon going.

'Be back later,' she said as she grabbed her book-bag.

'Have fun, baby sis,' Lilith smiled and kissed her on the forehead. She still insisted on calling her that, and Aleera had given up trying to change it, 'I'm sure I can keep myself entertained until then.'

'Oh, yeah?' Aleera said knowingly, 'who're you seeing today?'

'Haven't decided yet. See you at five.'

After Aleera left, Lilith looked down at a letter buried under a small pile of sticky-notes and bills by the phone. She picked it up, opened it and read it, her exquisite face turning into a grim frown, before she crushed the paper into a ball and threw it into a trashcan.

Lilith's new apartment was, as it happened, only down the street from Aleera's high school. The place- unfortunately- hadn't changed over the summer and was still just as grey and dull as ever.

Sadly, other things hadn't changed either, as Aleera noticed as she passed by the bike racks. Jamie Shane was hanging around with a few of his semi-sentient friends. She recalled that Gregory Smith wasn't with them, so that made at least some subtle difference. She idly wondered what became of him.

'Hey,' Jamie laughed, nudging a fellow idiot, 'check this out. Hey, bitch!' Seemed he'd noticed her passing. 'Hey!'

Aleera idly glanced in his direction.

'How many people can you fit in an SUV?'

Aleera slowed to a stop. She'd heard this joke before, and that blood-red river of rage inside her was begging for release on the chance that he may be going where she expected.

'Three in the back,' Jamie said. His fellow morons collapsed into fits of joke/drug-induced giggles. 'Three in the front,' he shook, containing his laughter, 'and your fucking boyfriend in the ashtray!'

The others never had a chance to laugh, before Jamie Shane's face was smashed into the railings, and Aleera, screaming and red-eyed, kicked and pounded at him as he snarled in pain. One of the others made a grab for her and received an elbow to the face for his troubles. Aleera swung Jamie away and delivered a solid, smashing punch to his face.

This time, she wasn't even thinking about calming down. It wasn't an option to be considered. He could take all the shots at her he might feel like, that stupid little bastard, but Michael... oh, no. Not that. If he even... if he *dared*...

That filthy, slimy little piece of shit!

Jamie Shane, his cocky laughter gone, was screaming and pleading by the time two teachers, with a great deal of effort, pulled Aleera away from him.

Well, that had been embarrassing. Losing it was one thing. Half the city's back-alleys were crawling with people who deserved to be on the business end of it. But going completely off the wall like that, in front of that many people... imagine being caught having sex in the locker room, only a lot more personal.

'You scratched his face,' the principal repeated. Ms. Wood, Aleera's favourite I-hate-kids-but-I'm-a-teacher, stood beside the desk. 'Do you have any idea how close you came to taking his eye out?'

Aleera had a hundred replies to that, mostly insinuating the point that, whatever damage she did up to and including cutting his undeveloped balls off, it would be entirely too good for him. But she was embarrassed, and more importantly angry enough to take the school apart with her bare hands if it really came down to it. She didn't listen to much of what they had to say- something about a week of detentions that she probably wouldn't go to- and left the office, slamming the door nice and hard.

Jamie Shane was sitting on one of the chairs outside the office, holding an ice pack to his cheek. Part of Aleera immediately screamed with questions of why he got an ice pack for something he brought on himself, and all that Aleera got was grief and that idiot kicking her in the stomach.

Shane looked up. He glowered.

'You think you're pretty fuckin smart, dontcha bitch?' he shouted loud enough for everyone to hear. 'Yeah, real smart, real tough, gets my brother sent to fuckin prison!' Oh, so that was where Ryan was, among his own kind at last. 'Yeah, you got guts, dontcha?' he pushed her.

He snarled like an animal, ready for its prey to fight or flee.

'I didn't get anyone sent anywhere,' Aleera said levelly as she walked past him without interest.

She took a calming breath as she stepped out into the relatively fresh air- fresh being as relative a term here as anywhere, as she must have walked through about three clouds of smoke.

'So what was that about?' a voice asked from one side as she passed the outer wall of the gym. Jasmine moved away from the wall to join her. 'I mean, did you really…?' she visibly fished for an expression.

'Not on purpose.'

'I heard you knocked his brother out.'

'That was on purpose,' Aleera admitted with surprising ease.

During their lessons together, Aleera and Jasmine had hit it off surprisingly well; being the only two people in the school of roughly the same species did that, apparently, or maybe because it was the first real conversation Aleera had partaken in with someone she wasn't related to in months. Or maybe it was just that Jasmine was one of those naturally friendly people among whom Aleera did not number. Whenever she moved, it seemed to be with an excitable energy. And she was always wearing those cute little outfits like this green-and-white number with…

Oh, don't you start that, she chided herself.

'What did he do, anyway?' Jasmine asked.

'Insults, switchblades, chunks of marble; take your pick.'

'A chunk of marble?' Jasmine parroted disbelievingly.

'He was an idiot.'

'Yeah, well that seems to be how most of the guys around here act,' Jasmine observed. 'Probably that perfume. I'm gonna go get something to eat; you coming?'

'I'll meet you there,' Aleera said, rather hurriedly all of a sudden, 'I need to get something from my locker.' She walked off quickly in the other direction.

She shouldn't be worried about it. She'd only just met Jasmine, and with Michael and Sara it had taken-

Not very long at all. She'd just been too wrapped up in her own problems to see it for too long.

The thing was, neither of them had ever commented on perfume or anything like it. Aleera didn't wear any.

The one thing she just might smell of was what any succubus did.

Pheromones.

Oh. Shit.

It was now well into Tuesday afternoon, and despite everything Aleera looked forward to the weekend as much as anyone else. It gave her the chance to be in the company of people who had two brain cells to rub together, even if it was just her sister. The portly biology teacher had tried to get across the subject of animal reproduction without people making some kind of lewd comment and giggling, clearly thinking that what they'd said was amazingly invented. There was a girl in Aleera's geography class, name of Cathy- one of those pretty airheads that plan to trade on their looks for as long as possible. She had a nice laugh, but she was a little too much on the dim side to be Aleera's type; she'd proved that when Aleera told her what veal was, and she'd responded with 'everybody knows cows lay eggs.' Half the class had laughed. Aleera had wondered why the idiot species was not yet extinct, and why nothing was being done about it.

Currently, it was the last lesson of the day, History, and Aleera was still feeling extremely stressed; and as many a report had attested, she didn't have much of a tolerance for it. She was leaning on one hand and tapping a pencil on the desk. From a few randomly-placed moments of attention, she'd gleamed that the history teacher was in the process of giving people assignments to be worked on in pairs.

'Gregory and Isobelle, you will present a report on Roman agriculture,' the teacher recited, choosing the names from the register. 'Jasmine and… let's say Aleera. You can give a report on Roman politics.

Needless to say, it all came rushing to mind immediately.

As the history teacher dismissed the class, Aleera tried to tell herself that her worry was unfounded. Maybe Jasmine had smelled something else, or nothing at all. The pheromones had never been detectable before; they never were for anything other than a full-blooded succubus. Lilith, she realised, might be the person to ask; it was hard to be embarrassed with her.

Or maybe there'd be nothing to ask about. She'd certainly picked a fine time to start being paranoid.

Being a succubus came with a few added features; a hell of a body in most cases, inherent bisexuality (to give what was essentially a sex-feeding demon a wider spectrum of "prey", presumably) and the emission of some very focused pheromones. In a full-blooded member of said species, the effect was immediate. For Aleera, half-and-half that she was, it tended to take a while longer. Considering that she'd never drawn much of a difference between that and slipping someone rohypnol, it was never a point of pride for Aleera, even if it couldn't be switched off.

'Hey,' Jasmine caught her as they left the classroom. 'You busy tonight?'

'What?' Aleera blurted out. Oh, subtle. Clever girl. Just blurt out "what"? Oh lovely, she was showing emotion again, she realised. That was never a good sign.

Jasmine stared blankly. 'The assignment.'

'Oh,' Aleera found herself saying just as dumbly. '*Oh*. Oh. Right. Sure.'

'Duh. What, you thought…' Jasmine pointed. Aleera suddenly found herself clamming up like an embarrassed schoolgirl. Well, yes, she was one, fair enough, but still. Her cheeks turned red. Mercifully, before anything potentially awkward could happen, Jasmine just laughed, said 'c'mon' and half-dragged her out of the classroom.

Aleera felt her cheeks pale again. Well, that was embarrassing. Maybe she could at least pray that it wouldn't be brought up again.

God, she'd actually blushed. When was the last time she'd done that? It almost suggested…

No. Of course not. Don't be stupid.

It wasn't that absurd, was it? She was a succubus, bisexual by birth, and Jasmine wasn't an unattractive girl. Nice eyes. And another delectable outfit today.

Now stop that, she snapped at herself. Stupid girl.

She'd somehow managed to get to the school gates without actually noticing. And to one side was something she was well-and-truly not in the mood for.

'You goin somewhere?' Jamie Shane spat as he walked up to them. 'Still a freakin dyke, huh?' he swaggered. 'She know what you did, bitch? She know what you did to my brother?'

Aleera stood still and folded her arms. 'Jamie,' she said flatly, 'you're in my way?'

Jamie Shane's face contorted in an arrogant, angry, sneering snarl. He looked vaguely like a cross between a dog and a very unhappy pig.

'C'mon then, bitch,' he spat, shoving her, 'come on!'

Aleera didn't react. She was actively trying to stop himself.

It must be stressed that Aleera had indeed been having a difficult week… not all week, but it was hard to see the week as a good one after Tuesday. And already, as she was fully aware, she was not an entirely-stable individual. She had an extremely low tolerance for frustration. Having this mentally-lacking individual shoving her, mouthing off and smelling vaguely of pot was a pleasant experience to few people, if any.

The result: a very strong compulsion to snap his damned neck.

Aleera always tried to fight this, but feelings like this came up more often than she'd have liked and she never really got the chance to indulge. She knew that it wasn't normal to have her favourite way of venting to be breaking noses, but she didn't normally care. She did, however, want to try and avoid the trouble that tended to come with doing so. Not from Jamie, certainly, but she'd only had a week back before summer following a two-week suspension for leaving his brother barely conscious.

The nagging voice screaming inside her brain to cut him off also wasn't helping.

'What you gonna do, bitch?' Jamie Shane spat in her face, 'what you gonna do?'

For God's sake, just shut him up and-

Then Jamie grunted painfully and doubled over, clutching something very personal. Jasmine, wearing a smug smile, gently nudged him and sent him falling over sideways.

'You have such nice friends,' she smiled sweetly to Aleera. 'Um- sorry if you wanted to do that yourself.'

'It's fine,' Aleera said levelly. At the same time, she felt a distinctly un-Aleera-like pang of sympathy for the poor simpleton. Even she never went for that target, even if it was more effective than seven years of Tae Kwon Do lessons.

Ignoring the assembled gaggle of students, Aleera followed Jasmine out of the gates and proceeded to show her the route to her sister's apartment.

'So is that true?' Jasmine asked after a slightly-awkward moment. When Aleera looked inquiringly at her, she clarified 'that thing he called you?'

Thing he'd called her? Aleera checked back. Bitch, skank, dyke- ah, that'd be it. Oh dear, embarrassing.

'Come on,' Jasmine smiled, 'you think I'm gonna run a mile or something?'

'You want to know?' Aleera asked. Wait, was she actually considering telling someone she'd known for all of five days? What was wrong with her?

'What, you are?' Jasmine raised her eyebrows.

'Bisexual,' Aleera confessed. Wow. That had certainly been said easily. For some reason, saying things to Jasmine didn't seem to be capable of being difficult.

'Now was that so hard?' Jasmine smiled. 'So, what do we start with?'

'What?'

'Down, girl, I'm talking about the assignment again.' Aleera actually found herself laughing as well this time. This was someone, she realised, who was genuinely unassuming. A welcome surprise, actually.

She wouldn't realise until later that, somehow, she'd virtually forgotten about the Guild.

They were back at Lilith's apartment within around five minutes. 'Lilith?' Aleera called as she opened the door, 'you in?'

There was a brief bustle, and Lilith emerged from the other side of the sofa. There was an inordinate amount of paper strewn over the floor. Aleera made a mental note to ask about it later.

'Hey, baby sis,' Lilith smiled, and then noticed Jasmine. 'Who's your friend?' she asked, looking Jasmine up and down.

'This is Jasmine, we've got to work on something. For school,' she added before Lilith could say anything.

'Cool. You two need anything?' she jerked a thumb toward the kitchen.

'I'm good,' Jasmine said, slipping off her shoes. 'So where are we working?'

'Sorry, living room's booked,' Lilith indicated to the mess of papers. 'You two can work in peace in Aleera's room.' Aleera prayed that she'd imagined the inflection at the end of the sentence as she led Jasmine through. 'You two play nice,' Lilith called as she returned to whatever it is she was doing.

'You didn't mention you had a sister,' Jasmine noted as Aleera shut the door behind them, seated on the edge of the bed. Aleera realised that she hadn't mentioned Lilith at all. Not out of shame, certainly; it honestly just never occurred to her to mention most things. It was never much of a point of concern to tell other people about herself.

'So is she…' Jasmine fished for a term, 'AC/DC?'

'Yeah,' Aleera said, sitting down. 'Runs in the family, you could say. How'd you guess that one?'

'Not trying to stir anything up,' Jasmine said, 'but I think your sister was mentally undressing me.' Well, Aleera thought, mentally was allowed. 'So, do you have a computer?' Jasmine asked. 'It'd make things easier.'

Aleera nodded and, on a desk on the other side of the room, lifting the top half of a laptop. The insurance had indeed covered the old one, though unfortunately (and typically) not much of her other possessions that had been burned down along with her old apartment.

After about an hour of work that had proven surprisingly productive, the two decided to summarise their notes and take a break.

'You want something to eat?' Aleera offered, 'I'll throw something together.'

'What, you cook?' Jasmine asked, lying on her stomach, looking down at a mass of paper and idly kicking her legs in the air.

'Why not?'

'You just…' Jasmine turned her head to one side, 'you don't seem like the kitchen type. So is that what you wanna do? After school, I mean?'

'Would be nice,' Aleera admitted. What she'd always wanted to do, she recalled, was open a restaurant somewhere. One that actually served good food. It was a childish ambition, but for some reason that had never actually stopped her. The devil's daughter running a restaurant. It sounded somehow macabre.

And then, the reason why she may never get to came flooding back to her. It was like a punch in the stomach.

In some ways, Jake's promise hadn't helped. It just made things more uncertain. There was now no way of even knowing whether she'd get to run her own life; even whether or not she did was out of her hands.

She was back to feeling powerless. And it was quite definitively not a pleasant feeling.

'Aleera?' Jasmine asked playfully, waving a hand in front of her face, 'anybody home?'

Aleera blinked. 'Sorry,' she shook her head, 'what were we talking about?'

'After school,' Jasmine reminded her.

'Right. So what do you want to do?'

Jasmine smiled weakly and looked away. 'Promise you won't laugh.'

'Why would I laugh?'

'Promise?'

Aleera, perhaps hypocritically, made a cross-sign over her chest. It wasn't that she didn't believe in a God, or a heaven or hell; she just couldn't quite help finding the idea of herself following a religion to be mildly obscene. There was bound to be a commandment against it somewhere.

Jasmine bit her lip. 'I want to be a designer,' she finally said.

Aleera looked at her expectantly. 'Why would I laugh at that?'

'Most do,' Jasmine shrugged. She reached into her bag. 'You wanna see?'

Aleera nodded.

Jasmine pulled out a thick pad of white paper and pulled back the first sheet. There were various pictures of tops, dresses and clever little features. One that caught Aleera's eye was a gothic eighteenth-century-style dress, but of a cut that no mother in the seventeen hundreds would let her daughter out in.

'This is good,' she said honestly.

'Oh, stop it.'

'I mean it,' Aleera said, 'I like these. You've got a talent.'

'What, you think?'

'Yeah. Honestly.'

Jasmine smiled gently and took the piece of paper back before Aleera could see the next page. She appeared to be blushing slightly. 'Thanks,' she said.

Aleera smiled back. For a moment, something seemed almost surreal. For some reason, neither of them could seem to think of anything to say. Only then did Aleera realise how close together they suddenly were, and how soft Jasmine's blue eyes were…

'Well I should probably get going,' Jasmine said, looking down at her watch, 'or my mom is literally going to kill me. Study again tomorrow?'

'Sure,' Aleera said without thinking. Jasmine smiled back, picked up her things and left, wishing her good afternoon.

What the hell had just happened? Aleera thought. Had she actually been thinking of… no. Don't be ridiculous. As if she would ever contemplate that kind of stupid behaviour.

Even if Jasmine did look so delectably…

Stop that!

After she went out, Lilith peered back over the sofa. 'Nice work,' she said knowingly.

'And you can cut that out,' Aleera said.

'What? She's cute. You never minded about the guys you used to go out with.'

'We're not,' Aleera said levelly, leaning over the sofa.

'You're not going to?' Lilith asked blankly, leaning back on the sofa and looking up.

'No.'

'Oh.' Lilith looked thoughtful for a moment. 'Can I?'

'No.'

Lilith shrugged and put her book down. 'So,' she said cheerfully, 'let's hear about this girlfriend of yours.'

'I told you, she's not.'

'Do you want her to be?' Lilith asked knowingly.

Aleera blinked. 'You're changing gears awfully quickly,' she observed.

'I like how you avoided answering the question,' Lilith raised her eyebrows. 'You've been out with people before. Remember Dante?'

'Do *not* remind me of Dante.'

'Fair enough. So answer the question: you like this girl?'

'No,' Aleera said quickly.

'Liar,' Lilith poked her tongue out. 'Come on, you can tell big sister.'

'She's straight.'

'And we're succubae, so that's an issue because...?' Aleera groaned and buried her forehead in her palms. 'I'm joking, kiddo,' Lilith grinned, 'it's called cheering you up.'

'I know,' Aleera sighed distantly. 'It's just- never mind.'

'Come on,' Lilith said, 'since when have you ever had to say "never mind" to me?'

'I don't know what to do about it,' Aleera shook her head. 'I really, really don't.'

Lilith nodded thoughtfully and pursed her lips.

'Actually,' she announced, 'I know exactly what you should do.'

Aleera looked at her. 'Which is?'

'Worry about that in the morning and cheer yourself up tonight,' Lilith beamed.

Aleera laughed inwardly.

'That's more like it,' Lilith smiled. 'I can tell exactly what you need, baby sister, and that's some nice, fresh ice cream. Chocolate?'

Aleera smiled. Ice cream; the ultimate pick-me-up. Of course, there was just one thing that could enhance it...

'Only if it has honey on it.'

"Pentagram" was a word spoken in different ways throughout the supernatural community of New York City. Ask a member of the Guild, and it would be a source of constant irritation. Ask a politician on the High Council eager for re-election, and it would be a hothead of crime and corruption as does not belong in a moral society. Ask any of its clientele, and it would be the best damn demon nightclub in town. And if you were to ask anyone in the know, it was run by the biggest "off-the-records entrepreneur" in the tri-state area.

The dance floor that took up the bulk of the literally-and-metaphorically-underground club was illuminated on-and-off by rolling, flashing red lights and filled with vibrant revellers indulging and intoxicated in a number of different ways with bass speakers loud enough to be heard in the dank back-alley above.

'Ok, remind me,' Makian shouted to Jake and Katya over the pounding "music", 'why are we here again?'

'Kheron,' Jake shouted back. 'He runs the place.'

'Right. And how exactly are we gonna find him?'

'Easy,' Katya yelled over the music.

To one side of the bar there was a thin staircase that led to a short corridor containing two rooms. The first was, as indicated by both the sign and the noises coming from within, the V.I.P. room. The other was a plain, unmarked wooden door.

Jake opened it swiftly and purposefully. 'Knock-knock?'

Two bouncers immediately moved in front of them. One cracked his knuckles demonstratively.

'No need to worry, gents,' came a polite voice from behind them. 'They've an appointment.'

The man seated behind the desk on the other side of the room glanced up briefly. His orange hair was combed back expertly, and he wore a suit of the type of quality that would see anyone else in Pentagram mugged or lying in a dumpster never to be heard from again. Without much reaction, he sealed an envelope and placed the lid back on a pen. Only when he was quite sure that he had silence and the undivided attention of the room did he speak.

'Mister Connolly,' he said leaning back in his chair and rhythmically tapping the pen on his desk, 'to what do I owe this enormous honour?'

'Nice turntable,' Makian commented, leaning over the record player. Nobody had noticed that it was quietly humming away with *Space Oddity*.

'Didn't know you were a Bowie man,' Jake observed.

'It's a fine record,' Kheron said as he tented his fingers. 'You know a man's cultured when he's got one of those. 1965. Vintage. So what can I do for you, gentlemen-and-lady?'

'You misplace some employees lately?' Jake asked directly. Kheron peered over the top of his fingers.

'Come again?'

'The other night one of your "businesses" got itself slaughtered.'

'I can't imagine what you're implying, Mister Connolly,' Kheron said expressionlessly, reaching a hand under the table to start a tape recorder, 'I'm simply a club owner, after all. Quite fully licensed and paid-up, I can assure you.'

'Owner of Pentagram,' Jake clarified.

'I can't be held responsible for *everything* that happens inside these walls; I'm only here now because you caught me at a good time. I do have other ventures to manage, after all.'

'Yeah, and we found one of them with all its members dead next to enough snow to make our own winter wonderland,' Makian cut in, 'sound familiar?'

'Well, I certainly can't tolerate any of my employees getting in trouble with the law,' Kheron said in a tone that made it clear that the argument had just been thoroughly won. Now that was evasion for you. 'Tell me: what exactly has happened to my employees?'

'Dead. Drained.'

'My, my, my,' Kheron shook his head, leaning back and tenting his fingers again, 'I offer my sincere encouragements, then. I understand that the Eighth Division- and D-Unit in particular- has seen better days. Correct?'

'Wraiths,' Jake spoke up. Kheron turned sharply to him. 'What do you know about them?'

Kheron looked inquiringly at him. 'I know they're not to be trusted,' he said flatly. 'Certainly not ideal business partners. Now, if we're quite finished, my car happens to be on a metre.' He reached under the desk and turned the recorder back off.

As all turned to leave, it was Katya that turned round and raised one finger. 'One question,' she piped up, 'what were your boys doing there?'

'I prefer to keep my ventures private,' Kheron said levelly. 'I'm sure you understand.'

'That place was stacked halfway up the walls with cocaine,' Jake warned, 'and we know you ran it.'

'Well then,' Kheron said, standing up. He held his hands forward, together at the writs, palms up. 'Arrest me.'

Jake didn't move.

'Oh, yes, of course,' Kheron smiled thinly. 'You're an earnest young man, I'll give you that. Here.' He slapped something into Jake's palm, 'treat yourself. *Ask for Rachael*,' he whispered knowingly.

Jake dropped the roll of cash onto the floor. It rolled away.

'I'm not done with you,' he said quietly.

'No need for that, Mister Connolly,' Kheron said courteously, 'gents, show my guests out, please.'

'We'll find the exit ourselves,' Jake said. He, Makian and Katya left the room.

Without a moment's hesitation, Kheron returned to his desk, sat down and signed one last paper. Then he put everything neatly away, leaned back in his chair and waited until the record finished playing.

6

Jake had spent most of the time since visiting Pentagram holed up in his study, poring over dusty old tomes. He'd read nothing he didn't already know.

Kheron, he'd long-since worked out, had done something. Something that brought this on him; that would be obvious. And if the wraiths were willing to take a gambit like that, they wouldn't just leave.

In the middle of his unhelpful research, he'd received a phone call from one Daniel Cassidy: 'We've got something.'

And something it was.

The warehouse had, at least according to the records, been condemned for some months. Judging by the look of it, it was virtually uninhabitable. Judging by its contents, it had been used for roughly the same purpose as the last place. Going by that evidence, using DNA evidence to figure out who these latest victims were would be a minor technicality.

'Two more,' Makian confirmed, 'both male. That gives us six in three days,' he bitterly handed a preliminary report over to Jake. 'Lucky the council isn't crucifying us already.'

'If this is another one of Kheron's rackets,' Jake pointed out, 'it gives us an excuse to question him again.'

'Not a chance,' Cassidy said bluntly.

'What?'

'You heard me,' Cassidy said flatly. 'We comb the building.'

Jake glared at him for a second. 'Huh. You really have replaced Khazahn, huh?'

'Shut it, Connolly,' Cassidy snapped. 'You know as well as I do that pressing him's like getting blood out of a rock. Besides, the minute we bring him in, he'll walk back out again if half of what I've heard of his lawyers is true.'

'This is the second place peddling Kheron's crack that we've come across so far,' Katya thought out loud.

'Is your familiar going to give us an after-school special on the dangers of drugs,' Cassidy asked sardonically, 'or are we going to get to work for once?'

Jake shot him a death glare.

'Can we track the supplier?' Katya offered.

Jake turned to her and took a sharp breath. 'Idea?' he asked.

'If we find the supplier, we can find out who they're supplying.'

'This is homicide, Sheba, not narcotics,' Cassidy said venomously. 'We have different departments,' he said slowly and clearly.

'Leave it,' Jake snapped, stepping in between them. 'And she's right.'

'Excuse me?'

'So far, this is what the wraiths have been hitting, even if we don't know why.'

'Stakeout time,' Katya grinned.

'You said wait and see,' Jake reminded him. 'Now we'll know what to wait for.'

'I'll consult dispatch,' Cassidy said bluntly. 'Don't see why we should protect these miserable bastards.'

'Or catch a group of wraiths that's already killed at least four people that we know of?' Jake reminded him. 'We need a break, and this could be it.'

'I prefer to listen to qualified advice,' Cassidy said bluntly.

'If we can put the testosterone aside for two seconds, gentlemen?'

All whirled round as one. Straightening his suit, Khazahn strode up with a black-cloaked Guild soldier on either side. Cassidy gave a brief glare, and then settled into defiant submission.

'The idea's sound,' Khazahn said authoritatively, 'and it's the only one we have.'

'Commander-'

'It's your call, of course,' Khazahn interrupted what would surely be a well-made speech from Cassidy, 'but I suggest we at least try to make some progress, don't you think?'

Daniel Cassidy nodded resentfully. 'Lieutenant Makian,' he ordered, 'get it organised.' He turned away. 'Keep me posted.'

Khazahn turned to Jake and gave him a subtle nod. Jake appeared not to acknowledge it until he walked past Khazahn. He did, as it happened, have a few things he'd have liked to say. Right now, though, he had more important things to discuss with Khazahn.

'About done, Mister Connolly?' Cassidy called. 'I suggest we clear out before searching the building.'

'No problem,' Jake said levelly. 'Oh, and by the way-'

He walked up to Cassidy slowly. Then he purposefully raised one hand, held the middle finger and thumb together, and snapped.

'Talk to my friend like that again,' he said quietly, 'and you will see exactly why the word "trouble" is stamped on my file.' With that, he turned and left before Cassidy could reply.

A thick, rusty chain was wrapped on the wire fence that led into the lot. Several seconds after Jake had snapped his fingers, half the links snapped.

Kheron's penthouse was certainly among the finest that upper Manhattan had to offer. Even if Jake hadn't seen the interior yet, he was aware that it was on the thirtieth floor in one of those buildings were, rather than try to buy and impossibly-exclusive penthouse, it would probably be cheaper to build one of your own. It was, possibly, also cheaper to build your own building as well.

'So just to repeat,' Katya said as she and Jake navigated the dull, brown-orange-tinted street in the sickly glow of endless street lamps, 'we know where this guy lives?'

'Yup.'

'And we know *who* he is.'

'Yep.'

'And the High Council- the actual, right-at-the-top High Council- knows who he is and what he does.'

'Yes indeedy.'

'And he isn't in jail.'

'Uh-huh.'

'And they say that the worst corruption the Guild gets is stuff like the Azrael Incident.'

'Bullseye.'

'And if you've worked for these guys for so long, you must really hate the High Council's guts.'

'Oh *my*, yes.'

The distance between them and the foyer of the building closed. Before they got there, the double-doors swung open on the arm of a valet.

Jake froze. Not so much out of fear, but because this was wholly unexpected.

The man held a long coat to himself. The end of a cigarette gave of wisps of smoke from his mouth. He, too, froze. Long-dulled eyes looked up sharply between greying temples.

'Khazahn,' Jake realised in a moment of disbelief.

Khazahn dropped the cigarette and stamped it out. 'Jake,' he said curtly. 'What brings you up to this neck of the woods?'

'I was about to say the same,' Jake said. 'Nice coat.'

'May as well all come clean,' Khazahn shrugged. 'Kheron.'

'An off-the-records visit?' Jake surmised.

'Cassidy told me about your discussion. I figured you could be right.'

'The head of the Eighth Division?' Jake arched an eyebrow. 'Mr. By-The-Book-Khazahn? Flouting the rules like… like me,' he grabbed the nearest available simile.

'We're not talking about a couple of magical pushers. There are wraiths in this city. There aren't supposed to be Wraiths in this city. You have no idea how badly the council wants this dealt with. Daeiol's been pounding on my door for days.'

'Uh-huh.' Jake said dryly. 'Why are you really here?'

'Pressing Kheron,' Khazahn repeated. Perfect poker-face.

'And?'

'What do you think? Like getting blood out of a rock. Same as ever.'

'How many years of this guy and we've never found ourselves with a speck of dirt on him,' Katya reflected.

'We did,' Khazahn answered. His voice rang with years-old bitterness. 'We had CCTV footage of him, personally, strangling an informant with his bare hands.'

'Seriously?'

'Deadly.'

'And he's still living up there?' Katya pointed disgustedly to the penthouse.

'"Questionable evidence",' Khazahn spat. '"Inadmissible". Tribunal threw the whole thing out, *and* we had to pay the son of a bitch five thousand for "mental damages". Like I said, kid: this isn't your run-of-the-mill scumbag. This is career filth. This is the kind of person who doesn't just break the law; he makes it work for him. And that's the kind that really laughs at us.' He lit another cigarette. 'Now if you'll excuse me,' he said as he brushed his way past Jake, 'I'm going to go and drink myself stupid.'

Aleera slowly pushed a few rashers of sizzling bacon around the pan. Cooking was one thing that she'd consistently enjoyed for most of her life, and it had always been her favourite means of escapism. The very few memories from her childhood that she actually held in fondness generally involved herself and her sister; she'd never forget when Lilith had first taught her to make chocolate cake. She could just stand and work away and generally, at last, not worry about something.

Two slices of toast popped up out of the toaster. She grabbed them in mid-pop and took some honey out of the cupboard. That had always been her single greatest vice: anything with lashings and lashings of honey.

The night had been little better than usual. Even in light of everything else, the nightmares persisted.

She slammed the sticky knife down on the side and buried the top half of her head in one hand as her chest constricted.

God damn it. They were dead, and for the week so far she'd practically forgotten. She'd loved them, for Christ's sake.

And, of course, when hearing she was being drafted she'd broken a friend's desk. Maybe there was something in the need to send her to those wretched psychiatrists.

On the other side of the apartment, the door into one of the two bedrooms open. Lilith emerged rubbing sleep from her eyes. 'You're already up?' she asked groggily.

Aleera turned round and pushed the unwanted thoughts back down where they belonged.

'Yeah,' she smiled slightly. 'Breakfast?'

'I keep telling you, you don't have to do that.'

'And I keep telling you, I enjoy it. So: bacon? Eggs?'

Lilith replied 'yes' to both just before the phone rang. She picked it up and answered with 'Hello? ...No, right number; hold on.' She handed Aleera the phone. 'It's for you,' she smiled.

Aleera lifted the phone to her ear.

Well, she hadn't been expecting this.

'Ok,' Jasmine said, 'quiz me.'

Aleera looked down at their notes to find something. 'Who permanently suspended democracy and became the first Roman Emperor?'

'Easy. Caesar.'

'Yeah,' Aleera nodded. Both of them knew that they knew enough about the subject by now to breeze through the presentation. Right now they were, if anything, killing time during lunch by going over a few things in the school library. 'Ok, let's take a break.'

'Might as well,' Jasmine shrugged, 'By the way, did you do that thing for Math yet?'

Aleera pulled up her book-bag and checked. She pulled out a sheet and held it between her thumb and finger. 'Let me guess.'

'Please?' Jasmine smiled a fake-innocent smile. 'I'll give it back tomorrow.'

Aleera handed her the sheet, and was quietly amazed at how familiar they seemed to have become in a little under half a week. It was only their third day of so much as knowing each other, and it was as though she'd known Jasmine her whole life. Not hard to see, then, why Jasmine already seemed to be better-liked at school. Then again, Aleera could, by her own admission, be kind of a bitch.

She had, by definition, not noticed that she hadn't even remembered her Guild problem.

'You researched a lot of stuff,' Aleera recalled, 'must have kept you busy.'

'Yeah, well I like to keep busy,' Jasmine said flicking a pencil over and over idly. 'Keeps the old bitch off my back.'

'She can't be that bad,' Aleera shrugged.

'No? I'm only living with her because dad's in jail,' Jasmine said flatly, flipping the pencil up in the air. 'I can't stand her.' She caught the pencil, then appeared to realise what she'd just said. She looked ashamed. 'Sorry,' she said, suddenly subdued, 'didn't mean to unload on you like that.'

'It's fine,' Aleera said, lying down adjacent to her. 'I know the feeling.'

'Yeah,' Jasmine said after a moment of "um" and "uh". 'I kind of figured, since you, y'know…'

'Live with my sister,' Aleera finished for her. 'It's fine. I actually used to have a place of my own. Guild housing.'

'The Guild?' Jasmine sat up, eyebrows raised. 'Seriously?'

'Not that I ever did anything,' Aleera clarified. 'It's… a long story.' Needless to say, she always left out the fact that she was the daughter of a mass-murderer. It was something of a conversation-killer.

'Wow. I finally know something interesting,' Jasmine smiled conspiratorially. 'I swear, draconic life in Boston was boring as shit.'

Aleera sat up as well. As suddenly as ever, it dawned on her again how easy it seemed talking to Jasmine. Holding back- except about her father, obviously- almost sounded impossible. 'You've got a mouth on you,' she observed. She then noticed that her eyes had suddenly been drawn to Jasmine's lips.

Her own lips felt suddenly dry. She licked them and suddenly noticed the quivering feeling in her stomach. She was suddenly aware that the top of Jasmine's latest self-tailored outfit was slightly see-through.

She snapped out her trance when the bell rang, and realised just how close together they were and how much they were both blushing.

All she'd have to do was lean forward a tiny bit more…

'Sorry,' Jasmine said quickly. 'I should get going. See you tomorrow?'

Aleera nodded, as dumbly she as she ever had done, and immediately distracted herself by packing her books away.

What the hell had that been? Pheromones were one thing, fair enough, but when had it ever been in her nature to make a move like that?

Although there was that little flutter in her stomach whenever Jasmine smiled…

She shook her head, wondering what in heaven and hell's respective names had come over her, and left the library.

The old playground had clearly seen better days. Rusted swings creaked back-and-forth and the weathered slide looked none too safe. Still, there were a number of children, playing, laughing and running back-and-forth.

Any public place was a good place for people-watching, and from time to time Aleera confessed that she partook; mainly because human beings were like a train wreck: she didn't dare watch, but couldn't quite look away. A couple of baby-brigaders, one with a cigarette in the same hand as a baby, idly pushed prams back and forth while talking about soap operas and ignoring their children when they spat or cried.

Why anyone would want to meet here, Aleera couldn't be entirely sure. Then again, it was a standard place to bring one's granddaughter.

She was about to meet someone, she recalled, that she hadn't seen since the... unpleasantness.

The day after it all happened had probably been the worst. She'd thrown up any number of times and, at a few points, actively considered suicide. It had been nearly impossible to imagine a time when that deep, sick pain wasn't everything.

Now she was marginally better. There was barely an inch of her that didn't still feel it. It was just that, now, she had something else to lose sleep over.

She'd finally met someone who wanted to be anywhere near her, and her biology was about to tear that down again. She had been about to start looking through colleges, and her future had been snapped away from her.

Not for the first time, everything was falling apart around her again. It just made her want to shut down and push everything away; in fact, the option became more promising each day.

About four days. That was how long she had left. God, she wanted to be sick.

Remembering why she was there, she forced herself not to think about it. Probably not healthy, but it had worked for the last week.

Calm down. Remember why she was there. Yes, that helped for a few seconds by sending her back to the start of that same train of thought.

An elderly lady, wrapped up in many layers of clothing and with silver hair crossed the playground towards her. Aleera saw her face light up when the old woman saw her.

'Good morning,' Aleera said, remembering to smile. That was what normal people did, correct? 'Nice to see you again.'

'Oh, stuff that nonsense and come here,' Mrs. Mcrae said in a thick Irish accent while pulling her into a bone-crushing hug. 'Good lord, I can't thank you enough,' she sniffed into her shoulder, 'after what you did, I... oh, God bless you, girl.' She pulled back and wiped her leaking eyes.

'Don't worry about it,' Aleera said reflexively.

'And don't you go talking about it like that. If it wasn't worth worry, would I have gone through all those Guild lines to see the girl that saved my little Chloe? You should be proud, by God.'

'I suppose,' Aleera said levelly.

Mrs. Mcrae shifted. 'Yes, that friend of yours told me. I'm very sorry about that,' she said sympathetically.

'Don't be,' Aleera said. Before saying the next part, she caught herself. Should she? Shouldn't she? She was an old woman whose granddaughter almost died. She should know. She deserved to. 'I should tell you,' she started, 'what happened- it was…'

'Not your fault in the slightest,' Mrs. Mcrae interrupted fiercely. 'Honestly. That Jake Connolly man told me about that as well, and you know as well as I do that that man- that *awful* man- would have gone after my daughter anyway. And I'll tell you what else,' she pointed a finger, 'my granddaughter owes you her life.'

Aleera didn't really have anything to say to that. It dawned on her for perhaps the first time that, for the first time in three months, she had no reply to that.

'She doesn't talk about it much,' Mrs. Mcrae said more softly.

'How is she?' Aleera asked.

'Coping very well, considering everything. She's with a therapist right now; says it'll be a few weeks yet before she's ready to go back to school. Said she repressed most of it. Can't rightly tell if that's better.' Aleera nodded slowly. It was a feeling she recognised.

'She doesn't talk much, still,' Mrs. Mcrae went on. 'She does sometimes, and she's getting a lot better. Talks about you sometimes. Goes on and on like you're some kind of superhero.' Aleera felt herself smiling fondly. 'Which reminds me: that's why I called you here…'

Mrs. Mcrae rummaged in an old, battered handbag. After a second she produced a piece of paper and handed it to Aleera. It was coloured bright blue, with balloons et cetera, and contained a birthday invitation. Ten-year-old Chloe had signed it by hand.

'Her birthday's tomorrow,' Mrs. Mcrae said. 'The therapist said it wouldn't be a good idea to have that many people, but I was going to get her a cake and a present or two, and- well, I know it's short notice, but- I think it'd mean a lot to her if you could make it.'

A smile tugged at the sides of Aleera's mouth. She didn't bother trying to fight it.

'I'd love to,' she said, pocketing the invitation.

'Wonderful,' Mrs. Mcrae smiled. 'Well, I know you're probably busy, but I don't suppose you'd have time for a cup of tea?'

Aleera smiled again. 'Sure.'

Tomoko cursed quietly to herself and paced around the autopsy room for the hundredth time.

She should have been able to figure this out a *long* time ago. For God's sakes, she was a Kawasaki Medical University graduate with an IQ that was unrealistically high. She'd mastered molecular biology while finding a date for senior prom. And here she was, with nothing to do but stare blankly at the withered corpses that had shown up so far.

The problem was that a medical genius was just that. Medical only.

The tests she'd been carrying out so far on materials from the warehouse had shown nothing. A little under thirty minutes ago, she'd figured out why and dragged the nearest available living being into the lab.

Makian let out a stifled breath. 'I've got nothing,' he said, just slightly embarrassed. 'Sorry.'

'There must be something,' Tomoko said fiercely, 'nobody kills five people without leaving a single clue.'

'Even wraiths?' Makian offered. 'I mean, who even knows about those things? Yeah, Jake, but he can't stand being in the same room as Cassidy or Khazahn.'

'Just think,' Tomoko insisted, tapping both sides of her forehead as she irritably circled the autopsy table again.

'We've been thinking all evening. We don't know a damn thing, that's where the problem comes from, see?'

'There has to be something on one of these-' Tomoko froze, verbally and physically, in mid-motion, then whirled to face Makian like an excited child as something in that genius brain clicked. 'Say that again.'

'We don't know about wraiths.'

'No, the other thing,' Tomoko said excitedly.

'…where the problem comes from?' Makian hazarded.

'Where it comes from,' Tomoko repeated ecstatically. 'We didn't do a sweep of the first place, but we got some material from the warehouse. See, if there was something on the wraiths, it'd just… well, drop of, but if we're lucky,' she excitedly shoved a slide under a magnifying glass, 'if we're very, very lucky…'

Makian regarded her curiously. 'I have no idea what you're talking about, but you're attractive enough that I'm going to stand here and keep listening.'

'I'm looking for anything that shouldn't be there,' Tomoko rambled on.

'But you said we couldn't get DNA from wraiths.'

'I'm not looking for DNA,' Tomoko buzzed, 'but like you said: source of the problem. Like...' she stood back, her face lighting up. 'Water.'

'Water?'

'Water,' Tomoko beamed. 'Show me our other find.'

'Onto something?'

'Oh, yes,' Tomoko grinned eat-to-ear. She really should have a T-Shirt that said "genius at work".

'Now just repeat that,' Daniel Cassidy said levelly, arms folded, in the middle of the autopsy room having received a half-laughing call from Tomoko, 'slowly and clearly. Do we have something?'

Makian was still in attendance, still trying to wrap his head around just how Tomoko had managed to do this that fast. You'd probably need to be a forensics expert to understand half the ten-syllable words that had been streaming out of her the whole time.

'Yes,' Tomoko said quickly, 'we have water.'

Cassidy looked blankly at her. 'Yeah, there's a cooler outside,' he said dryly.

Tomoko held up a small vial of water. Except that, in Daniel Cassidy's experience, water wasn't normally purple.

'The PH level is way off,' Tomoko explained at breakneck speed, 'this water's full of pollutants.'

'Because?'

'Because it's not water.'

Another blank stare. 'You just said it was water.'

'It's sewage,' Tomoko said. 'Just a little of it, soaked into the wood, but it's there, and it shouldn't be.'

Cassidy somehow seemed to grow taller as he thought. 'Can you back this up?' he asked, realising where she was going.

'We found fleas,' Tomoko said, 'full of blood that showed remarkably broken down blood cells that hadn't yet been digested-'

'Just nod when she pauses,' Makian whispered.

'-and the most likely way that would happen would be if they'd tried to feed on wraiths. To add to that, we found rat hairs as well. The hairs also showed levels of pollutants, contaminated water, waste, etcetera. Which means…'

'They're in the sewers,' Cassidy ended the sentence. 'Fantastic,' he added dryly, 'that just gives us God-even-knows-how-many acres of sewers and building foundations to trawl through.'

'But,' Tomoko said even more brightly, pulling out and unfolding a sewer map, 'considering how quickly it would have to be lost, we can narrow it down to…' she ran her finger round a relatively small area, 'here.'

Cassidy looked down at the map. He nodded in acknowledgement.

'That wasn't so hard, was it?' he said brightly.

Tomoko looked up at him. Something cold passed through her eyes. 'Excuse me?'

'We've been working on this for three days,' Cassidy said bluntly, 'and you turn this up now.' He paused and looked discerningly at her. 'What did you say your I.Q. was?'

Tomoko sharply opened and closed her mouth. Cassidy turned and left, muttering something under his breath.

'He truly is an asshole,' she finally said.

'That he is,' Makian said. 'If we get this right, you think they'll thank us by getting rid of him?'

7

'I'd just fallen asleep,' Katya complained in a groan as she and Jake entered through the grating stone door, 'and still nobody tells us what's happening.'

The room within was, again, not what one would expert. A handful of technicians, their heads framed by bulky, black headphones, busied themselves over a long bank of computers and such equipment mounted against a wall. Tomoko, Makian, Cassidy and a handful of other officers bustled around.

'Sewers,' Tomoko told them proudly. 'It finally clicked: the wraiths are hiding in the sewers.'

Jake paused and thought. 'Could be,' he observed, 'out of the sun, out of sight, plenty of vermin between meals-'

'Rats and otherwise,' Daniel Cassidy brought up with dry wit. 'According to police liaisons, they've lost track of a couple of homeless lately. A sewer worker up and vanished a few days ago.'

'Rats won't keep a wraith going,' Jake commented, 'so what now?'

'Five minutes of sleep, that's all I'm asking for,' Katya muttered to no-one in particular as she got herself a drink from a water cooler.

'Thought cats didn't like water,' Cassidy said sardonically. Katya bluntly flipped him off while drinking and sidled up next to Jake.

'And this is?' she asked.

'Ground control,' Khazahn announced. Jake turned round sharply. He hadn't even noticed he was there. 'Any tips from the master?' he asked, turning to Jake.

Jake gave him an icy glare, and then looked down at one of the several screens. 'You're sending people in?' he realised.

'We need to get hold of them before they move on. We may have missed them already,' Khazahn declared.

'How many?'

'Six soldiers. Any number of wraiths.'

'*Six*?' Jake repeated in abject horror. Part of him couldn't believe what he was hearing. The parts that could didn't like it much more. 'Against *wraiths*? When there could be any number?'

'What's the likely figure?' Cassidy asked.

Jake leaned on the console and covered his hand with his mouth. 'Could be just one, but there's no way less than, I'd guess, three, could have done all of this,' he said gravely. 'If it's a whole cabal, we could be looking at anything up to twenty.'

A hushed silence fell over the room.

'That's the worst-case scenario,' Cassidy said dismissively.

'And we should plan for it until we know what we're sending our people into,' Khazahn said levelly. An odd look was exchanged between him and Jake. 'We should pull the plug on this.'

'We have to deal with this now,' Cassidy snapped as he reached for the console, 'or would you rather let wraiths carry on with a killing spree in the middle of Manhattan, with the High Council riding our backs?'

'For all we know, we are sending our men into a charnel house!' Khazahn shouted.

'I am in charge of this operation,' Cassidy shouted back.

Jake felt something tug his sleeve. It was Tomoko.

'Jake,' she whispered quietly, 'Makian's down there.'

He turned sharply back to the monitor.

'Is that true?'

Khazahn felt a headphone buzz. 'Put it on speaker,' he said to one of the technicians. A switch was flipped.

'Right here, boss,' Makian's hushed voice crackled. 'And you can relax about that "twenty" stuff. Place looks deserted, man. Not a freaking wraith in sight.'

Makian found it tough to fathom why that anyone would be in the sewer by choice. The darkness was half-blinding, every surface was slippery, and most noticeably, the entire dank place stank. Someone near Makian gagged yet again. The metal masks/helmets that were standard-issue among Guild soldiers weren't helping.

The six soldiers, all garbed in black body-armour, hoods and flowing cloaks that kept them well-concealed in the darkness, rounded another corner.

A soldier staggered back. He slipped. A young one, if Makian recalled. Lawson. Rick, that was it. Raw recruit. College dropout.

'Shit,' Rick Lawson retched. 'Oh, *shit*, man. What the hell!'

'Move,' Makian ordered, running on the sudden surge of adrenaline and pushing himself through the soldiers.

The old, ragged clothes still clung to the withered corpse. The skin was dark, hardened and clinging to the bone. A filth-caked, scraggly beard was torn in places. The face was still screaming, illuminated with shadowy caverns by the soldiers' lights.

'Makian!' Jake's voice shouted into his helmet's radio,' what the hell happened?'

'We're Ok,' Makian said quickly, 'but we've got another body up here.' He kneeled down. 'Looks like a homeless guy. Poor son of a...'

Makian trailed off. He looked up.

Something moved.

'Uh, Jake...'

'Get them out of there,' Jake said fiercely. 'Makian, get out of there, now!'

'Belay that!' Cassidy shouted.

'The wraiths are there. Get them out of there!'

'Not if it brings those things down!' Cassidy roared.

'They don't have a hope in hell if they're ambushed,' Khazahn yelled, 'get them out of there!'

'Commander, this is my unit; you will respect my authority!'

'Hunt to Hound One, withdraw!' Jake shouted into the console.

'Connolly, step down or I will arrest you right now!'

'Your operation's failed, Cassidy!' Jake snapped. 'Hound-One, withdraw!'

There they were. Movement below. Lights. The lights stung.

They moved as one.

Makian looked up. He froze. His eyes widened.

'Oh f-'

A sheet of wraiths descended from the ceiling of the sewer. There was a shout from behind him. The wraiths screeched and reached forward and downward.

A mass of black fell on top of something. Makian whirled round, a three-pronged black staff as was given to all Guild soldiers held firmly in his hands. He took aim and fired a shimmering bolt of what could only be dubbed solid force. So did Rick Lawson. A wraith was knocked back. Brickwork shattered.

Behind him, the soldiers screamed.

The screams turned to static in the airwaves. There were sounds of shots being, fired, of shots and impact and horribly inhuman screeches.

'Hound-One, come in!' Jake shouted into the microphone. No reply. 'Hound-One, come in!'

'Fuck,' Katya covered her mouth. Her golden eyes trembled.

'If this fails…' Cassidy snarled.

'Then it's in your head,' Khazahn snapped. 'Your unit, your job.'

Tomoko suddenly burst in between them and shoved Cassidy. 'If he's dead,' she shouted, shaking, eyes blurred, 'I swear to God-'

'Will everybody *shut up?*' Jake roared over the cacophony.

The sounds of chaos continued.

Makian was running on pure adrenaline. The scene was one from a nightmare. A wraith lunged at him and received only the blow of a metal staff. Another struck him from behind. A blast of force from the only other staff still being held smashed into another.

Everything around them was a whirling of rags and foul-smelling black shapes. The nearest moved in. The others followed.

Instinct took over. Makian turned on his heels. His neck ran straight into an open hand.

Makian felt himself gag. A rotting face greeted him, parting rotten, yellowed teeth with breath that reeked of melting flesh.

Something struck the wraith. The bolt of power carried it into the wall with a solid, echoing "thud".

Makian whirled round himself at the sound of a scream. No time to think. Twin blasts sent the two wraiths on top of Rick Lawson flying away.

He struck the young man from the side. With a cry of 'hold your breath,' they struck thick, slimy water.

Makian held his breath. They both moved as fast as they could through what felt like gelatine.

Something grabbed his leg. He yelled as he it pulled him back toward the surface. His head broke free of the water. His mask was torn off, cutting his cheek. He felt the sharp, stinging pain. A hand reached for his face.

Makian's hand sent thick sewage splashing into the wraith's face. Something struck the wraith that had grabbed his leg. Rick pulled off his own helmet in a shower of thick brown water. Makian fired another shot. The wraiths dispersed.

They dived into the water again and swam, eyes closed, as long as they could, until, gagging for breath, his windpipe screaming, his brain starting to reel back and forth, Makian rose and inhaled a lungful of sweet, foul air.

He pulled himself onto the brickwork and helped Rick Lawson climb free of the sewage. He felt his heart pounding in his chest.

The air was empty. The stench of death remained.

8

'Ow.'

'Sorry.'

'Ow.'

'Stop it.'

'Ow.' Makian winced as the cotton swap pressed against the cut on his cheek.

'You do remember why you're in here, right?' Tomoko asked.

'Because you couldn't wait to get my shirt off?'

'That and you were swimming in sewage with a cut on your cheek,' Tomoko lectured. 'You'll be lucky if you're not vomiting for the next week or more.'

'I like how you didn't deny the shirt thing. Ow,' he complained again as Tomoko moved onto another cut.

'Could've been worse.' Makian shuddered, seemingly out of nowhere. 'Fuck,' he shook again, 'they train you, you know that, but… shit. Those guys were… those…' he shook again.

The sudden collapse lasted a moment. Then with a sniff, Makian sat back up straight.

'Six of our boys went in there,' Makian shivered. 'We got two of them back,' he finished despondently. 'Me and Rick.' He looked up, suddenly almost-panicked. 'Is he…?'

'He'll be fine,' Tomoko reassured him. She sat down on the bedside in the Guild's medical facility next to him. 'We almost lost you,' she said quietly.

'You didn't.'

'I don't care,' Tomoko said fiercely. 'I am going to see that son of a bitch Cassidy fry for this.'

The door into the room swung open. 'Hey,' Jake smiled. Katya followed and held something forward.

'They said grapes,' she smiled, 'but Tomoko can keep a secret, right?'

Makian opened the box and grinned. Bollinger '69. Nice.

'Hey, boss, Kat,' Makian half-smiled. 'Close one, huh?'

'You had us worried,' Jake said. 'How are you?'

'He'll be fine,' Tomoko smiled slightly, patting Makian's nearest knee.

'Recommendations?' Khazahn stepped into the room, hands in pockets. 'Nice work back there.'

'You kidding?' Makian groaned. 'I lost four men.' He buried his head in his hands and shook violently. 'Four fucking men died down there…'

'Doctor,' Khazahn said to Tomoko, 'if you would?'

Tomoko gave Makian a worried glance before moving closer to Khazahn, Jake and Katya. 'I'd recommend counselling and at least a week off active duty; for physical recovery and…' she hesitated, 'I'd say there's a definite possibility of Post-Traumatic Stress Disorder.'

'I'll refer the case to a counsellor by this afternoon,' Khazahn vowed. 'Now if you'll excuse me.' He moved towards the door.

'I'll be right back,' Jake said after a second, then followed Khazahn out into the corridor. 'Khazahn,' he called after him. The Commander stopped and turned round slowly.

'Let me guess,' he said. 'Aleera.'

'What did you expect?' Jake pressed as he caught up with him. Khazahn turned and walked further away.

'I didn't expect you to leave it so long,' Khazahn said without clear implication.

'And that's how you defend yourself after what you helped them do?'

'We're here to protect the magical community,' Khazahn recited, 'sometimes we have to go to extremes to do that. You know that at least as well as I do.' Khazahn sat down. 'Nobody ever said it had to be fair.'

'You've seen the psyche reports. She is seriously damaged, Khazahn. She admits it herself. What the hell did you think this was going to do to someone like her? If she were anyone else, she wouldn't even be deemed fit for Guild service.'

Jake glared at him for a moment. 'It was your idea, wasn't it?'

Khazahn nodded slowly. 'Yes it was.'

'You-'

'Wake up, Jake. This is the High Council; top of the ladder; no higher authority; it stops with those people. You can't keep on being this naïve.'

'No,' Jake said fiercely, 'I was naïve when I thought there was a line we didn't cross.'

'Kudra was the biggest threat we have faced in five hundred years!' Khazahn snapped, 'In *five hundred years*, we never had to deal with anything that did anywhere near the damage he dealt us. Do you really think the High Council is going to let regulations, processes and red tape get in the way of making sure that doesn't happen again?'

Jake didn't respond.

'I managed to talk them down from having her locked up,' Khazahn said, 'by suggesting the idea of drafting her. It took a lot of work, but I convinced them, because call me crazy but it sounded better for her than an eight-by-ten. Now just leave it alone,' he ordered bleakly, 'and don't make this harder than it needs to be.'

Jake stood still for a long, slow moment.

'She deserves a life,' Jake said fiercely. Khazahn looked up at him. 'We failed her before. She brought Azrael down. You know and I know that we owe her that much.'

Khazahn exhaled slowly and folded his hands.

'Yes,' he finally said, 'yes we do.' He stepped forward. 'But we have to let this be for now. This thing- the wraiths- it's too big for us to distract ourselves, and we don't know how much worse it's going to get.' Jake visibly hesitated. 'Jake,' Khazahn lectured with raw honesty, 'I don't expect you to forgive me after what I did. But in this job, we check the personal issues at the door. I know you got her assigned to be your assistant. If you can do that, she can still have her life. I need you to work with me on this, Jake.' He held up a hand. 'One last time?'

Jake shook the hand.

Aleera tore her way down the corridor and into the ward. There was nothing else there; just long, empty, inky black spots that her mind didn't bother trying to fill.

Her legs pumped beneath her. Her heart slammed again and again against the inside of her chest. She tried to form a coherent thought. She failed.

Nearly there, now. Nearly there.

However much she ran, it didn't seem to get any closer. It was five feet away now. Now ten. Now fifty.

Nearly there. All that she could feel was surging adrenaline and desperate fear and roaring, soul-filling rage.

She'd flown across Manhattan as soon as Jake had told her. Sword of Heaven. The Guild. All the lies upon lies upon lies, all those people who, knowing what she was, would kill her in a heartbeat if someone would only give them a gun.

Nearly there. She'd find him. He'd be fine. Then she could find the man that had tried to do this and tear his eyes out.

The sharp, green curtain was in front of her. She reached out, grabbed it and pulled it open so desperately that the fabric tore in her hands.

Michael was there. Lying on the bed. A black-crusted mass of blistered, red flesh that had been her friend, teeth held together in a mad, ashen grimace.

It started to descend upon her as she took the sight in. The despair. The hopelessness. The mad, howling grief.

She stepped forward as her mind scrambled for any thoughts of denial it could find.

Then it screamed. Then it jumped up, grabbed her and tackled her to the cold, hard floor.

'Look what you did!' its screaming voice roared in her face, 'look what you did to me, you bitch, look what you did!*'*

There was a hood over its head now, flailing as Aleera reached up and pulled it off. It tore away, and with it came the burnt, red and black flesh.

Then, beneath it, covered in blood, Aleera screamed and howled with nothing, nothing, but thick, black hate.

Then Aleera was taking a lungful of air, sitting up in bed and wrapped in quiet and darkness.

It had happened again. No surprises there. Ever since she tried to fall asleep, this had been happening. This was the third nightmare that day.

After a moment, she realised that the dampness on her cheeks was the result of a flow of tears that poured down her cheeks and over the marks on her neck. They stopped when she woke up, and she couldn't remember where it was that they'd come from. She tried to wipe them dry and succeeded only in soaking her hands.

Damn.

She shuffled back and rested against the wall as the images faded again.

What was this, the fourth time she'd had that dream? Not the first, certainly, and probably not the last either.

She got up early and took a shower, reflecting on how used to nightmares/flashbacks she was, even if they were usually a little more faithful to the original. Maybe her subconscious was just becoming more theatrical in its approach.

She was just getting started on breakfast, which consisted of lashings of honey with a side of toast, when Lilith got up. When her sister entered the kitchen, she studied the sight before her for a moment and then pulled up a chair.

'So what's the problem?' Lilith asked.

'Nothing,' Aleera answered, perhaps a bit surprised.

Lilith gave her a deadpan look. 'Uh-huh.'

'What makes you think there's a problem?' Aleera replied before taking another bite.

'Well, whenever there's a problem, you always say "nothing" right away if someone asks about it,' Lilith enlightened her, 'and you always eat a mountain of that stuff whenever something's wrong, and you weren't eating it yesterday, so I can tell there's something beside the Guild thing.'

Aleera considered this. 'You'd probably make a better psychiatrist than any of the ones I've met,' she said dryly.

'And we both know you're only saying that because they all suck. Now: what's up?'

Aleera shrugged. She could probably get away with being evasive for a little while longer, but with Lilith she never was. That was the kind of relationship two siblings had with nobody else caring for them for a long while.

'Jasmine,' she said.

'Knew it,' Lilith said proudly, laying back on her chair. 'You, baby sister,' she smiled, stealing a corner of toast, 'are smitten as a kitten.'

Aleera felt herself blush. 'I am not.'

'Don't lie to your sister,' Lilith scolded.

If it was possible, Aleera was blushing even more. She wasn't. Of course not. It was ridiculous. Idiotic. Preposterous.

None of that sounded overly convincing.

'Maybe a little,' she said meekly.

'You should go for it,' Lilith said bluntly. 'Maybe a birthday present to yourself.'

'Seriously, just stop,' Aleera groaned.

Lilith looked sympathetically at her. 'I get it,' she said quietly.

'I doubt it,' Aleera muttered.

'Come on; give your big sister a little credit. I've only had two guys-'

'It was five,' Aleera interrupted sharply.

'-Five guys back here since we moved in. Right: time for a heart-to-heart.' She leaned forward.

'Look, no offence,' Aleera said bitterly, 'but you never really seemed to worry about making it work to your advantage.'

'Well, that's because when I sleep with a guy, it tends to be just the once. Which, Ok, not for everybody. Now you,' she said, 'that's not what you're about. I can respect that. Not understand, but still. You want,' she searched for the word. 'A relationship- which, in all honesty, is a little strange coming from a just-under-eighteen-year-old, especially one who's half-succubus, even if you act like you're eighteen-going-on-thirty.'

'Pheromones,' Aleera recited, leaning right back on the sofa. 'I really wish I could turn them off, you know that?'

'Yeah. Sucks sometimes.'

'For you?'

Lilith paused in apparent reflection. 'Remember Sean? Nice guy, smart, biggest-'

'Yeah.'

'-you ever did see. Well- and never, *ever*, bring this up again- a little before I moved back, it got pretty serious. I mean really serious.'

Aleera looked at her with small-to-moderate confusion. 'I thought-' she'd learned not to bring it up, but it was still her recollection that Lilith had been unceremoniously dumped.

'Actually,' Lilith fidgeted uncomfortably, 'the day before, he…' she pursed her lips, 'he proposed.'

Midway through a mouthful of food, Aleera nearly choked. 'He what?'

'Down on one knee and everything,' Lilith sighed distantly. 'All romantic.'

'What happened?' Aleera asked, turning sideways.

'I turned him down.'

Aleera took a moment to think about this. 'Why?'

'Because,' Lilith said guiltily, 'I could never be sure. I never really knew how much of it was me and him, and how much was- just me.'

Aleera nodded understandingly.

'I was young. Well, young*er*. I was stupid,' Lilith confessed. 'I didn't know what else to do, so...'

'You turned him down,' Aleera realised.

'Yeah.' Lilith lidded her eyes shamefully. 'I wasn't happy to do it,' she said, her eyes glossing over, 'and it wasn't easy to do. I spent a long time, a *very* long time, thinking about it, and I think I figured it out what I should've done. I should have been honest,' she said. 'Right from the start. And the first part of that: guess who you need to be honest with.'

'Jasmine.'

'No,' Lilith tapped her lightly on the head, '*you*. Do you like this girl?'

'She's my best friend,' Aleera replied vaguely, 'and she's about the only one I've got right now.'

'You know what I mean.'

Aleera hesitated. It would be nice to deny it, of course, but the truth was that a few times, she had... noticed... Jasmine. Whenever she was in her company, she felt at ease, like it was impossible to be uncomfortable.

It had only been a week, and most people would probably have given an answer like "I don't know" or "maybe". But a big part of Aleera's personality was that she was a very cool, level-headed and logical young woman (or, by the reports of some, an icy bitch) who could step back and look at even emotional things like this very objectively. She could just look at the evidence and see what it said. And in this case, it was not so much saying things as standing on a pedestal and screaming into a megaphone.

But, and this was a very important and troublesome "but", she was still a teenage girl underneath that cold demeanour and frankly-spooky intelligence.

These two equally-important parts of her collided, argued, then settled down and grudgingly worked out an agreement.

'I think so.'

Lilith exhaled slowly and handed her the beer. 'In that case,' she said, 'you know what to do, huh?'

The impromptu bonding session ceased abruptly at the sound of the mail being pushed unceremoniously through the mail slot. 'I'll get it,' Lilith said, leaving Aleera to finish her breakfast.

'Anything important?' Aleera asked when Lilith came back in, leafing through the wad of letters in her hand.

She paused at one of them, and her forehead creased into what Aleera could best interpret as something between irritation and unease. For a second, she thought that perhaps she should ask, although if Lilith didn't feel like telling her, she wasn't going to pry.

Lilith inhaled sharply, tightening her grip on the mail. Then she folded up the envelope she was examining and stuffed it quickly into her pocket.

'No,' she smiled transparently as she put the rest of the mail down on the table, 'nothing at all.'

Ok. This was it. She just had to talk to Jasmine, be honest, and tell her the truth. After all, she'd told Michael and Sara about it, and they hadn't reacted all that badly.

Then again, she'd known both of them for considerably more than a week and hadn't almost kissed them out of absolutely nowhere. As it happened, she didn't know why that had bothered her so much; it was, by definition, just a kiss. Nothing for a succubus to get worked up about, surely. And yet, here she was.

Well, she thought, nothing ventured...

Unfortunately, before dealing with that, she also had one Jamie Shane to put up with. He was waiting at the bike stands for her again.

'Gonna be waitin for you at lunch, dyke,' he literally spat. 'Right here.'

'Wonderful,' Aleera said sharply and disinterestedly, and left him to it.

'You think you're runnin again, huh? You think you can just walk away, huh?'

Aleera hated to duck out on what sounded like an enthralling conversation, but she had places she'd rather be than talking to a deranged little crackhead. At the bottom of a river, for example. 'Morning, Jamie,' she said politely, enjoying his inarticulate rumble of anger as he walked after her. Dear Lord, he really didn't learn. Maybe it ran in the family.

Aleera turned. Jamie grabbed the front of her collar and pulled her forward, cursing in her face.

Now, Aleera knew precisely what to do in such circumstances as these. The first thing was to act surprised. Then, just as he snarled and was about to make his move, unladylike though it may be, she head-butted him. On the forehead was no good, of course; a good, solid blow to the nose was much better.

As Jamie fell to the ground, clutching his face and howling like a dog, Aleera moved on.

She found Jasmine by herself, grabbing a drink from a vending machine.

'There you are,' Jasmine said. 'You want a drink?'

'I'm fine,' Aleera said. The way her gut was suddenly feeling, she'd probably throw up if she swallowed anything.

Jasmine shifted uncomfortably. 'Look, sorry about yesterday,' she said, smiling faintly and giving an uncomfortable laugh. 'Hope I didn't, like, freak you out or anything.'

'No,' Aleera said, much too quickly. After all, it had been her own behaviour that had surprised her. 'Actually, I- I wanted to talk to you about that.'

'Oh,' Jasmine said, and then her blue eyes widened slightly. '*Oh*.'

"Oh"? What was "oh" supposed to mean? Unless-

Oh.

'I think that's kinda my fault,' Jasmine said nervously, 'I mean, you did say...'

'Yeah,' Aleera said quickly, 'listen, I know you're not interested, but I should probably tell you...' well, this was it. She could practically hear the whistle of an atom bomb falling.

Before she could finish her sentence, Jasmine was the one to drop a bombshell. 'What if I was?' she asked, blushing bright red.

Aleera felt like she was choking for a second. Something inside her chest did a back-flip. 'What?' she asked dumbly.

'Well, suppose I thought about it,' Jasmine said anxiously, 'and... I wasn't exactly not-interested?'

Aleera gulped. 'Oh.'

Neither of them got to say anything further, and for once Aleera actually thanked whatever higher power was at work when the chorus of catcalls started as the football team passed.

'Maybe this isn't the best place to talk about this,' Jasmine said. 'Are we still studying at your place tomorrow?'

'Sure,' Aleera answered breathlessly.

Jasmine smiled awkwardly and walked off, leaving Aleera to pick up what was left of her thoughts. And there was one thought, and one way of expressing it, that came through first.

Well, fuck.

After school turned out to be a pleasant distraction. She'd arrived at the apartment at four and had actually managed to pick up a present for Chloe. She'd had to get some advice from Lilith on exactly what to get for a ten-year-old girl, and remind her that it should ideally be tasteful. She'd eventually decided on a box of candy and a card into which she'd slipped a ten dollar bill.

Mrs. Mcrae opened the door and smiled. 'Hello,' she said, letting her in, 'lovely to see you again.'

'Thanks,' Aleera smiled back, putting her bag down.

'She's just in here,' Mrs. Mcrae showed her through. 'She's been dying to see you ever since I told her.'

Aleera glanced around the old living room. It seemed to have brightened up a little since her past visit.

Chloe looked up from the floor, where she was busily drawing something in crayon. She smiled.

'Hi,' the child said.

'Hey, kiddo,' Aleera said. Wow, that was easily. 'Got you something,' she handed Chloe the present. She smiled back, said "thanks" and opened it while Mrs. Mcrae offered Aleera a cup of tea. When Aleera replied, she was told to cut the Mrs. Mcrae nonsense and call her Shelly.

'So tell me,' Mrs. Mcrae- Shelly- said as she sat down, 'how've you been?'

Aleera was actually about to answer honestly before she remembered that there was a child present. 'Busy,' she said evasively, 'school and such.'

'Yes, I was wondering about that,' Mrs. Mc-Shelly- said. 'I wondered; do you work for the Guild?'

'Not yet,' Aleera said, technically honestly.

'You want to, then?'

Aleera caught herself. 'Not that much,' she said. 'It's a little complicated.'

'Are you a soldier?' Chloe asked innocently, sat between them.

'I will be soon,' Aleera replied.

'How come?' Chloe questioned her further, 'if you don't want to, why don't you do something else?'

Aleera made to reply. She froze in mid-breath. How, exactly, did she pass this off?

'I'm just working for them for a while,' she said the first thing that came to mind.

'What do you want to do?' Chloe asked while popping a piece of candy into her mouth.

'To be honest,' Aleera said, 'I always wanted to be a chef.'

'That sounds cool,' Chloe said, swallowing the candy.

'What about you?' Aleera asked. It was quickly amazing her how well she was getting on with the child. It had always been hard, for reasons not hard to figure out, to imagine herself as the child-friendly type.

But the thing that really made her feel was when she saw the gratitude in Shelly's eyes. She wasn't sure exactly what she felt, but she was definitely feeling it.

Children, she'd heard- and she remembered that she'd heard it at Sara's funeral- were the future. They were hope.

Slowly, it seemed to be starting to sink in what she'd done on that pier, while Chloe's questions continued to ring in her mind.

Surprisingly enough, the rest of Thursday, and much of Friday, passed without incident.

The one thing that was ever-present, of course, was the thought that, by Friday evening, only a night and a day left until she started work at the Guild. Then again, during the time that had elapsed she had taken on the opinion that this could be at least a slightly positive thing. Work with Jake a few hours, hopefully get to hurt some polluters of the gene pool…

It was strange, but for the last few days she'd been in a much more positive mood, and as much as she was trying to keep her mind free of such a conclusion, she had a good idea as to why.

The cause was studying with her again. They'd started to make quite a habit of it. This afternoon, it was something of a friendly argument.

'I don't believe I'm hearing this,' Jasmine giggled, 'it's simple, Ok? It's perfectly simple.'

'No,' Aleera held up a textbook, '*this* is simple. I've read *that* five times and I still don't have any idea what he was talking about.'

'That's stuff that we're not even supposed to be doing until college,' Jasmine pointed at Aleera's book, still laughing as she sprawled out over Aleera's bed, 'this is just basic.'

'I understand what he was saying,' Aleera said simply, 'I just don't see why he needs three pages to say it.'

'It's Romantic.'

'He's talking about having killed someone.'

'The other kind of Romantic,' Jasmine pouted playfully.

Aleera shook her head defiantly. She was still going to stick to her side of the story: college-level calculus made more sense than Shakespeare. It was at least written with sense-making in mind.

'You have no soul,' Jasmine said, arms crossed, 'no soul whatsoever. This at least has some relevance in the world after you leave the school gates.'

'How exactly does one apply Shakespeare to the real world?'

'No soul,' Jasmine repeated. 'No soul at all.'

Even though she would probably never wrap her head around Shakespeare, Aleera was just thankful that they hadn't picked up on their line of conversation from the previous day.

'You know, we still haven't talked about the other day,' Jasmine said. For a second, Aleera thought she'd done that on purpose.

'That's true,' she said. She didn't exactly feel capable of coming up with a particularly sharp or witty remark. 'Jasmine, I should probably mention…'

Jasmine's eyes turned down in what looked like disappointment. 'You're not single,' she speculated.'

'Actually, I am,' Aleera answered. She moved herself round to face Jasmine better. It was only after doing so that she realised how close together they suddenly were. Jasmine's eyes widened slightly, reminding Aleera of how blue and bright they were, and her lips curved into a soft smile. 'What?' she asked uneasily.

'You have pretty eyes.' Jasmine was almost whispering.

Aleera's mind more-or-less went blank, and she quietly answered 'you too.' The two of them went quiet enough to hear the traffic on the street outside, muffled by the window that kept them both locked into their tiny, awkward microcosm that neither one wanted to leave, whatever they might tell themselves. 'Now what?' Aleera asked, feeling her own cheeks grow warmer.

Then Jasmine's eyes lidded and she moved forward, until their lips were nearly touching. Aleera felt something buzz inside her before she instinctively moved back, and apparently not far enough. Jasmine closed the distance between them, and the next thing Aleera knew, her own eyes were closed and a soft, content sigh escaped her as their lips pressed together. She knew that she really should stop this. There was no way, absolutely no way, she was going to do that without… without…

God, her clothes felt confining all of a sudden.

Jasmine finally broke the kiss and moved back, smiling softly at her. 'What were you saying?'

Very much against her better judgement, or what was left of it, Aleera answered 'never mind' and kissed her again.

9

Aleera would have felt better if she'd woken up the next morning feeling awful or guilt-ridden. Instead, when she opened her eyes and blinked in the intrusive sunlight coming from the open window, she unfortunately felt fantastic, like something that had been kept tight and crushing her chest had finally been torn off.

That was the first thing she noticed upon waking up. The second was that she wasn't alone. The third was that it was Jasmine lying next to her, wearing the faintest, most content smile she'd ever seen. Immediately, exactly what they'd been doing the previous night came flooding back to her. She sat up as gently as possible, oddly reluctant to wake her... well, the term "girlfriend" probably applied by this point. In doing so, she confirmed that they were both completely naked.

Jasmine stirred with a quiet sigh, opened her eyes and squinted in the light. When she saw Aleera, she blinked a few times, sat up straight, and, realising why that had been a bad idea, pulled the duvet up over herself.

'Oh,' she finally said. That said it all, really. '...Morning.'

'Morning,' Aleera replied awkwardly as she pulled some underwear on.

Jasmine seemed to think for a moment. 'Yeah, we did.'

'I'm sorry,' Aleera said reflexively. Ah, there was the guilt. And where, her brain snapped at it, had it been last night? 'I-'

'What "sorry"?' Jasmine grinned, then leaned over the bed and kissed her. 'I mean, that was...' she searched for a word. 'Wow.' Aleera decided she might as well take it as a compliment.

'What time is it?' Aleera asked as she fished a top out of her wardrobe.

Jasmine checked the clock. 'Half past way-too-late,' she realised. 'Oh man, my mom is gonna crucify me when I get home. Where'd I leave my clothes?' she asked as she pulled a garment from the floor. 'Oh yeah,' she recalled in the middle of dressing, 'you mentioned it the other day, so...' she grabbed Aleera's shoulders, seizing her lips in a heated kiss. '...happy birthday.'

Aleera collapsed onto the bed, heard Jasmine leave, and let her pulse slow down a little. Then she finished dressing and stepped out.

'Morning, birthday girl,' she grinned. 'How does it feel to be legal?'

'Not bad,' Aleera said as she opened the fridge. 'It legalises what I like to do anyway.'

'So does that mean you'll be having your girlfriend over again?' Lilith asked slyly. Then she added 'and just because it's your birthday doesn't mean you can't share her.'

'She's *not* my girlfriend,' Aleera said in the manner of someone a good four years her junior.

'You think I'm about to believe that after the way you two were all over each other last night?'

Aleera felt herself turn red. 'How do you-'

'Her mom rang at one point and I came in to tell her. You two didn't even notice.'

Aleera turned round to look at her. 'You didn't.'

'Of course I didn't. I told her the two of you were out at the movies.'

Aleera sighed. That would be an uncomfortable family discussion. As opposed to this one here, she thought sarcastically, which isn't uncomfortable at all.

'Anyway,' Lilith said, hugging her, 'happy birthday, baby sister.'

'You're never going to stop calling me that, are you?'

'Not a chance.' Lilith ducked out of the kitchen for a second, 'be right back. Take a look in the fridge.'

Aleera looked back inside the refrigerator, and pulled out a box that had caught her eye before. Despite everything, she couldn't help smiling when she opened it and saw a big, fat chocolate cake covered in frosting and drizzled with honey.

'Here, baby sis,' Lilith smiled, stepping back into the room and handing her a small, neatly-wrapped package, 'happy birthday.'

Aleera smiled and started opening the present while Lilith picked up the mail.

In a rare phenomenon indeed, Aleera's face lit up. Inside, a small, gold pendant the shape of a heart gleamed lovingly up at her. Smiling, she attached it round behind her neck and traced the edges with her finger.

'Like it?'

Aleera beamed and clasped a hand around the pendant. 'Love it.'

Kheron didn't bother to look up as the door opened.

'Come in, Mister Connolly.'

Jake shut the door behind him. Kheron glanced up as if paying attention were an afterthought. 'I assume that this relates back to your wraith problem?' he asked idly.

'What do you know about it?' Jake asked bluntly.

'What I've told you.'

'And what else?'

Kheron looked through him and leaned back on his chair. He reached under the desk and turned on the tape recorder. 'Mister Connolly,' he said civilly, 'it's one thing to follow up on leads during an investigation, especially one as serious as this; commendable, even. It is quite another, however, to start throwing this type of wild accusation against a respected member of the community.'

'We found a ring across town with two crack dealers.'

'Dead, I presume.'

'And you know because…?'

'Would you be here talking to me otherwise? You're hardly a regular.' Kheron went back to his paperwork.

'Six people have died in under a week,' Jake warned, 'all of them in places that you run.'

'Which I trust you can prove before a tribunal,' Kheron said dismissively.

'At this rate, they'll hit this place by the end of the month.'

Kheron glanced up at him. He replaced the lid of the pen and sat back in his chair.

'That could easily be construed as a threat, Mister Connolly,' he said matter-of-factly. 'Now unless you plan to arrest me for something,' he pointed his pen toward the paper on the desk, 'I have an inordinate amount of paperwork to complete.'

Jake turned round slowly. The door slammed shut behind him.

Kheron muttered something indecipherably to himself and began twiddling with his pen.

This, he mused, was fast getting out of hand. Once was permissible. Twice was significant. Thrice was inexcusable. Still, it was a private matter, and he would see to it himself…

Mostly.

He did, he recalled, have the perfect ace up his sleeve. But first… a way dawned on him that this situation could work very much to his advantage.

Kheron chuckled to himself as the record player in the corner of the room kept spinning. Mr. Bowie again. *Ashes to Ashes.*

Sunday came, and Aleera was by herself making some attempt to pass the time. Tomorrow would be the big day, and she still wasn't entirely sure how to spend her last twenty-four hours of freedom.

As she got dressed, her cell phone jingled to life on the bedside table, with Jasmine's number flashing up on the screen.

Maybe she should answer it, she thought to herself. How much harm could a conversation do?

Or maybe they'd go somewhere, and Aleera wouldn't have the nerve to tell her the truth- *again*- and the whole situation would only get worse.

Damnit, how could she have been such an idiot?

How the hell could she not figure this out? She was half sex-demon for God's sake, and locking lips with someone she had a schoolgirl crush on had bent her out of shape like this?

Wait, crush? Where had that come from? It would explain a few things but that was something that… well…

She'd had feelings for people before, obviously, but this schoolgirl infatuation, butterflies-in-her-stomach and all, it had always been something that happened to other people.

And it was finally beginning to dawn on her that she didn't have a clue what she was doing.

She should really answer the phone, she thought, just before the jingle ended.

That was that. She wasn't avoiding Jasmine. No, of course not.

Considering how weak that sounded to her, it was little wonder Lilith hadn't been convinced.

This was it.

The sentence hardly did it justice. This wasn't just it, but "it". End of days; the final hour. Maybe a bit exaggerated, but it was hard to think that straight considering what the end of school that dull Monday forebode; and especially when thinking entirely straight wasn't your specialty and you instead tended to take the odd detour through near-psychosis. For the same reason, the entire affair seemed to look like a worse and worse idea the closer it got.

The other problem was that this Monday was as Mondays tended to be; right there all of a sudden, when on Friday Aleera had had far more normal concerns and Monday had been a nice, long way off. Nonetheless, Aleera found herself rather calmer than she perhaps should have been. It was one of those many times when it paid to not be so emotional.

Jake was waiting for her in the usual place; under the bleachers of the football field. He'd been on the phone the day before and said that he'd been there to meet her. Well, here goes nothing.

'All set?' Jake asked.

'As I'm going to get,' Aleera replied stoically. 'So are we teleporting?'

'Not into the Guild,' Jake shook his head. 'Besides, you hate it. C'mon, we'll walk; I can bring you up to speed on the way.'

'On what?' Aleera quizzed as they started off.

'Your first case,' Jake said simply, 'what else? The Guild's stuck us together, as always.'

'Sympathetic of them,' Aleera observed dryly.

'Actually, I think it's because you don't listen to anyone else there.'

'Neither do you.'

'Fair point. Anyway, you're gonna love this one.' His tone, of course, was one that suggested that Aleera would not remotely love whatever one it was.

'Ok. Let's hear it.'

'Sixteen dead people in a fortnight.'

Most people would have reacted in horror. Aleera's reaction of simply rolling her eyes said a lot about why she so worried the Guild. Just once, it would be nice to get together with her old friend and not be surrounded by corpses.

'And the real kicker,' Jake went on, 'is what killed them.'

A brief moment of silence passed.

'You're going to make me ask, aren't you?' Aleera sighed.

'It's a small pleasure,' Jake shrugged, 'and I thought I'd get at least one bit of humour in before I tell you.'

'And you're going to tell me…?'

As they exited the school, Jake turned to her and said, quietly, 'Wraiths.'

10

Aleera knew as well as anyone that the supernatural world was not a place of unicorns and happy little fairies and pixies (humans got one or two things right, but mostly by coincidence). Rather, it was largely made up of draconics, demons, succubae, and, just once in a while, wraiths would turn up. Now there was something to be avoided. Wraiths weren't just ordinary, garden-variety bad; they were why humans and most draconics saw demons as things straight from the bowels of hell. They were something to be loathed, feared and pitied for what they'd become, straight out of the darkest fantasies. To draconics, they were the very clearest example of why the Guild and its laws needed to be in place, and the consequences of the darkest side of magic.

Dark magic is powerful stuff. It was never "dark" because of any alignment, or any malign intent. It was just energy, a tool; this was just the kind of tool that gave a person power, and more of it than they could control. Dark magic could eat away at you. One use could change things inside a person. It was ancient, powerful, and for that reason forbidden. It could drain your own magic as its reserves; deplete your own soul, until there was nothing left.

Until you became a wraith.

When that happened, the magic would be all that kept you alive. Yours would be gone, and you would need more. The very basest, most primal instincts would kick in and you would do anything to keep it, to postpone the process of your soul rotting away and your body falling apart off the bone. Wraiths killed. They did it with a touch; sucked out the magic just to survive. A wraith, whoever they might have been before, would never stop. There would be nothing except feeding. No way of resisting any more than a compass can fight the urge to point north.

Wraiths, nowadays, were rare. In decades and centuries past they'd been feared as spirits and devils. The sickest of the sick. There was nothing in this world more wretched.

And there were at least ten of these creatures somewhere in Manhattan.

This, Aleera reflected, was her new job.

It turned out that the Guild did have a locker room. It didn't really fit the whole mystical image, but Aleera had expected it; she had the kind of practical mind that thought of these things. It was not unlike any other locker room; perfectly clear in communicating that its only purpose was to provide a room in which there were lockers.

She'd expected the uniform, too. Black fitted Kevlar, cowl and hood, metal mask, etc, a little tight around the chest- then again, everything was on her. Since she was to be on active duty, she was to wear it, evidently.

What did impress her, though, was the pair of long, thin slots folded over each other at the back, specially fitted for soldiers with her not unique, but scarce, ability, to allow the wings out without comprising protection to the back. Protection to the wings could be a problem, though.

Jake was waiting for her outside the locker room; no uniform for him a) because he was a freelancer and b) because he was good enough at defending himself that providing him with one would be a pointless use of a perfectly good set of body armour, and Kevlar didn't come cheap even to these people.

'All set?' he asked readily.

Aleera uncomfortably adjusted the uniform's chest piece. 'I suppose. Where to first?'

'Briefing,' Jake answered brightly, 'Khazahn and the new head of D-Unit will bring you up to speed, because it's been a hell of a couple of weeks.' He muttered something under his breath that sounded like "here comes the hurricane".

Through a short walk, he led her to what had formerly been Khazahn's office. 'Ok,' he said as he opened the door, 'Khazahn you've already met, so this is the new D-Unit Sergeant, Daniel Cassidy.'

Cassidy stood up from his seat. 'Ms. Maheste,' he said without a great deal of emotion. 'Nice to have you with us. Best not to waste time, then,' he said, picking up the file that sat on his desk, 'have you been informed at all so far?'

Not many pleasantries, Aleera noted. Most of the time that happened, of course, it had been clear that this was merely someone caught up in his work, reserved, or just plain arrogant. She recalled Chara, but this man was quite unlike him in the way he carried himself, and what appeared to cross his eyes when he looked at her; he didn't like what he saw, and he didn't *want* to. Aleera picked up on those things; after all, she was a smart girl. Not necessarily book-smart and not street-smart because when you were as intimidating as she was you didn't need to be. But she was smart because she was good at working things out with what was in front of her, and at figuring out what was going on inside people's heads- and then making it work to her advantage.

She stored this little tidbit for future references.

She opened the file as if automatically used to the environment. It was immediately satisfying to her to see Cassidy react ever so slightly. Maybe he'd been expecting her to be bitchy, oppositional, rude… she'd considered it herself. But Aleera had always been the eighteen-going-on-thirty type.

'Wraiths, isn't it?' she said.

'Right,' Cassidy said bluntly, 'a whole cabal of them somewhere in New York. We had a failed operation to capture them about a week ago. We're looking into it.' Jake and Khazahn both glared at him from across the room. 'Where they've come from, nobody's been able to figure out yet.' Tiny little inflection in the middle of that sentence. Someone didn't like his new co-workers.

'Dark magic,' Aleera surmised, 'New York's got a decent sized draconic population.'

'Actually, the victims were demons.' Cassidy clearly wanted it to be clear that there was a difference. 'Half a dozen of them over the last week. Mostly drug dealers and addicts. All we can assume is that they were in the wrong place at the wrong time. We also lost several of our own men.'

'In a failed operation,' Jake added under his breath.

'*So* we're currently looking into those circles,' Cassidy went on, making a deliberate point of implying that Jake hadn't spoken.

'Reasonable targets,' Aleera said offhand, 'bottom-rung; not to be missed; plenty of them in Manhattan to keep a whole cabal going, but not for long at those kinds of numbers. Wouldn't keep their intrinsic fields up.' She turned her dark eyes up to him. 'Sorry,' she lied, 'I was thinking out loud.' Well, it was a little satisfying.

'A rather educated viewpoint,' Cassidy said levelly. 'Intrinsic,' he repeated quietly and sardonically, 'big word for a teenager.'

'Not really,' Aleera said pleasantly, '"patronising" is bigger.'

'Aaaanyway,' Jake cut in like a desperate flood barrier faced with a sudden tidal surge, 'I think Khazahn was going to fill you in on the rest?'

'Most of the locations where we found the bodies,' Khazahn said, holding open another file, 'were operated by this man.' He handed Aleera a photo.

She took it and turned it over in her hand.

She started at the face beneath.

'Bad idea,' Jake said quietly to no-one in particular.

Aleera felt her chest tighten. That dark thing inside it stirred. Animals recognise their own kind. She tensed.

She handed the picture back.

'Kheron,' she said. 'I heard he was supposed to be in jail.'

'He was "supposed to be" a lot of things a lot of times,' Khazahn replied bitterly, 'he ended up with amnesty after the Secret War when he gave us a bunch of the others. Since then, he's been the biggest sentient piece of garbage on this seaboard. He's up to his neck in every kind of vice you care to name and has been for a good two years.' He snapped the file shut and slapped it onto the desk. 'As near as we can figure, he's somehow managed to put himself in the wraiths' firing line.'

'So do we arrest him?' Aleera asked simply. Khazahn looked uncomfortable for a moment in the seconds that ticked by. 'Right. Evidence?'

'He's a slippery little bastard,' Cassidy spat. Aleera wasn't naïve enough not to realise that the sentence ended with a silent "and that's all you need to know".

'So what, exactly, am I to be doing here?' Aleera pressed.

'You'll be working with Jake,' Khazahn replied, 'mainly assisting in this investigation and keeping to the sidelines except when absolutely necessary. We're a little short-handed at the moment, anyway.'

'Makian's off-duty for a week or two,' Jake explained quietly to her, 'nearly got himself drained.'

'We've already lost four men to this investigation,' Cassidy grated, 'and so far it's been two weeks in which our only solid lead has turned out to be a dead-end. Khazahn here tells me you've got a personal understanding of this type of psychology.' He left the implications unsaid.

'I prefer to think of it as a good deductive mind,' Aleera said nonchalantly, 'might be useful to have one around.'

Cassidy managed to squeeze in a few seconds of glaring before Jake gently tugged Aleera out of the room. 'Well, I think Tomoko can bring you up-to-date on the specifics,' he said hurriedly. He couldn't get her out the door fast enough.

'So that's the new head of D-Unit,' Aleera summarised.

'And you don't like him,' Jake hazarded. 'Can't say I blame you.'

Aleera leaned back on the door. She had a laser of a mind; the kind that immediately pinpointed the thing that she should be worried about, not just mildly irritated.

Kheron.

The thought made her sick to her stomach after all those years. Him again, after all that. She could feel her shallow breathing and the nauseous feeling creeping its way up her throat.

After what he'd done, he was still out there.

'You Ok?' Jake asked. The eyes, Aleera realised. She hadn't even felt them change. She nodded sharply and willed them back to the normal brown colour.

'You never mentioned Kheron,' she finally said.

Jake caught himself. 'No,' he said. 'I didn't.'

'How long did you know for?'

'Is that important?'

Aleera just glared at him. It was better than having to repeat the question, and still unnecessary; evasion said more than words ever could.

'Welcome to the Guild,' Jake said grimly.

'So that's what we do,' Aleera muttered, 'let Kudra's lieutenants off without a slap on the wrist.'

'Cassidy told you; he isn't easy to get hold of.'

'We all know what he did.'

'Doesn't mean we can prove it,' Jake said. 'We've had three separate cases thrown out by a tribunal.

Aleera didn't appear to move. Inside, she wrestled her angry, screaming soul back into submission. 'I didn't think I'd ever hear you give up that easily,' she finally said.

Jake took a deep breath. 'I tried a few times,' he answered, 'never worked. Kheron's... he's career scum. Nothing like Azrael.'

'*Kheron*,' Aleera hissed, the rage taking its chance to stream out of her, 'is running half of New York!'

'Yeah. He is. But right now, we have this to deal with.'

Aleera took a breath to calm herself. She quietened the screaming thing and felt herself shiver as she recalled the face.

It was about eight o'clock when Aleera finally returned home. She only even registered Lilith's presence when she collapsed onto her bed with a stifled groan.

'Hey,' Lilith said from the doorway. 'Good day at the office?'

Aleera pushed herself up. She remembered it. She'd been remembering it all day.

'I *really* don't want to talk about it,' she said coldly.

'That good, huh?'

'Seriously, Lilith,' Aleera said, 'I don't. Just- don't.'

Lilith glanced at the floor in understanding. 'Alright.' She closed the door. Growing up with someone like Aleera gave you a good idea of when it was a good idea to get out of dodge.

Aleera stood up. She sighed heavily and dragged a palm over her tired face. She ached, not on the outside but… she just felt drained, full of dull, lifeless anger at…

Kheron.

She punched the wall. Then again. Then twice more. That was good. Let it out. Calm down.

Damn it, why? Why him, of all of them? After what he did, he was still free? Still out? Still *alive*, after everything he'd done? While the Guild treated *her* like a criminal?

She was going to lose it. She was actually going to-

He was out and running a city!

She shouted something indecipherable and lashed out with one hand, claws erupting. The bedside lamp smashed.

Kheron was still out, after what he'd done. After everything she saw him do in her father's name. And she was supposed to be the dangerous one.

There we go. All out. She heaved one last time.

Lilith was waiting for her outside the room. 'Do I get to know what that was about?'

Aleera let out a bitter sigh. She dropped herself onto the sofa.

'Kheron,' she said quietly.

Lilith's eyes widened as she leaned over the sofa behind her. Aleera felt her sister's hand on her shoulder.

'He's gone, sweetie,' she said gently.

'No,' Aleera shook her head slowly. 'He's out.'

Lilith looked down at her. 'What?'

'He was never even in,' Aleera said disgustedly, 'he- they never even locked him up. Never.'

'You're joking,' Lilith said with stifled breaths, 'Aleera, tell me this is a joke and I'm on some stupid candid camera show or something, because-'

'He's out and he's involved in what I have to work on,' Aleera clarified, sick to her stomach.

'They can't make you do that,' Lilith breathed.

'They can.'

Lilith steadied herself. Her hands were tight around the back of the sofa. 'Kheron?'

'Yes.'

'He's not in jail?'

'He isn't.'

The only sound was of gritting teeth.

'Why the fuck not!' Lilith yelled at the room.

'He testified against the other lieutenants,' Aleera replied, 'and he got let off in return. Now he's- he's the biggest demon crime lord in America and he's involved in the case that the Guild's assigned me to.'

Lilith retched. She had, as far as Aleera ever knew, had no contact with Kheron. She'd be surprised if he even knew what he looked like. But Lilith was like a wolf cub- intelligent, cute, but kick at her sibling and she'd claw your damn eyes out.

'Get them to transfer you,' she said immediately.

'They won't.'

'The hell they won't.'

'I'm serious.'

'So am I,' Lilith said fiercely, 'where's the phone?'

'Just leave it.'

'Where's. The. Phone?'

'Just leave it,' Aleera snapped. 'There's nothing we can do about this until the case is over, so we might as well just leave it.'

'They are not making you relive that shit,' Lilith swore, 'you understand me? I've sat by so far, but they are not doing this to my baby sister.'

'*Lilith*!'

The room quietened. Aleera buried her head in her hands.

'I just don't want to talk about this, alright?' she said quietly. 'Not now. Just… I can deal with it.' She sat back up and rubbed her dry eyes. 'I can deal with it.'

'You know,' Katya said with a sideways glance, 'I can just tell how much you love working with Aleera.'

'Cut it,' Jake warned, turning over another piece of paper. He'd already read it twice.

Katya, sprawled backwards over the sofa, rolled over to scrutinously inspect the coffee table. There was something about that table, she was sure, that was almost instinctively inclined toward a natural state of being covered in clutter and papers. Apparently Jake had been doing research. She also noted that a number of old Guild case files littered the surface. She picked one up and examined it.

'Kheron?'

'Yesterday,' Jake started, 'Aleera said something about all the stuff Kheron did back during the war. I looked back at some old cases,' he said distantly, 'see if there's anything we can at least use to bring him in for questioning.'

'And?'

'Nothing we haven't already tried. So we have to get creative.'

Katya turned to him. She grinned.

'Are you suggesting… "our" kind of deduction?'

'Not like we'd be setting him up for arrest,' Jake said innocently, 'just questioning. Grill him over, see if he spills anything.'

'Will that work?'

'Daeiol's been screaming at everybody down the phone for a fortnight; this should at least calm him down.'

'And Aleera?'

Jake looked up defensively. 'What about Aleera?'

'Is this because of her?' Katya asked directly.

'No.' Jake went straight back to the files.

'Jake?'

'I'm doing this because we need to do something about the wraiths, and because Kheron has it coming.'

Katya shifted herself into a seated position and leaned against Jake's side. 'She can cope, Jake.'

'Should she have to?'

'She will if she ends up face-to-face with Kheron.'

'She won't have to be there.'

Katya made a noise somewhere between a sigh and a purr. 'If you're doing this for her, I understand,' she said softly, 'I honestly do. You feel responsible for the kid. I get that.'

'I know,' Jake sighed, reaching a hand round to gently tussle Katya's furry ears.

'Of course,' she purred, 'it would be fun to rub this in Cassidy's face.'

'And maybe bring Kheron down a notch.'

'Downsides?'

'Wasting Cassidy's and Khazahn's time and insanely pissing them both off.'

'Go for it,' Katya grinned wickedly.

Jake reached into his pocket as his cell phone rang. It was Aleera's home phone number, although he recalled that she should probably be in school. 'Hello? …Yes,' he said with mild apprehension. 'Can I… excuse me? Yes, but… I didn't…' now he sounded offended by something. 'Look… I understand that, but…' for the first time Katya could remember, Jake appeared to have not only lost an argument, and not so much an argument as a tirade against which he stood no chance. 'I see… Uh-huh…. Yes… I see… Right.' The call ended.

'Aleera's sister,' Jake said, ashen-faced, 'has one *hell* of a mouth.'

11

Aleera knew that anyone working in as stressful an environment as the Guild would need a way to unwind after hours. Still, she didn't expect to be back at Pentagram so soon.

There are a great many poor ways to start a day at the office. A mountain of paperwork. Getting to work late after being stuck in traffic. A computer crashing. For those in the Guild, the definition of a "bad day" obviously had to be somewhat tightened up; compared to demons, shades and wraiths, a few minutes lost on the freeway paled into insignificance. But the sight of eleven fresh corpses littering a closed-off dance floor was unmistakably a sign that the office was not going to be a delightful place to be.

A little over a week, and now a grand total of twenty-one corpses. Katya said it best.

'We,' she said, looking at the scattered sheets of white, 'are fucked.'

'A whole pack of wraiths on a crowded dance floor,' Jake observed, 'it's a miracle that they only got this many.'

Aleera squeezed past a pair of white-garbed forensics officers. The entire place stank of rotting, dry flesh and choked screams. She saw a few soldiers heave.

'Sorry.' One of them squeezed past her. He sounded young under the mask, not likely to be over twenty. His breathing was shallow, and his voice sounded stifled.

'Lawson,' Cassidy said abruptly, 'over here. See what you can tell us about this.'

Lawson. Familiar name. Aleera gave herself a second to think before recalling that this was the other name she'd heard to have come out of the first raid attempt in one living piece. Already, she noticed, back on duty.

'Sir?' Lawson said anxiously.

'Get back to forensics and tell them we're pulling out.'

'Yes, sir-' Lawson stuttered. He saw a withered, blackened hand still stiff and frozen in the process of scratching the floor, underneath one of the tarps.

He heaved. He gagged. He pulled his helmet off and ran for the door.

'In here,' Jake said quickly, stuffing a plastic evidence bag into his hands. Lawson looked at him, dumbfounded and confused for a moment. 'Evidence pertaining to a scene. Enjoy.' Jake left him with a bag and joined Cassidy and Khazahn.

'Please tell me we've got something here,' Khazahn pleaded tensely, 'because if not, this division can kiss its credibility goodbye.'

'We're still trying to track down everybody on the guest list,' a soldier said, 'but most of them are refusing to comment.'

'Not a lot that we could learn from them other than "wraiths did it".'

'We were supposed to have a man staking this place out,' Cassidy hissed. 'Where the hell is he?'

Jake pointed morbidly to one of the tarps.

'They actually hit Pentagram,' Khazahn muttered to the air.

'And we all know what that means,' Jake reflected.

'They won't stop here. They're after the man himself.'

'Talking of whom,' Jake said levelly. The crowd of soldiers shuffled aside to make way for six feet of demon in an impossibly-sharp suit.

'Gentlemen,' he said with unfaltering politeness, 'Welcome to the club. I do apologise for the conditions, but I'd just like to reassure you personally that you'll have my full support in this investigation.'

'Wonderful,' Khazahn said flatly, 'now get out.'

'Excuse me?'

'Get out. As in "leave".'

'Commander, this is my establishment, and-'

'And until further notice, it's not an establishment; it's a crime scene, off-limits to all unauthorised personnel. If you're not wearing a Guild pass, then get behind the yellow tape.'

Kheron inhaled slowly. Then, gradually, he stepped away.

'Very well. Do let me know if I can be of assistance.'

Kheron left, the rest of the room continuing to empty.

'Ok,' Jake said, distracting Khazahn, 'we should go, then.'

Cassidy nodded abruptly and turned back to the soldiers. 'Alright, people!' he barked, 'if you're not in a forensic uniform, then out!'

Aleera managed to get over to Jake past the shuffling armada. She heard another soldier gag in the background and felt like doing so herself. Even when you could remember it from your earliest memories, that stink got everywhere.

'Maheste!' Cassidy snapped, 'you deaf? Out!'

'She's with me, remember?' Jake interrupted. Cassidy glared at him for a second.

'You probably should go,' Jake said quietly, making his way over to Aleera, 'go back to HQ.'

'That bad?'

'You kidding? This is officially the worst three weeks we've had since the end of the war.'

'Hey!' They heard Cassidy bark along the edge of the dance floor, 'who the hell let a civilian into my-'

Aleera actually almost smiled when she recognised the man smiling and holding up a Guild scene pass.

'Hey, kid,' he chuckled, 'anybody miss me?'

'Who the hell-'

'Tomoko let me through,' Makian answered with a Gallic shrug.

'Well you're not back on active duty until Monday, so get the hell-'

'Well if that's how you treat a man who comes to you with a lead, no wonder this shit's still going on.'

The entire room fell silent.

'You have what?' Khazahn said.

'Well don't get your hopes up, because this is probably nothing, but I overheard something all nice and juicy-like.'

'You were here?' Katya cut in.

'Off-duty,' Makian said innocently, 'thing is- there's somebody who might know something.'

'Let's hear it,' Jake said before anyone else had a chance to talk, 'we'll let the forensics do their job, and frankly it reeks in here.'

Makian nodded, and everyone turned to the door. Aleera was surprised that it was her that he spoke to first.

'Heard you were onboard this week,' he said. 'To be honest, we all hoped this'd be over by now. How're you finding clusterfuck central?'

'How do you think?' Aleera said icily. Undeserved, but true. It had not been the nicest place to work, although she quickly corrected herself that she shouldn't be taking it out on Makian. 'It's been a long week.'

'Well, let's see what old Mak has in his magic bag, huh?' Makian beamed as the heavy metal door was pulled open and the assembled party made sure to avoid the tape around the last of the eleven corpses.

'Shinju!' Cassidy snapped unexpectedly as a white-garbed figure made her way inside, 'my office. Eleven p.m.'

'The hell's that for?' Jake hissed.

'Sending non-forensic personnel into a closed-off crime scene.'

'It was closed off for all of thirty seconds!'

'Man, I can't believe *I'm* the most professional person talking right now,' Makian sighed, shaking his head in dismay. 'Can't I leave you kids alone for two minutes?'

'Nice t' have ya back, Mak,' Katya squeaked, giving him a crushing hug from one side. 'So are we gonna be in suspense all day?'

'Well like I said, I was here the other night,' Makian started, 'and guess who gets called to meet with the owner. 'Course, he didn't know I wasn't working, but some bouncer with rocks in his head and lead in his ass explained it to him.'

'And you decided to trespass on a crime scene to tell us *this*?' Cassidy demanded.

'No, I decided to trespass on a crime scene to tell you *this*: while I'm outside the office, there's some other guy in there trying to string together an explanation of why Kheron shouldn't fill him with holes or something. And I started listening because he said something that really caught my interest: he says- or he says something like- what was it- "I didn't know it would do that to them. I didn't know it'd start all this". Then Kheron turns up some piece of shit music and I couldn't make out much else, but there was definitely something about this week's hot topic.'

'I hate to break it to you, Makian, but this is circumstantial at best,' Khazahn said bleakly.

'Enough to give us a search warrant, though. I heard the words "Dark Magic" come out of the guy's mouth, clear as day.'

'If we know who we're searching for,' Aleera pointed out. She'd gotten to that rather disheartening point as soon as she gleamed the nature of the story.

'Oh, but we do,' Makian grinned, pulling a cell phone from out of his pocket. 'What, you never heard of a camera phone?'

By now, Jake was grinning ear-to-ear. 'Got a voice recorder, too,' Makian said proudly, 'can't make much out, but you never know. We've got a good pair of ears here,' he nodded in Katya's direction.

'This is nothing concrete,' Cassidy said dismissively.

'No, but it's something,' Jake pointed out, 'and that's more than we had five minutes ago.'

Makian called up the picture on his phone. 'Here's our man.'

The phone was briefly handed round the group. Aleera only managed to catch a brief glimpse- dark hair, goatee, looked like he wore a lot of black; the camera had clearly zoomed in, so that would likely be helpful- before Cassidy snapped the phone away from her.

'I remember that guy,' Katya piped up. 'Thomas Smith. We busted him- what- five years ago?'

'This stays confidential,' he said, 'until we can be sure.'

'Fair point,' Khazahn conceded, 'we don't need this blowing up on us too.'

'Want me to follow up on it?' Makian offered.

'No such luck,' Khazahn said, 'you're still on leave.'

'So screw the leave.'

'No can do. Until the date's up, it's illegal for us to even take you into the building.'

'Khazahn, for-'

Aleera remained externally quiet. Internally, she screamed and that dark little thing ranted and raving. They couldn't take him back? They weren't allowed? But they were allowed to drag her away from her life just because they felt like she might be dangerous. Then these people had the gall to say that what the other side did was so awful, so terrible, with the only difference being that they were honest about it.

She put her private fuming aside for now, or rather pushed it down until it stopped screaming, and continued to walk after the others.

'Is it me, or is Khazahn wound up even tighter than usual?' Katya asked.

Jake's pager chose that moment to go off. When he looked down at it, he shrugged and said 'not half as much as he's going to be.'

Even Aleera had to confess herself somewhat surprised as the elevator, finishing its descent from within the Flat Iron Building, came to a stop and opened its doors to reveal the amount of activity going on within the Guild's headquarters. The entire place was a shifting mass of activity, which lead Aleera's adaptable brain to immediately conclude that something had presented itself as a great source of irritation for everyone there.

Even as she changed, the amount of hustle in the locker room confirmed that trying to talk to anyone would essentially be a useless gesture, but she did manage to catch a name amidst everything.

Guess who.

Unable to find Jake amidst the chaos, she'd found relative sanctuary by wandering into the forensics lab to see if anyone had replaced Harry Drake. It turned out that it was still just Tomoko down there.

'Alecra,' the doctor smiled when she saw her. 'I didn't think you'd started yet.'

'Only since yesterday,' Aleera replied, 'I heard you were having wraith trouble.'

'For the last two weeks or so. Today it's Jake that's set a new record for biggest kick up Khazahn's backside. The whole place is going nuts.'

'What's he done?'

'Brought the biggest, most-untouchable magical criminal in the country in for questioning on- and you'll love this part- tax evasion.'

Aleera felt herself grin, then remembered why she shouldn't be. Still, if Kheron was actually there…

He was there. In that building.

'Where is he?' she asked immediately.

'Holding-one,' Tomoko answered, putting away some piece of equipment Aleera didn't recognise, 'they're questioning him now.'

When she looked up, Aleera was already out the door.

Kheron. Right there. The one thing- the one thing left from what her father had done. In that building with her. It was somehow a thrill. She felt dizzy.

She was just going to see him. Not be in the same room, not do anything to him, just see him. Just see the man who'd done that to her along with Kudra, and then that could be the end of it.

Yes, this is a perfectly normal thing to be doing, a sarcastic little voice in the back of her head told her. This would solve everything.

As it transpired, Aleera wasn't the only person with that idea. At least a dozen people were crammed into the tiny room watching through the two-way mirror.

Kheron sat on one side of the table, leaning back on the seat as, on the other side, Jake Connolly was stood up "idly" wandering the room while Khazahn seated himself opposite him.

And there he was, Aleera realised. Ordinary orange hair. Ordinary green eyes. Sitting there talking like a human being. Not even in jail.

He turned. Aleera felt his eyes fix on hers. He couldn't see her. There was no way. They still lingered.

'Connolly,' she heard Daniel Cassidy saying somewhere in the gathering, 'is going to fry for this.'

'There you are,' a hand caught her arm. Katya pushed her way through a pair of soldiers next to her. 'Hope we didn't get your hopes up, but we're not gonna be able to keep him here. He's way too slippery for that. But it does give us a chance to press on him a little.'

'He knows something about the wraiths,' Aleera surmised.

'More than he told us, at least. Fingers crossed that those two get it out of him.'

'Think they can?'

'Well Jake just plain knows what he's doing, and Kheron's been riding Khazahn's back for years. This should be entertaining enough, anyway.'

Aleera fixed her attention on the glass and the sound coming from a small speaker.

'I'll say again: I am not saying a word,' Kheron said bluntly, 'until my solicitor gets here.'

'And I'll say again: why are these wraiths after you?' Khazahn asked again, clearly not for the first time.

Kheron shifted uncomfortably in the seat and leaned forward on the table. 'I'll go one better,' he offered. 'I'll give you the address.'

'Address?'

'As it happened, yesterday I received a very likely lead as to where your wraiths might be. You understand, of course, why I didn't immediately come to the Guild, given our... history of misunderstanding.'

'You found out where they are?' Khazahn snapped, 'how the hell did you find out who they are?'

'My revenues have been cut in half in less than a month, and you don't think this is a priority for me?' Kheron said, looking at Khazahn as he would at someone who'd just dribbled all over himself.

'Do you even get the idea of what's after you?' Jake cut in, 'because it's wraiths. If they're after you, nothing you've got will prevent them from coming for you.'

'Mister Connolly,' Kheron said, turning sharply to him, 'I assume you're aware of how easily that could be construed as threatening. So why don't I just give you the address, and we'll all be on our way. I do have business to attend to, after all.'

Khazahn glared at him, long, slow and deep. Then he tore a piece of paper from the pad in front of him, pushed it across the desk and placed a pen on top of it.

Kheron smirked. There was no mistaking it, or what it said. It said "you need my help. You can't do this without me". He scribbled something down and pushed the paper back toward Khazahn.

'It's an old gambling den; before it went out of business I believe it was owned by a gentleman of ill repute. I've heard a few whispers, as one does, that fit the description of a wraith.'

'We'll check it out,' Jake said simply. 'Make yourself comfortable.' He turned away. Khazahn moved slowly, standing up and pushing the chair back.

Then the door burst open inward to allow through a short, stocky man in a creaseless suit with hair that didn't look so much flattened back as drawn on his head with a black marker. Beady eyes moved from Jake to Khazahn to Kheron and back again.

'Commander Khazahn. Mister Connolly.' He said with sharp civility, 'I hope I'm not too late.' Jake muttered something like "oh shit". Behind Aleera, Katya did much the same.

'We're done here,' Khazahn said bluntly.

'I should imagine so. I trust you can explain yourself, Commander? Have you even charged my client?'

'Not as such.'

'Yet I just overheard a clear intent to hold my client, apparently indefinitely.'

'Only until we can determine whether his claim is accurate,' Khazahn said simply.

'Am I correct in understanding,' the fat little man glared with infinite perceived superiority, 'that you intend to hold my client without charge?'

'Your client's just given us some information pertaining to a top-level case,' Jake said simply as he pushed past him, folding the paper over. 'Bye.'

'Information, I'd like to point out, without being permitted to consult legal counsel.'

'Bye.'

'Mister Connolly, you may be outside the Guild, but you are not-'

'You still here?' Jake asked as he opened the door and stepped through.

'Mister Connolly-'

'Bye!' The door slammed shut.

The lawyer shook momentarily, flustering and regaining his composure. 'Well,' he said sharply, 'if you can find no reason to hold my client...'

Khazahn opened the door himself. 'Tax evasion,' he said sardonically. 'I'll leave you to confer.' He left the interview room.

Outside, the assembled crowd of soldiers parted to clear the exit. Khazahn moved to the side and placed the piece of paper in Daniel Cassidy's hand. 'I want every available soldier at that address ten minutes ago.'

Aleera tried to calm herself again. It didn't work. She still wasn't entirely sure why she thought seeing Kheron would calm her; if anything, the desire to sink her claws into him had grown.

And now there he was, entering the evidence room to, as calmly as if he'd walked into a lost-and-found, retrieve the effects that had been confiscated when he was brought in.

When the soldier behind the desk went to retrieve them, Kheron looked across the room to see Aleera leaning against the wall.

'Steve,' he said quietly to his lawyer, 'would you wait outside for a moment, please? I'd like to have a word with the young lady.'

'I'd advise you not to say anything without-' the lawyer began.

'Just saying "hello" to an old friend; a personal thing. You understand.'

The lawyer nodded and left. Kheron turned to Aleera and chuckled deeply. 'Well I'll be damned,' he grinned without moving his mouth, 'Aleera Maheste. I'd heard you were around when I came in. Good God,' he said as he walked slowly and easily over to her and held a palm flat beside his ribcage, 'I haven't seen you since you were this tall. My, my,' he looked from her head to toe slowly, pausing at a few points, 'how you've grown.'

Aleera didn't say anything. Her eyes turned red.

Kheron straightened up as if paying attention. 'You know, that is a wonderful trick, isn't it?' Aleera watched as his own eyes drifted from green to blood-red. 'Hardly unique, but it helps scare people, doesn't it?'

'What do you want?' Aleera said scathingly.

'I can't say hello to an old friend? Hell, your old man, God rest him, he was like a brother. I'd feel cruel if I didn't at least say "hi" to his little girl.'

'You've said it,' Aleera said, dripping with hate. 'Get your things and leave.'

'Busy, I take it. I heard you got into a spot of trouble recently.' Aleera felt her claws start to scrape against the brickwork behind her. 'I'll let you get on, but we've clearly got a lot of catching up to do- what's it been, five, six years? How old are you now? Anyway…'

He turned back to the desk where his effects had been placed. Damn the man, there wasn't even anything suspicious- a pack of cigarettes, a wallet, a cell phone, a set of car keys, what looked like tickets, and a piece of candy in a wrapper.

'…you should drop in sometime,' Kheron finished, handing her one of the tickets. Its most significant features were the words "Pentagram" and "V.I.P.". He popped the piece of candy in his mouth. 'Works as a substitute. I'm supposed to be cutting down,' he said, patting the pack of cigarettes in his pocket. Well, must be off.'

He walked out. The heavy stone door grated shut behind him.

The address to which Kheron had referred them was one Aleera had her suspicions about as soon as she recalled the other things Jake had informed her about. And the more she thought about it, the less she liked the situation. She had that kind of mind; the kind that took facts in and scrutinised every detail. Her encounter with Kheron, for instance; nobody would even need to think to realise that accepting the "invitation" was a bad idea.

Similarly, Kheron just happening to come across this information and then passing it onto the Guild, rather than take care of the matter himself? Hardly the man she remembered. And as soon as that happened, everything else about the case came into question, and there was much question to come into.

The main thing was the attacks themselves: so far, every attack had been focused on a drug dealership that could be traced back to Kheron. But, as she'd learned, there were others, easier targets, much closer to this location. There was any number of explanations- the wraiths, for all they knew, could have been deliberately throwing them a red herring, but the Guild had traced them to somewhere else entirely. And could Kheron have worked it out if the Guild, Jake, Aleera and Tomoko between them couldn't?

Well, at least the place existed, and the whispers of *"Hthwail-Yiens"*- that old, familiar third-eye spell that helped to see in ways the naked eye couldn't perceive- followed by "all clear" did seem to suggest that nobody would get shot upon walking in.

What all present could tell, though, was that there were at least a dozen figures inside.

And so, here they were. Aleera stood beside Jake as the ten armed Guild soldiers tensed, waiting for orders on pins and needles..

One wrong move against a wraith cabal and it would be as much use as any plan when a bullet was an inch from your head.

The door was surrounded. Upper floor windows covered. Apparently the idea was for this to be something more than taking more than one route into a charnel house. Aleera found herself hoping so. A lot of the other soldiers looked nervous. None of them would admit it, of course, even with the last failure on every mind. This was another time when Aleera preferred to remain detached; it at least helped to think of her next move instead of desperately gripping her staff like the others. Still, at least they'd given her a weapon. She decided to keep the wings in for now; no sense in being a larger target than was necessary.

'All Hounds, move in.' Khazahn's signal crackled through the radio in the side of the helmet.

The door burst inward. Above, windows smashed. With shouted orders, the rows of soldiers filed in through the doors, staffs raised and buzzing with energy as, with a shout of *"Sola"*, at least three soldiers sent harsh light flooding the room.

The screams of sudden panic coming from in front of the soldiers were the first sign that something was wrong. The second was the gathering of ordinary, badly-clothed, completely non-wraith draconics turning and shouting by piles of crates and packaging.

The first sign of something else going wrong was when the nearest one shouted 'Shit, everybody get the fuck out! We got Guild!' and thrust his hand forward with a shout of *'ThuraiShiahl'*. A wall of shimmering, solid force erupted from his hand- uselessly as a soldier at the front yelled *'Blaish'* and the blast collided against a momentary barrier of gelatinous, solidified air.

'Somebody lay down a suppression field, *now*!' Khazahn ordered. A pair of soldiers near the front thrust their hands forward and yelled '*WhualLiah*,' and as soon as another one of the building's inhabitants tried to cast a spell, all that happened was a useless spark on the end of his finger, courtesy of the suppression field, standard practice for field operations, suppressing any use of magic. The only reason it hadn't already been in use was because, against wraiths, the general consensus was that they should be taken down as quickly as possible, be any means necessary. No point disarming your own soldiers.

Luckily, enchanted items- i.e. Guild staffs- weren't affected, and the thirteen rather-dense men finally got it into their heads that now would be a good time to put their hands up.

By the time they were on their knees, hands behind their head, all twenty-plus Guild soldiers were in the room, most of them looking mildly dumbfounded.

'Khazahn,' Jake finally said somewhere in the crowd, 'I don't think I'm the only one getting worried here.'

'Right address,' Cassidy said darkly, 'somebody check this stuff.'

Immediately, the soldiers nearest the piles got to work. The first to pull something out inspected what looked like a teddy bear. Cassidy pulled it from his hands, grabbed the head and pulled it off, revealing a number of small plastic bags filled with white powder.

'Fuck,' Cassidy breathed under his mask, 'he didn't. Somebody tell me he didn't!'

'Same with these,' Khazahn shouted as he inspected something from another pile, 'all kinds of stuff- coke, smack, pills…'

'You,' Cassidy snapped, pointing his staff at the forehead of one of the arrested men, 'what is this?'

'I ain't telling you shit, man,' the thug shook, 'no way. No freakin' way.'

Aleera managed to push her way through the soldiers and reach Jake to voice the conclusion that she'd reached immediately when the first bear was opened. 'There's no way Kheron would send us to break up his own operation. Not something as big as this.'

'I doubt it's his,' Jake said grimly, 'am I right? Some kind of rival operation?' he asked, directed at the men on the floor.

'Nobody told us this was gonna happen,' one of the men blubbered, 'we was just- come on man, I can't go to-'

'He set us up,' Khazahn realised, snarling beneath his mask. 'Kheron set us up to find this place.'

'And arrest everyone inside,' Jake said tensely, 'get rid of the opposition.'

'We're seriously going to do a favour for Kheron?' Cassidy snapped.

'It's that or we let this place keep going, and if we did that the High Council would tear us a new ass,' Jake said. 'We take them in.'

'Son of a bitch,' Cassidy seethed, 'too good to be true. We all freaking knew it. He played us. Bastard played us like a vio-fucking-lin!'

'Get these guys out of here,' Khazahn ordered to the soldiers, 'get forensics down here and have them sweep the place, then figure out what we're doing with this stuff. Anyone not needed for that, out. Now.'

Slowly, the place started to empty, the dealers being led out shamefully. Then, in a moment of solitude, Khazahn shouted to himself and kicked the side of one of the crates.

Khazahn closed the door into the office behind him. It was, foremost, a great deal larger and more lavish than his own and, most disconcertingly, contained three people whose presence in Guild matters could not possibly bode well.

The High Council had indeed been taking a personal interest in the matter involving the wraiths, and the previous night's debacle looked to have been the tipping point.

Behind the desk, an Indian man of tall, stocky build stood up and nodded a quiet greeting. To the other side, a small, Asian woman in a form-fitting black dress announced her presence without a sound. *Now* Khazahn was worried. If Lady Tamara was involved, it was almost certain that, by the time the situation was resolved, somebody was going to lose their job. The presence of the third official- a tall man with quaffed brown hair decked out in an especially well-armoured Guild uniform- was peanuts by comparison.

'Commander,' the man behind the desk said. 'Thank you for coming. I assume you know why you're here?'

'Yes, General,' Khazahn said quietly. You didn't forget your formalities when talking to the head of the Guild.

'Commander,' the woman said with a small voice that still managed to fill the room and every ear in it. She stepped around Khazahn and the desk slowly and purposefully. Only when she was sure she had his undivided attention did she continue. 'I don't think it will come as a shock to you when I say that this council- my council- bends over backwards to keep your numerous political enemies off your back.'

'No, ma'am.'

'Or that you are given a frankly-insane amount of leeway with the kind of people your division employs with regards to freelancers that have given us at least as much trouble as benefit, and the current situation, whose risks I shouldn't have to remind you about.'

'No, ma'am.'

'*Or* that, following the incident barely three months ago, the Eighth Division has escaped with little more than an internal investigation.'

'No, ma'am.'

'And do you know what we ask in return for this?'

'No, ma'am.'

'At the bare minimum,' the High Chancellor snapped, '*we expect you not to run errands for mobsters!*'

Khazahn folded his hands behind his back.

'Commander,' Daeiol said from behind the desk, 'I think we would all like your version of the events that transpired last night.'

So Khazahn told them, as non-incriminatingly as possible, how Kheron had offered information as to where the wraiths might be located, and how every available soldier in D-Unit and then some had closed in on the place and found nothing but Kheron's rivals setting up a drug cartel, at which point they'd had no choice but to bring them in.

'And these dealers you came across?'

'According to what we've dug up, they're small-timers who were looking to go up against Kheron. It seems he just took advantage of the situation.'

'And you had Guild officers arrest his rivals for him,' Daeiol said scrutinously.

'We'd come across a draconic/demon-run drug ring. We didn't have much of a choice.'

'Commander,' Lady Tamara snapped, 'you are over a week into this investigation and have absolutely nothing to show for it.'

'I understand that.'

'This means that the time has come for decisive action. Colonel Hartwell?'

The man behind Khazahn hadn't even spoken yet. When he did, his voice was low, rough and grating.

'James Hartwell,' he introduced himself, shaking Khazahn's hand, 'Special-Ops. We'll be personally monitoring the investigation from this point on.'

Khazahn inhaled sharply. His hands turned into fists without his permission.

'This isn't necessary,' he said.

'The decision has been made, Commander,' Daeiol announced. 'As of right now, every move in this investigation goes through Special-Ops.'

'There's no need for this in the case.'

'Then you'll have nothing to hide,' Daeiol said levelly. 'I assure you, Special-Ops, as well as ourselves, will be watching.'

'I see.'

'And one other thing, Commander.'

Khazahn felt his stomach starting to tie itself in knots.

'If we hear so much as a whisper of anything else like this or the Azrael incident, then you can kiss your Guild career goodbye. Understood?'

Khazahn nodded slowly.

'Excellent. We'll let you get back to your work. We expect to hear from you by the end of the week.'

Aleera went back over the plan for the evening in her head. That night, she and Jake would meet with Thomas Smith, the week's dark-magic dealer de jour, and, assuming all went to plan, bring him in for questioning. Now she just had to pass the time until then.

Her first distraction came as she was on the way out of the building and heard a voice calling from behind her.

'Private Maheste.'

Aleera didn't bother guessing who it was; nobody else there who knew her addressed her formally. It was such a wonderfully subtle way of establishing that you didn't like someone.

'Sir.'

'I expect Connolly's taking you along to bring Smith in.'

'Yes he is,' Aleera replied curtly.

'Good,' Cassidy said levelly. 'I hope we can rely on you for this.'

'You don't need to worry about that,' Aleera said as she took a last sip of her coffee and threw the cup into a trash can, 'we're not all people-eating monsters.'

'Quite an assumption.'

'Is it, now?'

'You are aware of what you're suggesting?' Cassidy said in a voice that had suddenly become a storm. 'It sounds an awful lot like you're accusing me of something.'

'Not at all,' Aleera said innocently. Then, for no other reason than that she was in a mood, she added 'you made the connection' under her breath.

Cassidy seemed to grow taller. 'I don't take kindly to that being implied about me over a matter of race, Private,' he snarled. Then, suddenly so much more polite, he stepped back. 'Just as a reminder: discriminatory behaviour will not be tolerated.'

As Cassidy walked away, Aleera found herself overcome with the notion that their career together would not be an enjoyable one.

With little else to do, she wandered around for a moment and made a brief detour on the trip to nowhere in particular, picking up her helmet from her locker.

Aleera didn't believe in fate, but she was prepared to accept what then happened, because she did subscribe to the theory of convenient- or as was most often the case in her experience, horribly *in*convenient- coincidences.

The door of Khazahn's office was open as she passed by. Aleera thought nothing of it at first, until she heard Khazahn address her as 'Private. Or am I still allowed to call you Aleera?'

She pushed the heavy stone door the rest of the way open. She never did understand why they still made them like that; it was impressive, fair enough, but hardly ergonomic.

'Sergeant,' she greeted him.

'Haven't seen much of you since you've been around,' Khazahn said from the desk. 'Been busy, though.'

There was, Aleera noticed, something different. It was hard not to notice it, really, for anyone acquainted with Khazahn. No sharp, well-spoken monosyllables; no harshly-spoken commands. In fact, he was slurred, as if every word fought its way out and was left exhausted by the effort.

She noticed the half-full glass of scotch in his hand. He'd been drinking. Obviously. Out of character, though.

'Been a long week,' Khazahn said, clearly trying to justify the presence of the liquid. 'Wraiths. Bodies. *Kheron*.' He spoke the last name like the worst insult ever conceived by the mouth of man.

Aleera fished for something to say.

'Jake said you helped him convince the High Council not to bring me in full-time,' she said, as conversationally as possible.

'You should have seen him,' Khazahn sighed, 'he actually shouted- really, properly, shouted- at the High Chancellor herself. Nobody's ever shouted at that bitch, as long as I can remember.' Aleera smiled to herself. That was Jake all over.

'Thank you, though,' Aleera said. There was a lot of honesty in that sentence. It had never occurred to her to think about it that much- in all fairness, there was an awful lot else going on- that, after everything that had happened before, she really owed him something.

'It's fine,' Khazahn said distantly. 'You're a brave kid. You've got a bright f-future,' he spluttered, suppressing a cough. 'Ahead of y-' the next one fought its way through a barrier of phlegm.

Khazahn leaned forward, hand in front of his mouth, coughing. Then it turned to hacking, and finally a grating, burbling wheeze.

'Khazahn?' Aleera said, rounding the desk, 'are you-'

Khazahn raised one palm. 'Fine,' he said quickly, before another coughing fit struck him. After a long, awkward moment, it died away.

'Sorry,' Khazahn said, quick and flustered, 'swallowed an ice cube.'

Doubtful. Even if the semi-sober lie wasn't easy enough to see through, the look on his face said everything.

'No you didn't,' Aleera breathed.

The air became heavy and silent. Khazahn groaned and collapsed into his chair.

'I'm sorry you had to see that,' he finally said. 'Truth is, I've been...' he sighed heavily, 'sick.'

'Oh.' Aleera looked around for something else to focus on. 'Is it...?'

'Well, you know the kind of sickness you get better from?'

'Yes.'

'This is the other kind.'

The dreadful words sat heavy in the air. Aleera's eyes lidded as she shifted uncomfortably.

'I'm sorry,' she said.

'No, no,' Khazahn said, waving a hand, 'that was- I'm the sorry one. Shouldn't have dropped that on you.'

'It's alright. I asked.'

'Don't worry about this,' Khazahn said, 'won't change much.'

'Does Jake know?'

Khazahn paused.

'No. Listen, Aleera-'

'I won't tell him.' Aleera realised immediately. Some things just weren't done through a third party, if at all.

'Seriously.'

'I won't.'

Khazahn sighed again. 'Thank you. Now do me one favour?'

'What's that?'

Khazahn picked up Aleera's helmet and handed it to her.

'Show me how right Jake was,' he smiled faintly. 'Go and solve this thing.'

12

And so, Aleera's second day as a member of the Guild of Guardians was nearly over.

In roughly thirty minutes, she and Jake would be paying an investigative visit to Mister Thomas Smith and finding out exactly what it was that he'd taken it upon himself to deliver into the city. And, if any luck, her first case was finally about to start going somewhere.

Wraiths. Her first case, and she was dealing with wraiths. It was enough to almost make her miss the old pre-Azrael days, when all she'd ever had to worry about was which strung-out mugger she was going to brutalise.

She was taking some time out at the moment; it turned out that there was indeed some adrenaline to be found in busting up a drug cartel, and she wanted to be nice and calm. It wouldn't do to lash out if she heard or saw anything particularly reprehensible during her "shift".

She turned the page in one of her old favourite books, *Interview with a Vampire*, noticing how, although this one had come close, humans had never quite managed to nail vampires as far as she was aware. As she did so, she reflected on the excuse Jake had used to pull her out of school: apparently she had viral pneumonia. It sounded realistic, and still far-fetched enough to be believable. Then again, Jake had been doing this for a good few hundred years that she knew of. Maybe now that she was officially working with him, she'd find something out, although judging by how little Katya knew, she doubted it.

Reality invaded her contemplation when Lilith knocked on her bedroom door.

'You've got a visitor,' she said.

'Visitor?'

'Is there an echo in here? Yes, a visitor. It's your sex-buddy-in-waiting. I'll send her in.' She said the last part quickly as Aleera's eyes flashed red. Making a mental note of it, she changed them back when Jasmine came in.

'Hey,' she smiled, 'I heard you were sick.'

Aleera sat up. 'Yeah. I'm getting better, but apparently they won't let me back to school for a week or two.'

'Well, lucky you. I don't know how you managed there all that time.'

'What makes you say that?'

'Apparently we've acquired a few nicknames,' Jasmine said as she sat down, '"carpet-munching skanks" is one of the nicer ones. And someone held a cross to me and said I was going to burn in hell, which was memorable.'

'I've heard that one,' Aleera said under her breath.

And yet, despite the attempt to take this in her usual sardonic stride, she felt a great swell of what she took to be indignation. With it came a surprisingly clear image of what she would do to anyone she found talking to her girlfriend like that.

So now she really was her girlfriend? Part of her piped up. You stay out of this, she snapped at it.

'News travels fast,' Jasmine shrugged. 'Apparently someone saw us in the library.' Ah yes, that. Considering the day after, it almost seemed insignificant now. 'I had a hell of a time convincing my mom that it was just one of those rumours. Apparently I'm still grounded for letting it happen.'

'I don't see how it's your fault.'

'Well, tell her that,' Jasmine said bitterly. 'Anyway, I, uh, I tried to call you yesterday when you weren't at school.'

'Oh.' Think of something. 'I was pretty bad yesterday. I must've slept through it.' Actually, considering what her cognitive faculties had been like lately, that wasn't a bad excuse.

'That's fine. I was just worried that maybe…' she fidgeting anxiously, 'the other night, maybe that was too fast?'

'Um,' Aleera gulped. Wait, "um"? Had she actually just given that kind of response? When had she started acting like the love struck teenager she was? 'no,' she said quickly. Wait, yes it was. 'Yes. I mean, maybe. A little. Yeah.' Dear God, just shoot her now.

'Oh.' Jasmine looked down, 'I mean, that's fine, really. I don't want you to feel like- I mean, it's alright. I get it.'

'I'm sorry,' Aleera said quietly.

'Don't be.'

They both went quiet. The silence was long enough for Aleera to notice the ticking of her bedside clock.

'Do you…' Jasmine hesitated. 'Do you like me?'

'Yes,' Aleera said, more readily than she'd have liked, 'I do. Really. It's just- I had this friend, a little while ago, and...' wait, was she going to tell her this? What was she thinking? How the hell to explain this? '...well, he's... gone.'

What was that supposed to be? Some kind of excuse? Was that really what was wrong with her?

'Gone?' Jasmine asked.

'He died,' Aleera said.

Jasmine looked back at her for a second. 'Oh, Jesus- God, Aleera, I'm so sorry.'

'It's alright,' Aleera said, 'it's just, what happened between us- I mean him and me- it was complicated.' Ok, this was good. She'd brought it up, now just gently explain...

'I get it,' Jasmine said gently. 'If... if you want to take it slow, I don't mind. Honest.'

Aleera froze before she could get her next sentence out.

'Alright.'

Oh, she was going to kick herself for this.

Thomas Smith's up-market apartment was, according to what Aleera had heard, barely a street away from the one owned by Kheron. Aleera chose not to comment on the fact that the Guild actually knew where Kheron lived.

Aleera and Jake were outside the door of the penthouse. Her first arrest, Aleera thought. She'd always expected to be on the receiving end.

Jake knocked on the door, waiting a few seconds for a reply.

'Mister Smith,' he shouted.

There was no reaction.

'Mister Smith, this is the Guild. Open the door.' Still nothing. Shrugging, Jake placed a hand over the lock of the door and whispered '*Yhiehl*'. There was a brief flash of orange-yellow light from under his palm, and the lock clicked open.

'Shall we?' Jake asked, gesturing into the apartment.

Aleera took the chance to survey her new surroundings. It was certainly far from the dregs; spacious, tastefully furnished, modern furniture; the place was better than the one she was living in now. Even in the evening darkness, it was genuinely quite stunning. There were even sculptures on the tables. Aleera didn't honestly think anyone but eccentric millionaires even owned sculptures.

And this belonged to a criminal. A black-marketeer who, by all accounts, had turned a dozen people into those walking nightmares. And it was painfully obvious who lived in even more glamorous housing.

It made her think of how much of this Kheron had, and who he'd double-dealt and stepped on to get it. You didn't get that far in three years by being trustworthy. You got it by betraying everyone and everything.

And with the Guild's attitude, and the whole situation, she might as well be working for him. Here she was, eliminating his competition when she wouldn't lose an hour's sleep over feeding him to those things. But there were other people who'd die, and that took away every choice.

It was wrong. It was sick, wrong and a perversion of everything she and the people currently surrounding her were supposed to stand for. And it was still the best possible option.

It sickened her. It mocked her. It taunted her and spoke to that monstrous little part of her that just wanted to lash out at every sound, the rage that she'd stifled and pushed down with every waking moment, the monster that clawed at the inside of her chests and bayed for blood.

'You alright?' Jake asked, placing a hand on her shoulder. Aleera nodded automatically.

'Is this the right place?' she asked the first thing that came into her head. Ah, now there was a point. How long was it supposed to take them to find this man?

Jake looked around. Sure enough, there wasn't a sound coming from the place. All of a sudden, the shadows seemed a little deeper. Aleera became aware of a faint scent of smoke.

'Wait here,' Jake instructed quietly. He made his way over to one of the doors, testing to see if it was locked. It wasn't. He opened it slowly, peering inside.

'Oh, *fuck*.'

'What?' Aleera asked.

'Well,' Jake said with a slight shiver, 'we found him.'

'Are we bringing him in?' Aleera asked, although Jake's tone had been ambiguous enough to suggest otherwise.

'Probably not.'

'Why not?'

'Well,' Jake said, still staring into the room, 'I think the main obstruction is that he's dead.'

The apartment, already silent, somehow grew even quieter. A certain heaviness descended. Then, in the space of a breath, he was through the door into the master bedroom. The next thing Aleera heard was him swearing.

Upon following him into the room, even Aleera winced. Tom Smith- or what she could only assume had been Tom Smith- was lying on the bed, legs spread out and arms still frozen in the midst of a frantic thrash. Dark, dried skin, screaming face, it was all there.

Although...

Something in the dark caught her eye. She couldn't quite put her finger on it, but there was definitely something... something not quite right.

'Hold on,' Jake said quietly as he started to creep around the room. He reached into an inside pocket, pulled out a white rubber glove and pulled it on over his right hand. Avoiding fingerprints, she realised as Jake slowly entered the en-suite bathroom through the open door. Aleera immediately started to realise the possible significance of the door being wide open. The shower curtain, too, was open just slightly.

'*Sola*,' Jake whispered, an ethereal white glow spreading across his palm and sending out a shaft of light in front of it, casting long, contrasting shadows over the empty bathroom and the folds of the shower curtain.

Jake reached for it, the many folds of its surface cast in light and dark bars by the light spell. He gripped the edge of the curtain and pulled it sideways. White lights flooded the open shower.

'And here we go,' Jake said grimly.

The woman- at least it looked like a woman- was slumped against the back wall, blackened skin still in a twisted grimace and her left hand still clutching the soap rack; a long, thick metal bar was wrapped right in the other. Behind Jake, there were two points where something had clearly been frantically torn from the wall.

'Who the hell is that?' Aleera asked as she stared. Evidently, she thought, someone who'd been with Smith in the wrong place at the wrong time.

Immediately, Aleera's computer of a mind started to work over what was there to be worked over. She backed out of the bathroom and, confirming a notion already in her head, cast the flashlight over Smith's body. The first thing she noticed, just because a detached brain tended to notice things others didn't at first, was that his torso was exposed, but a pair of black jeans still adorned the lower half of his form.

Ok, a quick bit of thought, and there we are. Instant conclusion.

Tom Smith, quite clearly, had come home with a lady friend, possibly a lady of the evening from Pentagram. Stumble in, light one up as the faint smell of smoke in the air testified, then an evening of rumpy-pumpy, only to have it spoiled by the presence of a couple of wraiths. They drained Smith dry as he tried to fight them off, while the girl fled into the shower room, pulled the towel rack off the wall, tried to fight off at least one, then fell backwards into the shower and suffered the same fate as Smith himself.

Well, thank you for that obvious conclusion. She could be a detective.

She stepped out of the bathroom, whispered '*Sola*' and cast her own light spell over the bed. Then she noticed something else.

Oh, hold on now.

Well, well. Maybe she really could be a detective.

'Jake,' she hissed, 'look at this.'

Jake was by her side in a moment. Aleera shone her light over the glint of metal that had caught her attention. A long, sharp piece of metal, and there on his chest… deep grooves, ones not made by dried skin stretched over the rib cage. Straight, deep cuts down the length of his body.

Jake nodded affirmatively. They'd cut him. That wasn't normal wraith behaviour; the wraith's behaviour was one of doing things was to feed and get it over with as quickly as possible.

This had indeed been not only premeditated, but prolonged. This had been personal. That meant-

Aleera sniffed. Something in the air, all of a sudden.

Smoke.

Smoke that was still curling from a cigarette down by the side of the bed. Smoke from a cigarette that was still only just being burned.

'Do you see that?' Aleera asked Jake. She felt the adrenaline start to surge, claws itching as if to ask "now? Can we come out and play now?" Then came the thrill, the enticing possibility of finally, really being able to cut loose on…

On a wraith. On something that smelled of the rotten, decomposing meat it was made of. Something she'd smell a mile away.

Unless she was surrounded by smoke.

All the ideas and theories collapsed into one gaping, howling, mad idea.

'Somehow,' Aleera whispered feeling her heated breath inside her metal mask, 'I don't think they've been dead for long.'

Maybe just "not for long" enough for them to have heard them coming. No. No, ridiculous. Where would it hide?

Aleera moved slowly across the room. There. Just faint. One or two other soldiers appeared to smell it, too.

Her dark eyes focused on an old, ornate wooden wardrobe.

She crept toward it slowly. One step. Then a second. Then a third. She reached forward slowly. Her fingertips brushed over the handle.

Then the door exploded outward and the mad, screaming black thing was on top of her, howling into her face, scratching and tearing at her armour. A hand grabbed onto Aleera's forearm as she swatted at it, the other grabbing the edges of her mask and ripping it away, the metal edge scratching at her cheek. She smelled its reeking, pungent breath and flesh as chunks of dead meat fell away.

Then a sharp, solid blow, the wraith was knocked away, pulling Aleera's arm with it even as Jake swung the office chair again. The monstrous thing turned, screamed and reached for her face. Halfway there, it screamed again, howling as four thick, black claws sliced noisily through its flesh. It released her, falling back and screeching as Aleera's wings erupted.

No caution now. No hesitation. This was happened when the devil's daughter was running on pure adrenaline. The dark thing was in charge now, and it wanted only blood.

A set of claws struck it around the face, sending it falling back as it howled like a walking nightmare. The entire room seemed to whirl as Aleera readied herself, readied herself for the kill.

Oh, please, just this one, it was so perfect, perfect excuse, nobody would miss it, it would literally be a damn service… just please, let her just taste blood again… God, she wanted the blood…

Then the bolt of shaking force struck the wraith square in the chest. It screamed, hurled back into the half-open window. Glass smashed and fell in a glittering shower. A black mass of rags fell from the window.

And then it had passed, nothing left but the echo of the wraith's scream, and Aleera was left, standing there with the realisation of where she was and what she'd been about to do.

Would she have done it? Killed it? Cut it down then and there? Greater good and all that. Couldn't hurt anything but the wraith. Hard to see how it would be a bad thing, really.

She could be ashamed later. For now, she pushed the dark thing down.

Jake moved to the window. A shadow moved away across the rooftops. He shook his head. 'You alright?' he asked, turning back to Aleera.

'Fine. Is it dead?'

Wraiths were three things: tragic, gruesome, and hard to kill. They *leaked* magic. That made it so much easier to adapt in some ways, so much harder in others. Unfortunately, one of the easier ways was one that contemplated how much lighter you became when half your flesh had rotted away.

'No,' he said, 'but it's gone.'

Aleera felt herself cool down. Her cheeks burned with embarrassment at losing it in front of someone. Rationality came creeping back. 'It won't get far,' Aleera said, sliding back into relative normality as fast as she could force herself.

Aleera controlled herself. Although in fairness, having read her psyche reports, Cassidy should have known better than to treat her like that when she had one of her, ah, outbursts.

'Cassidy and Khazahn are going to crucify me,' Jake cringed. 'We just got a chance to find something out from one of these things, and I shot it out of a window.'

'So now what?' Aleera asked, looking over at Smith. 'Do we call in forensics?'

'Better had. See what we can find.' He looked around and exhaled slowly. 'You know something, Aleera, there are days that I hate this job.

'What the hell was that?' Cassidy demanded, 'why didn't you see that coming?'

'That does tend to be the point of an ambush,' Jake answered. 'Still, to try that, the thing must've been half-starved.'

'Great,' Cassidy snarled, 'just fucking marvellous. We're up to- what's this give us- twenty-three deaths including these, our only lead turns into a pair of corpses, so we have a dead end *again*, and we miss our chance to finally catch one of these things- which could've helped break this entire thing by tomorrow morning. Now: somebody had better tell me: *who the fuck thought it was a good idea to shoot it out of the window?*'

And you had someone under your command come within half a foot of being drained, Aleera thought resentfully.

After a few seconds of silence, Jake put his hand up.

'You?' Cassidy snarled. Aleera kept silent. Maybe she should say something.

'The wraith went for Aleera,' Jake said. 'Snap decision.'

'You fucked this case up for *her*?'

Everyone in the room tried to convince themselves that, when the room seemed to shake as Jake glared at Cassidy, it was a coincidence.

'Right. Expect to report to Colonel Hartwell. Now *somebody* please tell me something good!'

To one side, Katya looked down at the mess of items that had fallen out of the wardrobe during the burst of chaos. She made to say something, and pretended to think it was a good idea not to. 'Wait, you said "good".'

'Why the hell is she talking?' Cassidy barked.

'Button it!' Jake snapped, twice as loud as Cassidy. Aleera was fairly sure it was the first time she'd heard Jake shout like that. Then, in a voice that sounded as though it couldn't possibly be from the same person, he said 'what is it?'

Awkwardly, Katya leaned down and pointed Jake to a photograph from the pile. Jake conjured up another light spell and inspected it.

His face paled.

'Oh. *Shit.*'

'Will somebody please tell me what's on the goddamn photo?' Cassidy barked.

Jake held the picture up. Aleera moved around the soldier and fixed her eyes on it as well. She recognised the face. She'd seen it that same afternoon: Rick Lawson. Guild Private of D-Unit of the Eighth Division, Rick Lawson. Taking a briefcase from Kheron.

13

'You shot it out of a window?'

Jake shrugged, hands behind his back, as Colonel Hartwell leaned over his head.

'A little bit,' he admitted.

'What the *hell*?' Cassidy barked.

'The thing was on top of her,' Jake argued, 'what the hell was I meant to do? And before you answer, I wouldn't find it funny if you said "leave her".'

'Did you have to shoot it out of the window?' Hartwell snapped.

'That wasn't intentional,' Jake pointed out.

'Too bad.'

Hartwell walked round the desk slowly, stopping and seating himself on the edge. He took a moment to make sure he had complete silence.

'Do you know how many charges there are on record against you?'

Jake turned his eyes upward, mouthed a few calculations and replied 'ninety-seven.'

'Ninety-*eight*.'

'That was a grievous misunderstanding, and that's beside the point because you can't even prove that was me.'

'Really?'

Jake studied Hartwell for a moment. 'What? Now you're threatening me?'

'I'm doing whatever's necessary to move this investigation forward, up to and including having you removed and replaced.'

'Yyyyyyeah,' Jake shrugged again, 'thing is I don't buy that. I mean, not to gloat, but I've probably cracked more weird, confusing and generally unusual cases than everyone else in this building put together. Hell, I was doing this before you were even born.'

'And why is that?' Hartwell asked, 'because we've all been itching to put an investigation together.'

'Wouldn't be the first time someone's wasted time trying.'

'Do not push me, Connolly.'

'Who's pushing?'

Hartwell nodded slowly. 'Sergeant Cassidy, would you excuse us?'

Cassidy nodded curtly and walked out of the room. Once he was gone, Hartwell stood up.

'You know your problem, Connolly?'

'I'm a workaholic?'

'You think whoever's in charge is just somebody you get to mess with.'

'Not all of them.'

'And you think- you think the reason I'm threatening you here is because I'm one of those by-the-book assholes from the movies who can't stand anyone who bends the rules, right?'

'Dunno, is it right?'

'I am like this, Connolly,' Hartwell glared, 'because we had twenty-three civilian deaths this week. Right now, I have more complaints, accusations, reports and other crap to deal with than I ever have done since the day I took this job. And right now, this place is full of people like that. You don't see the issue if one of them loses their job, because as far as you're concerned, politics is just made up of signatures on pieces of paper.'

He walked back round behind his desk. 'You think you don't have to answer to anybody. Maybe you don't. But the rest of us? We *do* have to answer to someone. Deal with that.' He sat down. 'And find my wraiths. Dismissed.'

Jake nodded politely, walked out and shut the door behind him.

To the great surprise of no-one, Cassidy was there waiting.

'I still can't believe you threw this whole case out of the water just for that little bitch,' he griped.

'Don't,' Jake warned venomously.

'Seriously. Just let the bastard thing eat her and then slap the cuffs on it.'

Without a word, Jake waved his hands and Daniel Cassidy found himself slammed into the wall.

'Know something?' Jake glared, 'I am entirely sick of you. I really am. I am sick of the way you talk to my student, my familiar and my team-mates. If you don't like the people you're working with, then leave, but if I hear you making one more snide, vicious little remark, I will remove your arms and have them beat you to death.' He lowered his hand, dropping Cassidy to the floor. 'Back off of the kid,' he said coldly. 'Last warning.'

As a pleasant enough surprise, Aleera was back home by twelve. She always had to be careful when she flew home during the day, as a rule of thumb, an invisibility spell intended to bend light worked best when there was less light to bend.

'Lilith?' she called as she entered the apartment.

There was a sudden shout and a sound of confusion from Lilith's bedroom. When she heard the sound of hushed conversation and sheets moving, Aleera realised the situation and entered her room- although, on the way, she saw that the same letter from that morning was still on the kitchen table; she grabbed it and disappeared behind her bedroom door.

Outside the room, she heard Lilith apologise to the young man she'd been sharing the room with as the door closed. She ignored it and focused on the letter.

Alright, so she should feel guilty about reading her sister's mail. But she and Lilith… they never hid things from each other. Not one thing hadn't been shared between them in Aleera's eighteen years of life.

And finding out something like this was enough to make her wish she'd left well enough alone. On the top-right corner of the paper was the emblem of *University of Phoenix.*

Aleera covered her mouth. There were things Lilith had told her that definitely didn't fit in with this. And they didn't live close enough to Arizona for Lilith to attend a college there, although three months ago Lilith had been living in Phoenix.

The door into the room clicked open. Aleera instinctively stuffed the letter behind her back.

'Little early, aren't you, baby sister?' Lilith asked as she straightened her tube top, 'seriously, we were just getting start-' she stopped in mid-sentence when she saw the look on Aleera's face. 'What's wrong?' she asked, rampant sexuality thrown out the window the minute she knew there was something wrong with her sister.

Aleera bit her lip and lidded her eyes guiltily. She slipped the piece of paper out from behind her back. Lilith's eyes widened as she covered her mouth with one hand.

'Oh.'

Still feeling far from guiltless, Aleera handed the paper over. Lilith took it and sighed heavily. 'Alright,' she said, sitting down next to Aleera. The younger thinned her lips and folded her hands over each other uncomfortably. She recalled that if she found out secrets about most people, she'd just confront them about it. But when it was Lilith, she was back to being a baby sister again. Add in a little bit of shame and she couldn't even look her sister in the eye.

Lilith put the paper down. Printed on it was:

Dear Ms. Maheste,

We have not yet received a reply to our previous letters asking you to return to our university. We still hope that you might reconsider as your achievement in your chosen subject has been outstanding. If you wish to continue at the University of Phoenix, please contact us through the number below.

Kind Regards,

Kenneth Rogers, University of Phoenix Administration.

Aleera still looked away from her sister. It was longer than she'd have liked before she spoke.

'You dropped out of college?'

Lilith sighed. As if it might help, she turned the paper over.

'Yeah.'

Ah, here we go. Now she could say something.

'You dropped out of college?'

'Yes I did,' Lilith answered.

'I didn't-' Aleera paused for a moment and gathered her thoughts. 'I didn't even know you went to college.'

'I didn't go for long. I just heard…'

'What had happened?' Aleera finished the sentence for her. 'Is that why…?'

'That's why,' Lilith replied.

'Lilith,' Aleera said, 'did you drop out because of me?' Maybe she should have been a little more circumspect, but as always, she still couldn't feel awkward about anything talking to Lilith.

'Yes I did,' Lilith answered without as much as a trace of embarrassment.

'You dropped out because of me?'

'As opposed to what?' Lilith snapped, 'Aleera, you were nearly killed!'

'How did you think I'd feel when I found out about this?'

'So I was just supposed to leave you to it? After somebody burned your home down and nearly killed you?'

Aleera couldn't reply. Even if she tried, she just plain didn't have an answer to that.

'I dropped out of college to come back here,' Lilith said, 'and I still don't regret it.'

'You didn't even tell me you went to college.'

'Because if I did, you'd have known I left it, and…' Lilith thought momentarily, 'I knew we'd end up having this exact conversation we're having right now.'

'How did you think I'd feel when I found out?' Aleera asked.

'Honestly, I didn't think it mattered. You needed me and I came down here. Simple as that.'

'So you just gave up what you wanted to do?' Aleera said.

'Doesn't matter.'

'It does to me.'

'I abandoned you, Aleera! Nine months ago, I just up and left. You were seventeen and I just left you alone and fucked off halfway across the country with a guy who turned out to be a complete dick. I was the worst fucking sister you could've had.'

'You were not-'

'I was. We both know it. You just won't admit it because, for some reason I can't wrap my head around, you're not mad at me when, let's just face it, I failed you. I always said I'd take care of you, and then… I was a stupid, selfish bitch. Then I heard that I wasn't even there when that lunatic was trying to kill the only family I have.'

'And that's a bad thing?'

Aleera immediately regretted saying it, because it was one of those things that could, in this context, only be misinterpreted.

Lilith steeled herself. 'You think so?'

'I don't mean it like that,' Aleera said, 'but Azrael would have killed you like he did Michael and Sara. So, yes. I'm glad you weren't here, because if you had been, I'd have had to watch them put you in the ground as well.'

Lilith sighed. She slid next to Aleera and put her arm around her. Aleera leaned onto her sister's shoulder as she was pulled into a soft hug, Lilith kissing her gently on the forehead.

'I still shouldn't have left,' she said gently, 'I should have told you, baby sister. But I'm not going to abandon you again. Ok?'

Aleera nodded slowly as Lilith's fingers ran through her hair. 'Ok.'

Rick Lawson's apartment was about a half-hour's drive from Guild Headquarters. Maybe a little longer with New York traffic and the roads had looked pretty bad today.

Consequently, Jake had come up with a better idea.

In the alley behind the apartment building, the only thing other than the dumpster, and therein perhaps the occasional rat, was an old ginger tom that mooched around the side of an overturned trashcan.

The air shimmered, everything convulsed, and finally three semi-solid outlines came into focus, glowed, and collapsed into a trio of at-least-mostly human forms.

Daniel Cassidy pulled off his helmet and, grimacing, wiped respective layers of yellow vomit from the metal and his face. Jake, next to him, collapsed onto all fours, gasping for breath and wincing from the effort. Katya staggered, gagged and held onto her forehead before she helped Jake up.

'Could've bloody warned me,' Cassidy groaned as he leaned against the alley wall. 'Feel like I just got out of a cab driven by a monkey on acid.'

Jake ignored him. Cassidy sounded fine, and Katya was clearly well enough to help him, so he quickly checked himself; head, legs, arms, body, hands, feet, fingers, hair, nose. All there.

There was a reason teleportation was just about the trickiest spell to learn. Unless one had actively attempted to use it, it was nigh-impossible to appreciate how difficult it was to keep three distinct sets of molecules from falling apart or mixing together, especially when one set was your own and you were having a very literal out-of-body experience at the time. That was the reason he only managed to teleport three.

Still, at least they weren't after wraiths this time. How Jake had been convinced that there was a need to teleport them, he'd probably never know.

'Ok,' he groaned, then inhaled sharply and grabbed the side of his head. 'Ow. Pain. Pain is bad. Ok.'

'Can you stand?' Cassidy checked. The sentence was as impersonal as such a sequence of words could be.

'Technically,' Jake groaned, clicking his neck.

'Same,' Katya said a little weakly, adding 'thanks for asking' under her breath but, hopefully, loud enough for Cassidy to hear.

'Right. Apartment 15-I. We go in, we arrest the little twat, and we get out.'

Shaking his head in dismay, Jake followed, still cringing.

Behind them, the old ginger tom, unfazed, made its way across the dumpster and through a tear in the mesh gate at the end of the alley.

It stopped, rubbing a paw on its cheek, next a black limousine that had been parked on the other side of the block. A gleaming metal door opened, and the creature looked up with a quiet purr. Beckoned, it jumped into the car's wooden interior, onto the leather seats, and curled up as its master scratched it behind the ears.

Kheron looked down at the cat, then moved his hand to the top of its skull, his middle finger between its eyes. Honestly, Jake Connolly seemed to think he was the only person in New York with a pet cat. Of course, Leonardo here, being one hundred percent feline, had a much simpler mind, one that could quite easily be checked with just a little…

He focused. A swirl of monochrome, mad, oh-so-very-curious images covered the back of his eyelids.

And there they were.

Now, he thought to himself, what might Mister Jake Connolly, his lovely familiar, and a Guild Officer be doing there?

'That's a good boy, Leo,' he said affectionately, ruffling the cat's fur. He sat back and thought, fidgeting irritably as the tiny, cheap plastic headphones hissed in his ears. He pulled them out sharply; how these things, sounding like nails on a chalkboard compared to a real record, had ever taken off, he'd never know.

There was a buzz from the small intercom on the back of the front seat. The driver might have only been a few feet away, but Kheron was a man who liked his privacy. He sighed irritably and pressed the button.

'Yes?'

'Just got a call in, sir. You wanted someone to keep an eye on the Police Scanner for the district around Maheste's place?'

Kheron perked up.

'Yes.'

'You might want to hear this.'

The black screen separating driver and passenger slid back, and Kheron took the phone from the driver's hand.

Beside him, the iPod hummed away as Leo dozed, and the tune of *No More Heroes* faded away.

The knock at the door was loud, sharp and unmistakable. Rick Lawson found that he jumped the second he heard it.

No, he told himself, calm down. He'd said that the whole thing was foolproof. In, out, done, unseen, never spoken of again.

Except...

Except it hadn't been, had it? With what he knew...

He could tell them.

It'd be the last thing he'd ever tell.

He wished he could tell them. Wished he could just muster the guts for the two minutes it would take. Just. Tell. Them.

He opened the door of the apartment.

He went cold.

'Rick Lawson,' Daniel Cassidy said sharply, 'you're under arrest for corruption. You have the right to an attorney. You have the right to remain silent; anything you choose to say can and will-'

Lawson bolted. He shoved his way past them on pure adrenaline. No thought, no plan, just run. Run now. Run!

Cassidy spun round, shoved Jake to one side, and thrust a fist forward. '*Sheahm!*' A solid, straight blast of orange light erupted, leaving shimmering shockwaves into the air, and struck him in the back. There was a shower of sparks, a flash of light, and a pained howl from Lawson as the magic of his own body was stabbed and ripped. Then he went limp and collapsed onto the floor.

'Jesus Christ, man!' Jake snapped, 'you didn't have to-'

'He'll be fine,' Cassidy barked, 'now let's get this little bastard back and find out what he's been up to if we have to take him apart!'

Aleera still wasn't exactly on top of the world when she arrived at Guild headquarters. She was guilty; of course she was. How was she supposed to be alright with Lilith having given that much up for her?

So why did that small part of her want to smile when she thought that someone would do that for her?

Still, for now she could put it out of her mind. That was one thing to be grateful for about this new job; that kind of problem paled to utter insignificance in the face of a horde of life-sucking monsters. Descending onto the roof of the Flatiron Building, she allowed her wings to slip seamlessly into the skin of her upper back and again recited the '*Tyasans*' spell. With a brief shimmer of air, she became visible again just as she finished putting her top back on. No need to let it get shredded by her wings when she had her most-accomplished spell to preserve her modesty.

She entered via the fire escape on the rooftop and, from past experience, located the elevator. She recalled that she had her own clearance now: 'Red Clearance. Plato Five-Zero-Nine.'

Most of the faces she found familiar turned out to be huddled around the same two-way mirror she'd seen before her encounter with Kheron. She recalled that she still had those tickets. Maybe she ought to mention them to Jake.

'What's going on?' she asked as she negotiated her way into the room.

'Lawson got brought in about two hours ago,' Makian said, 'and Jake's drawn the short straw so he's going in.'

'I can't believe this,' Katya shuddered. 'I mean, of all the times.'

'Doesn't matter,' Cassidy announced brusquely, 'find out what the bastard knows and what he was taking in that case, and do it now.'

'We could always bring Kheron in,' Jake pointed out, 'find out from him. Another chance to press him.'

'I'll remind you,' Khazahn snarled bitterly, 'if we're going to pull the likes of him in again, we need to be able to prove he's been doing something illegal. I don't see how this can help a damned thing.'

Jake looked away from the two-way mirror and glanced over at Khazahn. He looked pale. Shaky. As if he might jump at the slightest movement. Jake shook his head and paced across the room.

'We get one shred of proof,' Jake insisted, 'we can have Kheron in here within the hour.'

'And have him out again in the next one.'

'Lawson can give us concrete proof.'

'Jake, this is *Kheron* we're dealing with!' Khazahn barked.

'Exactly! How long have you spent chasing him? How many years? For all we know, we could take him down today. So why the hell are you just sitting here?'

Khazahn didn't answer.

'I'll see what he's got to say for himself,' Jake said.

'Works for me,' Cassidy commented as he glanced over Lawson's file. 'Christ, look at this. Bloke never so much as returned a library book late.'

'Fine,' Khazahn finally said, 'don't say I didn't warn you. Five minutes.'

Jake nodded. He rounded the immediate corner and swiped his access card into the electronic panel on the door, keying in a long-memorised code. With a buzz and a click, the door swung open.

Rick Lawson looked up with a sudden, sharp fear. He seemed to calm himself down quickly enough.

'Freelance Lt. Jake Connolly,' Jake said, pressing the "record" switch on the tape recorder on the desk, 'interviewing Suspended Private Rick Lawson. Interview commenced at…' he checked his watch, 'nine a.m.'

'I- I want my lawyer,' Lawson said. It wasn't an order, or a command, but just the first thing he could find to stand behind.

'You turned that chance down earlier,' Jake pointed out. 'Any particular reason?'

Lawson struggled to say anything. 'No.'

'We have a photo,' Jake said, holding up one of the evidence bags, 'of you accepting a briefcase from a known criminal. Sound familiar?'

'N- No.'

'We have security footage of you at Pentagram on the night of September the second. Any reason you were there?'

'It's a good club.' Lawson's answer was completely transparent.

'So you were there,' Jake said. Then, without pausing, he continued. 'What was in the briefcase?'

'I don't know.'

'Did he give you a briefcase?'

Lawson struggled to reply again. This time, he failed. He took a deep breath and stared at the floor.

'Kid,' Jake sighed, sitting down on the edge of the table, 'this is big. You realise that?'

Lawson nodded.

'You know that the Guild could put you in jail for- honestly, something this suspicious, under these circumstances, probably as long as they like.'

'You can't prove I did anything illegal,' Lawson blurted out.

'Right now, it's more a question of whether you can prove that you didn't. Can you?'

Lawson swallowed a lump in his throat.

'Where's the briefcase?' Jake asked.

'I don't know.'

'No?'

'I don't,' Lawson repeated.

'Did you give it to someone?'

Lawson nodded.

'Who?'

'I don't know his name.'

'Can you describe him?'

'I didn't see his face.'

'Rick,' Jake said sharply, 'I really do not want to send you down when you've been here for all of six weeks.'

'I-' Lawson stopped in mid-sentence. 'I just can't say.'

'If you've got nothing to hide,' Jake insisted, 'tell me what was in the briefcase.'

'I can't,' Lawson said pleadingly, 'I just can't, alright?'

Jake sighed, threw out his hands, and asked 'why?'

'You don't get it!' Lawson shouted, 'you don't get it! He's- H- He'll *kill* me!'

Jake paused. 'Kheron? Look, we have more than a few options for people in your situation-'

'You can't protect me! Not from him!'

'All we need is his name on the record from you,' Jake said, 'and-'

'I can't!' Lawson yelled, 'He's desperate, alright? I mean really desperate! He's not gonna take a chance, especially me! Please, you have to let me out of here!'

'You won't be any safer out there than-'

'If I stay here,' Lawson begged, 'I'm dead. He'll kill me!'

Jake remained quiet. He took a deep breath as Lawson buried his head in his hands.

'I thought I could cope with this,' he shook, 'but he- he's going to kill me…'

Aleera watched intently as Lawson gave a slight, quiet shake, and myriad questions charged through her mind.

Take a chance? On what, exactly? He knew something, obviously, and Kheron clearly stood to lose something from this situation. And desperate? If anything, he'd seemed cocky. Hardly a man struck with fear. So unless he was onto something big…

But he wasn't going to talk, she realised. He was afraid, and whatever he was so scared of, it was worse than anything the Guild could threaten him with. She couldn't blame him for *wanting* to be arrested in that situation, but the way he was reacting to that, like whatever he was fearful of could still reach into the room and grab him…

And yet there was something, some tiny, unknown thing that she couldn't put her finger on, but that teased her from the edge of knowledge and said "if you only knew."

14

'Wow,' Jasmine stared. 'You look ready to kill something.'

'Close enough,' Aleera mumbled under her breath.

'What?'

'I feel crap enough,' Aleera covered up hastily. 'Bad night at work.'

After returning from her outlandish new employment, Aleera had persuaded Lilith that she was just going out for a while. This little diner had long been a favourite spot of hers; unlike many of its contemporaries, it actually served edible food from time to time, and it was a convenient place to meet up with people.

She wasn't exactly sure why she called Jasmine to meet there. After all, Jasmine was about the only person she even knew through something other than relation or the Guild.

'Rough orders, huh?'

'Actually, I started somewhere else yesterday.'

'I thought you liked working there.'

'Long story,' Aleera said simply.

'In other words, "not telling". That's fine- look, I'm just gonna get straight to the point: you feel like skipping first-thing biology on Monday? Because I'm sick of that guy staring down your shirt every lesson.'

'You do that all the time.' Aleera knew that was a mistake as soon as she said it, purely because it promised to prolong a conversation about something she was nearly as unhappy about as Kheron.

'Yeah, but I thought I was allowed considering- yeah. Besides, I get jealous because I sit behind you- although I do have a good view from back-'

'I get it,' Aleera said sharply, apparently more so than intended.

'Wow. Bad day, huh?'

'You don't know the half of it.'

'You can tell me.' Jasmine's smile fell when she noticed her reluctance. 'Come on, you've told me worse.'

'I really haven't.'

'What? Girl-trouble?'

'No.'

'*Boy* trouble?' Jasmine asked with mock suspicion.

Aleera bit her tongue. Before she could say anything, it just slipped out. 'I'm working for the Guild.'

Jasmine froze.

'What?'

'The Guild.'

Jasmine stared back at her. 'Say that once more,' she instructed.

'I work for the Guild.'

'That's...'

'That's where I've been for the last few days.'

Jasmine's face was a mask of awe- at least until she grabbed Aleera and gave her an excited kiss.

'That... is... so... fucking... *awesome!*' she squeaked.

'Not really.'

'It's the Guild!'

'They're-' Aleera paused. Now how to put this, exactly? She could think of a few adjectives, none of which did justice to her thoughts or were acceptable in civilised conversation. '-they're not the best people to work for.'

'Oh. You mean because of the-'

'Among other things. It's nothing, really.'

'Nothing?'

Aleera sighed. Well, a fresh perspective would be nice- and it did seem to be getting increasingly hard to lie to Jasmine and those big blue eyes.

'This guy got let off,' she explained in the most moderate terms that still held some honesty, 'he'd done something bad- something *really* bad.'

'How bad?'

Aleera bit her tongue again. It still didn't help. 'He killed people,' she said, 'a lot of people. And he hurt this- this girl. This little girl. She was only about eleven.'

'Oh.' It seemed that Jasmine couldn't think of anything else to say. She covered her mouth with one hand.

'And then- because he informed on someone else- he wasn't even charged,' Aleera said with disgust.

Jasmine paled. 'Jesus.'

'Not quite the word I'd use.'

'Fuck,' Jasmine whispered.

'Closer.'

'No, seriously. You were actually there?'

'No. I just heard about it yesterday.'

'They just let this guy go?'

'They did.'

'Oh my *God*.' Jasmine shuddered. 'That poor kid!'

Aleera nodded bleakly.

'I think you were right,' she finally said.

'About what?'

'We can skip biology on Monday,' Aleera suggested, 'go to the mall or something.'

Jasmine smiled. 'Cool. And… that sucks. That thing you said.'

'That it does.'

'If you want to talk about it-'

'It's alright.'

'You *can* talk to me about stuff, you know.'

'I know.'

'I mean,' Jasmine suddenly blushed a little, 'I figured we were kind of a- a couple… or something. Ever since…'

'I thought so,' Aleera admitted. Oh, very clever. That was going to help things, wasn't it?

Well, in a sense they did seem to be. Couples had sex, they met up in diners at night…

'Cool,' Jasmine smiled. 'Ok, I gotta go. See you tomorrow.' She gave Aleera a quick kiss on the cheek and left.

On the way out, Aleera found herself outweighing the merits and consequences of this idea. While hardly a model student, she didn't tend to skip classes, mainly because there was little to do in the day- she recalled that she hated just about every movie she had ever seen. And yet she'd suggested it…

For that matter, what the hell had she just been thinking? She screamed at herself. Letting things slip that easily? Telling someone she worked at the Guild-

Well, they were a couple, so…

She never told anybody anything.

But this was different. How, exactly, she still couldn't be sure, but…

Well, on the one hand, Aleera had now finished her third day working for the Guild. On the other hand, of course, it was rapidly turning into the most disastrous week in the organisation's history. Anyone would think Aleera was a jinx- then again; the thought had crossed her own mind a few times over the years.

Aleera couldn't help wondering how Khazahn had gone about reporting the whole mess: "the good news is that we have a lead, the bad news is that we have a renegade number in the same unit again, our only others leads got either killed or blasted out of a window- by us- and the body count is just getting ridiculous" just didn't seem to be the kind of thing that the High Council would hear gladly. She'd shared a brief phone call with Jake, during which she'd managed to determine that the situation at headquarters could be summarily described as "a complete and utter chaotic mess". Beyond that, Khazahn and Daniel Cassidy were both apparently screening every surface for any trace of evidence against Rick Lawson.

Now, after all that, what she was really looking forward to was a nice, quiet evening at home to mull over all the other little nuisances that tripped over each other in her mind.

And instead…

Well, for fuck's sakes.

This… this irritated her. It didn't make her blood boil, because frankly, compared to much of what she'd seen in her life, this was kids' stuff.

But the words *"Dyke Bitch"* spray-painted on the front of her apartment building were still enough to get her claws itching. Not so much as the smashed windscreen of her sister's car, of course.

On the plus side, she didn't have to figure out who was responsible, because he was still there. Jamie Shane was as persistent as his brother; she had to give him that, at least.

''s right, bitch,' Jamie snarled, 'what you and your fuckin dyke sister get when you-'

The sentence remained unfinished as Aleera grabbed his shoulders and, swiftly and almost mechanically, drove her knee into his balls.

Over time, she'd figured out why Jamie, like his equally-unintelligent sibling before him, had never gotten it into his head that messing with Aleera was bad for his health. It wasn't the fear that wasn't there; it was just that, like a dog, he reacted to fear by biting at the source of it. Even if it broke his teeth.

That, Aleera would tolerate. It almost brought her a sense of bemused interest.

But this crossed the line. *Nobody* brought it to her home, and nobody so much as vaguely threatened her sister.

And he was still standing there and laughing.

Oh, you stupid, filthy, little…

'You *vicious little bastard!*'

Aleera's fist smashed into his face with a crunch of breaking nose, before she grabbed his hair, bunching it as painfully as possible in her hands, and slammed her knee into his forehead. Then she tore out the chunk of hair, threw him against the wall and hit him again.

Do it. Knock his teeth out. Bust his scrawny little head in!

He threatened her sister?

The outrage screamed over the blood pounding in her ears. That pathetic little *shit* actually dared to do this? Thought he could come to her home?

She should fucking kill him for this!

She felt the claws itch in her fingers. He should. Why the hell hadn't she done it already? Just because he couldn't take her, she was supposed to pity him enough to let him threaten her and Lilith and Jasmine, just because his worm of an older brother got what was coming to him?

She kicked him in the ribs as he fell to the ground, listening with sick glee as he coughed and groaned.

No. No, that was enough. No way in hell was this little wretch worth the trouble.

'What the hell is wrong with you?' Aleera hissed as she pulled him to his feet, 'how is anyone stupid enough to keep starting this when they come off worse every time?'

'You think I'm gonna stop?' Jamie shouted. 'Why the fuck should I stop, ya skinny fuckin psycho-dyke?' He shoved her and stepped back, blood from his nose trickling over his face. 'Huh? That was my fucking brother and our school, bitch, you get the *fuck* out! You-'

'Jamie,' Aleera said levelly, still fighting that urge to cut his stupid little face open, 'you're embarrassing yourself.'

No fear. Not so much as a trace. Aleera just talked to him like a naughty child that was standing on the table.

She saw Jamie's face contort.

There was a glint of metal.

The switchblade turned in Jamie's hand as he seethed and snarled, his fingers wrapped around it as it wavered in the air.

'Yeah,' he spat, 'yeah, you see that? You remember that? Thought you were so fuckin smart when you got my brother in prison for one of these, huh?' he slashed the air with it. 'You scared, bitch? Huh? You scared?'

Aleera didn't react. Her deep, dark eyes traced the path of the blade as an idle curiosity.

'Yeah,' Jamie shook, 'yeah, you're fuckin scared…'

Aleera fixed his gaze.

'You are fuckin scared, you bitch…' not a statement anymore. Not mockery. Something desperate. The flicker of fear was in his eyes, not hers.

'*Stop just standing there!*' he screamed, face like a mad dog. The blade thrust forward.

Nobody in the slowly-gathering crowd could follow what happened. Aleera grabbed Jamie's wrist, thrust the blade down over her right hip and, at the same time, brought up her other knee and slammed it into his jaw. Then, with the momentum already gained, she spun round, kicked him in the side and sent him falling to the ground.

Still clutching the knife.

Please. An idiot with a knife. She'd faced the blade of a demon-slayer. The previous evening she'd looked the most nightmarish creature in the world in the face and not even flinched. This was nothing. He was nothing.

A nothing practically screaming for her to hurt him. Yes, that sounded good…

The rage had flooded her from the second Jamie swung, riding the tide of adrenaline. The rage was screaming already: go ahead. Do it.

'*Skank!*' Jamie howled, lashing out with the blade again. Aleera dodged and grabbed his wrist effortlessly. Really, this was becoming nothing more than a nuisance, she thought as he struggled pointlessly. The adrenaline fired up again, that sudden surge of feeling so powerful, making him so weak, the thought that… God, she could have her claws in his stomach in a second. Nobody would see. So easy to blame on his own blade. She could do it, and that thought was like a drug. 'You lemme fucking go, you bitch!' he screeched, 'you see, I'll cut you and then I'll cut your fuckin dyke girlfriend!'

The rage exploded. From that moment on, Aleera wasn't in charge. It was the dark thing, a wave of pure, mindless, instinctive, thoughtless rage, that pushed his wrist down and sent the blade into his leg with the sound of tearing, wet flesh. Jamie screamed. The bloodied knife fell and clattered on the asphalt.

The torn skin wasn't enough. The scream wasn't enough. There was no temptation now; this was past that. Everything, every problem, every wraith, every shred of guilt, was forgotten before one burning truth:

Nobody threatened someone she loved.

Her elbow smashed into Jamie's face. His nose splintered into a mess of bone and blood. He staggered and screamed again as the pain in his leg stabbed again.

'You fuckin happy now, bitch?' he roared, 'you send my brother to jail and you *stab me in the fucking leg, you fucking skank*!'

He gasped painfully as Aleera's hand grabbed a fistful of his hair and pulled him up on his knees. He screamed again as his thigh was stretched.

'You brought this on yourself,' she hissed, raw, seething hate still rushing through her, 'because you're an idiot who doesn't know when to stop. And that is why your brother is in prison. If you threaten my girlfriend again,' she said venomously, every fibre of her screaming to slit his throat right then, 'then… *then*… I will cut you open.'

She pushed his head down, stood up and sharply walked away.

Then it happened.

She heard Jamie stand. There was a scream from somewhere among the people who'd gathered to watch the commotion.

She turned round.

She saw the gun wave in his hand.

She saw him squeeze the trigger.

The gun fired.

'Oh! My! *God!*'

'I'm sitting right here,' Aleera said dryly, flinching at the sudden pain in her ear.

'Can you see this?' Lilith said, louder if anything.

'I'd like to reiterate what I just said about volume and ear proximity.'

'You were *shot*?'

'He missed,' Aleera said defensively.

'Someone shot you?'

'He missed me.'

'Bullshit. Look at this!' Lilith insisted. 'Doesn't it hurt?'

'I already put a healing spell on it,' Aleera explained, 'it doesn't even hurt.'

Lilith looked straight at her. Oh, very well, so she knew when she was being lied to.

'Alright, a little. But it's fine. It was only a scratch.'

'You! Were! Shot!'

'It was a scratch. If that.'

'Your sleeve is soaked! Did you at least disinfect it?'

'The healing spell took care of that,' Aleera said, 'look, this isn't that big of a deal,' she repeated as Lilith stood up, 'the guy with the gun came out of it a lot worse than I did.'

That didn't stop Lilith from standing up from the kitchen table and getting out some disinfectant.

'Don't you dare.'

'Hold still,' Lilith commanded.

'Come on... Ow.'

Aleera was adequately well-versed in healing spells, but there was still a thin cut from the bullet that gave her a sharp sting when the disinfectant made contact.

Once Lilith was done, she put the disinfectant away and shook slightly.

'What happened to this city?' she shuddered. 'This used to be a decent place.'

'No it didn't.'

'God, this was on our doorstep!'

'He won't be doing it again,' Aleera promised.

That, at least, was true. After that, even Jamie wouldn't be dumb enough to try anything like this.

The lucky thing was that everybody had looked away and generally been too busy covering their eyes and screaming when Jamie fired. The second was that Aleera had been just far away enough, and had just quick enough reflexes, to shout 'Blaish' and raise her hand enough. The third was that, with a room-temperature I.Q. and a leg that had moments earlier had a blade in it, Jamie's aim was far from perfect.

Of course, the shield only had a fraction of a second to form, and bullets are far from slow. Still, the air at that point had become dense enough to at least slow it down, and that, coupled with Aleera's quickly moving to the side, resulted in what would have been at best a shot to the shoulder and at worst a bullet into her chest or neck becoming a still-painful, but nowhere near as bad if only due to its non-fatal nature, tear into her arm.

Aleera had screamed. She did, after all, have her limits, and the thing about bullets was that they weren't like knives; they didn't go straight in, but twisted as they tore through the skin and the flesh.

It was a mix of pure adrenaline, Jake's teachings, and her near-psychosis that allowed Aleera to make the equation of pain equals anger; anger equals violence that propelled her from that moment on. Before Jamie fired again, she shouted 'ThuraiShiahl' and, praying that nobody was looking, sent the wall of force slamming into Jamie, carrying him off his feet, still gripping the gun.

Then, confused and angry, he'd struck the ground, still clutching the gun, and it had gone off. With the barrel pressed against his side.

Ouch.

'Who was this guy?' Lilith asked as she proceeded to examine the "mortal wound".

'The sheriff of idiottown.'

'You said he got arrested.'

'There's a new sheriff in town. His brother.'

Lilith shook her head. 'You really do keep some lovely social circles, don't you?'

'I suppose.'

'I'm getting you off Guild duty with this,' Lilith declared. 'No arguments.'

'It's barely even a scratch.'

Lilith moved her own fingers over the wound. '*Xiaol.*' Blue sparks danced over the cut, and Aleera winced as the faint mark of her injury tightened itself up further. 'They won't let me off anyway,' she said further. 'One person I know isn't there, and that took a near-death experience.'

'That's what you had!'

'Not really.'

'Fine,' Lilith said, standing up and throwing her arms up in the air, 'what do I know?'

Aleera shifted uncomfortably. Understandable as a reaction though it was, it was hardly Lilith-like.

'Something bothering you?'

'Besides the fact that my baby sister has a bullet wound?' Lilith yelled.

Hardly fair. All that was there now was a thin, white mark on her arm. Another scar for her collection, Aleera thought distantly.

'Is something else wrong?' Aleera hazarded.

Lilith was about to reply. She hesitated. 'No.'

'No?'

'Sorry, but I just find the idea of my baby sister getting shot kind of distressing. I'm a little protective that way.'

'It's fine,' Aleera insisted, 'it doesn't even hurt. Really this time.'

And that, Aleera thought as she went on reflecting, had been the scene. She turned over in bed again.

When Jasmine had said, quite shockingly enough, that she was in love with her; she didn't think she could have possibly felt any lower. Turned out, she was wrong.

On the one hand, she knew that she shouldn't have been listening to a word Kheron said. He was, after all, a sack of deceit wrapped in one twenty-four-hour-seven-day lie that, were there any justice in the world, would have long-since been locked up to see how long it would be before he considered drinking a can of motor oil. But on the other, all he'd really been saying was exactly what Aleera had spent too many sleepless nights thinking about, whenever something went wrong in her life and she was feeling at her darkest.

And the main problem here was that Aleera had a worrying tendency to spend entirely too much time listening to what the other hand had to say. It always seemed to have a persuasive argument up its sleeve, while the first hand had nothing to offer but boring old common sense.

Yet there was one tiny little sense of un-Aleera-like pity for the idiot who was probably in hospital right now. Between him, Lilith, Michael, Sara and Jasmine, hanging around Aleera didn't seem to be good for you.

15

Well, thank heaven for small mercies. Thursday, at least, had come and gone without much incident. Aleera had called Jake first thing in the morning to ask where they were with the case, and apparently it was more of the same. Rick Lawson was so scared that they'd have more luck trying to extract information from a brick wall, and barring some miraculous way to find out where the wraiths were, nobody had any idea of what to do next.

Actually, Jake did seem to have one idea, and that was to drag Kheron in, kicking and screaming if necessary. Unfortunately, Cassidy and Khazahn both insisted that doing so would be a waste of time and effort and his slimy little lawyer would get him out within the hour. As much as it turned Aleera's stomach, they had a point.

They were practically picking up the man's dry-cleaning, after all.

So, Jake had suggested that she come in later, as another body crammed into the growing crowd behind the two-way mirror wouldn't accomplish much. Besides, Cassidy would probably be a lot happier for not seeing her.

So it was around lunchtime that Aleera finally arrived.

When she got there, she found Jake feverishly poring over some notes in his office. On one side of him was Katya, looking at the occasional file but mostly sitting on the desk and absently kicking her legs, and on the other, to Aleera's surprise, was Makian.

'Hey, kiddo,' Makian smiled, 'miss me?'

'You're back?' Aleera allowed herself to smile for what felt like the first time in an age. Wait a minute, "kiddo"?

'Just this morning,' Makian answered, 'although considering what I came back to, can't say I wouldn't rather be sitting around watching the naughty channel.'

'Lawson?' Aleera asked.

'Think so,' Jake said absent-mindedly as his eyes darted from side-to-side over an open page, 'still.'

'I get back for two minutes,' Makian sighed, 'and I'm back running around the desks for this guy.'

'And what, exactly, are we looking for here?' Aleera asked as she looked down at the reports.

'Anything,' Katya shrugged, 'Jake's had one of those "I have an idea but I'm not going to pause long enough to explain it to my familiar" moments again.'

'I said,' Jake replied, 'we're looking for something hidden.' He was tapping his old coin on the edge of the desk.

'I get that,' Katya pouted, 'what I don't get is how we're supposed to be able to find it, which just sounds like it defeats the purpose of it being hidden in the first place.'

'We just need to look for something that wouldn't ordinarily be noticed,' Jake answered, still not taking his eyes of the sheet in front of him or ceasing to fiddle with the coin, 'something that someone could've buried in the paperwork.'

Aleera sidled up the desk and leaned over to more closely examine the aforementioned paperwork. When it became apparent that nobody was going to say anything, she finally asked: 'why?'

'Lawson.'

'Correct me if I'm wrong,' Aleera said in exasperation, that, *again*, Jake wasn't telling her a damn thing. 'But Lawson happens to be presently locked up in an eight-by-ten cell.'

'He's not telling us anything,' Katya explained helpfully, 'Jake thinks he's scared.'

'He's college age and he's looking at a twenty-year stretch in the cells,' Aleera pointed out, 'I can't say I wouldn't be stressed in his situation.'

'No, he's scared of something else,' Jake muttered, tapping the coin against his temple, 'nobody with nothing to hide looks as worried as he did, I promise you.'

'And what is he scared of?'

'I am, at this moment, trying to figure that out,' Jake replied.

'And when you say "scared"…?'

'I mean, afraid for his life,' Jake replied, 'not of jail. He just kept saying "he's going to kill me",' he shook his head ruefully, 'said we couldn't protect him.'

'Of Kheron?'

'Didn't sound like it,' Jake replied, 'something just doesn't feel right. Khazahn and Cassidy didn't listen to a word, of course.'

'You do say that a lot.'

'Usually right, though,' Jake pointed out.

Aleera shrugged and turned round, absent-mindedly clicking her tongue. After a minute, Katya turned and sat next to her.

'Coffee?' the feline offered.

Aleera shrugged and followed her to the coffee machine.

'Long time no girl talk,' Katya smiled.

'We've all been busy,' Aleera pointed out.

'True enough. You do seem stressed today, though,' Katya said.

'It's been a long week.'

'Boyfriend trouble?'

'Girlfriend trouble, actually,' Aleera said as she took a cup of coffee. 'Besides, first week on the job and everything.'

'Long and slow, and still a mansion of mayhem,' Katya sighed. 'I have to remind Jake to sleep sometimes. It's like having a little brother all over again. Speaking of which, how's Lilith?'

Aleera paused. The notion of that piece of paper came back to her. 'Fine,' she finally said.

They finished their coffee, making the occasional bit of chatter. When they got back, Jake didn't seem to have made any progress.

Eventually, the excitement of watching Jake reading old reports became too much for Aleera.

'Am I needed around here?' she asked.

Jake sighed and leaned back. 'Sorry,' he yawned, 'slower today, I know. Everybody's feeling down.'

Aleera recalled the atmosphere when Chara and Harry Drake were first found out. In this line of work, it wasn't exactly comforting to know that the person holding a weapon behind you might be working for the other side.

'You can go if you like,' Jake offered, 'I'll cover for you.'

'Thanks,' Aleera nodded, 'I'll probably be back later; I just need to talk to Lilith about something.'

'No problem. Catch you on Monday.'

Aleera nodded, favoured him with the friendliest smile at her disposal and left.

It turned out, however, that she was to have someone else to talk to on the way out, as Tomoko had taken that time to take a break from her duties.

'Bad day, doctor?' Aleera asked as she caught her on the way to the locker room.

'No fresh bodies,' Tomoko answered, 'we've had to bring in analysts from six units across two divisions just to get through all of the poor dumb bastards, and apparently some of them never saw a female biologist before. Other than that, can't complain. They have it worse,' she pointed out in reference to the ever-growing number of at-hand corpses.

'True.'

'And yourself?'

'Adjusting,' Aleera replied. 'You seem different,' she noted. While emotions weren't Aleera's specialist subject, and she didn't really tend to be that in-tune with people, she could still observe the occasional change; a brighter choice, more of a tendency to smile.

'Cheered up, I guess,' Tomoko answered with that same newfound brightness.

'Did you know Makian was back?'

'Yes, actually. We've been... getting on a lot better lately.'

'Really?' Aleera asked shrewdly.

'"Really" what?'

'Nothing.'

'Well, how've you been doing?' she asked, 'I've been up to my knees in dead bodies, so sorry I haven't seen you since...' she bit her tongue, 'last time.'

'Nothing much,' Aleera answered, 'besides this.'

'Well, glad someone's still in one piece,' Tomoko smiled faintly. 'I'd better get to work, not that we're likely to find anything. Catch you on Monday?'

'Sure.'

Tomoko turned to the lab, groaning and pinching the bridge of her nose as someone inside shouted something.

Aleera had actually been thankful for this, but around midday, thankful-Aleera was apparently to be replaced with stupid-Aleera, starting when she got a call from Jasmine.

'Aleera, what happened?' Jasmine said hurriedly over the phone, 'someone said that little psycho came to your place! Are you alright?'

'I'm fine,' Aleera reassured her, 'he came off worse. Again.'

'Oh, Jesus... oh, thank God. Are you sure?'

'Yes, I'm sure. I barely have a scratch. Really.'

'Do you want me to come over?'

Aleera checked the clock. 'Don't you have biology?'

'I can ditch. Besides, the amount of studying my mom makes me do- I could probably teach that class.'

'Ok,' Aleera said, knowing full well that she shouldn't, 'come on over.'

She was starting not to think of doing this as stupid anymore. It didn't seem to be making any difference to her actions, and she wasn't sure what she expected to happen. She was hardly going to blurt out the truth to her right now.

Well, why not?

Because she hadn't done at any of her other chances. She'd ask herself what the hell she was thinking, but she was getting a little tired of that.

She was going to sit there with Jasmine, she thought bitterly to herself, look into her eyes and not be able to think of anything else. Again. Did that equate to love? Shouldn't she know that?

All these thoughts rolled around her head, until they articulated themselves the only way they could.

'This sucks.'

Jasmine covered her mouth and trembled. A faint gasp escaped her as her blue eyes widened and blurred.

'Oh my God...'

Aleera rolled her eyes and sighed. 'I hate to think how you'd have been if he actually shot me,' she said bluntly.

'He did shoot you!' Jasmine half-screamed. 'What the hell do you think that is? You've been shot! In the arm! By an actual gun! With an actual bullet!'

'I can heal it,' Aleera said flatly. 'It only grazed me.'

'You have a bandage on your arm! Do you know how lucky you were?' Jasmine asked.

'Nobody saw me,' Aleera replied simply. 'Could've been worse.'

'I'm talking about the bullet,' Jasmine said sternly.

'Oh.'

'"Oh"? That's it?'

'It's been quite a day,' Aleera said defensively.

Jasmine sighed and shook her head, covering her mouth with one hand. 'You nearly *died*.'

'Nearly's Ok.'

Jasmine tried to say something, but it came out as an angry, inarticulate "aargh". 'What is with you?'

'Nothing.'

'You were shot!'

'I know,' Aleera said sardonically.

'And you're sitting there like nothing happened!'

Oh, yes. That would probably be it, wouldn't it?

'Sorry.'

Jasmine sighed. 'I don't get you,' she muttered, 'I really don't.' She softened and smiled. 'You're just lucky I love you,' she said sweetly, kissing Aleera on the cheek.

'It's this, or we don't get to go to the movies on Saturday. I'm going.'

'You are not.'

'Yes I am.'

'If you do not get that looked at, I swear to God that I will dump you,' Jasmine snapped.

'I'll get Tomoko to look at it.'

'Who?'

'Guild. Forensics.'

'That's not a doctor.'

'It is.'

'Not the kind that you need!'

'She probably knows more about medicine than half the doctors at Mercy General.'

'Fine,' Jasmine said loudly, throwing her hands up in the air, 'go and see your cop doctor instead of a real one. Just don't come crying to me when your arm falls off.'

'Deal.'

Jasmine exhaled slowly and relaxed a little. 'I wouldn't really dump you,' she said after a second.

'I know.'

The conversation played itself back over in Aleera's head. One thing in particular stood out.

Jasmine loved her? She'd actually said it. Did she? Could she? It was just the pheromones, it had to be- but she'd said- did she really- she loved her? No. No, it couldn't be. The thought was too big, too stupid, too laughable. God, did Jasmine really think she was in love? Was Aleera doing that to her?

She felt sick. This was what she'd done? What the hell had she been thinking? How could she have been so stupid, so selfish, so…

Because she was in love with-

'Do you wanna go to a movie tomorrow night?' Jasmine asked, snapping her out of it. 'I mean, if you're well enough and your Guild miracle-doctor says it's alright?'

She should really have said no. That would be a very sensible thing to do.

Or maybe the logical thing to do would be to time it better? When she could be sure she was thinking clearly?

On some level, she realised that she was trying to make a logical argument to herself about doing something incredibly stupid. Worse, she was being very persuasive.

'Sure, what movie?'

Yep, now she'd landed herself in it.

'Who cares?' Jasmine shrugged, 'they're all terrible.' It was entirely possible that Aleera was reading too much into what had been said, but Jasmine's reply made it sound an awful lot like the movie wouldn't be the focus of her attention.

It still didn't seem to be stopping her.

'Ok,' Aleera said, 'see you tomorrow.'

'Cool. I should get back. My mom would kill me if she found out I ditched.'

Jasmine smiled and left, leaving Aleera to try and convince herself to listen to the intelligent part of her that was telling her how unbelievably stupid she was being.

No, not stupid.

She was being a stupid, selfish, sick little bitch, and honest to God, whatever she tried, she just couldn't help herself.

Maybe Aleera should have come here sooner, or at least more often. Hell, how could she not have done?

Whenever she visited the cemetery, she could almost picture herself becoming lost amongst all the chiselled, worn and battered headstones. Ironically, it was a good place to think about life.

Not far away from her, someone had apparently found it hilarious to smash someone's gravestone to pieces.

It was evening now, and Aleera sat still on the bench, watching the sky turn orange and looking at the gravestone in front of her. There were days when it still sank in, the thought that someone she'd cared for was lying prone, facing upwards, six feet beneath it. Whenever she tried to think about them being up in heaven with angels and open-armed grandparents, she found herself coming back to the knowledge that they were stuffed into wooden boxes and surrounded by dirt and bugs and worms, their skin slowly rotting off.

How could she not have come here? Three months ago, she and Michael, or she and Sara, were supposed to have meant something real to each other. She and Michael had been a couple, and Sara… she'd never apologised properly for that. For doing to Sara what she was now doing to Jasmine, only now it was even worse.

Why the hell did this have to keep happening to her? The pheromones, she could deal with. But why did her friends have to put up with that as well? And why could she not just deal with it when these things happened, instead of waiting for something to come along and ruin everything? How did she not grasp something that was supposed to be such a basic part of life? Why did everyone seem to understand how to do it but her?

And Michael and Sara… how did she end up losing them the way she did, one right after the other, with so much that could have still happened? And now this- what was this supposed to be? Was this what "love" translated to for her? It had only been months and now she was making the same mistakes again, like cheating on her own victims.

'Well, aren't you a sight for sore eyes?'

Aleera looked up sharply. She tensed when she saw who was walking towards her up the gravel path. 'What's the matter, kiddo?' Kheron chuckled. 'You look like you've seen a ghost.'

'Leave,' Aleera ordered, her eyes turning vivid red.

'Hey, relax. What, I can't stop by for a chat?'

'Bite me.'

'I could take offence to that,' Kheron lectured, 'but seriously. If I wanted trouble, would I have come here all by my lonesome?'

'What do you want?' Aleera demanded, biting back the desire to vent all this frustration on so very deserving a target.

'Just to catch up.' Kheron sat down next to her on the bench, folding his legs. 'How's work?'

'Secret.' Aleera didn't intend to elaborate.

'Fair enough. Tell you what: why don't I give you a lift?' Aleera turned to look at him, and Kheron caught her gaze. 'I'd like to discuss a problem you and I share.'

Aleera regarded him for a moment. The wraiths, she realised. What, now he was offering information? To her?

She shouldn't go with him. It would be even dumber than the way she'd been acting lately. Then again, she was an intelligent, resourceful young woman. Whatever coercion Kheron might use, she'd be able to use her better judgement, right?

'Let's hear it.'

16

Aleera had seated herself in the back of Kheron's limo and soon found a plump ginger tom rubbing its head against her leg. She'd distracted herself by scratching it behind the ears on the way. Apparently it was named Leonardo, or "Leo" as Kheron preferred to call it. She'd always preferred animals to people.

The limo was just about the biggest she'd ever seen. Onboard refrigerator and everything; Kheron had offered her a drink, but she'd refused.

Their destination had turned out to be Kheron's penthouse. Once again, probably the most lavish Aleera had ever been inside. Lilith's entire apartment could probably fit in the living room alone. A massive, panoramic window surrounding the room and covering most of the wall gave a bird's eye view of the city stretching away. Like a tyrant looking down on his kingdom.

Aleera felt that little bit of disgust again. Khazahn was probably still in his office, drinking himself to a death that was already around the corner, and here was Kheron, miles up in his immaculate penthouse with a record player on in the corner.

'Are you sure I can't offer you a drink?' Kheron offered again.

'I'm fine, thank you.'

'Very well. I suppose you still don't want me to have someone look at that arm?'

Aleera glanced down at the bandage around her upper arm. She'd applied a healing spell or two since the shot, enough to stop the bleeding, although there was still a scratch and the arm was still stiff and stung when it moved.

'No.'

'Alright, then. Make yourself at home,' Kheron said as he poured himself a Martini. 'Good stuff, this. Premium olives.'

'What, exactly, do you want?' Aleera asked icily.

'I take it we're not in a conversational mood?'

'I have been shot in the last hour,' Aleera pointed out.

'Fair enough. You know, seriously,' Kheron chuckled, 'I still remember when you were a little girl. Gave your old man no end of headaches.'

Aleera's eyes flashed red. 'Don't mention my father,' she hissed. It probably wasn't that tactful, but it had been an exceptionally stressful day.

'Ah, yes. You two never did see eye-to-eye.'

'What. Do. You. Want?'

'Well, I was going to make at least some small talk. Such a thing as manners, you know. But still, if you're going to insist...' he sat back in a chair, took a sip and smiled up at her. 'I thought I'd do my civic duty and tell you a little something pertaining to this case of yours. Maybe catch up at the same time.'

Aleera regarded him, betraying just the right amount of interest.

'My old friend Khazahn's unit,' Kheron said with a slight grin, 'has a wolf in the fold.'

'If you mean Rick Lawson,' Aleera pointed out coldly, 'we know.'

'Actually, I wasn't referring to him,' Kheron said with a sideways smirk.

'Who?'

'Oh, I'll let you figure that out for yourself. I think you'll be pleasantly surprised.' Kheron took another sip.

'And you think I'm going to believe you?'

'Why wouldn't you? Because the Guild are the "good guys"? Please. You know as well as I do that they'll cross their own lines the minute things start getting ugly.'

Kheron stood up and walked around the room, slowly and deliberately, diverting his gaze to the window and the sea of blackness and light.

'Aleera,' he said, 'let me give you some advice. It'll help you make sense of the world, and it's time you realised it. I realised it. The thing is: between those people out there, and you, and me, there's so much less difference than you seem to think.'

'I am *not* like you,' Aleera glared.

Kheron rolled his head inquisitively to the side and looked expectantly at her.

'Are you going to let me talk or not?' he asked dryly. 'The thing is: you've got this idea in your head, just like everyone else, that the world is split into good people and bad people- and it's not. Your father realised that. You see,' he stepped towards her and gave the slightest grin, 'it's not good people and bad people. It's just the bad people.' He paused and let the words ring in her ears, then turned back to the window.

'Just look at it,' he went on, 'this is supposed to be a city of good and decent people, human or draconic, and I'm standing on the very top of it, literally and metaphorically. It's a great, rolling sea of evil, lies and corruption. Oh, it's deeper in some places, fair enough, but it's always there, and in some places it's so, so much deeper. And still, people like you and Jake get the idea into your head for all this integrity and good intentions and say "this is the opposite, this will triumph". The people out there will follow anyone who serves their interests, out of some mundane, everyday evil. Not the stuff of the real greats like Kudra, just a kind of mass-produced darkness that's in every last one of them.'

He patted Aleera on the shoulder. 'You see,' he smiled, 'this city, and every city like it, needs someone like me to keep it afloat; to take all that evil and manage it, and shape it into something vaguely capable of sustaining itself. You and Jake and Khazahn, you need people like me, because I'm the sort of person that keeps things going. Not the High Council, people like me, and the day I'm gone, someone else will take my place. The only thing good people are good at is stopping the bad people. People like me and your old man, we have plans, whether it's to rule the world or to just get richer, but the Guild... nothing long-term there. No way of keeping things afloat once all the bad people are locked up.'

'And you,' he chuckled, 'you're the most amazing one. You do everything you can to fight that bad thing in you. Oh, it's there, it's in everyone, but it's more solid than it is in everyone else, and you know it as well as I do: you're something of a higher calibre. You're not the same dull, garden-variety sinful. You're not even tainted. You're the kind that does the tainting. You're evil. Born from evil, marked by evil, living and breathing evil. So much deeper than anyone else that you howl in the night because it's slowly consuming every last part of you. You respect the good people because you don't know the way of the world, and what has it ever given you? You're not good. If anyone in this world is good, it's never going to be you. You're an evil little girl trying to be good, and failing.'

He turned back to the window. 'I'm sorry if this offends you,' he said honestly, 'but that's the way of things. Honest and true.'

Aleera took a calming breath. 'Are we done?'

'Feel free,' Kheron said, nodding to the door. 'Nice to see you again.'

Aleera walked straight over to the door without saying anything further. In the corner of the room, Kheron's record carried on playing.

Aleera spent the walk home trying to convince herself that, in some way, she was Ok. She wasn't. Of course not. She still felt sick. Lilith had given up her whole life for her, and she'd been so self-absorbed and wrapped up in her own problems that she didn't even know Lilith had ever been to college- or that she'd given it up so that she could jet across the country the moment she heard that Aleera had been in trouble.

No wonder Lilith had seen fit to hide this from her; how was she supposed to take it? She'd given everything up because of her.

After Lilith left, Aleera had sat in her room and just thought of what Kheron had said to her. Those words came ringing back to her again. It had been the same after she'd been at the Guild; everywhere, people were lying for one reason or another, and now, here was the one person Aleera really did know, in her heart of hearts, to be good, and what had she done to her?

Just like Kheron said- what was she, if she wasn't poison? Everything she touched ended up tainted- Michael, Sara, Jasmine, Harry Drake, and now Lilith. That was it. The tipping point. There was one thing, one very simple thing, that she had sworn to herself never to do, and that was bringing suffering upon her sister- the one person who had ever actually cared for her.

The thing was- and she realised it then- she'd been doing that to someone who didn't even realise it. She'd been doing it to Jasmine since they met. When that thought hit her, whatever barrier had been keeping common sense out of her mind was shredded to pieces.

Alright. Enough. She'd had it. She'd spent the last week surrounded by liars, criminals and monsters, and what she'd been doing the entire time was as bad as any of them. She sickened herself with every moment of it. She had, and there was no other way of looking at it, been taking advantage of someone who thought she was in love with her.

She swore. She shouted and punched the bedroom wall until her anger at herself had drained.

And then she'd known what to do when she went to meet Jasmine.

'Hey, you,' Jasmine smiled sweetly when she opened the door.

Aleera took entirely too long to say 'hi', mainly because she noticed how Jasmine had modified one of her homemade outfits so it was as far up the knee and down the chest as possible without actually exposing anything. The colour was perfect for those gorgeous blue eyes as well…

Stop it. No more of this. She was there for a reason, and she was going to do it even if it tore her apart as it had been doing all day.

'You're a little early,' Jasmine smiled coyly as she shut the door behind Aleera, leaning on it for a moment as Aleera tried to avoid glancing up the back of her skirt, 'the movie's not 'til tomorrow. Good thing I was home alone,' she giggled as she wrapped her arms around Aleera's neck.

Aleera moved her head to the side. If she kissed her, then it would be exactly like all those other times. For once, she was going to do the right thing.

Yes, she was going to break someone's heart to do the right thing. That made perfect sense.

Shut up! She screamed at herself. She was doing this.

Jasmine would never forgive her if she did this.

She'd never forgive herself if she did it.

Oh, so she was just doing this for herself? No point considering Jasmine's feelings about it, then?

Shut up! What the hell kind of stupid justification would that be?

'What's wrong, babe?' Jasmine asked, kissing Aleera on the cheek. 'Another bad day at the office?'

'…No,' Aleera said shakily. She reached up, took hold of Jasmine's arms and gently moved them away. She felt her chest quiver. Her stomach was tying itself in knots. 'I have to talk to you,' she said at last.

'Just talk?' Jasmine asked playfully.

'Yes.' Aleera was as serious as she'd ever been.

'Oh.' Jasmine fidgeted uneasily.

Aleera took a deep breath. This was it. Now or never.

She didn't have to. She couldn't do this. How was she supposed to-

She was doing it. End of discussion.

'Jasmine,' Aleera said slowly, 'I can't go.'

'Oh,' Jasmine said disappointedly. 'You know, you could've just called and said you couldn't make it.'

'That's not what I mean,' Aleera said. She kept her eyes behind her back and avoided meeting Jasmine's eyes. 'I mean, I…' say it. Just spit it out. Say it!

Just say it!

'…'

Say it! Why in God's name couldn't she just say it?

'I just can't do this,' she finally managed to force the sentence out.

'Well, we can do something else,' Jasmine offered, 'we could-'

'No. I mean *this*. I just… I can't. I can't do this.'

Jasmine's blue eyes lidded as the truth sank in. She bit her bottom lip and folded her arms, as she'd do when finding herself suddenly cold. 'Oh.' She swallowed something in her throat. Her eyes started to shimmer and she covered her mouth for a second. 'You mean…' she blinked, dampening the edges of her eyes, 'you're breaking up with me,' she finally said. 'Is that it?'

Aleera's lips and throat were dry. She tried not to look at Jasmine's face. 'Yes,' she finally said.

Jasmine was trying not to cry. 'Why?'

There it was. That one dreaded question.

'Does it matter?'

'Of course it does,' Jasmine said immediately. 'I mean, if it doesn't…' she bit her lip again, 'if it didn't, would you be doing this?'

'You really want to know why?'

Jasmine shook her head sharply. A few strands of hair stuck to the tears that had started to leak out of her eyes. 'Don't- please, don't,' she said as her bottom lip started to quiver.

Aleera didn't look at her.

Jasmine took a breath that turned into a sob halfway in. 'I love you,' she choked, thick wet trickles starting to coat her cheeks.

'I know.'

Jasmine blurted out another tearful burst. 'Do you love me?' she asked.

'I do,' Aleera said, 'I really do, but…'

Tell her. Just tell her. She'd understand.

She'd hate her.

That was the idea, wasn't it?

Tell her, damn it!

'But what?' Jasmine cried, 'Aleera, why are you-'

'I can't tell you,' Aleera said without thinking. "I'm a succubus" is what she probably should have said, and was really a much better explanation, but sadly that irritating little thing called shame got in the way again.

Jasmine covered her mouth. Fresh tears ran down her cheeks and over her fingers. Then she sniffed and wiped the tears from her cheeks and said: 'Get out.' She took another deep breath. 'Just- just get out, you- you *bitch!*' she suddenly shouted with more anger and pain in her voice than Aleera could have ever imagined. 'You fucking *bitch!*' Jasmine yelled. 'If it's over, then fine. Dump me. Here. Right now. I get it. I just got dumped. You know what? Fine. I get that. But don't you- don't you stand there and give me this "it's not you, it's me" bullshit just because you've had enough of me. If it's over, say it's over, don't just- God, you- *I fucking loved you, you bitch!*' she screamed loud enough to make Aleera flinch. 'Get out,' she repeated. 'Get out.'

Aleera didn't argue. She didn't say a word. She walked past Jasmine, opened the door and left. Hard to argue at a time like that, when she knew she deserved every word.

The last thing she heard from inside Jasmine's home was the girl who'd loved her sobbing.

That was it, then. Over and done with. Her work was finished. Right thing done.

So why, then, did it feel like all she did was cruelly snap a heart in two?

Was that the right thing? Was leaving Jasmine heartbroken and crying the decent, honest, kind thing to do?

For God's sake, Aleera had said she loved her. She'd kept that from everyone- kept it from her damn self- the whole time. And when she said it just then, she'd meant it.

She'd been in love. Honest to God, in love. How much of a once-in-a-lifetime thing must that be for someone like her? And then she'd thrown it all away.

That dark, sick heart of hers was awake again, and laughing in triumphant glee, because something else, something good, something decent, had just been torn out of her.

When Aleera got home, she entirely ignored Lilith's queries as to where she'd been, locked herself in the room, and finally collapsed against the back of the door, buried her head in her hands and did something she'd never done for this kind of reason; something that suggested there was something in her now that she could never have imagine having in her before.

She collapsed to the floor, held her head in her hands and cried.

17

Aleera hadn't expected things to seem much better when she woke up on Friday morning, but even she was surprised at just how lousy she felt.

She woke up at about nine. The nightmares had been the worst all week. She'd woken up at least four times, and when she finally climbed out of bed she was covered in a thick, cold sweat. She was in the shower when, as it does, everything came creeping back into mind.

Oh, God, what the hell had she done? She'd… she'd said she was in love? And she'd meant it!? Was she ill? Well, no, not ill, at least not physically, though maybe…

Did this have to be so damn confusing? No wonder she'd never been in love before… so she was now, then… oh, for-

No, seriously, what had she done?

Well, she'd broken up with her girlfriend, still not come clean with the truth, and figured out entirely too late what had been going on in her own stupid head at the same time.

This was… this was just plain awful. She'd dumped and been dumped, at least one of each, and it had never been anything close to this. Every time she was around Jasmine, there'd been that flutter, that surge of excitement in her chest, and now there was just this… nothing. The absence of it was the thing that really hurt. This, she couldn't help feeling, just might be what an honest-to-God broken heart felt like. She'd known hate, and she'd known love, and it turned out that it was love that did the real damage. Wasn't that a bitch?

She eventually managed to pull herself out of such a funk long enough to leave the shower, get dressed and somehow make it all the way to the kitchen table. It was going to take a whole bowlful of honey to get herself through this.

'Morning, smiler,' Lilith said brightly when she saw her. Then she got a good look at Aleera's face and realised that this was a stage or two above a "bad night" Aleera. 'What's wrong?'

'Nothing,' Aleera said instinctively as she opened the fridge.

'Uh-huh.'

'I'm fine,' Aleera repeated.

'Uh-huh.'

Aleera sighed. No, there was no point to keeping this to herself. Besides, this was Lilith. That was an inarguable point in and of itself. Plus, even at a time like this, that logical, rational thing called "being an antisocial near-psychopath" broke through, and she knew that it wouldn't do any good to herself or anyone else if she spent the whole day walking around like this.

She sat down on the table. Lilith seated herself on the other side and waited for her to talk.

'I broke up with Jasmine,' Aleera said.

Lilith nodded slowly. 'Badly?'

'It was historic.'

'Did you break up with her,' Lilith asked tentatively, 'or was it, y'know, the other way round?'

'It was me,' Aleera answered, resting her head in one hand.

'Why?' Lilith asked. 'I mean, really? You two were... you were crazy about each other.'

'Shockingly,' Aleera muttered sideways, 'that doesn't make me feel a lot better about it.'

'Why, though?' Lilith asked again.

'Because I was being stupid,' Aleera replied. Her voice managed to betray more bitterness than she'd have liked. Wow, bitter after one day. Only a real bitch could manage that. 'I was being really, really, really stupid.'

'Three really-s?' Lilith noted. 'Ouch.'

'Remember when we talked about the pheromones?' Aleera reminded her.

'Oh,' Lilith realised as the implication slowly sank in. '*Oh.*'

'Yeah.'

Lilith thinned her lips and folded her hands. 'That doesn't sound like you,' she said. 'And I know I'm not exactly in a position to judge, but... like I said.' She quietened herself.

'I did say I was stupid,' Aleera said.

'Yeah, but that isn't something you'd do. You- you never do that. Even with D- with your ex,' she stopped herself from mentioning the name.

Aleera tried to stop herself. It didn't work; the whole thing had been tripping over itself in her mind all night, it had only just resolved itself there, and it wasn't about to be delayed again.

'I loved her,' she finally said. She felt her eyes starting to blur. Oh God, she was actually going to start crying? Over a relationship? Like a normal person? 'I loved her, and I- God, what did I do?' she groaned as she buried her head in both hands.

Lilith sighed, walked round the table and put an arm around her sister. 'I understand,' she said, distantly remembering that same talk. 'I really do. I know you think you were stupid, but believe me, you're not the first and you won't be the last.'

What was probably about to become a real sisterly heart-to-heart was interrupted when the phone started to jingle in the corner of the room.

'I'll get it,' Lilith said, standing up, 'it'll be for you.'

'How'd you figure that out?' Aleera asked as she finished drying her eyes. It was going to be a long day.

'It was for you earlier,' Lilith answered as she picked up the phone, quickly explaining why she didn't wake Aleera with the inescapable logic of 'you were sleeping.'

That done, she listened into the receiver. 'Hello? …Yeah, she's here now. …No, I haven't told her yet… yeah, just up; I'll put her on.' She handed the phone to Aleera.

Told her what, exactly? Well, no time like the present to find out, Aleera thought to herself.

'Hello?'

'Hello, Aleera?'

That, honestly, was the last voice Aleera had been expecting to hear any time soon. 'Mrs. Mcrae?'

'What did I tell you?'

'Sorry. Shelly.'

'Better. Now: I'm sorry to call you out of the blue like this.'

'That's fine,' Aleera replied, 'what can I do for you?'

'Well, I wouldn't be bothering you normally, but there is something I was hoping to ask you. I know it's short notice, and you're probably busy and I'd understand completely if you said "no", but I was wondering if you wouldn't mind taking care of Chloe for me tonight?'

Aleera felt herself tense. She blinked in a moment of honest confusion. Break-ups, demons, crime lords, wraiths, that was all fine, but this was downright surreal. 'You mean babysitting?' she asked to confirm whether her ears were actually functioning.

'Well, yes. My sister's just been taken into hospital, you see, and apparently it's nothing the doctors can't fix but they do need a next of kin. I wouldn't be asking but I only found out today and every other sitter I could find was booked.'

'You want me to do it?' Aleera parroted disbelievingly.

'Only if it isn't a problem. I understand you're probably busy, and there are some people on the next floor, but… well, then I remembered how well you two were getting along on her birthday, and- well, if I'm honest… there really is nobody else I'd rather have taking care of my little girl.'

Wow. That was… well, it was fourteen words she'd never expected to hear in a row. Seriously, her?

'Well- I'd-' Good lord, was she actually speechless? Her of all people? 'Sure,' she finally blurted out in a moment of spontaneity. 'I'd love to.'

'Great,' she could actually hear Mrs. Mcrae smile, 'can you be here at about seven?'

'Sure.'

'Lovely. Chloe's been so excited; I'll see you then. Thanks again.' Then she hung up.

Aleera put the phone down on the table and shook her head.

'Babysitting?' Lilith asked, eyebrows arched.

'I know,' Aleera said, quite possibly in shock.

She'd agreed? She'd just agreed to it? Her, in charge of an eleven-year-old? *Her*? Seriously, what was the thinking behind… well, maybe it was understandable that Mrs. Mcrae would have the idea, but still.

'Never really pictured you as the babysitting sort,' Lilith said idly.

'Tell me about it.'

'You're actually doing it?'

'Might as well,' Aleera mused, 'it'd probably take my mind of yesterday.'

'Well, I say go for it. She trusts you. Can't say I blame her.'

'Seriously?'

'You saved her granddaughter's life,' Lilith reminded her, 'without you there, that kid would be dead. I mean, yeah, you say it was because of you that she was in trouble, but honestly, that's only inside your warped brain.'

Again, Aleera didn't find any way of objecting.

Jake yawned loudly as he entered the living room, stretching one arm after sleeping on it the wrong way.

'You're up already?' Katya asked in disbelief, halfway through a bowl of cereal. 'Do you actually need to sleep?'

'Somewhat,' Jake shrugged, cracking his neck. 'I miss anything?'

'Not around here,' Katya shrugged.

'And work?'

'Do you ever switch off that freaky machine brain?'

Jake, in the middle of opening the fridge, turned round to regard her. 'You didn't answer the question,' he noticed.

'And?'

'And, since this is you not answering the question, I can only assume that I won't like what I hear when you do answer the question. Am I on the ballpark?'

Katya stuck her bottom lip out. 'Well,' she admitted hesitantly, 'don't get upset- and that part I can't stress enough- but I did get a phone call from Makian, asking me to break it to you gently that Rick Lawson's gone,' she blurted the end out in the span of a second.

Jake froze, an upturned glass of orange juice overflowing a glass. 'What?'

'He's not at the Guild,' Katya replied, wincing, 'and nobody knows where he is.' She bit her lip. 'You're mad, aren't you?'

Light flashed over Jake's form. Katya squinted her eyes shut, and a second later Jake was standing there fully clothed.

'Thought so,' Katya sighed as she swallowed the last mouthful of her breakfast. 'You're not going without breakfast.'

'I'll be back in a minute,' Jake reasoned. '*Appiras*.' The air convulsed, and Jake was gone.

Katya sighed and dropped the spoon into her bowl. 'Don't worry about me,' she muttered irritably, 'I'll make my own way there.'

Across New York, Jake burst into being on top of the Flatiron Building, irritated, shaken, twenty-two floors up and with a splitting headache from teleporting himself halfway across New York first thing in the morning- even if one person was easier to transport. Oh, and it had to be raining, of course, just to complete the experience.

Heading down the fire stairs, he quickly came to the hidden elevator, the walls sliding open soundlessly at the password 'Silver clearance, Archimedes Eight-Seven-One'. The silver elevator descended and opened into the central hall of the Guild's New York headquarters. Perfect hiding place.

The door into Makian's office was still open. Tomoko and Makian were sharing a coffee inside, and it would take Jake several moments to notice their proximity to each other.

'Jesus Shit,' Makian half-shouted as Jake burst into the room, 'man, you about scared the living-'

'Where's Lawson?' Jake interrupted.

'What?'

'Lawson.'

'He's gone,' Makian said sheepishly. 'I did call to tell you,' he added as Jake stormed out of the office.

Just as Makian predicted, the cell that had formerly held Private Rick Lawson was empty. More as a way of venting than anything else, Jake punched the wall, the "thud" echoing around the empty room.

Great. Oh, this was also just so great, wasn't it? Their one lead. Their one, single lead, and now he'd just strolled out? Oh, this was-

'Missing someone?'

Jake whirled round. Khazahn entered the room with the slight lurch and pale countenance of a man who hadn't had nearly enough of a good night's sleep. 'Whoever got him out of here took the camera out. We've already searched his apartment, and he's not there.'

Jake shook his head ruefully and leaned against an arm on the two-way mirror. 'The High Council's going to eat us alive for this,' he muttered.

'That they are,' Khazahn nodded.

'I don't believe this,' Jake breathed, 'in a three-week investigation, we get one lead that doesn't turn into a corpse, and instead it turns into an empty cell.'

'We are… we are done,' Khazahn said in dismay, apparently not noticing any of what Jake had said. 'Once Hartwell gets wind of this… damn. What the hell do we do now?' he broke into a shout and slammed his fist on the glass. 'This unit's hanging by a thread as it is.'

'We find Lawson,' Jake replied, 'we find him quickly.'

'And if we don't?'

'Cross that bridge when we come to it,' Jake shrugged, 'but where would he go? I mean…' at some point he'd started fiddling with that old coin as he always did, 'he was scared out of his wits, like he knew someone was gunning for him. Why take this kind of a chance? I mean, let's face it, this is probably the most secure building in New York.'

'We can figure that out when he's back *in* the building,' Khazahn said with new and surprisingly spontaneous resolve. 'Right now, we find him.'

'He's just gone?'

'Just like that,' Jake confirmed, leaning on his desk and fiddling with that old coin of his.

It occurred to Aleera, as a side-note, that she hadn't been at Jake's apartment since starting her first case. It was just as messy as before. They were doing this here because Jake didn't technically have access to the Guild's personnel files. What he did have, however, was a laptop and a friend who knew his way around the Guild's computer system and knew not only how to get into the records, but also how to erase any trace of his having done so.

'Anything?' Jake asked of Makian, whose fingers still tapped away on the keyboard.

'Our boy had a girlfriend in Brooklyn, name of Hannah Clarke, parents divorced in 1983, older brother serving a tour of duty in Afghanistan. No known criminal activity prior to this, not a regular at pentagram or any other hotspots, no contact with Kheron or his associates at all... like Cassidy said, dude's squeaky clean.'

'Any idea where he might have gone?' Jake prompted.

'No, but if he's smart, he's long gone by now. It's, what, two-thirty? Guy's probably across the state line, even if he had to go on foot. We put a stop on his passport and all his credit cards before we brought him in.'

'They can do that?' Aleera asked.

'It's the Guild, and this is officially an emergency situation. They can do pretty much whatever the hell they feel like. Sorry, Jake, but this isn't gonna help.'

Jake nodded. It had been a long shot, but it was worth a shot.

'Speaking of the emergency,' Katya piped up from her position lounging over the back of a chair, 'anybody noticed something? It's been like two, maybe three days since the wraiths turned up?'

Makian froze. Jake just nodded again and turned that old coin over.

'There are a lot of homeless people down there,' Aleera pointed out, perhaps a little too freely, 'rats, too.'

'Alligators in the sewers,' Makian pointed out.

'It needs to be a magical caste,' Jake answered. 'A normal human would only sustain them for a few hours. Rats and such, even less.'

'Could they have died off?' Aleera suggested. It could be, if they hadn't fed in that long.

'Considering how this case has gone so far, I don't see us being that lucky.'

'So remind me again why we're wasting time on Lawson?' Makian asked.

'Because he's our only chance to find out where they came from, which *just* might help us work out where they are.'

'Well, we know they're in the sewer.'

'We've got people in the sewers searching, but do you know how long those things go on for? It's like saying "they're in the city" and hoping that narrows it down.'

'And that's assuming they're staying in one place,' Aleera added.

'Well aren't you two a barrel of laughs?' Makian shook his head dismally.

'We'll find him,' Jake said sharply, 'if he's within a thousand miles of here, we'll find him.'

Aleera had arrived at the Mcraes' apartment at seven o'clock as scheduled, was greeted with as much kindness as she'd ever seen, and, at the moment she'd been dreading, was left alone to take care of an eleven-year-old.

But the scary thing- the real, terrifying, shook her to the bones, shiver-inducing thing, was that it wasn't that difficult.

Aleera had never really pictured herself in the role of a caregiver; though she was fully aware that at some distant point in history she herself had been one, small children always seemed like something strange and alien. It was probably that whole childhood innocence thing. She never did get much of that. The thing was, though, that little Chloe seemed to have it in spades.

It hadn't even been hard taking care of the girl; she'd mainly sat there drawing or watching TV all night. A perfectly ordinary eleven-year-old child, and for Aleera, that was food for thought. Clearly not everybody came out of childhood horrors as a near-psychopath.

As per Mrs. Mcrae's - *Shelly's*- instructions, she put Chloe into bed a little after nine o' clock.

'Aleera,' Chloe said as she was reaching for the light switch, 'can you turn the nightlight on?'

Aleera spotted the small light plugged into the wall socket. 'Sure,' she said and switched on, filling the room with a surprising amount of light for something that small.

'Thanks,' Chloe said as she fidgeted under the covers. Aleera went downstairs and started flicking through channels.

So, what to do now, exactly? Shelly wouldn't be back until morning, and she was by herself for the night now that Chloe was in bed. It wasn't exactly as if she had a boyfriend, or a girlfriend, she remembered bitterly, to sneak in.

Oh, dear. Here we go. This was the part of the night she'd really been dreading: the part where she was to be left alone with her thoughts. No problem. She just had to not think about her. Don't think about her, don't think about her, don't, don't... She was thinking about her.

She flicked through a few channels to see if anything caught her eye, but it only served as a reminder of why she didn't watch much T.V. Eventually she managed to switch on the news, which, even if it was as miserable as ever, served as enough of a distraction. Before long, she was finally starting to doze off.

Then she heard the scream from the other room.

She was in Chloe's room in a heartbeat, where the child was sat up in bed, crying and clutching the sheets.

'Chloe,' Aleera said, kneeling on the bed next to her, 'are you alright?'

Chloe nodded and wiped her eyes. 'I had a nightmare,' she said sheepishly.

'It's alright,' Aleera said gently, remembering what Lilith had always done for her, 'it was just a dream.' She put an arm around her until she felt her stop shaking. 'Better?'

Chloe nodded and sniffed.

'Can I come in the living room?' Chloe asked.

'Ok,' Aleera said, leading her out of the room. Chloe was clutching a stuffed animal of some kind in one hand. Aleera sat her down on the sofa next to her and put an arm round her.

Chloe looked uncomfortably at the roof. 'Do you ever have dreams like that?' she asked.

'Like what?'

'I dream about him sometimes,' Chloe answered distantly. 'Like one where I turned round a corner and he was there.'

Ah, yes. Him. It was hard to be surprised by the idea. She'd had unspeakable things done to her when she was ten years old. Of course that wasn't just going to go away. There were two living examples in the room.

It was wrong. Not just like what the High Council has done, but honestly, evilly, something that should not happen. A child, an innocent child who'd never done a thing to anyone, shouldn't have to wake up screaming at night. She didn't deserve to have some depraved lunatic tear her life apart when it had barely begun.

'Do you ever have those dreams?' Chloe asked.

'Sometimes,' Aleera confessed. For now, she decided to leave out the fact that most of hers were about someone worse. She was doubtful that, in Chloe's mind, the words "worse", "than" and "Azrael" belonged in that order.

'I keep dreaming about it,' Chloe said, 'like he's coming to get me again.'

'He's not,' Aleera said gently, 'he's not going to come back, Chloe. He's gone.'

'What if he isn't?'

'He is. I promise.'

Chloe fidgeted again and rested her head on Aleera's side. 'Thank you,' she mumbled. It was possibly the most honest thing Aleera had ever heard.

A couple of minutes drifted by slowly. The next time Aleera checked, Chloe was sound asleep. Amazing, part of her thought. She'd actually managed to console a child after a nightmare. Rather worrying, really, to think how good she was turning out to be at this whole babysitting thing.

Then again, said another, she was only there because she was so directly involved in the reason the poor girl was having nightmares in the first place. Surely there was some psychological reasoning stating that Chloe should be terrified of her.

Aleera ignored them both, switched off the T.V., leaned her head against the back of the sofa and drifted off.

The sound woke her up, sharp and sudden. She woke to a pitch-black room and took a second to remember the circumstances as her eyes adjusted. The slamming came again from the door. It wasn't a knock. It was louder, harder and larger. With a third, the door shook. Oh, now this was perfect, part of Aleera's mind grumbled. Seriously. Again, she was near Chloe, and now someone was trying to break into the child's home.

The poor dumb idiots didn't even know what was waiting for them, she thought as she let the claws extend from her hands. She unbuttoned and removed her blouse- no sense in shredding it- and let the black, leathery wings unfold.

She stepped forward slowly, fighting to control the adrenaline. That dark little part of her was going to enjoy this so very much…

Then, before she could do a thing, the door exploded inward, the chain snapped like a piece of string, and the wraith burst through.

18

A number of things come to mind when one has no shirt on and has unexpectedly come under attack by a wraith. Chief among these were questions concerning where it had come from and what it was doing there. These, of course, paled in comparison to Aleera's realisation that she was in mortal danger, which in all honesty had a tendency to trump most things. As it happened, she really didn't have all that much going for her; a wraith grabbing hold of one's bare skin was tantamount to an instant fatality, and in what could only be termed a massive miscalculation, Aleera, not anticipating this kind of assailant, had removed her upper clothing so as to avoid her wings shredding it to pieces upon emerging, resulting in entirely too much skin being exposed.

She was fairly sure that not many succubae so vehemently regretted getting topless.

All things considered, a number of things had conspired not in Aleera's favour. Fortuitously, she did have five very useful things on her side. One: a pair of wings. Two: razor-sharp, six-inch claws, ten total. Three: the kind of brain that, even after being unexpectedly woken up in the middle of the night, kicked into high gear quickly. Four: a solid grasp of offensive and defensive magic. And fifth: a willingness to use all of the above to whatever ends necessary.

The claws were used to the most immediate effect; a good, sharp swipe sideways through the air caught the nearest wraith in the face; a trail of blackened blood followed their arc as they met no resistance from rotten flesh. Nonetheless, a wraith could still feel pain if nothing else, and it fell to the side, screaming and clutching its face in the most primal, agonised way Aleera had ever heard.

No time to let it get to her. Especially since three of the things had just burst in. The wings came into play next; a good, solid flap carried her back enough to give her that little bit of distance. Then, with a shout of "*Blaish*", the second of the wraiths struck a shimmering barrier of solid air. Even as the barrier flashed out of existence, the next thing it felt was the side of a trusty size seven shoe striking its left temple.

The third one was luckier. It sailed over the others on a straight course for Aleera. A pair of wings knocked its arms to the side as Aleera grabbed it by the chest and, as she'd practiced for years, rolled with the blow, sending the thing flying past her and into- into the living room. Stupid!

'*ThuraiShiahl*!' the wall of force struck the wraith side-on, sending it and apparently a lamp crashing into the opposite wall.

No. No, no, no, not good, not good at all. Two directions to attack from now. Two targets to choose from. And those two behind her would still be-

Shit.

She was tackled to the ground, the darkened world screaming as a rotten, grey face screamed at her. The hand grabbed hold of her forearm.

'Feed!' the wraith howled, chunks of flesh falling from its mouth, 'this time we feed!' Not a second later, it was punctured by a set of claws- literally, in the bottom of the limb and out the top- from the opposite hand. It released its grip immediately and, not bothering to lift the hand, fell back.

Wraith muscle, long-rotten, was nothing resembling strong. It gave no resistance as it tore, the bone snapping out of the weakened joint as the entire thing slipped off of Aleera's claws and into the wall opposite, its former owner howling in pain, turning into a savage snarl as Aleera's foot struck it in the face.

The next moment, Aleera was on her feet again, shifting her weight perfectly. The next, she heard Chloe scream.

She had just enough time to see what she was aiming for- the wraith, leaning over the sofa, prying the protective pillow out of Chloe's struggling hands- before the wings took her rocketing across the room. No flight, just an assisted leap, claws first.

The wraith's scream was cut short as Aleera's claws pushed themselves through its cheeks, mouth and eyes and erupted out of the back of its head. The whole foul mass, still moving, collided with the wall, claws sinking into the plaster. Levering herself against the wall with one foot, Aleera pulled the claws out on strings of tendon and brain.

One down. No compunctions now. No time for conscience. This was when it really came down to it. Forget reason, forget decency, and forget everything except the real, ultimate, life-or-death truth of the situation: either she killed these things, or they killed her *and* Chloe. And that was a choice that was no choice at all.

The other two were already shooting across the room. Another "*ThuraiShiahl*" struck them both, carrying them both back towards the front door.

Now or never. Think. Quickly. What helped with wraiths? Light. Most eyes are at least momentarily blinded by any sudden change, whenever anyone suddenly turned the lights on in a dark room. Imagine that, she thought, with eyes that had already half-rotted out. Besides that, wraiths hunted best in the dark; hence, no real tendency to look on the bright side of life.

'*Sola*!' She shouted as she ran forward. The wraiths howled as soon as the shimmering white light struck them. They howled and thrashed and covered their eyes. Then, as suddenly as they'd been there, they fled.

Not for long, Aleera thought before she could give herself a pat on the back. Wraiths didn't give up, especially if one of their own now had a set of holes through his head. The bitter part was that she'd probably done the poor wretch a favour. The point was: they'd be back. Soon.

The first thing Aleera did was turn the lights on, if only so that she could see better. No sense in giving the other side all the advantages they could get. And whatever other tricks she had planned, she knew she'd better carry them out quickly, because the time before the wraiths' attempt at retribution could probably be counted in seconds.

'Chloe,' she said, rounding the sofa. Chloe was huddled up on the sofa, her face streaked with tears. Oh God, what would this do to her?

Focus. She could panic when avoiding certain death was no longer an immediate issue. 'Chloe, look at me. Look at me,' she said, holding the child's head in her hands. She responded. Good. 'Come on,' she said, leading her by the hand into the kitchen. Chloe managed to follow. Good girl.

Ok, now where? Keeping Chloe in the room with what was about to happen was by no means a good idea. Somewhere to hide. Hide in… small things. With doors. Cupboards. Kitchen.

She turned on the kitchen light as she led Chloe in, picking up her top on the way. It would at least cover some skin, but compared to the Guild armour she'd been wearing last time, it suddenly felt so very flimsy.

Wait.

Last time?

It had said "this time". "This time we feed". So it remembered a last time? The penthouse, she recalled immediately. It knew? It remembered? If so, it had been there to remember, so…

How, the question screamed in the back of her mind, did it find her?

Worry about that later, came the reply as Aleera opened one of the cupboards, pushing to the side whatever she could and spilling the rest onto the kitchen floor.

'Ok, Chloe?' she said, coming up with the first thing at hand to calm the child, 'come on, Chloe, look at me,' she said, holding her shoulders, 'listen, don't be scared, alright? None of this is real. It's just- just a big, silly thing the grown-ups are doing. Now listen, because this is really important: climb in there,' she said, turning Chloe towards the cupboard, 'close your eyes, cover your ears and stay really, really quiet. Ok, can you do that, sweetness?'

Chloe nodded, still crying.

'Good girl,' Aleera said. She kissed her on the forehead, helped her into the cupboard and closed the door. Then she pulled the blouse back on and did it up as effectively as she could. She didn't bother with the fact that it was inside-out.

Now what? Time was short, that was a certainty. Weapons. Anything to give her an edge. Edge. Sharp. Knives.

Immediately, she grabbed whatever was at hand and could be remotely useful. Any source of help- and then, the words "help" finally exploded into mind.

She reached into her pocket and found no cell phone. 'Shit…' not in the other one either. She must have dropped it, rather understandably, in all not-inconsiderable confusion.

Oh, wonderful. So she was stuck with two-against-one. Still, a minute ago it had been three, so she'd at least partly shifted the odds in her favour.

Here we go. No more scared little girl. There was times when it really did pay to allow that dark little thing inside to be in control.

Besides, now she could *really* cut loose.

Any. Second. Now.

There. Movement. Outside.

Out of the kitchen! Aleera's mind screamed. Away from Chloe!

The movement reached the edge of the door.

'*Tyasans*,' Aleera whispered, feeling the light fold around her as she faded from sight. Element of surprise. Play to her strengths.

And then, Aleera knew, the time had come to throw reason out the window and hand the reigns over to nice, violent psychosis.

The first thing to hit the wraith was a plate, smashing to pieces as chunks of porcelain sliced through its cheek and scalp. It screamed and turned, and on some level it dawned on Aleera that the time she'd spent working on her aim may not have been suspicious. This, however, was tempered when the knife struck the wraith in the head, slicing clean through as it screamed and clutched its forehead and a mass of gore embedded itself in the wall behind it.

Now.

Before it had a chance to recover, Aleera was on it, riding a tide of blood-red rage that she didn't bother trying to resist. No point now. No calm. No reason. Do it. Either she killed them, or they killed her. Just, perfect killing.

Arcs of wraith blood and flesh were strewn out to the sides as Aleera's claws sliced into the wraith's chest, jarring to a stop as- oh Jesus, *they were caught in the damn ribs!?*

'*Whoahn*!' the wraith was hurled away, the claws scraping across bone. There. Ten nice gashes in the chest and stomach and a sliced-open head. Try getting up from that, the dark thing screamed and cackled. Oh, Aleera just loved this!

Kill them! Kill them! Kill, kill, kill them!

Yes!

She was upon the wraith in a second, clawed thumbs jabbing into its eye. With a sick, wet tear, they were out, thick, sinewy strands dangling from them as the wraith screamed again.

Were Aleera functioning as rationally as usual, she might have taken heed of the fact that this was a wraith. Singular. Instead, it was too late that she looked up to see the third and final one collide with her.

Her back struck the floor as the claws stabbed into the wraith's side. It screamed, but didn't stop.

The hands wrapped around her neck.

Then everything went cold.

The world fell silent in an instant; a long, slow echo of the wraith's howl as she felt the fingers tighten around her. She felt her skin pulsate, felt her blood coagulate as her muscles constricted.

She felt her heart beat twice. Then once. Then not at all.

Oh God. Oh God, oh God, oh-

She screamed. She screamed as she felt herself being torn out, every fibre of her ripping and tearing and forcing its way out through the scream.

The pain was endless, screaming and white-hot. It filled everything. It *was* everything.

Everything was pulled, kicking and screaming, out of her, with every part of her heart and brain burning, and Aleera screamed like never before.

And through it, pulled out so sharp and painful, were so, so many screams.

She felt everything.

Everything she'd felt in life. Every rush. Every pleasure. Every pain. So. Much. Pain.

She saw everything slide out. Her father laughed as his fist struck her face. Then he pulled her up by the hair and forced himself in.

She sat by Lilith's side and cried.

Kudra's men surrounded her, scratching and pulling at her, ripping out clumps of hair as they tore at her with depraved lusts.

She cried, sat in the corner and wept, pleading with her mother to stop, to leave Lilith alone, knowing that it was going to be her next.

Everything went past. She was in that old kitchen with Lilith, baking a chocolate cake for the first time.

She was looking at Jake and Katya for the first time.

She was eleven years old, falling asleep in her sister's arms.

She was seventeen years old, spending lunch with Michael and Sara.

She was in the Guild's medical room, kissing Michael with such passion.

She was thirteen, being struck round the face by her mother.

She was fifteen, lying in bed with Dante.

She was pinning Dante to a wall, punching him in the kidneys and telling him never to go within a hundred miles of her sister again.

She was ten, huddled in fear as she heard her father coming up the stairs.

She was fourteen, sitting alone and depressed after her first girlfriend dumped her out of the blue.

She was sixteen, mastering the invisibility spell for the first time under Jake's watchful eye.

She was fourteen, hearing for the first time that her father was dead.

She was just turned eighteen, feeling Jasmine's lips pressed against hers a week before she broke her heart.

Jasmine…

Everything she'd done. How deeply she'd hurt her, and- God, she would never see her again.

She was eleven years old, watching her father commit an atrocity and unable to stop him.

She was what she had always been at heart, now more than ever with everything else torn away: she was a weak, powerless, terrified little girl.

And she was… God, she was going to die this way. Powerless. Weak. Scared.

Screaming.

The last of it was pulled away.

She felt everything stop.

…

And then, she felt it scream back. She felt it pull back. She felt it fight back.

It lashed out from the heart of her, curled up, chained, and now free. Now with the chains broken, with the walls of its prison stripped away.

The dark thing inside, screaming and unconfined, lashed out. Pure, endless darkness lashed out from the pit of Aleera's soul.

Aleera's eyes opened. They turned again. Blood-red irises shifted, flooding pupils and irises and whites with thick, inky black. She took a sharp, screeching breath as cold, harsh air invaded her lungs.

There was a long, slow heartbeat. The dark thing screamed and tore through Aleera's soul, making sure she felt every shred.

For the first time, it touched her mind, and she knew what it was.

It was something pure, screaming and howling constantly. It was something that had long-since ripped out her soul and sat in its place. It was what it had made her so very long ago.

It was evil.

It was the bowels of wretchedness all chained up and ready to be freed. It wasn't just darkness and anger and the desire to do wrong. It was what the very word *evil* was first supposed to mean in frightened whispers. The very fires of hell.

It was the thing in the dark that made men afraid since the earliest times. It was the part of every human being that made it turn away from good. It was the sins of those who knew better, but still did it. It was the tears of the damned and the screaming of the forsaken.

It was her own soul.

The wraith screamed, releasing her as the raw dark burned at its hand. Decayed flesh exploded outwards, revealing dirty yellow bones and dripping sinews. The hand flailed back, burning and sizzling with black smoke.

It screamed again as the black light curled through its body, throwing its limbs into wild spasms. Then there was a third scream, and it fell to its back, scrambling and sobbing.

'You can't be,' it half-shouted, half-whimpered, 'so strong... so... so dark, you're... you...' it howled again, clutching its arm as it crawled desperately, like an injured and desperate animal wounded, 'what are you,' it trembled and sobbed, *'what are you!'*

Then, sweeping and screaming, it was gone.

Aleera was gone, lying still on the floor of the wrecked room, feeling the dark thing curl back up and drag everything else back with it.

There was one final stab of blistering pain.

And then the world faded to black.

19

The dark began to slip away.

What was it? Or what had it been? Something inside. Still there? She could feel it, stirring and rumbling inside her.

It had beaten it. Driven it off. Hurt it like nothing else could. It used her limbs to kill two of them and then, with nothing else to do, lashed out on its own, all fear and rage and dark and *power*.

And now it was chained up again.

What could do that? What would keep it chained like that?

The dark slipped away. The light faded in and stung the back of her eyes.

Don't open them, then. Stay here. Stay with the dark.

She opened them with an inward, stifled breath and sat upright as the blinding light poured in.

The fear welled up without hesitation. Her eyes flashed red as she shook violently. Wings and claws erupted on instinct.

'Aleera,' the voice said, 'easy. Easy, come on.'

The pure, burning light started to recede. Her eyes adjusted. The room came into view. White walls. White ceiling. Light-green curtains around a white bed, a now-torn soft-blue gown covering her. All there. Inside. No screams, just her own breath and a rhythmic, fast beating that grew steadier as she calmed.

She exhaled slowly and pulled the claws and wings back. The remains of the hospital gown fell away.

'That's better,' Tomoko said gently from beside the bed, 'welcome back.'

Wait, Tomoko? What was Tomoko doing there-

Doctor. Medical. Medical room.

Before anything else had a chance to happen, the curtain was pulled to the side with a sharp rustle. Faster than any wraith, Lilith flung her arms around her sister.

'Oh my God!' Lilith sniffed, tightening her already-crushing grip, 'Aleera, I- I thought-'

'Yeah,' Aleera said bluntly. For what was quite possibly the first time she could remember in a while, she was speechless, not out of anger, surprise or embarrassment, but because she was honestly drawing a complete blank.

Jake, Katya and Makian were on the other side of the curtain. Lilith released her grip when Aleera, only just noticing the pain herself, hissed at a sharp stab in her back.

'Is she alright?' Lilith asked urgently.

'Nothing worse than a few cuts and bruises,' Tomoko replied, 'we couldn't really risk doing anything to her own magical field until her condition stabilised.'

'Good,' Lilith sniffed. Aleera realised she'd been crying.

'Yeah,' Aleera said again. This time she managed a faint 'hi' as well. 'Um… is anyone going to tell me why I'm here?' she croaked. Her throat was dry.

'In all honesty,' Jake said, 'we were hoping you could tell us.'

'Nobody's telling anyone anything,' Lilith said sharply, 'hello? Near death experience? Sound familiar?'

Aleera sat up fully. What *had* happened? She remembered… nothing. The whole thing had become a total blank from the moment she opened her eyes.

Think. Think back. She'd been at home- no, she hadn't, she been out, she'd been at- she was babysitting. Didn't sound right. No, that was it, definitely. Then…

Then chaos. All swirling images, swiping claws, ripping flesh, and foul, screaming…

Wraiths! The word exploded into her mind.

'The wraiths,' she blurted out, 'they were in the apartment!'

'No kidding,' Makian piped up. 'We found two of them in there. You do realise, right, that that alone means you've had more success than this entire division altogether?'

Everyone turned and looked incredulously at Makian.

'Just thought I'd cheer the kid up,' he said sheepishly.

The apartment. Not just here there. Chloe!

'What happened?' Aleera asked, shaking. Oh, God, what about- 'what happened to-'

'Everybody's fine,' Jake said. 'Chloe's grandmother picked her up yesterday, and she doesn't have so much as a scratch.'

'Yesterday?'

'You were more-or-less out of it,' Tomoko said tentatively, 'it's Tuesday morning.'

Aleera nodded slowly as she groggily absorbed the information. Wait. She'd been attacked, caught, namely caught in a Manhattan apartment, and now she was… 'How did I get here?' she'd remind herself later that it was probably more socially acceptable to have a few more minutes of disorientation before making that kind of observation.

'The kid found you a few feet from a couple of dead wraiths,' Katya spoke up helpfully, 'dialled 911. You were taken to hospital as soon as the paramedics got over the sight of a couple of dead; they called the next-of-kin, and that's Lilith. She finds out, and the next thing we know, Jake gets woken up with your big sister screaming at him down the phone. So we go to the hospital and figure out what happened; clean-up took care of the bodies in the apartment and hopefully aired the place out, and finally we had a load of stupidly-scared human memories to adjust.'

Jake shrugged. 'What she said.'

Dead wraiths. That was it. That was right, she'd- she'd killed them? Still no remorse. Good. Remorse would be a real bitch at a moment like this. Was that her that killed them? She remembered being there, stabbing the claws into it, but it was like looking back through a thick, grey cloud.

Hold on. Hold on, hold on, hold on now.

She was attacked by wraiths. Two- no, three, because the last thing she remembered, its hand was on her neck. Then…

Then, everything was just a dark, rushing blur.

The point was that she'd been attacked by a wraith that had no solid reason not to suck out every last juicy drop of essence, and she was still alive. She was fairly sure that not even her soul was enough of a sordid mess to give one of those things indigestion.

Aleera's hand moved unbidden to her neck as she thought. There; she could feel it. A remaining tightness in the skin.

'That…' Tomoko hesitated, 'that'll go down in a day or so. There might be some superficial scarring.'

'Can I have a mirror?' Aleera asked. Tomoko hesitated for a second, then reached anxiously towards a table and handed over a metal-set mirror. Aleera lifted her neck up, turning her eyes down as far as they would go as she inspected her neck.

There. Four of them on one side and one on the other: thin, discoloured white bumps, like burns.

Another scar for her collection, part of her noted.

'How am I not dead?' she asked.

'Well don't complain,' Lilith said.

'Actually,' Jake admitted, 'on that, we're clueless.'

'We thought maybe one of them was injured while it was…' Tomoko prevented herself from naming the process, 'but it was a good few feet away from you. Odds are, there was a third, and for some reason it started, then never finished.'

'It just left?'

'Any ideas?' Makian asked haphazardly.

Aleera shook her head. Every time she tried to focus, all it earned her was a dull headache.

'No idea,' she confessed. It was true; she honestly, try as she might, couldn't form the faintest image of what had happened.

'Ok,' Lilith announced decisively, 'everybody out.'

'I need to take down the pulse and blood pressure,' Tomoko said shyly.

'Alright, you stay. Everyone else, out.'

'Not to sound like Khazahn,' Makian said, 'but if she-'

'Then she's still an eighteen-year-old who's alive right now by a miracle. Out.'

Everyone left. Wow. Not even Aleera had ever managed to do that to Jake without needing to raise her voice. Maybe it ran in the family.

Lilith stayed behind as Tomoko jotted a few figures down, reassured Lilith that she was fine, and left.

'She should be fine,' Tomoko said as she walked out past Jake and Katya, 'but I'm going to recommend leave, and she'll probably need counselling after that.'

'I'll set it up,' Makian said. 'Lucky, huh?'

'She got attacked by a wraith,' Tomoko pointed out.

'And she lived,' Jake added, arms folded and clearly thinking out loud. 'Since when does a wraith victim live?'

At that moment, the door into the medical room swung open, and there was quite probably the last person Aleera would want to see.

'Where is she?' Cassidy asked.

'In there,' Jake indicated toward the tent. 'Her sister's with her.'

'Good. I need to speak to her.'

'About what?'

'About the lead she lost last night.'

'What?' Katya butted in, 'that she lost? What the hell!'

'She works for the Guild. She's accountable. Deal with it or go back to chasing mice.'

Katya hissed, flexing her sharpened fingernails.

'Actually,' Jake piped up, 'you know what? Go ahead.'

'Thank you,' Cassidy breathed, walking toward the curtain, 'glad somebody in this place as a bloody brain in their head.

'How do you feel?' Lilith asked.

'Faintly like crap,' Aleera confessed. 'Seriously, is this what a hangover feels like? Because I can't remember a thing.'

Lilith, unexpectedly and unavoidably, hugged her again.

'Oh, thank God,' she sniffed, 'I thought for a while that-'

'I'm fine,' Aleera said. 'Just a little jarred, I guess.' Fancy that. Her, jarred. The un-jar-able Aleera.

The last thing she remembered, she thought, was-

Its hand on her throat. Sucking everything. Everything, her whole life an endless stream of pain, sucking past her and-

She shook. No, that was a sob. An actual sob coming out of her? Get a hold of yourself- another one.

'Sssh,' Lilith said softly. 'It's alright. It's alright.'

Aleera choked back the next one. There was no point to it.

The whole thing reeled over in her mind again. That feeling, everything torn out of her, leaving just that empty pit, that screaming dark thing inside, and the fear. The raw, naked, helpless fear that she'd felt for all that time.

She'd been pulled back to being *that* way. Back to being a scared, helpless little girl.

She cried. After a minute or so, it slowed and stopped, and she embarrassedly wiped the soaking streaks from her face. The fear started to die away again, replaced with a dull, heavy tiredness.

The curtain rustled open at the foot of the bed. Lilith turned to the new arrival.

Aleera's eyes narrowed. This was quite simply the last person in the building she wanted to be within a thousand miles of.

'I'm going to have to ask you to step outside, miss,' Daniel Cassidy said with forced politeness.

'In a moment,' Lilith reasoned.

'I need to ask your…?'

'Sister.'

'I need to ask your sister a few questions.'

'Oh, no,' Lilith replied sharply, 'I don't think so. You're not asking her anything so long as she needs to be in here.'

'I appreciate your sentiments,' Cassidy patronised, 'but your sister is a Guild employee, and is also a witness to a major incident.'

'No,' Lilith rebutted, 'she's an eighteen-year-old who almost died last night.'

Aleera wasn't at all sure of whether she ought to be angry or embarrassed.

'Ma'am, your sister was involved in a serious incident,' Cassidy repeated.

'And that's exactly why I'm not stepping foot outside this room.'

'I need to speak to her,' Cassidy said again.

'And what, exactly, do you have to say to my sister that you can't say with me in the room?'

'Your sister,' Cassidy repeated, already straining to keep himself in check, 'is an employee of the Guild of Guardians, and as such needs to be accountable for her actions.'

'Her actions?' Lilith repeated. '*Her*?' her voice at least doubled in volume.

'Move it,' Cassidy barked, pointing to the curtain, 'or I will arrest you right now, you little tart!'

Oops.

Lilith inhaled slowly, folded her arms, and…

Two minutes later, Daniel Cassidy stepped, ashen-faced, out of the ward where Aleera was being treated, firmly in the mindset that it was by far the wisest idea to leave her alone until she had made a full and proper recovery.

As he regained his composure after what could best be described as a tirade of the most abusive language encountered in the draconic sphere of experience, he immediately stormed off down the corridor and tracked down the person who'd suggested that, if he wanted to talk about Aleera Maheste losing a potential lead, he should talk to the girl who was in the ward with her at the time. The suggestion, of course, had come from Jake Connolly and his familiar.

'You do that to me again,' he growled when he found them, '*ever*, and I will take the both of you up to the top of this building and throw you off the fucking roof!'

He marched off and left Jake and Katya to exchange knowing glances.

'Too cruel?' Jake asked.

'Not even a little,' Katya answered positively. Her face fell almost immediately. 'She'll be Ok, right?'

'Yeah,' Jake replied, 'I mean, if she can make it through that, she can manage a day or two in recovery.'

'Only that long?'

'I checked it with Tomoko and gave her a transfer when we brought her in,' Jake replied. 'For now, I say we leave her alone.'

'Seconded. Poor thing must've felt like she was in hell,' Katya shuddered. 'I never heard of anyone actually coming out of something like that.'

'It's been a while since anyone has,' Jake replied. 'A long time.'

He took a long, slow sip of coffee. Katya noticed that he was tapping his old coin against the side of the cup.

'You think…?' Katya started.

'Could be.' Jake lowered the coffee and set his jaw, turning the coin over in his hands. 'I don't know. I really…' he shook his head slowly and pocketed the coin, deep, grim thoughts rolling over each other in his mind. 'I really don't know.'

'What about Lawson?' Katya asked, 'do we have anything there?'

'Still nothing,' Jake answered. 'We'll just have to see what we can dig up.'

'Nothing at Pentagram?'

'We checked, but the guy's scared senseless of Kheron. He's not about to go near him.'

'We need to find him.'

'Clearly.'

'No, we *seriously* need to find him,' Katya said. 'Really, seriously, we need to find him after this.'

Jake regarded her and let out a stifled breath.

'We will.'

'They nearly killed her.'

'Yeah,' Jake said guiltily.

Jake leaned back on the wall and resumed tapping the old coin. Five hundred years of life with an awful lot of complications crammed into it gave you a certain amount of instinct when it came to matters like this, and the real nagging fear behind Katya's insistence, the burning crisis behind Cassidy's bravado, and the bleak worry behind Jake's own grimace was simple:

They'd found her.

They'd looked for her and known where to find her. They'd tracked her down. They'd managed to find her.

That meant they could find any of them.

Jake shook his head ruefully and turned the old coin over in his hand. Every time, every damn time it looked as though this case was as bad as it could get, something else came along to drag it down a little more.

'I don't need to stay in bed,' Aleera complained again as she emerged from her room, dressed but still drying her hair with a towel. She took particular care around her neck, and was pleasantly surprised to see that, as Tomoko had predicted, the marks had, albeit slightly, gone down.

'You're off-duty anyway,' Lilith declared, 'and there's no way I'm letting you out of the house. Knowing you, I'll probably have to nail the bedroom door shut,' she added under her breath.

'I'm fine.'

'You are not fine,' Lilith near-yelled, 'you almost got killed! Even that Jake- who by the way has a very nice ass, I wish you'd introduced us earlier- can't remember a time anyone ever lived through that!' she finished by pointing to the marks on Aleera's neck. Aleera regarded her inquisitively for a moment. Lilith was the only person she knew who, discussing something that serious, could make an offhand comment like that and not lose an ounce of the severity. That, and she did have a point.

'I can stand, can't I?' she said defensively. 'I don't know why I'm not back on duty by now.'

Lilith just stared. 'You *are* kidding.'

'Not at all.'

'March,' Lilith ordered, pointing at Aleera's room, 'and there's no way you're getting back on duty or leaving this apartment, so get back in there and sleep.'

'I spent the whole of yesterday sleeping.'

'Aleera, I am not arguing with you. Move it!'

'I can-'

'*Aleera!*'

Aleera ended her sentence willingly. She couldn't remember the last time Lilith had shouted at her like that. And either it was her imagination, or she appeared to be trembling and avoiding looking at her. Her own hands folded over each other behind her back and she shifted one foot uncomfortably.

'You almost died,' Lilith said more quietly. 'Do you even realise that?'

'Of course I do.' She did. How little attention would she have to have been paying not to realise it? She just didn't see what all the fuss was about. She'd nearly died on at least two occasions she could think of off the top of her head, and people did die every day.

'Just… don't do this to yourself.'

'Do what?'

Lilith didn't answer. 'Just rest for a while,' she said instead, as quiet as Aleera had ever heard her. 'Please.'

Aleera gave in. She had no rebuttal against that all-powerful non-command.

'Alright.'

Lilith didn't answer. Her eyes were lidded and she thinned her mouth.

'Are you Ok?' Aleera asked hesitantly.

'Yeah,' Lilith said quickly, wiping something out of the inner corner of each eye. 'Yeah, I'm fine.'

'I'm sorry,' Aleera said without thinking about it.

'I know.'

Aleera opened her arms and hugged her. 'You know I don't mean to do that,' she said.

'I know, baby sister,' Lilith sniffed. 'But you nearly died. Again.'

'I didn't,' Aleera said, hoping it might be helpful.

'And I wasn't there,' Lilith said quietly. 'I wasn't there again.'

Aleera knew better than to say it, but it definitely wouldn't have helped if she had been there. If anything, she would have almost certainly been a free meal for the wraiths. But Lilith wouldn't hear of that, not in a million years. She was Aleera's sister, and the closest thing she'd ever had to a mother- which, in all honesty, she had been since Aleera was fourteen.

'Now go and get some sleep,' Lilith instructed gently, 'and then you can introduce me to Jake properly. And maybe that familiar, too. Cat-girl. Yum.'

Aleera laughed out loud. Well, it lightened the mood enough, and honestly, she'd been waiting for Lilith to say something like that all day.

'By the way,' Lilith said, taking something off the table, 'someone you know left this for you.'

Aleera took the object, inspected it as she turned it over in her hands, and couldn't quite help smiling.

It was a hand-made get-well card, complete with pink crayon and tiny plastic sequins glued to it. The kind of thing she could just picture a child working over on the table. A little bit of glitter scraped off on her finger.

She didn't quite know why it made her smile like it did, but somehow it got even better at it when she saw Chloe's scribbly signature on the inside.

After another incident like that, Chloe should have been scared to death of her. If the child had any sense in her head, she'd never want to be within a hundred miles of Aleera again.

But the fact that she did put a warmth in Aleera that she still couldn't figure out.

When that was over, she did indeed relent and retired to bed. She finished drying her hair, pulled off her top and jeans and climbed into bed. When she turned out the light, it was just her, the frames of light around the door and window, and her thoughts. And those thoughts chose now to turn in a troubling direction.

The wraiths. At the thought, the marks on her neck seemed that little bit tighter.

They'd found her. Ergo, they had been able to find her. Therefore… therefore they'd find her again. Possible? Probably. Although… no, they wouldn't. Not after that. If they had a collective brain cell between them, it would be a cold day in hell before they thought of doing anything that stupid.

Now, think, why attack her? Out of everyone, why her? A threat? A message? A message to the Guild, she realised. Scare tactics. Well, that was nice. Her near-death experience, even if not her first, was just a scare tactic. That was almost enough to make her want to do that to the third one all over again.

Wait, the third one? She knew there was a third one? Well, yes, of course, that had all been explained to her, but she remembered it, suddenly screaming out of the blue. There'd been a third one.

It had been on top of her, its hand around her throat, and... and then what? It had been... afraid. Screaming. Thrashing before it fled with its tail between its legs like a kicked dog. What the hell was she supposed to have done to do that to one of those monsters? What could do that to what was essentially walking, undead darkness?

The answer was painfully simple: something even darker.

She shivered at the thought. Something else. Think about something else. What she'd do to that thrice-damned wraith if it was still alive. No, not that. *Yes*, that. Kill it! Kill it! Tear it apart! Rip out its heart and eat it in front of it!

No. Calm. That's better. Soon she'd be back on duty, and...

Hold on. Back on duty. Soon. After this? After something that caused Lilith this much worry? Granted, when it came to Aleera, a bee sting was sufficient incentive to hire the mafia to kill the bee, its friends and its family. But back in just a few days? That was what Cassidy said when she was leaving the...

She was a soldier, still a potential target, almost a murder victim, and they'd just let her walk out. Immediately, her blood boiled. Those bastards! Obvious, so obvious, right from the start! Who in their right mind would send an eighteen-year-old raw recruit up against a dozen-strong cabal of wraiths? Again, a simple answer: someone who wouldn't lose a wink of sleep if that recruit didn't come back. They practically wanted those things to snack on her, she thought, eyes turning red. They damn well wanted her dead!

No, she caught herself, no, don't be stupid. This was madness. Specifically, probably acute paranoia. It was ridiculous.

They were against her.

Oh, no. She was not starting that "they're all against me" garbage. She'd been putting up with a lot of things, and on top of it all she wasn't about to have another argument with her own psyche.

But they were. She'd always known they were. They hated her very existence. They were every bit as much an enemy as the wraiths.

Stop it!

They'd killed her. She knew what to do when someone tried to kill her. Just do what she did with the wraiths on Sunday night. The Guild had the same intention. It'd be the same thing. Self-defence. Justifiable. And it was oh so very much fun, wasn't it? Watching their faces tear and feel their hot, sticky blood all over her claws... God, yes, killing those things like she'd killed Azrael, the rush, *God, killing is fucking better than sex!*

No! Stop it! Shut up!

She'd kill them if she had half a chance. That hate, that rage, would get out and kill again... *again*. It had done it. The thought came flooding back to her. It had lashed out in that desperate moment. That terrible, dark, evil thing had saved her life, and now it was the only reason she was still there.

She felt sick. She felt the blood on her hands. She felt... deep down, she felt... *good*. And with that, she felt so, so scared.

What was this, she asked as she'd asked a hundred times, that had so long ago gone so wrong inside of her?

Then, again, she was back there, a frightened little girl lying on some floor, crying and doing God-knows-what to a wraith, or fighting off a killer, or begging her father to stop. She was scared, so scared, as she hugged herself and trembled back and forth.

Then, as quickly as it had begun, the episode passed, leaving Aleera to sit there in the middle of her bed, wipe her tears and quietly, desperately reassure herself that this would pass.

20

Jake closed the file and leaned on the desk, momentarily resting his head between his hands and tapping the old coin against his forehead.

Thought after thought kept swirling around in his head. The first thing to do, he decided, though it was never easy for him, was to organise his train of thought.

One: Rick Lawson was somehow involved with Kheron.

Two: Someone in the Guild had aided in Lawson's escape.

Three: Kheron was connected to the attacks being carried out by the wraiths.

Four: The wraiths had attacked Aleera.

And, hidden somewhere in the tangle of thorns, was that vital, elusive Five. The problem was that without it, nothing was making a lick of sense.

Lawson was involved with Kheron. Fair enough. But that didn't explain how the wraiths had managed to find Aleera. The only way they could have had any idea where to even start looking was if they had access to Guild knowledge. And thus far, the only people who could have access to that knowledge were Rick Lawson, Kheron and whoever had let him out.

But Kheron was hardly in league with the wraiths. For one thing, they'd halved his business in the city in a matter of days and then torn his nightclub apart. Kheron might have never looked as though he had a hair out of place, but the foundations beneath his feet were rapidly being ripped apart. Besides, wraiths didn't go into business with people; you didn't reason with a wraith. You didn't have time to reason with it before it tried to suck your soul out.

So how, he asked himself yet again, had the wraiths managed to find Aleera? That, right now, was the big question. He wrote it in a piece of notepaper and drew a circle round it.

There was something he didn't know about the situation. It was something glaringly obvious; something that was staring at him from an inch in front of his nose but had the light switch well and truly hidden. If he knew it, if he could find out, then that would be it.

But thinking about it didn't necessarily mean working it out.

He'd started going through old files again, skimming through until he found something that might somehow be of help. Still nothing. Not an un-crossed "T" or un-dotted "I".

Thing were never that well-organised. Not in an organisation like the Guild. Something that size, with so many employees that tended to skate the edges of their jurisdiction; there were always some figures that didn't quite match up, or a suspect not accounted for, or a warrant that nobody could quite remember where they left. But there was nothing here. It was spick and span. Pristine. *Polished.*

Somebody had not only done something, but they'd gone to some enormous lengths to cover it up. This was expert. Professional. This was someone who knew what they were doing.

'Are you still in here?'

Jake looked round as Katya leaned over the back of his chair, resting her head on his shoulder and curiously scanning the papers in front of him. 'I could swear, you're getting paler by the hour,' she said.

'I haven't found anything,' Jake sighed in frustration, 'nothing unusual for weeks. Since when is the Guild's paperwork this neat?'

'You're cute when you're paranoid,' Katya giggled.

'I'm serious,' Jake said, folding the old coin over in his fingers.

'I'm not,' Katya said bluntly picking up a pen and fiddling with it.

'Why?'

'Because you're always serious.'

'It's a serious matter.'

'I know,' Katya shrugged, standing up straight.

'Should I not be serious?'

'Be as serious as you like, so long as I get to stick around and keep you from blowing your brains out from over-seriousness.' She lifted up one of the pages. 'What's today's quest, then?'

'Still looking for anything that explains what happened to Aleera,' Jake replied. 'Thing is, there's nothing. If Lawson's involved with Kheron, that doesn't exactly mean he's working with wraiths. I mean, who works with wraiths?'

'Ultra-masochists?' Katya hazarded.

'Again, I'm serious.'

'Me too. You know, there are people on the internet that will actually pay to be a snack for a vampire. And I'm supposed to be weird because I like a scratch behind the ears now and then.'

Jake paused and folded his fingers over the coin. 'Why are we discussing vampire fetishism?'

'I don't rightly know,' Katya admitted. 'Easier than talking about what happened to Aleera?'

Jake didn't answer. He returned to the files. 'They did put me in charge of her,' he finally said.

'Yeah, but you've always felt responsible for her,' Katya said. 'It's like you're her dad. Not, y'know, the dad she had, but like a nice dad.'

'Hey,' Jake protested.

'Come on, you are. Why else do you think you and her sister are the only people on earth she ever listens to?'

Jake shook his head and dismissed the thought. Of course he felt responsible for Aleera, but he and Katya both knew the real reason. It was just that, as a general rule, they didn't discuss it.

The problem was that they might have to.

There was one way that he could think of, only one extremely worrying way, that she could have fought off a wraith when it had a hold on her. And it worried him more than a whole cabal of those things.

If it got out, if she learned of it…

He didn't like to think it about her, but Aleera had never had the healthiest of mindsets, and what had happened before with Azrael and Michael and Sara and Chara, that couldn't have done any good. And now this... nobody had so much as survived a wraith attack in years. Her soul- her actual soul- had very nearly been ripped out of her. What would that do to her?

Everywhere Aleera seemed to turn, more and more damage was being done. He knew for a fact that the girl was like a brick wall. Unfortunately, he also had to consider what happened when a brick wall was repeatedly struck with a sledgehammer.

It was then that the door burst inwards, Makian leaning on the frame for support as he scrambled to stop himself.

'Cassidy says he wants everyone involved in this case- which is everybody- in briefing, ten minutes ago.'

Aleera tore her way down the corridor and into the ward. There was nothing else there; just long, empty, inky black spots that her mind didn't bother trying to fill.

Her legs pumped beneath her. Her heart slammed again and again against the inside of her chest. She tried to form a coherent thought. She failed.

Nearly there, now. Nearly there.

However much she ran, it didn't seem to get any closer. It was five feet away now. Now ten. Now fifty.

Nearly there. All that she could feel was surging adrenaline and desperate fear and roaring, soul-filling rage.

She'd flown across Manhattan as soon as Jake had told her. Sword of Heaven. The Guild. All the lies upon lies upon lies, all those people who, knowing what she was, would kill her in a heartbeat if someone would only give them a gun.

Nearly there. She'd find him. He'd be fine. Then she could find the man that had tried to do this and tear his eyes out.

The sharp, green curtain was in front of her. She reached out, grabbed it and pulled it open so desperately that the fabric tore in her hands.

Michael was there. Lying on the bed. A black-crusted mass of blistered, red flesh that had been her friend, teeth held together in a mad, ashen grimace.

It started to descend upon her as she took the sight in. The despair. The hopelessness. The mad, howling grief.

She stepped forward as her mind scrambled for any thoughts of denial it could find.

Then it screamed. Then it jumped up, grabbed her and tackled her to the cold, hard floor.

'Look what you did!' its screaming voice roared in her face, 'look what you did to me, you bitch, look what you did!*'*

There was a hood over its head now, flailing as Aleera reached up and pulled it off. It tore away, and with it came the burnt, red and black flesh.

Then, beneath it, covered in blood, Aleera screamed and howled with nothing, nothing, but purest black hate.

Then Aleera was taking a lungful of air, sitting up in bed and wrapped in quiet and darkness.

It had happened again. No surprises there. Ever since she tried to fall asleep, this had been happening. This was the third nightmare that day.

After a moment, she realised that the dampness on her cheeks was the result of a flow of tears that poured down her cheeks and over the marks on her neck. They stopped when she woke up, and she couldn't remember where it was that they'd come from. She tried to wipe them dry and succeeded only in soaking her hands.

Damn.

She shuffled back and rested against the wall as the images faded again.

What was this, the fourth time she'd had that dream? Not the first, certainly, and probably not the last either.

Oh, God-

She rested her head in her hands and shook. Thick, salty tears leaked through the gaps between her fingers as she sobbed and rocked herself back and forth.

No, stop it, stop it you stupid girl, and get a hold of yourself-

God, what had that thing done to her?

It was like she was a child again. All fear and helplessness and despair and poison.

And she was, because there wasn't one person she knew that hadn't in some way, however small, suffered because of her. Michael, Sara, Lilith, Jasmine, Jake, Makian, all poisoned. All tainted the moment they'd touched her.

That dark thing inside rumbled contentedly. With everything it touched, it got to feed. It got to spread its poison and that dark little part of her…

It loved it. It loved seeing them suffer, it loved staring at those burned corpses, it loved cutting through those wraiths' old, stale flesh and brittle bones, and it loved watching the blood pool beneath Azrael.

No. No, *it* didn't. Because *it* was *her*. That evil, howling monster was as much a part of her as her brain or her heart. She'd be dead without it, just like the two monsters it had cut down.

It was disgusting to think about it. Like selling her soul to the devil.

There was a soft knock at the door. Aleera sniffed and sat up straight, drying her eyes as best she could. 'Come in,' she said.

The door clicked open as Aleera turned on the bedside lamp. 'Hey,' Lilith said. 'Feeling any better?'

'A bit,' Aleera lied. 'What time is it?'

'About four,' Lilith answered, placing the back of her hand against Aleera's forehead.

'I don't have a fever,' Aleera protested half-heartedly.

'Well, excuse me for worrying about my baby sister,' Lilith said, 'besides, you still look like hell.'

Aleera groaned and rubbed her head. Now that she thought about it, "like hell" was more or less how it felt.

'If you're up to it,' Lilith mentioned, 'you have a visitor.'

'Who?'

'You'll see,' Lilith said slyly. 'Want me to send her in?'

Her? 'Sure.'

'Two seconds,' Lilith smiled. She stood up and walked out, leaving Aleera to think, just for a moment.

"Her"? Who did she know that was female? The only girls other than Lilith she even knew were Katya, who never seemed to be apart from Jake, and-

No. No, that was just a ridiculous notion. There was no way it would be...

'Jasmine?'

'Hi,' Jasmine said shyly from the door. 'Um... I can go,' she offered, 'if you'd rather...'

'It's alright,' Aleera said. It was? Wow. That was news.

'Oh my God,' Jasmine stared. In all fairness, a rudimentary feel on her neck did seem to indicate that the burns had decreased in size again.

'The doctor says that'll clear up soon,' Aleera said reactively.

'Yeah, I heard you were in the middle of something,' Jasmine said hesitantly as she sat on the foot of the bed.

Aleera sat up straight and covered up as much of herself as possible. 'You heard right,' she said after a few seconds of fishing for a response. Then the implication caught her. 'How did you know that?'

'Lilith told me,' Jasmine admitted.

'When?' Aleera pressed.

Jasmine bit her bottom lip. 'Yesterday,' she confessed. 'I... kind of called.'

Oh. Aleera looked away, a surprising amount of embarrassment creeping up on her. 'I wasn't here,' she said. Her own voice had never sounded so quiet.

'I gathered. Lilith told me what happened when...' she looked down at the floor awkwardly, 'when I couldn't get hold of you here, I tried your cell phone.'

'Why did you do that?' Not a smart question. Ok, something else to focus on right now would be very nice, please…

'I was hoping we could talk,' Jasmine admitted. 'I know it sounds really stupid, since I was the one who got dumped, but… I hoped we could still talk. About what happened?'

Aleera nodded slowly. Her throat suddenly felt dry. 'I didn't do much of a good job explaining myself,' she admitted.

'I'm probably just being dumb,' Jasmine said, 'but you were about the best friend I've had in about a year.'

Aleera blinked. Her? Seriously? She must have had some really awful friends, if that was the case.

'I was just hoping…' Jasmine shifted uncomfortably, 'maybe we could still just be friends? I mean, even though the way things ended, that was pretty epic.'

'That it was,' Aleera admitted. 'Maybe we just… took things too fast.' Oh, really? Maybe? Dear God, she must have had her head on backwards.

'I guess,' Jasmine said quietly. 'To be honest, I was just…' she stopped, then forced herself to continue, 'I wanted to know why.'

'Oh.' Aleera felt her insides gnawing away at themselves more by the second. 'Right.'

The silence that descended seemed to grow heavier with each passing moment.

'Someone else?' Jasmine hazarded.

'No. Actually, no, it was-' Aleera shivered for some unknown reason. 'It was me. Really, it really was.'

'So why?'

'It's…' Aleera still avoided looking at her, 'personal.' Then she remembered just how awful she'd felt when she didn't tell her the whole truth before.

Say it!

Don't be stupid. She hadn't needed to say it before!

Oh, yes, and that had turned out just beautifully, hadn't it?

It'd hardly kill anyone if she did tell her.

No, but it'd probably end up with Jasmine running a mile.

Shut up! She snapped at herself. She owed it to her to tell her the truth, and that was that.

'The thing is,' she said, 'you remember when I told you I was half-demon?' Jasmine nodded. 'Well, the other half...' she chewed on her tongue, 'I'm half-succubus.'

Jasmine looked at her for a second. 'Oh.'

Aleera took a deep breath. Part of her had, foolishly enough, thought that she might feel better for getting it all out in the open. No such luck.

'So...' Jasmine started.

'Right. Pheromones.'

'Seriously?' Jasmine thought back. 'They seem effective.'

'I know.'

'So that's why all those idiots-'

'More or less,' Aleera said. 'The thing is, most succubae don't really have the best track record for relationships.'

'You too?' Jasmine seemed surprised and a little embarrassed by her own question. 'Sorry.'

'It's fine,' Aleera said quickly, 'it's just that a little while ago, I had this- this friend. She was straight, but... things got complicated.'

'Must've been awkward,' Jasmine said. She fidgeted slightly.

'It was,' Aleera said distantly. 'So I just...' she forced her suddenly-dry lips to move, 'I didn't want to do that again.'

'But we...' Jasmine avoided saying anything outright.

'I know,' Aleera said guiltily. 'I... I still don't know why,' she said. Ordinarily, she'd rather have cut off her own tongue than say this out loud, but it seemed she'd gotten used to not being ashamed of anything around Jasmine. 'Couldn't help it, I guess.'

'So that's why you ended it?' Jasmine asked hesitantly.

'Yeah.'

Aleera shifted again. She was feeling more and more awful by the second. Looking back on it now, what she'd done seemed even more stupid than ever. What had she been doing to her? She might as well have slipped her rohypnol- what the hell had she been thinking?

Jasmine looked at the floor again. Aleera couldn't entirely be sure, but she looked... hurt.

'I should probably go,' Jasmine said. 'Are we still...' she swallowed a lump in her throat, 'y'know, friends?'

'If you want,' Aleera said. She smiled faintly.

'Good,' Jasmine smiled. 'Still, I should probably...'

Then, suddenly, it all welled up yet again.

Aleera shuddered as that raw hate screamed and tore into her with what she'd done. You stupid girl! You brainless, selfish little-

She trembled as a sudden wave washed over her. Something awful welled up inside her and forced itself out in a burst of tears.

'Aleera?' Jasmine gasped, 'are you Ok?'

'Yeah,' Aleera gasped, 'it's just- it's what happened the other day-' her sentence was cut off as she blurted out another soaking wave. Everything filled her up to the brim as she found herself breaking out in a long sob.

'Hey, hey,' Jasmine said gently, 'come here,' she offered, holding her by the shoulders.

'I'm fine,' Aleera shook, trying to keep it from overcoming her, 'I just- oh *God…*' it all finally won out, drowning her hopelessly as she collapsed into Jasmine's arms. All of it, all that hopelessness and misery built up over eighteen years, poured through her with no resistance left. 'I'm sorry,' she sobbed, 'God, Jasmine, I'm so sorry,' she whispered into her shoulder. It was all she could do until it passed.

When it ended, she sat back and the misery gave way to embarrassment. Lord, what in all hells had she done now?

'Sorry,' she said immediately, 'God, that was embarrassing.'

'Yeah,' Jasmine said slowly, 'I guess so.'

'It's just been kind of… happening,' Aleera explained as best she could while its effects were still wearing off, 'ever since what happened.'

'It's alright,' Jasmine said. 'But… I should probably go, anyway. Are you gonna be Ok?'

'Yeah,' Aleera sniffed, 'I'm fine. Honestly.'

'…Alright,' Jasmine said nervously, 'when are you back at school?'

'Probably a few days,' Aleera said. 'See you then?'

Jasmine smiled, stood up and left. When she was gone, Aleera's head near-collapsed onto the pillow and left her to reflect on, if nothing else, the awkwardness of what had just happened.

The fact that she'd been in her underwear the whole time hadn't helped, either.

The Guild's briefing room was, like the rest of its New York headquarters, surprising in appearance to the uninitiated. It had, of course, all the basic features; lots of chairs for one thing. A big screen, a projector, etc. But, generally, since its last refurbishment, the room was a surprisingly passable working environment, right down to the chrome walls and ceiling.

The fluorescent lights were annoying, though. Jake glanced sideways at Katya, who fidgeted unpleasantly. The constant buzz was bad enough without superhumanly sensitive ears.

Presently, a number of Guild soldiers were settling down. Khazahn, Daniel Cassidy and a man Jake recognised from elsewhere- Hartwell, that was him; they'd brought in Special Ops, for all the good it was doing- stood at the front of the room.

'Who's that one?' Katya asked quietly.

'James Hartwell,' Jake whispered, 'big fromage from Special Ops.'

'Really?' Katya asked innocently, glancing back over at him and pretending to suddenly recall the events of the case thus far. 'Wow, those guys are useful, huh?'

At this point, Daniel Cassidy stepped to the front.

'People,' he announced in a sharp, strong voice that filled the room, 'I'll be blunt.'

'For a change,' Katya said under her breath.

'We've located a man we believe to be suspended Private Rick Lawson,' Cassidy continued, 'according to five eyewitness reports, a man fitting his description has been seen at a hostel in Queens.'

Queens, Jake noted. D-Unit's jurisdiction only covered central Manhattan.

'Because of this, we have organised a joint operation with F-Unit. Five of theirs, five of ours, and two of Colonel Hartwell's own hand-picked officers. That is who will be conducting this operation. The objective is straightforward: search and recover. We go in, we find Lawson, we arrest him and we find out what he knows if it takes all night.'

'There are about thirty humans in this building; that in mind, Colonel Hartwell will be assigning a number of spellcasters and specialists to perform memory alteration, and-'

Unnoticed prior to the hushed announcement, an aide arrived and whispered something into Colonel Hartwell's ear. He, in turn, turned and relayed the message to Cassidy.

Cassidy said something as inaudibly as it could be said while still remaining a shout. Then he turned around and announced, virtually shaking, 'Jake Connolly and Lieutenant Makian, you will report to my office immediately.'

Without another word, the officers disembarked.

'What do you suppose that was about?' Katya asked.

'No clue,' Jake admitted, 'be right back.'

He opened the door of the briefing room, joining Makian in the outside corridor. 'Any clue what happened?'

'I was gonna ask you the same,' Makian shrugged, 'you know, I dunno about you but I've only been back a week and I'm already sick of these Special Ops guys. Seriously, every time I ask one of them a question, all they ever say is "don't ask". It's at the point where I've given up on asking them if they can spare a quarter for the coffee machine.'

'First wraith case in about thirty tears,' Jake reminded him, 'they want to look like it's being dealt with.'

'All I'm saying is, they haven't even made their damn selves useful,' Makian said, 'Hartwell showed up the day after we raided the penthouse and ranted about us shooting that thing out of the window instead of slapping the cuffs on it.'

'Seriously?'

'Hell, yeah. It was one of his amateur Rambos that shot the thing!' Makian protested as he pushed the door into Cassidy's office.

'Gents,' Cassidy announced from behind the desk, 'we have a problem here.'

'Define "problem",' Jake said wearily.

'Our liaison just heard back from the N.Y.P.D.,' Colonel Hartwell said, 'there was a fatal shooting at that hostel last night. According to our witnesses…'

'Please tell me you're joking,' Jake cringed.

'Same guy they reported seeing,' Cassidy seethed, 'with a bullet in his brain.'

Jake froze on the spot.

'We're heading to the mortuary now,' Cassidy said. 'You two are both witnesses to Lawson's involvement in the case, so you get to come along for a positive I.D. Good for you. Can you teleport us?'

'Five people?' Jake noted, 'depends. You want your spleen to be in the same place?'

'Preferably.'

'Better drive, then.'

'Wonderful,' Makian said, 'we'll drive. Through Manhattan. At rush hour. I love my job,' he added under his breath with all the sarcasm in the world.

In the garage, the vehicle chosen turned out to be Khazahn's. Peugeot 207, as Makian noticed. He was about to add to the comment when Jake surreptitiously elbowed him in the ribs.

'See what else you can afford on this salary when you're under investigation,' Khazahn had said bluntly. The type of car hadn't really made that much difference, as traffic was heavy enough that it took the better part of an hour to get to the mortuary.

Inside, it at least wasn't as stuffy as the car, or as apprehensively silent, if cold and smelling of disinfectant. Awkwardness incarnate, as Makian commented to Jake on the way in, was sharing a confined space with three of one's superior officers.

The mortician led them through to what Makian so eloquently described as a "people freezer" and pulled out one of the slabs.

The cover was pulled back, and there was Rick Lawson's face, mouth slightly open, eyes still frozen in shock and fear. Trickles of dried blood still spider-webbed over his face from the dark, coagulated mass of tangled blood, flesh, skin and bone that tunnelled into his brain.

'Jesus,' Makian gulped, 'poor son of a bitch…'

Khazahn shook his head and set his jaw. It dawned on Jake that he'd barely said two works all day.

'Kheron,' he growled quietly.

'Think the poor dumb bastard was running?' Makian proposed as the cover was pulled back up.

From somebody, Jake noted. The notion was already starting to creep up on him that, by the time he found out the name of Rick Lawson's murderer, he'd be surprised.

The feeling was also present that the very thing he was missing had been in the knowledge of the man who was now lying in front of him with a tag on his toe.

Of all present, it was Cassidy who best described the mood in the room, with yet another lead lying dead in front of them.

'I,' he growled, 'am so fucking sick of this happening!'

21

She'd actually locked the windows.

Aleera sat back down on the bed and shook her head in bemusement. Given her aptitude with invisibility spells, she'd been sure that she could at least stretch her wings for a few hours. Instead, all she was left with was some old magazines, an iPod that she'd never bothered to download any songs for, and her laptop. She still didn't even have MySpace.

Lilith had popped in now and then to keep her company or, more often, check that she was resting. Aleera knew she couldn't be upset with her; each of them, when it came right down to it, was just about all that the other had. Of course she was going to be concerned. She'd just have liked to have been able to get out of her room for an hour or so. Twice, she'd convinced herself that she was sweaty and taken a shower, purely out of a lack of anything else to do. The fact was that she was just no good at being an invalid. The only light side she could come up with was that the marks on her neck were indeed clearing up nicely.

The real kicker was that, ordinarily, she had no problem with spending the whole day at home. It was only when she knew that it wasn't her own choice that she felt herself itching to get out the door. Maybe it was just that argumentative streak acting up.

So far, she'd just been alternating between that cabin fever and the remaining aftershock of nearly having her soul consumed, which as it turned out really could be a downer.

The worst part was that it just came out of nowhere. One second it was pushed nicely out of the way, then periodically something would open the floodgates and she'd just collapse.

The door clicked open softly.

'You awake?' Lilith whispered.

'Still,' Aleera answered, sitting back up. 'Sorry I kept you cooped up here all day.'

'Oh, please,' Lilith said nonchalantly, 'Steve's bedroom can wait for a few days.'

Aleera looked blankly at her for a moment.

'The psychiatrist's receptionist?'

'The same.'

'The psychiatrist's gay receptionist?' Aleera said disbelievingly, putting the right amount of emphasis on the word.

'That's the one,' Lilith announced proudly, 'he's gay, but his boyfriend's bi, and it's amazing what people tend to be willing to do mid-coitus…'

'You can stop there,' said quickly.

'You're still your old inexplicably celibate self, then,' Lilith pointed out. 'Thought you dealt with that.'

'I wish.' The sentence didn't appear to bother waiting to have its passport checked before leaving Aleera's mouth.

'Okay, I'm gonna be honest,' Lilith said, 'I've never- seriously, never- seen you this hung up.'

'I know,' Aleera groaned. True enough. When was the last time she got this much grief out of a relationship? Then again, when was the last time she'd had one?

'Well, we'll see what happens,' Lilith said offhand.

'Meaning?' Aleera asked with a note of suspicion.

'Just saying,' Lilith said with innocence that nobody with her "romantic" past should possess. 'So are you feeling any better?'

'Fine,' Aleera said immediately. After Lilith stared blankly at her for a moment, she hastily added 'mostly'.

'Still bad, huh?' Lilith asked, sitting next to her.

'Kind of,' Aleera admitted. 'I'll get over it.'

Lilith sighed and let Aleera rest her head against her shoulder. 'You're worried, aren't you?' Aleera asked.

'Can you blame me?' Lilith asked honestly. 'I nearly lost you.'

'It's not about that though, is it?' Aleera asked. 'How I've been for all that time, and now this…'

'Doesn't matter,' Lilith said simply. 'You're my sister, and I love you. Nothing changes that.'

Aleera gave a distant sigh and thought about what Lilith had told her, and that dark thing inside that still kept purring.

It didn't scream. It didn't howl with anger at hearing that, whatever it did to her, it wouldn't change this, that this was one thing it would never infect. It just did what it always did: it sat in her heart and fed on this newest piece of sweet, sweet evil to crawl inside her.

The record player sat singing away in the corner of the room. Kheron paid only slight attention to it as he leaned back and finished a glass of brandy. He placed the empty vessel on the floor on its side and allowed Leo to help himself.

Tapping his fingers against the surface of the desk, he leaned back and thought.

Well. Well, well, well.

This was going to change things, without a doubt. What, exactly, was this supposed to mean? It was, at least, a confirmation of what he'd been suspecting for a while now. But still… this was supposed to be a game with rules. An ongoing battle of wits, if you will, between two worthy opponents. The last three years of Kheron's life had been a constant, well-played game of chess, and he didn't much feel like having it all thrown out the window because somebody didn't feel like playing by the rules anymore.

"Whatever happened to the heroes? …Whatever happened to the heroes?"

Kheron sighed to himself and continued to mull all the facts over in his head. Of course, the really fun thing was that the Guild would most likely suspect him and come knocking any minute now.

Poor Rick Lawson. He was a bright young man. Big future ahead of him. He made a mental note to send a nice wreath to the funeral.

He chuckled to himself. This really was going perfectly, wasn't it? The Guild were about ready to crap themselves, and after learning of this whole development they'd probably be running around like headless chickens.

There was a knock at the door.

'Send them in,' Kheron said without looking. No less than seven sets of feet could be heard marching rhythmically into the room.

'Anything else, sir?' the bouncer asked.

Kheron turned his head and surveyed the new arrivals. Daniel Cassidy, Jake Connolly, Lieutenant Makian, Ms. Katya and a pair of uniformed Guild soldiers who, thanks to their helmets, remained unidentifiable.

'Nothing for now,' Kheron replied, 'but the Guild more than probably hold me accountable for their employee's regrettable fate, and I expect they've come to either arrest me or beat me up. Am I on the ball there, gentlemen?'

'Kheron,' Khazahn declared, stepping forward, 'you are under arrest on suspicion of involvement in the murder of Rick Lawson. You have the right to remain silent; anything you choose to say can and will be given in evidence.'

Kheron stood up slowly. 'You certainly managed to come to a conclusion quickly this time,' he noted, 'would you like to pin the matter of the wraiths on me as well?'

'Why'd you do it?' Cassidy asked casually as he slapped the handcuffs onto him, 'keep him from talking?'

'Sorry to disappoint, Sergeant, but I don't think I'll be telling you all that much until I'm allowed to see my lawyer,' Kheron said politely, 'oh, and would somebody be so kind as to unplug my record player? And I'll probably bring Leo here,' he indicated to the ginger tom currently mooching around his feet. 'The Guild hardly seems to have a "no animals" policy,' he said sideways, glancing at Katya.

'Well, judging by what I know of you, we're not the only ones who use our tongues to-' Katya silenced herself when Jake glanced warningly at her- though he himself had to suppress a snicker. It was a good one.

'Fine, bring the damn thing,' Cassidy instructed, 'and somebody turn the music off.'

Makian shrugged and pulled the plug out of the socket just as the lyrics of *No More Heroes* died away.

'Please, Tomo,' Makian said as he entered the autopsy lab, 'tell me we've got something. Anything. Seriously, I'd take what he found out for lunch this morning, because unless we get some evidence, Khazahn's about ready to cut somebody's balls off.'

'Charming,' Tomoko said levelly.

'Do we have anything?'

'Well, he had beef for lunch. Lousy beef. Does that help?'

'Ok, seriously, anything?'

'Basically,' Tomoko said, looking over her notes, 'not a clue.'

'What, nothing?'

'No fingerprints. No foreign DNA. No signs of struggle. It looks like Lawson didn't even see what was coming until it hit him. Perfect shot; instant death. That means this was definitely premeditated.'

'Did he have anything on him?'

'Nothing suspicious. Although,' Tomoko pointed out, 'we searched his apartment, and we did find this.' She picked up and handed over a small evidence bag.

'Burnt paper?' Makian asked sceptically.

'Burnt matchbook paper, and only mostly burnt,' Tomoko said, 'we found it beside a trashcan with a few other personal effects in much the same condition.'

'He was burning something,' Makian summarised, 'covering his tracks?'

'Looks like. This is sloppy work, which in my experience says he was panicking. But,' she said, brightening up, 'we do have this.'

A much larger evidence bag, and inside, a square, silvery digital camera. 'It was running a wireless feed from on top of a closet,' Tomoko explained, 'it would have been recording at the time of the murder.'

'Footage?' Makian asked urgently.

Tomoko shook her head. 'That's the problem with these things; it stopped transmitting by the time we got there, and there's no way of tracing the signal.'

'Wait,' Makian said, stuttering as his mind raced to keep up, 'you mean he knew this was going to happen?'

'Possibly.'

'And he still ran from us?'

'Right.'

'This is insane,' Makian shook his head, 'this is big. Real big.'

'I know.'

'And we still don't have anything to actually link Kheron to this.'

'We don't have anything to link *anyone* to *anything*. This was quick; professional. Somebody knew what they were doing. Nothing to even prove that they ever spoke,' Tomoko said gravely. 'The only thing that could prove it is that case, and we still don't know what was in it, where it came from or why anybody wanted it. *But*,' she announced more brightly, 'we did find the briefcase itself, because as well as arresting Kheron, we got a big, fat, juicy briefcase.'

Makian lit up. 'What?'

'Don't get excited. It was empty. We knew it was a long shot; whatever was in there, he was bound to have removed it. If he heard that Smith was dead, he'd have taken steps to keep us from finding anything out. With the quality of that photo, it's a stretch to prove that it's even the same case.'

'So we have sweet fuck all.'

'If that. Whatever Lawson wanted to tell us,' Tomoko said regretfully, looking down over the pale face of the body, 'apart from whoever was chasing him, it looks like it died with him.'

Makian nodded and looked at Lawson's face. At least it wasn't as bad as looking at one of the wraith victims, he thought to himself. He looked calm. Peaceful. Like some gigantic weight had been lifted from him.

He checked his watch, mainly for something to do. 'They'll be interviewing Kheron,' he said, 'I'd better go.'

'Sure,' Tomoko said. 'Anything else?'

'Not unless you're gonna hand me your phone number along with this mountain of evidence.'

'You should be so lucky,' Tomoko smiled thinly. 'Anyway, sorry I couldn't find anything useful.'

'You haven't done any worse than the rest of us, if that helps,' Makian said in dismay. 'I'll go see what New York's top asshole's got to say for himself.'

Makian left the autopsy lab and fetched a cup of coffee on the way through. Jesus, this was seriously turning into the Guild's biggest quagmire in years. Somebody, he knew, had better come up with something fast, or the High Council were going to take every scrap of authority they had and shove it up the nearest available ass.

'Anything?' he asked as he ducked into the room behind the two-way mirror. 'Because- and please, nobody scream- forensic searches haven't turned up shit.'

'Nothing yet,' Jake said as he looked through the glass. Beside him, Katya had seated herself on the edge of the desk as Kheron's cat gave her a low hiss. She bared her own fangs and hissed, quickly sending the "mangy little bastard", as she'd dubbed it, fleeing under the table.

On the other side of the glass, Khazahn was currently locked in combat with that most vile and evil of all human invention: the attorney.

'We know for a fact,' Khazahn said, not for the first time, 'that you have previously associated with Rick Lawson. We have, I'll remind you,' he picked up the evidence bag containing the photo, 'this photo of you and him exchanging a briefcase.'

'My client doesn't deny that he handed a briefcase to the late Mr. Lawson,' the lawyer said. 'This does not prove any criminal actions.'

'And then, while under investigation over these same events,' Khazahn elaborated, 'Lawson disappeared. Two days later, he is found murdered, having been hiding in a hostel in Queens.'

'This is purely circumstantial,' the lawyer said, 'and in no way pertains to my client.'

'What,' Khazahn demanded, 'was in that briefcase?'

'My client has no comment on that matter,' the lawyer said again. 'If you have nothing with which to charge my client-'

'Actually,' Kheron finally stopped smirking and jokingly raised his hand, 'could I have a private word with Jake Connolly, please?'

'I'll get back to you,' Khazahn said. He marched out and slammed the door behind him.

Jake shook his head and lost himself in thought as he made his way to the door. This didn't seem right. Khazahn, even if Jake had never particularly liked him, was a man who was good at his job. He knew how people like this ticked. He'd seen him rip confessions from all kinds. But this... this was sloppy. Amateurish. He'd been clutching at straws from the moment he walked in. He was desperate.

'Son of a bitch,' Khazahn snarled, fists clenched, 'we're getting nothing from this guy.'

'Let me talk to him,' Jake offered.

'You won't get anything out of him,' Khazahn warned, 'the lawyer won't even let anyone say two words to him.'

'Well, he asked to talk to me,' Jake pointed out. 'Stands to reason.'

Khazahn nodded slowly. Jake passed him, pushing the door open. As he sat down, Kheron nodded at him, and then turned to his lawyer.

'If you wouldn't mind, Steve?' he asked.

'I recommend-' the fat little man started.

'I know what you recommend. This won't take but a minute,' Kheron said.

The lawyer, stifling an objection, hurriedly bustled out of the room to regain his composure.

'Ok, what?' Jake demanded.

'You're all such great conversationalists round here, aren't you?' Kheron noted, leaning forward.

'You wanted to talk to me. What do you want?'

Kheron turned his hands over each other and glanced at the mirror, then the security camera.

'I'd rather this wasn't recorded,' he said.

Jake looked blankly at him. 'Tough.'

'Five minutes. One bit of personal information, and you can do what you will with it.'

Jake leaned back in his chair. At some point he'd started turning the old coin over in his fingers. Then he switched off the tape recorder and nodded to the mirror. After a second, the light on the camera went off.

'Now spill.'

'Before you ask,' Kheron said, 'yes, this is indeed to do with poor Mister Rick Lawson.'

Jake glared into his eyes. Something in the pupils burned with a cold flame.

'And no, I didn't kill him,' Kheron replied, 'you probably knew he was dead before I did.' He wasn't lying, Jake realised. For once. 'But I'll tell you what I do know.' His voice dropped to a whisper. 'Just what I told Aleera.'

Jake froze. At once, a hundred awful possibilities came to mind.

'Oh,' Kheron realised, 'she's not told you, then. Then again, word on the grapevine is that she was at the centre of some confusion herself.'

'What did you tell her?' Jake demanded. His voice nearly became a shout.

'Just this,' Kheron whispered, 'you, my friend… have a snake in the grass. And it's not Rick Lawson. Somebody let him out, didn't they?'

'How do you know that?' Jake demanded.

'Well, you weren't about to release him, were you? But I didn't kill Rick Lawson, my good man. Far from it.' He leaned back in his chair and chuckled. 'I mean, alright, I could be lying, fair enough. But the truth of it…' he gave another chuckle, 'the truth is that you're so screwed that nothing I could say and still be believable could make it even a little bit worse for you.'

'Who is it?' Jake demanded.

'Now, you see,' Kheron laughed lightly to himself, 'that's the thing about you. Always with the "good guy", "one of our own wouldn't do this" stuff. They're good men. Big deal. Those wraiths? The ones who've killed more than thirty people this past, what, three weeks?' he leaned forward. 'What do you think they used to be? You think they were all animals? You think circumstances had nothing to do with where they ended up? You'll see: when you introduce enough desperation, enough motive, you strip away all the nice frilly edges, and you'll see what you're left with. Because when the chips are down, really all the way down, all you "good people"… you'll do anything if you can convince yourself that you have to.'

Jake, unfazed, stood up. 'Who. Is. It?'

'Well, it would have to be someone who wanted Lawson to keep quiet about something. Because that crossed your mind a while ago, didn't it?' Kheron smiled darkly, 'he wasn't running from me. If he was, he'd have come straight here. No, no, no…' he shook his head, 'he was terrified of somebody right inside this building.'

'Who?'

'Think about it,' Kheron replied vaguely. 'Who's in the kind of position to do something like this? Think about it. Look at the pieces and see what's there.'

Jake's mind raced over itself. Nothing of any remote value came up.

'No ideas?' Kheron chuckled, 'oh, well.'

'If you hold out on this-' Jake spat.

'I'd like to see my lawyer now, if you don't mind,' Kheron said matter-of-factly. 'Feel free to turn the camera back on.'

Jake tightened his fists until the edge of the coin stabbed into his palm. 'Fine,' he finally said as he stood up.

22

You're doing *what?*'

'Going to work,' Aleera replied simply as she finished her sandwich. Lilith had, finally, allowed her out of her room upon being convinced that Aleera's condition was no longer entirely deplorable.

She had, of course, left out a few things.

Did Lilith really need to know, after all, how she'd spent the night? Probably not, because she had no intention of being the bearer of bad news. She'd... it was shaming for her, really, even to reflect on it.

She hadn't been like that in years. She'd known that this would be a little bit difficult to cope with, but this... this had really taken her back to the bad old days, back to being curled up in a little ball crying quietly to herself.

She'd been freezing. She'd wrapped her arms around herself, covered herself in two sets of sheets and shut the windows to keep out any draft. Then, every time she finally started to grow just the tiniest bit warm, she would make the smallest, the most inane of movements, and a fresh wave of biting cold would shoot through her body.

She was cold. So, so cold...

At some point, she knew logically that she must have fallen asleep, even if she didn't feel like it, because she'd woken up that morning, even if she soon wished she hadn't.

While not freezing from some invisible snow anymore, she was covered in a cold, reeking sweat that had soaked through the bedsheets. She'd thrown them into the washing machine before Lilith got up, and then enjoyed a nice, long, cold (ironically) shower to wake herself up.

And that, she hoped and prayed, would be that. No need for Lilith to find out, and she was now fairly confident that she was over the worst of what was likely nothing more severe than post-traumatic stress.

Yes, because that wasn't serious at all.

Fair enough, but in all honesty, she had had worse.

Aleera's way of thinking was, as she often reflected, a little bit cold. No pun intended. She rarely saw fit to allow emotions to enter the thinking process, mainly because whenever they did, things like the mess with Jasmine the result, and she didn't feel like putting up with that any more than was absolutely necessary. So: the goal had been what exactly? Track down the wraith that left her in that state and let it beg for mercy? Yes, that was a good idea. And Aleera's way of approaching a problem was simplicity itself: "there was an obstacle. Now it is gone. There is no obstacle now." Even the neck scarring was less noticeable.

'You are not going in,' Lilith declared flatly. 'No way.'

'I'm fine,' Aleera said brusquely, 'look at me. I look fine. I feel fine.'

'You can't just decide you feel better and go marching back out there after you nearly got killed!'

'They didn't set any kind of date,' Aleera pointed out. Actually, that was true; they didn't. She made a mental note of that.

'And if you're not "fine"?' Lilith demanded, 'then what? What if it gets worse?'

'Then I'll come back home,' Aleera said simply.

'…What is the matter with you?' Lilith finally screamed, arms out.

'Nothing,' Aleera insisted, 'that's my point.'

Lilith stepped forward until she was barely an inch from Aleera, when that extra inch or two of height on her side could make the most difference.

'You. Are. Not. Going. To. The. Guild.'

Aleera tried to come up with a reply, but there was nothing that trumped the placement of a period point between each word. Lilith had her pinned.

'Fine,' she said. 'Can I just go out, then?'

'Just "out"?' Lilith said sceptically.

'I've been stuck in my room for a day and a half.' And that, Aleera thought irritably, was even more of a pain when you a) didn't want to be there, and b) knew that you were actually, physically capable of sustained flight. 'It's just a little cabin fever, that's all.'

Lilith folded her arms and tapped one foot on the floor.

'Just for an hour or so,' Aleera promised. 'I'll take my cell phone.'

Lilith sighed. '*Half* an hour.'

'Deal,' Aleera said brightly, kissing her on the cheek and quickly ducking through into her room to change into something more flight-appropriate. Lilith unlocked the window while she changed into her waistcoat with the low back, and after promising again to be back in a half-hour, she applied the invisibility spell and took flight.

And a second later, she felt her hair whip around her face, the wind roaring and screaming past her ears as her wings stretched and caught the breeze like leathery parachutes, her upper body jerking as they caught the breeze. Then she felt herself sail, unimpeded, rising steadily with only empty air beneath her feet, spreading her arms, stretching her neck and relaxing in the tosses and turns of the wind.

She closed her eyes for just a moment, letting herself enjoy the feeling of rising freely, and when she opened them, the city was spread out beneath her, a shining, bustling stretch of concrete. Bridges stretched across the sea like living veins, and brilliant sunlight dazzled on the surface.

Really, she didn't come up here nearly as often as she probably should. What human was ever going to see, hear and feel this? New York City, in all its legendary splendour, from five hundred feet in the air. The cool wind around her, and all those people, with their own lives and thoughts and perspectives and feelings, all so far down there that she couldn't even see any of them.

All of them, every one, so very small...

It was a kind of rush, thinking that. Just look at them, so small and tiny, bustling about like that through dank back alleys and squalid streets. And here she was, hundreds of feet above them, completely hidden from their sight. So high, completely invisible, looking down on all those tiny, tiny people...

The feeling of it was indescribable. She was *above* them, by so, so much... this... this must be how God felt!

Steady, she thought, quickly derailing that train of thought before it went anywhere unpleasant.

But why be steady? Just look at them. How tiny they were. Just think- just think how many Ryan Shanes or Azraels there must be in a city this size. One in her school, with its number of students, so just think what ratio that would have to be, and all the people in this city, there would be hundreds of them. Maybe thousands.

Thousands of little venomous insects scurrying around beneath her. Nothing but an indeterminate, shifting mass. Like ants, that was the description she'd heard. If only. At least ants knew how to organise themselves.

They were tiny. Small. Stupid. Wretched. Nothing.

No. No, no, no, this wasn't right. When had she started thinking like that? That wasn't her. She'd never really liked them, but this... she was actually thinking about...

And why not? Her hand seemed to twitch involuntarily. One spell. One dropped object. Who could ever work out what happened? And name one of them that she knew of, just one, who wouldn't have it coming.

No. That wasn't her. That, that was something… it was something her father would say.

That was it. That simple, basic, all-consuming fear was all that was needed to silence it.

The evil little seed inside her growled. Go on, it tempted her. They'd do it to her, given half a chance.

No! She focused and forced it down, forcing it to stop hissing and snapping at her. Damn you, get back down there and stay there!

Rationality started to slip back in. She'd actually, she shivered, she actually… she'd never thought about that before. She'd been angry. She'd known that blinding, mindless rage that just made her want to lash out at whatever was nearest. But she never… she never seriously thought about doing something like that.

What had that bastard wraith done to her?

With the thought, she was suddenly cold. Then colder still. No, not this, not again- no, it wasn't, she told herself, it was just cold up here. Time to lose some altitude. Pick a rooftop that didn't look too shabby and land.

God, so cold…

Then without a note of warning, it welled up again and screamed and tore at her insides. That cold, that endless cold inside and out, and that mad, screaming fear.

She wrapped her arms around herself without thinking and, with her wings, forced herself down. Down, down! Get down, get warm, get- *get away!*

It stayed there, wracking and sobbing with her eyes, screaming and crying. Stop it, stop it, stop it!

So cold, so dark, so helpless, so- so scared…

What had it done to her?

Wings. Wings had stopped. Falling!

The air whipped harsh and cold around her face, lashing at her arms as she folded the wings out. She jerked and felt something stab painfully inside her shoulder. Land. Nearest rooftop. Land!

The wings caught the air again and she landed, hard and fast, the spell blinking out of its function on impact. She tucked herself into a ball and rolled over until she struck the hard, cold side of something.

Gasping for breath, she tucked herself in at the side of the air conditioning fan, wrapping her arms around her legs as she trembled.

She was so scared, so scared, what was happening? So afraid...

Then it passed, leaving nothing behind but the slow trembling.

Aleera pulled herself up on the side of the air conditioner, steadying herself as the wings withdrew and slipped seamlessly into her back. Slowly, the dull, panicking nausea passed. She felt the scar on her neck burn at her.

She retched and realised at the last minute that something hot and acidic was rushing up her throat. She turned, doubled over and let the bile spew onto the corner of the rooftop, pouring over the insides of her mouth. She spat out anything left and collapsed against the side of the metal box, breathing in and out slowly as the last tremors of the episode passed.

There we go. All over.

So maybe she wasn't entirely past it; it was still better than last night. Still, she should most likely go home. Yes, that would be sensible, she thought.

Although, alternatively, she could go and start towards giving the wretched thing that did this to her what was coming to it. That worked. And any reason not to do it? ...Not that she could think of.

That was it, then. She still had plenty of time in which to be back, and on a good day she could get a decent speed. Just pop in to do her duty. It would be nothing to do with getting back at the wraiths.

No, nothing at all. Never would she do such a thing.

Of course, if the opportunity came up to take her frustrations out on its blood vessels, who was she to say no?

Alright, then. Decided. Drop in, see how things were going, and be back within the half-hour. Admittedly, she did feel a tiny pang of guilt for what was essentially lying to Lilith, but she hadn't actually sworn to go- or not to go- anywhere specific.

She extended the wings again, re-applied the invisibility spell and took flight. Nice and steady, she reminded herself. She didn't need any more practice with her emergency landings today.

Luckily enough, she reached the top of the Flatiron Building without any further incident. When she landed, she immediately found herself reminded of her impromptu descent by a sharp stab in her shoulder. She winced and flexed it. It seemed mostly alright, if a little stiff. She'd probably just strained it at some point during her rapid descent. Nothing that couldn't be fixed; she gently placed one palm on the shoulder- alright, so there was a small twinge involved- and said '*Xiaol*'. The pain immediately faded away.

She entered via the fire escape on the rooftop and, from past experience, located the elevator. She recalled that she had her own clearance now: 'Red Clearance. Plato Five-Zero-Nine.'

The hidden doors opened soundlessly, and the spotless, gleaming metal of the elevator surrounded her in fluorescent light. With only the slightest lurch, it descended, twenty-two floors speeding past before it slowed to a halt and the doors slid silently open to reveal the long, stony chasm that was the central hall.

She didn't bother detouring to the locker room to get her uniform; after all, she wasn't going to work, just as promised. Just to see how close she might be to choking the life out of that miserable wraith- no, not that, just to see how things were going. A perfectly innocent visit to a friend at work.

She found Jake in his office, spinning his old coin between his fingers. He dropped it when he looked up and saw who was in the doorway.

'Aleera?' he asked dumbly.

'I hope you don't mind me dropping in,' Aleera said, 'I was going a little bit stir-crazy at home, so I thought I'd see how things are going here.'

'They're not,' Jake said bluntly. 'We lost Lawson. Then we *lost*-lost him.'

'As in "lost"?' Aleera asked, seating herself on an empty chair.

'Fatal shooting,' Jake elaborated, 'and not a shred of evidence to tie anyone to anything.'

Aleera soaked up the information. So how many dead leads did this add up to, now, throughout the course of the investigation?

'How did we lose him?' she asked.

'Straight to business, huh?' Jake said jokingly.

'Sorry. It hasn't been the best week,' Aleera admitted. 'How's everyone coping after this?' she asked. As she recalled from Jake and Makian's reactions to the incident with Chara and Drake, these kinds of events were a nightmare for any agent of law enforcement. The idea was meant to be that you could safely trust the man who carried a weapon behind you. And so far, they'd had one of their own turn on them and then turn up with a bullet in him. It would be enough to tax anyone. The job was supposed to at least try to provide some level of security, and this was the opposite of security in quite a number of ways.

'About as well as you'd expect,' Jake answered. 'Katya's just off mooching around the lab.'

'You've been here all day?'

'I swear, it's like the council's trying to drive everyone insane,' Jake sighed. 'Daeiol's pushing for a full inquiry as soon as the case is over.'

'So what did happen with Lawson?'

'Someone let him out,' Jake said, 'and it looks like he took the chance himself, because I think he wanted to get out of here.'

'You said that,' Aleera recalled, 'you said he seemed scared.'

'The man was out of his mind. The thing is, I don't think it was from Kheron, because if it was, this place is about as safe as any other.' Considering the influence Kheron had, Aleera debated whether that was a positive thing or not. 'Of course, now we've got no way of finding out who it was that he was running from.'

'Any thoughts?'

Jake nodded slowly and held the coin between two fingers. 'We brought Kheron in,' he explained, clearly trying to fit two damaged jigsaw pieces together in his head at the same time, 'and… he said,' he said hesitantly, 'that we have a turncoat.'

Aleera mused on this. That was what he'd told her, too. The Guild, as she knew firsthand, was no stranger to corruption, but this, right from the word "go", had seemed somehow different. There were probably any number of soldiers, however much the idea disgusted her, who were on Kheron's payroll. That, more likely than not, was the reason he wasn't staring at the inside wall of a prison cell. But this was something decidedly different. Kheron wouldn't tell them about someone working for him.

'It's not someone working with Kheron,' she reflected, 'but somebody who wanted to prevent us from finding something out.'

'Right,' Jake said, clearly somewhat impressed. Aleera did have quite the mind for this sort of thing.

'How, exactly, was Lawson broken out?' she pressed.

'He wasn't. He was released. Somebody even turned off the cameras.'

'So this was somebody who knew what they were doing; they'd have known the ins and outs of this place.'

Clearly, that told her the same thing as it did Jake, as they both looked up and said 'officer.'

'Somebody's hiding something,' Jake recalled, 'I went through about a year's paperwork yesterday, and there was nothing out of place anywhere I looked.'

The pragmatics of the matter weren't wasted. That shouldn't be, Aleera realised immediately. There was always something hidden in the Guild. This meant that somebody had gone to a great deal of effort to make sure something stayed hidden.

This was big.

Except… it wasn't. Not necessarily.

'It's not a move against us,' Aleera noted, thinking out loud as much as anything else, 'to see it through for this length of time, it would have to be big. Too big to bury like that without a soul knowing about it. And if it was hidden this well, it would really have to be someone who knows the Guild's procedures like the back of his hand. Maybe…' there. Hold onto that thought, because this one just might be it. 'Maybe this is something independent. Someone following their own agenda.'

'I thought as much,' Jake said, 'so what agenda's that?'

Aleera sat back in the chair. 'I couldn't really say,' she admitted, 'but I'd go so far as to guess it had something to do with a briefcase.'

'And Rick Lawson was involved,' Jake realised. 'Maybe that was why he was killed.'

'To keep him quiet,' Aleera said. 'That could have been it.'

They all seemed to fit. Again, like a jigsaw puzzle, and now they'd managed to get all the straight bits and corners, making the edge of the picture… only there was a piece missing, the heart of the image, and without it, it was impossible to tell quite what they were looking at.

Wait…

Aleera's computer of a brain was shifting into high gear.

'Did you look at the accountancy files?' she asked.

'First place I checked.'

'I thought so,' Aleera said, 'I think you were barking up the wrong tree.'

Jake looked up. His eyes held curiosity, intrigue, and that mischievous spark of "here we go". 'Do tell.'

'Maybe this agenda of whosoever it was,' Aleera explained, 'this could be something personal against Kheron.'

'Something Lawson was a part of as well,' Jake realised. 'That's a hell of a long shot.'

'Could you follow it up?' Aleera asked.

'We do know someone who's good with the paperwork,' Jake said brightly.

'Makian.'

'Right. Maybe we'll dig something up.'

Aleera's mind raced back, all the way back to Tom Smith and his dealings and the briefcase. Because he was a dark magic dealer, and whatever was in the case was something he would have known about. Find whoever was behind all of this, she realised, and they would find the origin of their wraiths.

'Only…' she said without thinking, 'that still leaves us with the wraiths.'

'If we find out where they came from,' Jake replied, 'we just might find them. So far, this is the closest thing we've had to a solid lead.'

Aleera nodded. Now it was just a matter of patience and logic. After all the uncontrolled emotion she'd been putting up with of late, it would be a pleasant change.

So, who did she know of who was high up in the Guild? Somebody who had a personal motivation against Kheron.

Well, there was always…

Oh no. Oh, no, no, no. Oh. Holy. Shit.

'Jake,' she said quietly, 'I think I know who might have done this.'

Jake looked blankly at her for a moment. 'Someone with authority,' Aleera said, 'someone who knows how things work in the Guild. Someone who has his own issues with Kheron.'

She saw Jake pale as the realisation hit him. He sat up straight and tightened his fingers around the old coin.

'Khazahn,' he said quietly.

'Could that be it?' Aleera suggested, 'he could do something like that from the position he's in now, and he's got more than enough motivation.'

'He was trying something against Kheron,' Jake realised, 'maybe something that has to do with all this wraith stuff.'

'Speaking of wraiths,' Aleera pointed out as she realised, 'that attack on me-'

'You mean the reason why you should be at home right now?'

'Yes,' Aleera admitted grudgingly, 'that was the first attack since the one at the penthouse. That was nearly a week ago.'

'There's a lot of homeless and animals in the sewers,' Jake said, 'enough to keep them going in-between. But I hear what you're saying.'

'Maybe they're…' Aleera decided on a suitable euphemism, 'saving their appetites.'

'Or building up,' Jake replied, 'each attack's been worse than the last so far. The first was just four small-timers. By the end, they're hitting Pentagram and taking out his biggest dark-magic runner.'

Aleera allowed her thoughts to sidetrack just a little. Smith's killing, she realised, had been personal. That was obvious enough. *What have you been doing, Khazahn?*

'There's going to be another one coming,' Aleera surmised.

'Soon,' Jake agreed, 'and it'll be big.'

The sentence hung over the room like a heavy cloud.

'I should probably be getting home,' Aleera finally said, if only to break the silence.

'Sure,' Jake said gravely, 'I'll get Makian to take a look, and I'll tell Katya you were here.'

Aleera nodded, managed the best smile she could, and closed the door behind her as she left.

Well, she'd come to find out how the case had been progressing, and now she had her answer. The answer was a clear, loud "abysmally".

Now: she wasn't going to think that this visit couldn't get any worse. No, really, she wasn't. Because immediately after she so much as though it, it would.

It turned out that it was about to get worse anyway, because she chanced to encounter Daniel Cassidy on the way out.

'What the hell are you doing here?' he demanded the moment he saw her.

'Nice to see you too,' Aleera said sharply. Well, technically she wasn't there as his subordinate at that moment. 'Just dropping in to see someone.'

'This building is classified,' Cassidy snapped.

'I am still a Guild employee,' Aleera regarded him. His face darkened by a shade. Oh, this was fun, she thought. 'So I believe I'm still permitted to be on the premises, right?'

'You're supposed to be on leave,' Cassidy said flatly, 'and by the way, I'll be sure to contact my superiors about it.'

Aleera froze as she walked past him. 'About what?'

'A number of things,' Cassidy said darkly, 'homicide, for one.'

Aleera felt her fingers twitch. 'That was self-defence,' she said in as controlled a manner as possible.

'I'm sure. Of course, it also lost us our only potential lead in a major case. And there's also the matter of your sister- no, half-sister, if I remember- deliberately blocking an officer in the execution of his duties.'

Oh, wow. Aleera almost pitied him. Much the same kind of pity as seeing someone poke a tiger with a stick, getting his hand bitten off, and then thinking "that poor, dumb bastard".

'Excuse me?' she said darkly. Her eyes were already flooding with red.

'I've made myself clear,' Cassidy said. 'You're dismissed.'

'No,' Aleera said bitingly, 'oh, no.'

'Excuse me, Private?'

'Let me make one thing clear,' Aleera said, stepping forward slowly, 'I'm stuck here. Which means you're stuck with me. Whether you like it or not. Whether I like it or not. So, because there's nothing that either of us can do about it, I'll take whatever shots you feel like throwing at me. Insults, abuse, whatever you have, assuming you're not stupid enough to lose your job over this childish vendetta of yours, all fine. But,' she was less than a foot from him by now, and somehow seemed to tower over a man at least half a foot taller than her, 'you do not- *ever*- make so much as the vaguest threat against my sister.'

It was probably the only time in his life Daniel Cassidy had been intimidated by someone ten years his junior. To his credit, he appeared to shrug it off after a second.

'Or,' Aleera suggested, 'you could just tell me right now: what is your problem, *sir*?'

'You know,' Cassidy snarled.

'Do I?'

'Call me old-fashioned, but I'm just not thrilled to have a bloody psychopath in my unit,' Cassidy barked, 'especially-' he bit his tongue.

'Oh, for God's sake, just say it,' Aleera said, 'go ahead. You won't be the first or the last, and we both know what it is. Spit it out.'

'Fine!' Cassidy snapped, his voice as loud and booming as Aleera had ever heard it, 'you're Kudra's fucking daughter! There! That's who you fucking are, you twisted little bitch, and we all know you're as messed up as he ever fucking was! I come in every day, and I see the face of his fucking daughter staring back at me, after everything he did, and they don't just still let you walk around, knowing who you are and what you are and what you do, and now they expect me to just act like you're one of my unit, after what I saw your father- your fucking father- do! That what you want me to say?'

Aleera nodded slowly. It was petty of her, and more than a little spiteful, but most of what was coming out of Cassidy's mouth was a viewpoint to which she was not unfamiliar. Besides, as rants went, it wasn't really the best she'd heard. Lots of swears, though.

She could react. Shout back. She had grounds to, after all. If the council wasn't already tempted to line her up in front of a firing squad, she probably had grounds to take him to court. Instead, she decided on something even more frustrating.

'I'll see you when I'm back at work, Sergeant,' she said, stepping past him to the elevator.

'That's it?' Cassidy shouted after her, 'you're just walking away, you little bitch? Do you even know who he was? You know what he did? *Do you know what he fucking did to my brother?*'

Aleera slowed to a stop. Well, there it was. Certainly explained a lot. Again, not the first case of this that she'd come across.

'I can imagine,' she said darkly.

'No you can't,' Cassidy snarled, 'because you didn't find him after your fucking flesh and blood got through with him.'

Aleera steeled herself up. She didn't reply.

'So what do you say now?' Cassidy said.

'I say that you should find a good therapist,' Aleera said icily, 'and just as confirmation, I didn't kill your brother. The man who did that died three years ago.'

Alright: even for her, that had been a little cold. But the alternative was... well, what? She was hardly going to say that he was right after that tirade. Besides, she'd never been that good at relating to people on personal issues like this.

She entered the elevator and ignored Cassidy's remaining presence until the doors closed and it started. Cassidy stared at the closed doors for a moment, and then turned around.

'What was that about?'

Makian had just emerged from a doorway, halfway through a donut.

'I think you can tell,' Cassidy said bluntly, pushing his way past him.

'Ok, seriously,' Makian piped up. Cassidy slowed down. 'Look, I can vouch for the kid, alright? She's not like Kudra was.'

'When I want your opinion, Lieutenant,' Cassidy snarled, 'I'll ask for it. It's bad enough having to listen to that fucking little demon bitch telling me she's not like her old man.'

Makian's eyes turned down. He threw the last of the donut into a trashcan and turned away.

'Heard that before,' he muttered.

Cassidy stopped again. 'What was that?' he demanded.

Makian turned round. A sudden quantity of what could only be called "guts" welled up, to a degree that surprised even him. 'I said I've heard that before,' he said. 'What you were saying to her.'

'Don't you dare,' Cassidy snarled, marching up to him. 'Don't you dare say another fucking word, you-'

'You do!' Makian said, louder this time, 'you sound like-'

'Don't!' Cassidy roared.

'You do, man!' Makian shouted over him, 'you do! You sound just like-'

'You-'

'*You sound like Azrael!*'

Cassidy fell silent. His fist was raised and an inch away from being swung forward.

'I'll be in my office,' he said gravely.

As Cassidy marched away, he passed the half-open door of Khazahn's office.

Inside, Khazahn leaned on his desk, shaking his head in dismay.

Damn it. He'd been able to hear that from up here. Damn it. Too late now, he knew that for a fact.

Still, he knew it wouldn't be his problem for much longer. That was oddly comforting, really. Soon enough now.

Damn it.

It was all going wrong. All of it. He was so out of time, so close, and now… now everything had just gone so wrong. None of this should be happening. It wasn't what he'd signed his name on that dotted line for.

He bowed his head in quiet despair and poured another glass of scotch.

23

'I,' Katya announced, lying across one side of the desk with her hair and legs dangling over different sides, 'hate this.'

'I know you do,' Jake said as he folded papers between his hands.

'We've been doing this for *days*,' Katya pouted, 'can we at least do something?'

'Until we turn something up,' Jake replied simply, 'there's nothing else we can do.'

'You're just doing this to get out of cleaning our place, aren't you?'

'That and find something out, which hasn't happened in the three days since we got the idea to start looking.'

'And it hasn't occurred to you,' Katya said, 'that just maybe, the looking through papers idea isn't actually going to be any help?'

'Yes it has.'

'So…?'

'"So" nothing,' Jake said flatly, 'this is all we can do.'

Katya remained silent. The only sound was the rhythmic ticking of a wall-mounted clock.

'So nothing on… the thing Aleera mentioned?' she asked hesitantly.

'No,' Jake said without elaboration.

'You think it might be true? Katya asked.

'I hope it isn't,' Jake answered honestly. 'I really do.'

'So you think…?'

Jake sighed heavily and snapped the folder shut, adding it to the pile. 'It makes sense,' he replied, 'and it's about the first thing in this case that does.'

Katya hesitated for a second. 'Do you still… remember?' she asked, 'what happened before?'

'I haven't forgiven him for that, if that's what you're getting at,' Jake said.

'You haven't said anything,' Katya said quietly. 'I mean, how long is that gonna go on?'

'I had to work with him to get the job done,' Jake said without emotion, 'if I have to put what happened aside, then I can do that.'

'So you haven't,' Katya said. Jake glared up at her. 'Sorry.'

'It's fine.'

'Do you think it's true, though?'

Jake remained silent for a few seconds. 'I don't know,' he said, 'I really don't.'

'I know what he was involved with before,' Katya said, 'there was a lot going on with that, and really, I don't think he wanted to do it. Do you really think he'd actually do something like this himself? I mean, we're talking about actually killing a man!'

'I don't want to believe that Khazahn could have done his,' Jake answered. 'Come on, we might as well go,' he said, standing up, 'grab a pizza on the way back?'

Changing the subject, Katya realised immediately. Well, she could hardly blame him. Times like this were simply what came of living with someone who always bore the weight of the world on his shoulders. 'Sure.'

'Hey Jake,' Makian called as they closed the office door behind them, 'you leaving?'

'Just about to,' Jake replied, 'why?' It was then that he noticed that Makian was running up to them, apparently out of breath.

'I think we've got something,' Makian said.

Jake's face was a frozen vision of amazement. 'You think what?'

'This way,' Makian said, directing them towards the interview rooms, 'this girl came in about an hour ago with a CD of camera footage.'

'There was a camera in Lawson's room at the hostel,' Jake remembered.

'And this girl,' Makian said quickly, 'claims to be the one whom our friend Rick Lawson formerly had the honour of schtupping.'

'His girlfriend.'

'On the nose,' Makian said with the accompanying gesture. 'So, if we're really, really, stupidly lucky, which would be a hell of a change, we just got video footage of murder and murderer.'

'Outstanding,' Jake proclaimed as they bumped fists.

In the interview room, Rick Lawson's girlfriend was sitting behind one of the thick metal tables. She was a pretty girl, with a suspiciously tight pink sweater and light hair. She looked up and started shifting uncomfortably in her seat.

'Are you…?' she asked nervously.

'Lieutenant Makian,' Makian replied, 'and this is Jake and Katya Connolly.' Jake nodded. Katya gave a small wave. 'It's Hannah, isn't it?'

The girl nodded. 'Hannah Clark,' she confirmed.

'And you're... were,' Makian corrected himself as he realised his verbal error, 'Rick Lawson's girlfriend.'

Hannah nodded and sniffed. Her eyes were red, and Jake realised she'd been crying. 'We started dating last year,' she said.

Katya was the first to sit down. 'I know this must be hard,' she said sympathetically.

'I don't know-' Hannah sniffed, 'I don't know who- who killed him.'

'He gave you that CD, right?' Makian asked. 'The one you gave us?'

Hannah nodded again. 'I burned it onto the disc myself,' she choked, 'he said the camera would send the footage, and I should-' she broke off into tears, 'I saw what was on it- he-'

'We'll find out who did this,' Jake promised.

'I know,' Hannah said, managing to force herself not to cry for a moment, 'he said if anything happened to him, then- then I should bring the disc here and ask for your names.'

'And only us?' Jake asked.

'Yeah,' Hannah sniffed. 'Look, he- he'd been acting... weird.'

'Weird?' Makian repeated, 'how?'

'I- I don't know,' Hannah shook.

'I know this is difficult,' Katya said gently, 'but this could really help us work out why this happened.'

'He was just- different,' Hannah said, 'he was out all the time. It was like- like he kept needing to look over his shoulder for something. Like he w- was scared,' she choked back more tears, 'he was scared of something, and I didn't know what, and now-'

'I'm sorry,' Katya said, handing her a tissue as was all she could do for the poor girl.

'Just tell me something,' Hannah said through still-leaking eyes, 'did he- was- did this happen because of what he did here?' The room went quiet immediately. 'After he started here,' she cried quietly, 'he changed. He just l- looked so desperate and so- scared and- it was ever since he came here, like he was hiding something,' she blurted out. 'So was- was that it? Was it because of this?'

'...We don't know,' Jake finally said.

'I was, wasn't it?' Hannah sniffed, 'I kept telling him it was dangerous, but he said-'

'Listen to me,' Jake said softly, leaning on the table, 'I don't know who killed him or why, but he was a good soldier and we will find out. I promise you, that whether they're part of the Guild or not, we will find whoever did this. I promise you that, Hannah Clark.'

As they left, Makian pushed the door shut behind them. 'You think she could've been right?' he asked tentatively.

'Easy way of finding out,' Jake said, 'CD?'

'Evidence locker,' Makian replied. Jake shrugged in agreement; it was, after all, the safest place for it.

It was a short walk to the evidence room, obscured from sight by a door that looked to contain at least half a foot of reinforced stone, and which Jake knew to actually have a centre of solid steel. Even the High Council couldn't find grounds to argue with that kind of security.

Inside, a single shaft of light was surrounded by the dark folds and glinting edges of metal shelves, filled with swirling iridescent dust. A moment later, light flooded the room as Makian threw the switch.

'Ok,' he announced grandly, 'our little treasure trove should be right about…' he paused by one of the shelves. He froze.

His hand was still reaching out, and now hovered above an empty patch of metal.

A long, slow moment of silence drifted by. With no other sound but the rhythmic ticking of the clock in the background, Makian said it best.

'Well, fuck.'

Aleera still couldn't quite believe that it had actually worked. She'd only been a couple of minutes over time, and there'd been nothing to betray the fact that she'd actually been sneaking off to the Guild. In all fairness, upon reflection the whole situation did sound quite ridiculous, but the job was done.

There were only two problems. The first was that irritating stab of what she could only assume to be guilt that came from lying to her sister. Normally, Aleera was enough of a self-admitted icy bitch to distance herself from it as she did most things, but she'd never liked the idea of keeping anything from Lilith. She recalled actually feeling guilty for not mentioning that she was being hunted down by a deranged serial killer. Fair enough, it wasn't the kind of trivial matter that traditionally slipped one's mind, but it had been for her own safety. This, as she rationalised it to herself, really wasn't anywhere near as serious. It wasn't like she was sneaking out to do drugs or mess around with some idiot boy.

The other problem was the fierce anger still gnawing away at her insides and demanded she draw blood for the tearing of her soul and the scarring of her neck. Rather than take action towards her vindication, the entire visit had only served to enlighten her about just how entirely catastrophic the entire situation had become since it all started.

She'd hoped- not really expected, because she was the realistic, practical kind- that it would bring her a little bit closer to taking her consolation prize out of a wraith's skull. Instead, it had left her even more irritated than before.

So, successfully brushing it off as more cabin fever, she'd fished out her sports bra and started a furious sequence of push-ups, sit-ups and a couple of long-ingrained Tae Kwon Do moves, followed by a cold shower once she'd worked up an adequate sweat.

Still, she reflected as she dried off, the visit had at least reduced the irritation she'd felt at being stuck inside from dusk to dawn. It was now just a matter of seeing if Lilith would let her out again. And, if she did earn the esteemed privilege of leaving, surely getting a few extra minutes in at work could be a positive thing?

Once she'd suitably de-stressed herself, then re-stressed herself by reflecting on the matter, Lilith had deemed her well enough to help out with dinner. Gratifyingly, she hadn't been subject to another episode like the unfortunate one a great number of feet above the city. Needless to say, she'd been sure to forget to mention that to Lilith. Aleera managed to serve up a casserole and, having not realised how much of a day it had been or how long it had been since she'd last eaten, was surprised by how dramatically she could feel her blood sugar levels rising. Lilith still insisted on doing the dishes, so Aleera just decided to fish out an old favourite book.

She was about halfway through the first chapter when the phone rang.

'Hello?'

'Hey, it's me,' the voice on the other end said.

'Jasmine?'

'Yeah. I was just wondering- how you were doing.' There was a very definite pause in the middle of that sentence. Aleera put it to the back of her mind for now.

'Fine,' Aleera said, 'I'll probably be back at school tomorrow.' She made sure to say that quietly enough to ensure that Lilith wouldn't hear. Better safe than deafened.

'Cool. So, uh, I was thinking I might come over? I mean, if you want.'

'Sure.'

'We've still got that history thing to do. I know you said you have a good G.P.A. and everything.'

'Ok.'

'Sure. So tomorrow?'

'Fine.'

'Great, because it's just, y'know, school and friends and-'

'Yeah, that's fine,' Aleera said. 'I'll see you then.' Fortunately, saying that let her hand up before the conversation became any more forced.

That was that, then. Now, if her damn heart would stop fluttering-

It suddenly dawned on her that Jasmine was anything but "over it". Of course, she was. Obviously. It wouldn't be right for her not to be. Absolutely.

'Fuck,' Makian announced. 'This is shit, man. This is raw, pure shit.'

'And you kiss your mother with that very same mouth,' Katya noted dryly.

'Just making a point,' Makian said defensively. 'And that point is that this is-'

'I can guess.'

After finding that the only lead was, for what was at the very least the third time, gone, Jake, Makian and Katya had returned to Jake's office. Of course, before that there had been the customary frantic search of the evidence locker.

Jake, meanwhile, had had Makian print some logs off from the computer system, as that controlled the passcodes, security cameras, etcetera, etcetera. The main conclusion he'd come to thus far was that whoever was behind this, they did indeed know what they were doing, because there were no records of anyone keying themselves into the evidence room.

'Unless,' he announced as the notion descended on him, 'the record of the access was deleted.'

'Except there's no record of anyone with that kind of authority entering the system,' Makian pointed out.

'Well, obviously, otherwise there'd been no point in deleting it in the first place,' Jake pointed out sagely. He sat back and continued to muse for a while.

'Somebody took it,' he said, 'that's an obvious one. And it was definitely somebody high up. For the kind of access that this would need…'

'Above Cassidy?' Makian asked.

'At the very least,' Jake answered grimly, 'Commander. Head of the Division.'

'Which basically narrows it down to Khazahn, Hartwell, Daeiol or her Royal Bitchiness the High Chancellor,' Makian established.

'Khazahn,' Jake muttered to himself. 'What the hell have you done?'

Somewhere in front of him, the full story was still dangling, and try as he might, he couldn't quite reach out and grasp it. So near, yet so far, and somehow he knew, by the time he reached it, so very much too late.

And just like that, it was morning.

Aleera allowed herself a few moments of idle contemplation as she flicked through a calendar. Among other things, it emerged that it had now been two weeks since she'd first learned of the draft. Amongst everything else, she was forced to admit that she'd more or less forgotten how angry she'd been at that weekend, mainly because she was at least that angry now.

Still: two weeks.

Add in the time since she'd first learned of this, and it was months. Months of her damn life. Not that she'd probably have done all that much with it, said a sage part of her. Except maybe sort out her personal life, a second butted in. Yes, a third said sarcastically, and maybe then she'd have cured world hunger.

Somewhere in the mental confusion, the thought spoke up that, of the four weeks thus far, only the first three had seen any kind of activity on the part of her wraith friends. A week without feeding, she thought, reflecting on what she and Jake had talked about. Any day now.

In any case, the school had gotten in touch at long last, and she was due to be back in school in about a week. Lilith had objected, but Aleera had miraculously won the argument, as a) there was little to be done about it, and b) there'd been no more episodes since the one while flying, and fate was capable of such kindness that Lilith didn't even know about it. Aleera, of course, was more than happy to let that one stay buried. Otherwise she'd never be allowed to jump out of the window again (this was probably the only circumstance under which that was unreasonable).

When she finally went to meet Jasmine, estimating that she'd probably be out of school by now, it was a pleasant change of pace to be able to leave the apartment and be open with her intention to actually go somewhere. Amazingly, Lilith hadn't objected nearly as much. It was about a twenty-minute walk, but Aleera had to admit that she was so happy to actually be out that it seemed to fly past.

Jasmine's mother opened the door to her, and it was only then that Aleera remembered that they'd never actually met before. The impression that she'd received from Jasmine seemed to be reasonably accurate, however. The woman was in her forties with short, curly light-brown hair and the kind of expression that came exclusively from instant disapproval machines.

'Hello,' she said in a manner that wasn't overtly unfriendly, but was hardly intended to make anyone feel welcome. 'Jasmine,' she called upstairs, 'your friend's here. Would you mind taking your shoes off?' she asked Aleera.

As a brief scrambling of feet started upstairs, Aleera politely slipped off her footwear.

'So,' Jasmine's mother strained to say, 'Jasmine tells me you're a demon.' It sounded like she was being accused of something illegal.

'That's right.' It seemed like the politic thing to say.

Jasmine's mother glared at her in a way that suggested that she was very much an unwanted guest. Aleera responded by tensing herself just slightly and giving a returning look that suggested that she was also a young woman not to be trifled with in such ways. Jasmine's mother shifted uncomfortably after a moment.

Any further body language sparring was curtailed when Jasmine emerged at the bottom of the stairs.

'Hi,' she said brightly, 'c'mon up.'

Aleera followed her upstairs, taking more delight than was probably appropriate in the irritation that practically oozed from Jasmine's mother. She'd gotten her to this level without giving any cause to be thrown out. It was a small victory, but lately she'd had to take them where she could find them.

'So how is everything?' Jasmine asked as they sat on her bed.

'Not bad,' Aleera said. Well, at least it was true now. 'Another week, and I should be back at school.'

Jasmine nodded and fidgeted, letting out a heavy sigh.

'Are you alright?' Aleera asked.

'Huh? Yeah, yeah, just- yeah, I'm fine,' Jasmine answered.

'"Just" what?'

'Well, it's nothing compared to what's been happening with you,' Jasmine said, 'it's just that my mom's had her obsessive act back on lately, and I've been busting my entire butt finishing that history thing.'

'Finishing?' Aleera parroted. She'd thought as much. 'You finished it already?'

Jasmine looked away and blushed slightly. 'Kind of,' she admitted. 'Like I said, I know you have a really good…'

'I'm sorry I've been so busy,' Aleera said honestly.

'It's fine. I mean, working for the Guild; that must be a hell of a job.'

'It is lately,' Aleera confessed. 'So…'

'I just thought maybe we could hang out today,' Jasmine answered the question before she asked. She'd have been a lot more convincing if she didn't seem to be becoming so tense so quickly.

'And talk?' Aleera guessed.

'Yeah.'

'About…?'

'We could,' Jasmine said awkwardly.

Aleera felt her own lungs seem to tighten. The air in the room seemed to have grown thicker and warmer.

'We did talk about that,' Aleera said quietly. 'About what happened. Between us.' For some reason, it suddenly felt as though it needed clarification.

'I know,' Jasmine said, 'it's just…' she seemed to struggle for a moment, then simply altered everything and forced it out in a short burst of 'forget it.'

'Forget what?'

'Nothing,' Jasmine said defensively.

'Is this why you asked me to come round?' Aleera asked.

'It's just- it's nothing,' Jasmine said quickly, 'I just thought, since we agreed we were still friends, maybe we could talk about… I don't know, stuff.'

Aleera sighed. She'd always been, at the same time, good and not so good at reading people. Body language, all the subtle little nuances, fine, but nowhere near as skilled at interpreting the emotions behind them. She could only do that in the cases of people she really knew well, and, despite the relatively short time that had elapsed, Jasmine appeared to be one of them. So it was pretty obvious, therefore, what was really on her mind.

'I'm sorry, Jasmine,' she sighed.

'It's fine.'

'No, I mean, I'm *sorry*,' Aleera said.

Jasmine looked down at the bedspread. Her hands fiddled with the button on the side of a homemade pair of trousers.

'I shouldn't have called you,' she said quietly. When she looked up, she hastily added 'I don't mean like that. I just wanted to say something and… it was stupid of me. It doesn't matter.'

'If you wanted to say it that badly, it must have done,' Aleera said simply. Emotional detachment could make one a handy debater as well.

'It's just about what happened,' Jasmine said. 'How we ended things. Why.'

'I told you,' Aleera said.

'I know,' Jasmine said bitterly. 'You said it was the- the pheromones or whatever. You said it had happened before.'

'It did,' Aleera said.

'With your friend,' Jasmine recited. 'You said she was straight, and… yeah.'

'That's what happened.' Aleera really couldn't be sure why she was supposed to be defending herself here.

'And you thought that was what was happening with us,' Jasmine concluded. She folded her arms and looked away.

'Wasn't it?'

Jasmine looked back up at her. She looked… annoyed. Angry.

'You just assumed,' she said under her breath.

Now that was an interesting one. 'Assumed what?'

'You just assumed,' Jasmine said heatedly, 'you just assumed I was straight, didn't you?'

Ok, now Aleera was surprised. 'You're not?'

Jasmine looked blankly at her for a moment. 'You actually didn't get it,' she finally said. 'You really don't get it, do you? You-' as if remembering to turn off a stove, she quickly got up and turned on the stereo by her bed. The music of Snow Patrol blared out at a particularly high volume.

'And this is for...?' Aleera couldn't help asking after the first few lyrics.

Jasmine looked embarrassed for a moment. 'I never really... came out. Much,' she admitted, downcast. 'My mom doesn't know, Ok?'

'Oh,' Aleera realised. Well, now she felt just plain stupid. 'You're...'

'Gay. A lesbian. A dyke. Whoop-de-fucking-do for me.' Jasmine dropped herself back onto the bed.

'Sorry,' Aleera said quietly. 'I didn't really-'

'My point,' Jasmine said bluntly, 'Jesus, you could see it from space!'

'Jasmine,' Aleera started, 'that doesn't mean-'

'I know,' Jasmine said, 'but you never even stopped to think, did you? You never stopped to think that it might have been real. Did you ever think of that? Honestly? Did you ever think that maybe, just maybe, *I was actually in love with you?*'

Aleera felt a very deep, very dark pit opening up in her stomach. She hadn't. She really hadn't. And she should have. On reflection, it should have been about the first thing she'd considered.

It was hard to find anything to say in reply.

Jasmine shook her head and stood up again, avoiding looking at her. 'I'm sorry,' she said, 'this isn't why I called you.'

'Why did you?' Aleera asked hesitantly.

Jasmine took a moment to reply. 'I wanted to see you,' she finally said. 'I still did, after everything, and- and you just didn't think about that, did you?'

That pit opened even wider.

'I loved you,' Jasmine sniffed, and Aleera realised she was faintly crying. 'I still think of stupid reasons to pick up the phone and call you, just so I can see you for five minutes.'

Aleera's eyes lidded involuntarily. The music playing did nothing to end the silence.

'I just- I don't believe this,' Jasmine said shakily, turning round and leaning back on her wardrobe. 'My mom- every night, she just used to sit downstairs and drink and pretend that my dad didn't cheat on her, and that he still loved her, and she just sat there being stupid and lying to herself that everything was fine and- and I told myself I wouldn't do that. I didn't think I could just be that blind.'

The room grew quieter still. That pit continued to widen.

'I should go,' Aleera said after a while.

'Yeah,' Jasmine said. 'I think so.'

There was nothing left to say. Aleera stood up, picked up her bag and left.

24

Aleera moved her tongue around in her mouth to get rid of the old, stale taste of the tongue depressor.

'Well, based on today and the blood sample we took when you were in here before,' Tomoko said, 'I'd say you're fine. The scarring's settled nicely, too.' It was true; what had been thick burns a few days ago were now little more than a few lines of discoloured oval shapes.

'Does that mean I can come back to work?' Aleera asked.

She'd previously booked herself in for a full physical in the Guild's medical facility. Lilith had had to allow it, since by the time she found out Aleera was already leaving to attend.

'I can't say I'd recommend it,' Tomoko replied, 'but it'd be doable.'

'You are not starting yet,' Lilith replied from her other side. She'd insisted on coming, of course. Aleera had more or less expected it.

'I just need to get out for a few hours a day,' Aleera insisted. She was, after all, going uncharacteristically stir-crazy.

'Chances are, you wouldn't be directly involved in much,' Tomoko admitted, 'that's why I was free to do this. We haven't had anything positive since a while before you were attacked.'

'Guiding light of the supernatural world,' Lilith muttered under her breath. 'Aleera, you are not going back.'

'I can deal with it,' Aleera insisted. 'Besides, I'll still be working with Jake, right?'

'Yeah, because he did so much good the last time you were in here,' Lilith snapped.

'I'm going back to work,' Aleera said simply. 'That's that.' She stood up, put her shirt back on and picked up her pass.

'Aleera!' Lilith called after her as she walked out. 'Aleera, wait a minute!'

'I know what I'm doing,' Aleera replied sharply, 'so just relax.'

'Oh, yeah. Relax. I can do that. Are you out of your fucking mind?'

Actually, that was possible. 'You can't stop me from coming back to work,' she said cuttingly, and then instantly regretted it. Just lucky for her that Lilith knew her too well.

'What's it gonna do for you?' she said as she followed her.

'What?'

'You know what.'

Aleera stopped and turned round. Lilith had a point. While Aleera didn't mind that, she never liked it when other people's points proved hers to be wrong.

'You're doing this to find those wraiths, aren't you?' Lilith asked.

'I don't know what you mean,' Aleera said. Wow, now that really was a weak defence. Really, she should be ashamed of herself for relying on that one.

'What have I always said to you, Aleera?' Lilith asked, arms folded. 'Don't take me for an idiot. I know you, and I'd have to have been pretty damn stupid not to know you were here yesterday. And I'm not going to get mad, because I know changing your mind is like trying to break down a brick wall with my face. My point is: I know what you're trying to do. You're trying to find the wraiths. *That* wraith.'

Aleera's eyes turned down without her permission. Hardly surprising, really, that she should have worked that out, even if it did make her feel that much worse.

Jesus Christ, she thought, but she was a fucked-up girl. Lying to one of the few people who gave a shit that she was alive so that she could work her way towards killing something. She felt low, probably deservedly.

'You think I shouldn't?' Aleera said. It wasn't a rebuttal of any kind.

'What do you think?' Lilith asked. 'Would it help if you tracked it down?'

Aleera bit her bottom lip and folded her arms. She felt suddenly hollow.

'And be honest with me,' Lilith said gently.

Aleera hesitated. The true answer forced its way out. 'Maybe,' she said.

Lilith's face said it for her. Somehow she looked cold.

'They're going to kill people,' Aleera said weakly. It didn't even need to be said that it wasn't her reason.

'Are you scared?' Aleera asked.

'No.'

'You look it.'

'I know.'

'I can deal with this,' Aleera said, 'once this is over, Jake can get me out, and the Guild can just go to hell.' It seemed like there was something more to be said. 'I don't want to stay here,' she said. 'But the faster this ends, the faster I can get out.'

Lilith nodded slowly. 'I'll see you at home, then,' she said.

'Alright.'

Lilith left silently. There, then. She'd see her sister later, and before long everything would be fine. So what was that pit still doing there?

God, she hated this. She hated being such a twisted little monster. She hated the bastard Guild for bringing this on her. And she *really* hated those fucking wraiths!

And then something clicked.

Find the wraiths.

Like they found her.

They'd found her. They'd known where to look. They'd known who to look for. All fair enough. But…

What was it that she'd heard about wraiths? They tended to set up a hideaway. Right. And they didn't stray too far from it. So where she was attacked, that would have to be…

The lair would have to have been near the prey.

Idea.

She took right off down the corridor. Everything shot by in a blur until she found Jake's office and practically kicked the door off its hinges.

When that happened, Katya nearly fell off her chair and Jake dropped his old coin to the floor. 'Aleera?'

'Idea,' Aleera said quickly. 'I need a map.'

'What are you doing here?' Jake asked as he started printing something off. He knew better than to argue when Aleera was talking that quickly. 'What map?'

'Where I was attacked,' Aleera replied hastily, 'and Tom Smith's penthouse.'

Jake's face froze into a gasp of realisation as the answer struck him. He immediately called the information up on the screen, his fingertips dancing over the keyboard.

'So, about the question?' Katya fished.

'Back on duty,' Aleera answered quickly, 'as of today.' There, that was the exposition lightning round out of the way. She snatched up the map as soon as it was out of the printer and picked up a marker from the desk. Her dark, intense eyes scanned over the map as she circled first Tom Smith's penthouse, then Chloe Mcrae's apartment.

At least half a mile from each other.

Aleera shook her head. She'd known it to be a long shot. The wraiths wouldn't have gone across all that distance. They were still moving from place to place. They still couldn't find them down there, skulking through the sewage...

Another idea.

'Sewer map,' she said urgently. A claw managed to sneak out and scratch anxiously at the desk's surface as she pulled it out of the machine and placed it on top of the other map.

Her dark eyes lit up.

'Take a look,' she said, handing Jake the maps.

'Anybody gonna bring the resident cat-girl up to speed?' Katya piped up.

'The wraiths won't stray far from their lair, nest, whatever,' Jake said at lightning speed. 'We thought they were still moving because of the distance between the penthouse and the apartment.'

'Ok, and...?'

'And we never thought of this,' Jake explained, 'they're hiding out in the sewers, and the sewers under this city run for miles. You'd never believe the size of some of them. And as it happens, those two very far apart, very different places,' he held up the maps, 'are on the same sewer line. They're still in the same place, somewhere along this tunnel.'

'Which means,' Aleera prompted.

Katya's feline ears perked up. 'We've got them?' she squeaked.

'We should go to Cassidy with this,' Jake said. 'It'll bust this whole thing.'

'You two go,' Aleera suggested. 'He'll probably be more likely to listen to you.' It was probably the more advisable course of action, considering that Daniel Cassidy didn't seem to hold her opinion in high esteem. She wondered, was he really the sort to jeopardise something like this over a grudge?

Yes, it seemed more than likely.

Jake and Katya left quickly, and that was that. Aleera couldn't help feeling a little pinch of pride, noting that she may well have just led to the solving of her first case.

And the entire Eighth Division, with assistance from Special Ops, couldn't figure out where those things had been.

Lilith's sideways comment seemed to have been richly deserved; was the safety of the magical community really in these hands? Because… damn.

Cassidy leaned forward, resting his arms on the desk. He glanced coldly from Jake to Katya, and then back again.

'It hardly seems likely,' he finally said.

'But it *is* possible,' Jake pointed out. 'It makes sense; it's a single sewer tunnel that stretches for more than long enough with a million and one sections that nobody's been into for years.'

Cassidy mused for a moment. 'Whose idea was this?'

'Aleera Maheste's,' Jake said. Cassidy almost seemed to flinch.

'Right,' he finally said.

'It's the best chance we've had so far,' Jake said. It was a good argument, but it suddenly sounded much weaker than it probably should have.

'How long were they in their last hideaway?' Cassidy asked monotonously.

'A little under a week, best guess,' Jake answered. 'There could still be time; they're not going to know we've found them.'

Cassidy leaned back in his seat.

'I think we should wait for a more professional opinion,' he finally said, turning down to some papers. 'I'll get back to you.'

'Don't you dare.'

Cassidy looked up. 'Excuse me?'

'Cut the shit and tell me why you really didn't just listen,' Jake ordered.

'We need a professional opinion if we're going to undertake another operation like that, especially with the High Council still poking their noses in. It's called "politics".'

'If I'd said that I'd thought of it, or Makian, you'd be marching up to Hartwell or Khazahn to draw up a strategy right now,' Jake said. 'Answer me that.'

'Well forgive me for not jeopardising another squad of men on the advice of a rookie,' Cassidy said bitingly.

'No, you're just risking this entire case because you're a fucking overgrown child!' Jake spat.

Cassidy near-leapt to his feet.

'Question my judgement again, Connolly,' he seethed, 'and we'll see how long it takes for an immortal to rot in one of those cells.'

'Call it in! Or if you want a "professional opinion", run it by an officer. This is sound, and you know it. The only reason-'

'Get out of my office.'

'The only reason you're not listening-'

'Get out now, or I will call security.'

'-is because this came from Aleera.'

'Out!'

Jake fell silent.

'Think about it,' he finally said. 'Since I've done my part even if you're not listening, I'll be going.' He walked out slowly, and Katya followed. When Katya reached the door, she paused and glanced back at him. Something approaching a wry smile briefly crossed her face.

'What?' Cassidy snapped.

'You were seriously the best they could find?' Katya asked.

'Excuse me?' Cassidy replied in a "why are you talking?" tone.

Katya's eyes narrowed. 'Nothing,' she said, and then she followed Jake out of the office and left Cassidy to get back to his work.

25

With little else to do, Aleera had decided to wander the Guild Headquarters for a little while. She noted that she probably should be getting back home soon, but she found herself oddly reluctant. There was still that odd little thrill to be had, knowing that she'd already done better at this job than the entire unit.

Yes, that was why she was still here. Congratulations, her excuse actually made her sound worse than the real reason.

Well, alright, maybe it might be just a little bit awkward talking to Lilith. Still, she'd always been good at looking at things objectively, and it wasn't something she could put off forever.

Hmm- she and Jake hardly spoke, she'd upset Lilith yet again, and her first relationship in months went down like an exceptionally heavy lead balloon. She really wasn't good at this relationship stuff.

In fact, she realised then that she'd barely thought about any of it since the wraith attack. That seemed to say enough about her.

Thus far, she'd convinced herself that she'd been feeling low as another one of her side-effects. It seemed less and less plausible as time went by.

On her impromptu trip, she came across the open door of Khazahn's office. Well, she could probably kill another ten minutes or so before having to go back and face the music.

Khazahn was sitting behind the stone desk, typing something on his computer. He glanced up at her. 'Come in,' he said levelly.

Of course, this wasn't just an exercise in time-wasting. She would make sure to bear in mind that she didn't know the exact level of innocence of the other party in the encroaching conversation.

Still, Aleera liked to think of herself as a scalpel; Vicious and rather painful under the right circumstances, but also able to probe into the little nooks and crannies.

'I heard about what happened,' Khazahn said, glancing at her neck. Even considering all else, there did seem to be some genuine honesty in his voice. 'How are you feeling?'

'Well enough,' Aleera replied, 'I'm back on.'

'Already?' There it was. Pleasant, but just a tiny bit of worry.

'Just started,' Aleera said, idly examining the cover of a copy of *Faust* that was lying on the table. 'How's the job going?'

'Bad,' Khazahn said bluntly. Not much said there.

'I heard about what happened with Rick Lawson,' Aleera said tentatively.

'Yes,' Khazahn said. His gaze remained intently fixed on the computer screen. 'Our lowest moment, you might say.' Just ambiguous enough.

He was tense. Anxious. Waiting, like a coiled-up spring. These were hardly even professional techniques that Aleera was using; he was practically screaming to confess to somebody. He was guilty as sin.

And he was scared. Desperate, even.

'Anyway,' Aleera said. Ok, now this would be the pinch. 'Apparently we received a CD from a witness the other day.'

Khazahn looked up just a little bit quickly. 'Did we?'

Aleera nodded. Khazahn's eyes were unfocused. Trying to find something other than her to look at.

Khazahn, what have you done?

'Yes,' she said, 'it turned out that it wasn't that helpful.'

There. That slight deflation. Like a weight lifted. Unmistakable relief.

'Shame,' he lied. 'It could have helped. Do we know what might have been on it?'

'Lawson's murder,' Aleera replied.

'Really?' A slightly higher-than-normal pitch in the voice there.

'Jake believes that whoever was responsible could have known who gave Lawson the briefcase that was in the photo. He thinks they might know the reason behind our wraith problem.'

'If only,' Khazahn said with a synthetic sigh.

Nice try. The main was scared out of his wits.

'The witness was interviewed, apparently,' Aleera said. 'It was his girlfriend.'

Khazahn looked down in a different kind of remorse than the bereavement over a fallen soldier. 'I see.'

It was all there, wrapped up and stamped.

He was guilty. But he was also… repentant. And afraid.

Khazahn turned away, covered his mouth and coughed.

Desperation, Aleera thought.

'Well, I should probably be going,' Aleera said quickly. 'It's about time I left.'

'Alright,' Khazahn spluttered. As Aleera was above to leave, it turned into a fit of hacking into a tissue.

'How's the…?' she started.

'Still as terminal as ever,' Khazahn replied simply. 'Shouldn't think I'll be in the line of duty for long.'

Aleera wondered if she should feel guilty for engaging in impromptu espionage with someone in his condition. 'I haven't told Jake,' she offered.

'Thank you,' Khazahn said croakily. 'I think everyone's got enough to deal with right now.'

Aleera thought on this.

'Yes,' she said, 'I suppose so.'

Aleera's mind had been virtually tripping over itself since she walked out of Khazahn's office, all with thoughts of Wraiths and Kheron and Pentagram. And, eventually, something had, out of the clear sky blue, presented itself.

Khazahn wouldn't confess. Whatever he was doing, he was risking all to do it. He'd not throw it away for the sake of preserving his guilty conscience. But she did know someone else, who, if the wind was in the right direction, just might be in the mood to divulge something.

It had remained, understandably, forgotten, stuffed into her locker at the Guild, if only because the location to which the ticket permitted entry was her least favourite of destinations. People always had a tendency to forget the little things, but now there it was, and after lying awake reflecting on Kheron's involvement in all that come to pass of late, the idea had finally struck Aleera to make use of her private Deus Ex Machine.

Because on her first day in the Guild, Kheron had handed her a V.I.P. ticket to Pentagram, and she intended to make use of it.

The idea was massive, unwieldy and insane on a number of other levels, but nothing quite ruled out the possibility that, just possibly, Kheron had wanted her to be at Pentagram at the appropriate time. All those cryptic clues, his hints to a snake in the fold or a wolf in the grass or what have you, he was playing against Khazahn. Of course he was. The man was a monster, not an idiot. Dirty money or no dirty money, you didn't get to his position by being stupid.

So maybe, just maybe, he would be ready to talk by now. If she'd figured out that the wraiths were steeling themselves up for something, it stood to reason that he'd have worked it out by now.

Thanks to a well-functioning pair of wings and an invisibility spell, she arrived at Pentagram before long, fortunately with no more incidents like her more memorable recent flight. She landed in the middle of the dank back-alley, silently thankful that she'd worn something with a low back. She didn't feel like taking anything on within a several-hundred-foot radius of Pentagram.

The doorman tried to stop her on first sight, before she held out the small ticket. She'd considered doing something belligerent when she felt his hand on her backside on the way in, but decided against it for now. This visit could well prove monumentally important, and it wouldn't have helped to anger the man in charge of deciding whether she entered or not.

Besides, she could always give him a good kicking if he tried it again on the way out.

Inside the club, the pounding music was deafening, and the area around the dance floor (more appropriately labelled the "grind against each other" floor) was virtually impossible to navigate thanks to the darkness, crowd and flashing red light. Alas, whatever twisted sense of humour passed for the gods clearly smiled upon her, as she managed to find the stairs without more than one person offering her a suspicious-smelling drink.

When she found it, she had to admit that the V.I.P. lounge was a different place altogether, though primarily in that it reeked of a higher class of drugs and sex. Still, she couldn't help noticing one or two of the young women on the payroll. She counted about three or four succubae in all.

'Aleera,' Kheron greeted her as he looked up. 'So glad you accepted my invitation.'

Well, this was it. Aleera silently prayed that she would get through however long this took and still resist the urge to smash his face in.

'I need to talk,' she said sharply.

'I thought as much,' Kheron chuckled. He stood up and led Aleera out of the V.I.P. room, across the small corridor and into his office.

In here, it wasn't quite as bad. It was probably the only room in the place that was furnished with even a remote amount of taste. Kheron's turntable sat in the corner, playing quietly to itself.

Aleera showed the best manners that could probably be asked of her under the circumstances, waiting politely as Kheron seated himself and gave Leonardo a scratch behind the ears.

'So,' he finally said, 'what can I do for you?'

'Rick Lawson,' Aleera said sharply.

'You're a little bit late for that,' Kheron replied with a half-chuckle.

'What was he doing here?'

Kheron sighed, shook his head and leaned forward. 'What do you know?'

'Khazahn.'

Kheron looked up at her. He gave a wry smile. 'Your father always did say you were a clever one.'

Aleera let the "F"-word slide for now. 'What was he doing?'

'Breaking the rules,' Kheron said in mock disgust. 'God only knows why, but your friend Khazahn has taken it upon himself to take our long-standing game of metaphorical chess to the next level, and he's ended up shooting himself in the foot because you, Jake and your associates are such a clever bunch. Which is a shame, because I always enjoyed our encounters.'

'Did Khazahn kill Rick Lawson?' Aleera demanded.

Kheron tented his fingers. 'No idea.'

'Don't play games with me,' Aleera said darkly, turning her irises blood-red.

'I'm not psychic,' Kheron said bluntly, 'though I have to say, it'd make sense. The whole thing was his doing, after all.'

'What do you mean by that?' No, really, what did he mean by that? Because this could very well be it.

'You don't know,' Kheron grinned faintly. 'Well, I suppose that does explain why he's not in jail yet.'

'What does?'

'He's overplayed his hand,' Kheron said quietly, 'he tried to do something big, and it backfired. So he destroys the evidence, because if what he's been up to were to get out, he would be finished.'

'What. Did. He. Do?' Aleera leaned over the desk.

Kheron chuckled faintly. He pulled open a drawer, reached in and produced a large, brown envelope.

Aleera surveyed it for a moment. 'And in return?'

'Nothing at all,' Kheron smiled dryly, 'I'm just glad to have done my civic duty.'

Aleera took the folder.

'Now, if you'll excuse me,' Kheron said as he stood up and opened the door, 'I have a gorgeous young blonde awaiting my attention.'

Aleera left silently, walking away from the doors. As the pounding bass of the dance floor began to encroach on the edges of her hearing, opened the envelope and pulled out its contents.

Photographs. Five of them, all showing the same thing.

Khazahn, from a number of high angles, handing an open briefcase to Rick Lawson. An open briefcase full of random, indiscriminate objects.

Enchanted objects, Aleera realised. Must be. Black market.

Immediately, her cold computer of a brain took in all of the clues, arranging them into one tiny, neat little pattern.

Of course.

She felt sick. The realisation was huge, mad and terrible.

Khazahn had given Rick Lawson black-market magical items. Dark magic. And he'd passed them on to Kheron, who'd had Tom Smith distribute them.

And black magic consumed people. Ate away at them. Tore out their souls and changed them. That was how they became wraiths.

Oh God, that was it, wasn't it? That was so clearly, obviously it. Desperation led to this sort of thing. So desperate to catch Kheron, so desperate to tie up that one loose end in the time he had remaining…

So desperate that he'd do something like this. A frame-up. Maybe permissible under circumstances, but one that had long-since grown out of control.

Still salvageable, though, because the wraiths would blame Kheron. And then the worst thought sank in, because if the Guild did a bad enough job of tracking them down, nothing would stop them from slaughtering Kheron and everything he had to his name. All he had to do was make sure it was untraceable.

But his little toy soldiers had been too good. They'd found what he'd so struggled to hide. They'd found proof of his dirty dealings, so then, with so little time left, he'd had no choice, and Rick Lawson had to die.

It couldn't be. Khazahn wouldn't do this.

Unless he was desperate. And realising how Kheron had manipulated him, maybe that would be just enough to send him over the edge.

She wanted to be wrong. She tried to find some way to make it all not make sense.

God, he-

This was too much. It was insane. These were supposed to be the- it couldn't be-

'Surprised?'

Aleera whirled round. There was Kheron, leaning against the wall.

'You knew,' Aleera seethed, 'you knew about this!'

'To some extent. Took me a while to make the connection, so I do have to give the man credit.'

Aleera tried to say something. Some kind of reasoning, some argument. Nothing came out.

'Oh, don't look like that,' Kheron chuckled, 'I told you: these aren't the good guys. They just like to think they are. What, you think Khazahn wouldn't do this?' he chuckled again and stepped forward, hands in his pockets, 'that's what happens. People are wronged, or they get desperate, and… well, you've seen it, haven't you? How insane people will get. How self-destructive. Just look at yourself,' he grimaced, 'I bet I can guess what the one thing on your mind's been since that wraith nearly sucked it out. Am I right?'

Aleera flinched. The pit in her stomach widened, and something inside started screaming.

'But just look at this,' Kheron chuckled, 'lucky you. You get to be the good girl. Hand that in, expose everything and send the bad guy down.'

Then the realisation hit. Of course he wanted her to hand this information in. Do his job for him. Again.

'No,' she said flatly.

'Fine,' Kheron shrugged, 'let Khazahn get away with it. Let him try something even more stupid than this.'

Oh God-

Aleera felt herself tremble. He was right. Dear sweet God, he was right.

It couldn't be. How could this, doing something for someone like Kheron, how could that be right? How-

God-

Aleera turned and ran to the door. Kheron sighed, shaking his head.

'Sorry, kiddo,' he muttered, 'them's the breaks.'

Aleera couldn't get out of there fast enough. As she reached the door, the smell of the stagnant, garbage-carrying air was almost fresh.

The metal door creaked open. She gasped, still trembling. For God's sake, she was barely eighteen, how the hell was she supposed to do this?

She felt the doorman's hand on her ass again. Like lightning, all that mindless, all-consuming anger focused itself and lashed out like a coiled-up snake.

The six-and-a-half-foot wall of muscle that was Pentagram's security could never have expected it. There was no way he could anticipate Aleera pulling his hand straight down, the rest of his unprepared body with it, striking her knee into his face, and then…

When the doorman looked up with the savage snarl of a kicked Labrador, something with Aleera's face and mad, black eyes looked down, gave a maddened, primal scream of '*Eiah!*' and, with an invisible wave, sent him flying across the alleyway hard enough to crack the brickwork on the other side.

Aleera froze as soon as she heard the sickening "crunch". Everything turned cold. She felt something hot and acidic in her throat.

Then the doorman groaned, a faint, pathetic sign of life.

What had she almost- what *had* she done?

Eiah. She'd said it. Dark.

That wraith- damn it, what had it woken up?

Sick to her stomach, she turned, unfolded her wings, cast '*Tyasans*' and took flight.

Calm down. Damn it, calm down!

Aleera had been telling herself that since she left Pentagram. Eventually, it had started to sink in.

Just her "problem", she told herself. All that anger, all that confusion just looking for an outlet. It was just that, this time, she didn't have time to prepare herself for it. It had been random. Unexpected.

And now it had passed, and she'd be fine. Yes, that was it. Now calm down.

Eventually, as she'd arrived, her heartbeat had settled and reason was nonchalantly creeping back into the chaos of her head.

Night was long settled in when Aleera arrived home. A cursory check of her watch informed that it was approaching eleven p.m. Hence, she entered as discreetly as possible. She needed a drink of water, or anything, really. Just to calm herself down.

There we go, she thought as she slowly opened the door. Nice and calm. Nice and controlled.

It was funny, she noted as she made her way slowly through the living room, how things always looked different in the dark. All the smiling faces on magazines and indiscriminate shapes in windows never seemed to be on her side when the lights went out.

She crept over towards the door to her room and, to her credit, felt that she did so very stealthily indeed. It was the kind of skill that generally went hand-in-hand with an affinity for invisibility spells. She was about there when a clicking sound filled the room with painfully bright light.

'Aleera?' Lilith said groggily sitting up on the sofa. Staying up waiting for her; that was just like Lilith.

'I thought you were in bed kind of early,' Aleera said in an effort to establish some manner of dialogue.

'Got a little tired out while you were at work,' Lilith admitted. Ah, so she'd had another young man or woman over. It was something you just got used to with Lilith.

Aleera twiddled her thumbs behind her back as she walked over and sat down on the sofa. Christ, but this was going to be an awkward one.

'I'm sorry about what happened earlier,' she said.

'It's alright,' Lilith said in a shallow breath.

Aleera looked at the floor. There was one thought that had been weighing on her mind all day, and it wasn't a particularly pleasant one.

'Lilith,' she said, 'do you worry about me?'

'Of course I do,' Lilith sighed, sidling up next to her. 'You're my baby sister, remember?'

'I mean *worry*,' Aleera said. 'About the way I am.'

Lilith's face fell. Aleera's... tendencies... were known between them. Of course they were; Lilith knew her better than anyone. But as a general rule of thumb, they were never discussed.

'Sometimes,' Lilith finally said in a hollow voice.

Aleera didn't say anything.

'I still love you,' Lilith said. 'I mean that.'

'I know,' Aleera answered. 'But you know that I'm...'

'Aleera,' Lilith said, more fiercely now, 'I've seen all the papers that random idiots have written on you, and I don't give a fuck about what they say in any of them. You're my baby sister, and nothing changes that. Ever.'

'They're right, though,' Aleera said. She didn't really need to justify the statement. Both of them knew it.

'I don't care,' Lilith declared.

'Maybe you should,' Aleera said quietly.

Lilith sighed. 'Remember when you were a kid?' she asked, 'and we spent all day at my friend's place making a chocolate cake?'

Aleera remembered. It was one of the few happy memories she had.

'Far as I'm concerned,' Lilith said, 'that's who you are. When they wrote all that shit about you, you were still my sister, and you're not a bad person. You're not.'

That nagging part of Aleera still didn't quite know who Lilith was trying to convince.

'I can't-' Lilith held something back for a second, 'I can't think that you're a bad person, alright? I just can't.'

Aleera decided against saying anything else. 'I'm sorry,' she finally said. 'I really am.'

'It's Ok,' Lilith said tenderly.

'I really didn't want to upset you earlier,' Aleera said, resting her head on her sister's shoulder.

'I know.'

'I mean it.' And she did. Lilith was the last person in the world she would ever deliberately hurt. 'I just…' she stopped. No, she didn't need to hear this.

'Go on,' Lilith said.

'I just get mad sometimes,' Aleera said, deciding to simplify the matter. 'Especially lately.'

'You want to tell me about it?' Lilith asked.

She could. She could tell her all about how, just sometimes, there would be that feeling, that desire, that urge to hurt someone. Not necessarily kill, but just some dark thing inside her that honest-to-God wanted to do harm to somebody. That something evil.

'It's fine,' she said. That could definitely wait until another day.

'Ok,' Lilith answered, giving her a gentle kiss on the forehead. 'Better?'

Aleera nodded sheepishly. 'Better.'

'Good. Now get yourself to bed,' Lilith smiled.

Aleera smiled back, stood up, stretched briefly and retired to her room. It had been a long day, and even she had to admit that there was a lot to be said for the appeal of a solid night's sleep.

She undressed, turned of the lights and climbed into bed.
As the lights went out, that dark thing stirred.

26

It was one of those mornings where you wake up grudgingly. Yet again, it had been far from a flawless night, even if this time there weren't quite as many nightmares to put up with. Still, Aleera felt at least marginally better than when she went to bed.

It was also, she vaguely recalled, Friday. Almost a whole four weeks had now passed.

One thing she'd definitely thought about doing was dropping into the Guild, if only to see how well her search suggestion had gone down. Still, her hours nevertheless started at four whether she was in school during the rest of the day or not, so it gave her time to grab a decent breakfast.

It had been a while, Aleera reflected, since she'd really been able to sit down to a proper meal. It had somewhat taken a back seat in light of all the rest of the chaos. She had plenty of time to prepare as well, after waking up at about six.

She'd considered the irony a few times that her favourite pastime was something as inherently wholesome as cooking, when considering her dual lineages she should probably be sex and violence personified. But it had always been a good way for her to forget her troubles, and there was no denying the fact that lately she did have quite a bit of forgetting to do. Her most beloved way to waste a few hours was to lock herself away in her own little space, taking whatever was in the fridge and make something out of it.

She should probably have been on pins and needles, considering that this could very well be the day on which she concluded her first case. Imagine that: her, the devil's daughter, being the one to negate the threat. She'd love to see the expression on the High Council's collective face if it turned out like that.

Nevertheless, all else was pushed to the side in favour of settling on a Spanish omelette accompanied by two slices of toast, the latter mainly to have something to slather in that most wondrous of things that God in his wisdom had named honey.

Besides, she'd need a good breakfast under her belt for today, because she'd at least made up her mind. As much as she hated the idea, Jake needed to see this. He knew Khazahn, and the situation, better than she did. She'd show him the photos, and the final judgement could be his with no blood to wash off of her own hands. Done.

After breakfast and a shower, she left the house and arrived at the Guild's headquarters in an hour or so.

Well, this was it.

A quick trip to the roof, then down in the elevator, and here she was, all ready to go.

Now, where was Jake's…

Oh.

The entire building was, almost literally, abuzz. Black-cloaked figures scurried in every applicable directions; some barking orders, some taking them and others apparently just trying to look busy.

Immediately, there was only one reason for this that Aleera could come to think of and it began with "w" and ended in "raiths". Maybe her little idea really had been taken seriously.

She managed to navigate a path through the crowd until she found Jake's office. Most likely, she'd have to get into uniform any moment now, but for now, this would take precedence. It wasn't like the presence of one already possible-traumatised demon/succubus was likely to make that much difference.

'Private Maheste,' Cassidy's voice said just as she was reaching for the door. Of course, she only really knew one person who addressed her that formally.

'Sergeant,' she replied.

'When did you get here?' Cassidy asked.

'Just now. I've been back on duty since yesterday,' Aleera said politely. 'What's going on?' she asked, feigning innocence. The visible vein on Cassidy's forehead was well worth any potential repercussion.

'Your lead on the wraiths,' Cassidy said. To his credit, he managed to get through the sentence without swearing, which looked to have been quite some feat. 'We're moving in today. Safer searching during daylight hours.'

'Oh.' Well. She could get used to this, being listened to. 'Well, good.'

'Right,' Cassidy said with more forced civility, 'I'll expect to see you in the briefing. Thirty minutes, if you can control your temper,' he said as he stepped past.

'Excuse me?' Well, it was understandable really; of course the idiot was going to try and pick a fight.

'Kheron reported your assault on one of his bodyguards last night,' Cassidy replied simply. 'I suppose you wouldn't know anything about that.'

'Self-defence,' Aleera said, thinking on her feet.

Cassidy looked at her with an expression she didn't like one bit. 'Well, I'll thank you to keep yourself under control,' he said bluntly. 'Hardly surprising.'

'I beg your pardon?' Aleera said as he stepped away.

'You heard me,' Cassidy replied, without turning round.

'You're welcome,' Aleera shrugged, again reaching for the door. That would be it, she knew it. Oh, come on, do something, you-

She heard Cassidy marching up to her.

'Listen to me,' he snarled, 'you fucking-'

'Oh, grow up,' Aleera spat. Probably not a good idea, but she was far from being in the mood for this nonsense. 'Put it aside and actually concentrate on doing your job.'

She grabbed the door handle.

In the window, she saw Cassidy move.

She ducked and dodged to the side, sweeping away on one leg as Cassidy's fist struck and smashed the glass surface. Snarling, Cassidy turned after, and, quicker than she could follow, lashed out with one fist. The blow caught her hard on the cheek with a sharp, solid "thump". Aleera's vision blurred momentarily.

Damn, but that was fast. She'd even tried to block, but wow. That primitive part of her was impressed.

The dominant part of her, on the other hand, wanted to do something much worse in return.

It looked like it would get its chance as Cassidy pulled another arm back for another blow. Then all that changed as Cassidy was suddenly carried off his feet by something unseen, skidding to a stop as a crowd of soldiers parted.

Jake lowered his palm, the rush of wind ceasing.

'You vicious little bastard,' he growled.

'Oh, shut the fuck up, you self-righteous twat,' Cassidy snarled back, getting to his feet. Before he could do anything, a shimmering bolt of force flew between them.

'What the hell is this?' Colonel Hartwell demanded, lowering his staff. 'Huh? Anybody?'

Khazahn stepped out of the crowd. His eyes turned immediately to the discoloration starting to form on Aleera's face, and then to Cassidy.

'Cassidy,' he said darkly, 'office. Now.'

Cassidy turned away slowly. A dark, burning glare remained focused on Aleera. Then he walked away, slow murmurs rippling through the ranks.

'I think everybody has a job to do,' Hartwell snapped to the crowd, marching away as the sea of black armour parted.

The door into Jake's office opened again, with Katya being the next out. 'What happened?' she asked, before seeing Aleera's face. 'Oh my God…'

'What?' Makian asked as he followed her, 'oh shit, man, he didn't-'

In the quiet sea of murmurs, Jake moved unnoticed over to Aleera. 'Come on,' he suggested, 'we'll get you to Tomoko.'

'Alright,' Aleera nodded and followed. She could feel a damaged tooth, and her cheek was rapidly swelling. Fortunately, a few licensed enchanted objects were permitted to be used for healing spells in the medical facility.

Of course, now was probably as good a time as any.

'Here,' she said, handing Jake the envelope, 'you'd better take a look at that while we're in there.'

'Lemme see,' Katya said, taking the envelope and opening the top. She pulled out one of the photos, and her honey-coloured eyes widened. 'Oh…'

It wasn't far to the medical facility. Tomoko happened to be grabbing some supplies, and applied something to Aleera's face. The pain and swelling vanished in a matter of seconds as Katya anxiously handed the wad of photographs to Jake.

'Jesus,' Jake breathed, looking up at Aleera, 'where did you get these?'

'Kheron,' Aleera admitted. 'He left me a pass when he was here before. I think you were right; Khazahn's out to get him. I think he's behind this.'

'No,' Jake said immediately, 'no way.'

'Maybe not intentionally,' Aleera reasoned, 'but this would explain it. If this was some kind of sting operation, something off the records, Khazahn would know how to cover it up.'

'But why?' Jake insisted, 'what the hell would make him do something like this?'

Aleera didn't reply. Maybe she should have done, on reflection.

'Sorry,' Tomoko piped up, 'but I'm completely lost here- what, exactly, are we talking about?'

'I told her most of the stuff up to this,' Makian said helpfully, 'and when I was looking through the accountancy stuff,' all eyes turned to him, 'well, there was a decent-sized transfer from Khazahn's funds to two other officers.'

'Two?'

'Rick Lawson,' Makian said awkwardly, 'and Thraiel Lathos. Half-demon. Been A.W.O.L. ever since.'

'That didn't turn up in the records,' Jake said, before realising the implications of that for himself. Another cover-up. Maybe the worst part of Khazahn's mistake.

'So what now?' Katya asked after a long, heavy moment of silence.

'Now, hopefully, we find the wraiths,' Jake said emptily, placing the envelope inside his jacket, 'and then I deal with Khazahn.'

27

Aleera sat in the locker room, fiddling with one of the straps that were, rather badly, designed to secure her uniform's gauntlets. If she was going to be fighting wraiths, considering what had happened before, Jake had insisted.

On the plus side, she thought, she would hopefully be out of the damned thing by mid-afternoon. From what she'd gleamed, everything had been planned out and all was in readiness. A quick Search and Destroy, or Search and Recover, or Search and Something, mission was the order of the day.

And that was it. Oh, there'd be a few people there, sure enough, but for once nothing to get embarrassed over. Could anyone really be that upset with her for slicing a wraith open? In all fairness, she'd already done it twice and nobody seemed that upset with her.

That nagging voice again brought it to her attention that she was only thinking of killing something as something to be "embarrassed" by. She still hadn't stopped itching for a chance to tear into another of those things. It had been fun the first time, hadn't it?

Fun? No, not fun. Killing something wasn't "fun". Satisfying, maybe, but anything worse than breaking a limb, and even then only if its owner really had it coming to him, wasn't supposed to be "fun".

She still wanted to do it, though. She really did. The scars on her neck almost seemed to bristle.

It was fair, wasn't it? An eye for an eye and all that. Biblical, almost.

And yet, it oddly felt as though she was only thinking that she wanted to do it. Not really feeling it.

Then again, it was hard to be in the mood to unwind. That dull, heavy stillness in the air had remained ever since her talk with the others. That sense of impending wrongness.

That considered, the temperature, even if only for those immediately involved in the conversation, did seem to have dropped by a considerable number of degrees. This was going to be a difficult day; that much was certain. By the looks of it, though, at least this could be it.

Nonetheless, it hardly seemed to have the buzz she'd been expecting.

Aleera finished securing the gauntlets and, with the rest of the uniform now assembled, removed the metal helmet from her locker. For a moment, she held it in her hands, idly turning it and examining the reflection in its polished surface.

Something about her face looked different in the uniform. More severe, maybe. Colder. Darker. What was it that Kheron had said? The one thing that had been on her mind ever since the attack? It suddenly seemed that much harder to muster the enthusiasm.

It seemed her assumptions had been right; it wasn't such a nice feeling to be marching into battle and not be able to trust the man your orders were coming from.

She held the helmet under one arm and left the locker room. The walk to the briefing room was a short one, and when she arrived, it appeared that the delay between announcing the mission and starting the briefing had merely been a formality, as it was full to bursting point already.

With no small degree of effort, she eventually managed to find an unoccupied space against one of the walls. Even then, it was hard to see the front of the room thanks to the mass of black-clothed forms in front of her.

When the dull hubbub started to settle, Aleera stood on her tiptoes to peer over some heads and saw that Khazahn was standing at the front of the room, with Colonel Hartwell to one side. No sign, she noticed, of Daniel Cassidy.

That certainly did present a couple of possibilities. Well, it made her wonder about the consequences of his actions, anyway; something he may have done well to think about beforehand. Suspension, she seemed to recall Jake mention, was the penalty for assault, and that was only if she didn't press charges. Luckily for him, even though she would gleefully admit to being rather pleased to see him get the book thrown at him, if only figuratively, she wasn't quite vindictive enough to try to cost him his job. It was far too much fun to get him worked up instead.

The last of the noise died down, and Hartwell stepped forward, hands behind his back, and gave a couple of cold glances around the room.

'That everybody?' Hartwell asked sharply as Aleera found an empty space amongst the sea of soldiers. 'Right. We're moving fast here, so I'll keep this brief: Commander Khazahn and I will be spearheading this operation. There will be a total of thirty soldiers and seven Special Ops members involved, and the Captains of your individual units will issue direct instructions.' So he was shoehorning his Special Ops men in again, Aleera noted. Probably more to save face than anything else, although judging from their prior performance it was frankly staggering that the High Council was letting them anywhere near the investigation.

At the press of a button, the display screen behind Hartwell lit up with part of a very recognisable sewer map. It was still odd getting used to this "being listened to" business. Aleera could imagine herself getting used to it, though.

'We believe the targets to be in this area,' Hartwell went on, and as if by magic a relatively small alcove was coloured vivid red. 'Specified members will be prepared to active *Sola* spells immediately.' Well, obvious enough. Wraiths don't like light, that about summed it up. It had worked well enough for Aleera, anyway.

Except that this time, she recalled, there would be about a dozen of the things. The annoying memory resurfaced that they still didn't know exactly how many of the things they were hunting down, although as Jake had previously reasoned it to her, anything over a dozen wasn't that likely; they'd have had to come up for a larger meal were that the case.

Twelve of them at most, she thought, and they'd done all this. '

'The objective is Search, Recover and Kill if that becomes necessary,' Hartwell continued. 'I shouldn't have to remind anybody in this room that these things are about as dangerous as it gets, so caution is the obvious course. We do this quick, we do this safe. Any questions?'

There were none.

'Right,' Hartwell declared, 'report to myself or Commander Khazahn for positions.'

As he moved back, Aleera glanced over at Khazahn, still unmistakable. He was composed, alright, but almost overtly so; everything creaseless and tightly buttoned, with only the occasional wideness in his eyes to betray anything.

This really was going to be one to remember.

Almost time, Aleera thought to herself again. She, of course, was to be alongside Jake during the raid. With any luck, it would be a simple case of get in, kill/capture wraiths, and get out. Of course, whether they'd have any luck was debatable, considering the case so far.

On the way to his office, she passed the coffee machine and found Makian downing yet another cup. 'Isn't that hot?' she asked.

'Boiling,' Makian said, shoving the cup under the dispenser and putting another quarter in the machine.

'How many have you had?'

'Enough,' Makian said quickly.

'Are you alright?'

Makian hesitated. He took a deep breath. 'Yeah.' He finally said, 'yeah, I'm fine. Just... this is it, huh? Gonna go and kill us some wraiths... down there...' he shuddered.

'Makian?'

'It's nothing,' Makian blurted out quickly, 'just a little... shaken up. That's all. I'll be fine once it's over.'

Aleera let a few seconds of silence tick by. 'You don't have to go,' she said. 'You can tell Cassidy. He'll understand.'

'The fuck he will. Jesus...' he shook again, crumpling the coffee cup in his grip. 'Oh God,' he breathed, leaning on the machine. 'I'm not- fuck...'

'It's alright,' Aleera said in what she hoped was a soothing voice. 'Do you want me to get Jake or Tomoko?'

'No,' Makian blurted out, 'no, it- it's fine. Seriously.' He smiled weakly and walked off.

'Name?'

'Lieutenant Makian.'

The roster officer checked the clipboard. The room was still abuzz with activity. 'Nnno, there doesn't seem to be any Makian on here?'

'There isn't? I mean, this was the post I was given, so-'

'You're not on here,' the officer shrugged, turning over the paper.

'Wait-'

'There, see? I told you...'

'It says here you've been signed off the operation.'

Makian blinked. 'W-what?'

'Says here "health reasons". That sound right?'

Makian shook his head. 'Hold on.'

He walked away, striding quickly across the room, and soon found who he was looking for. She was easy enough to spot- just look for

Jake and the girl standing next to him being looked at unpleasantly by Sergeant Cassidy.

'Aleera,' he said, 'can I have a word?'

Aleera looked back at him. 'Sure. Jake, I'll be back in a second.'

'No problem,' Jake said, returning to his conversation with Cassidy.

They stopped once they were far enough away. 'You got me pulled off the operation?' Makian hissed.

Aleera turned her eyes down. 'I talked to Tomoko about it. She said it would be best if-'

'Best if I chickened out. Yeah, great. Really fucking brilliant, thanks.'

'It's not like that,' Aleera said. Well, now was the time to see if she could pull this kind of conversation off. 'You're not ready.'

'What's that supposed to mean?'

'Tomoko said "post-traumatic stress disorder". You lost four men. She said it was a normal reaction.'

'What, you could tell?'

'The way you were acting- yes. I could tell something was wrong.'

'Yeah,' Makian glared at her, in a moment of anger, and said 'because you'd know all about that, wouldn't you? Psyche report says you're *real* good at understanding what's up with other people.'

Aleera's stare turned cold. Immediately, Makian felt a swell of guilt as she followed her arms.

'Apparently,' she said icily.

'No- listen, kid, you know I don't- I didn't mean it like that.'

'You did,' Aleera said. 'I understand.' Actually, she did. Possibly more than any "professional" psychiatrist would. 'You're scared, and you've got good cause to be scared. You're so angry that you don't even know who to be angry at. That- I understand that,' she said. Well, here was the moment of truth. She reached up to the collar of her uniform and pulled it down just low enough to show the marks on her neck.

Makian nodded slowly. 'You're still going, though.'

'It took a lot of arguing with Jake. Besides...' she trailed off.

'Besides what?'

'Nothing. Look, I need to get back over to Jake.'

'Alright,' Makian said. He nodded again. 'And kid- thanks. I think- if I'd gone down there- that could've messed me up. So... thanks. That was... that was good of you, what you did there.'

Aleera gave a faint smile. 'No problem.'

As she turned round, Aleera thought over just why she was going down there and Makian wasn't. Like he'd said: if he'd gone down there, it would have messed him up. Maybe badly. But Aleera- well, she was more or less there already, wasn't she?

The sewer reeked.

Aleera probably would have covered her nose if it would have helped. The mask that prevented her from doing so didn't help much either. She heard a few of what she presumed to be new or rather pampered soldiers gagging. She felt like it herself, but as she often did with such things, she sharply told herself to deal with it and that she could take all the time she wanted to throw up when she didn't have more important things to do.

The Guild's approach was a classic Pincer movement; ten from one end, ten from another. Aleera was part of the larger group. When both arrived, the idea was that the wraiths would be penned in and turned into the near-dead, supernatural equivalent of wooden ducks in a shooting gallery.

No retreat for them, either. The duct was long-since sealed off and out of use. Aleera felt that shameful adrenaline start to rise again. That wicked little thrill of the hunt. Soon, she said to her twitching hands, taut around her staff, very soon now. The scars on her neck sizzled with anticipation.

Although part of her would just settle for not being knee-deep in raw sewage anymore, there was something just as satisfying a while ahead of her.

Daniel Cassidy, formally commanding one side of the operation, Khazahn on the other, while Hartwell coordinated things via radio. Occasionally he would glare icily at her, and Aleera would just look blankly back at him. According to a few whispers, he was looking at the potential loss of his job altogether.

Of course, Aleera had her scepticisms. There was no way the Guild would throw away a competent, if unpersonable, high-ranking and well-reputed officer for, well, Aleera.

On a similar note, she was still rather glad that Cassidy wasn't behind her.

After about two dozen more strides through the thick sewage, the unit came to a stop. 'Hunt, this is Hound-2,' Cassidy's voice hissed across the radio, 'in position.'

'Copy. Hound-1 in position,' Khazahn's voice replied.

This was it, then. No going back now.

And then Aleera realised that there wasn't a wraith in sight. They'd have seen them coming, no doubt. But they'd have no way of escaping. The only option that would leave was attack. If one of them was willing to jump out of a closet in front of a group of Guild soldiers for a quick meal, how much more confident should a dozen of them be?

And yet, the place was empty and silent. Not a sickening scream to be heard.

Were they wrong? Or too late yet again?

That dark little part of her that really hated frustration was about ready to tear the head of the nearest living thing. She steadied herself, focused and tried to convince herself that she was wrong.

The pungent alcove was just ahead. Shafts of light cut through the thick, inky blackness. The two groups of soldiers were less than twenty feet apart. At a silent gesture from each commander, they readied themselves.

'Hounds, move in,' Hartwell's voice crackled.

The soldiers moved as one. Staffs clicked and began to buzz with power to a chorus of rustling cloaks and sloshing sewage. Shouts of '*Sola*' rippled out, and Aleera herself had to squint before the sudden flush of dazzling white.

The light flooded an empty alcove.

Aleera glanced round as Cassidy barked to a couple of soldiers to search the room. It seemed he wouldn't be particularly cooperative when it came time to give up his position.

Perhaps an invisibility spell was in use, she thought. It was a stretch, but she still whispered '*Hthwail-Yeins*'; "third eye". That was the standard counter to basic invisibility. Her vision faded quickly into grainy black-and-white, with dull ripples around every movement. That was what happened when light bypassed the rods and cones; no colour. And in this case, no wraiths either.

Nothing.

Nothing!

'Nothing!' Cassidy snarled, kicking angrily at the sewage. 'The damn place is empty!' For a moment, Aleera could have sworn she saw him scowl at her. She wondered how long it might be before this would be her fault.

Then came the scream.

A soldier towards the back of the unit was grabbed, hurled backwards and into the churning sewer water as the screaming, decayed thing on top of him scratched and scraped at his armour.

'Jesus Fuck!' someone shouted. 'Kill it!' yelled another. The wraith's hands grabbed hold of the helmet, forcing it- and its open, not at all waterproof eyeholes- under the water.

Then, like an avenging bolt of lightning, the bolt of force shot out of nowhere, struck the wraith and carried it backwards into the wall. It hissed and spat, recoiling in the light as thirty-seven weapons focused on it. Some of them fired, the wraith diving into water as the brickwork shattered.

'Cease fire!' Cassidy barked, 'cease fire and stop this shit right now!'

The wraith surfaced, screeching, and was promptly kicked in the temple and sent falling sideways. Somewhere nearby, entirely unnoticed amidst the chance for blood, someone pulled its near-victim up out of the water.

'Move,' Cassidy said darkly to the snarling thing, 'and everyone in here will blow your damn head off.'

The wraith looked up. Sunken, dead eyes narrowed. Insects and grubs crawled around between rotten flesh. 'Too late,' it hissed, 'too late, Guild man.'

Cassidy's staff swung and collided with the side of its head. 'Where are the rest?' Cassidy demanded as the thing thrashed in the water.

'Too late,' the wraith said again in a voice that was almost a giggle, 'too late.'

'Where. Are. They?'

'Gone,' the wraith seethed, 'long gone. Left here long ago. Went to hunt.'

'*Where?*'

'The last one,' the wraith wheezed, pushing itself to its hands and knees. 'Last one. The big one. Couldn't go,' it wheezed and whimpers, 'didn't feed too long, couldn't…' it shook and almost seemed to sob, 'couldn't go. Too weak. Said they'd get him for me. Drag him back here, he said, said we'd all have a piece of him, but couldn't go, couldn't get him, too weak, didn't feed…'

'Get who?' Cassidy shouted. 'Get who?'

'Get *him*,' the wraith gasped weakly, 'get him for what he did. Tear out his soul. Tear out his because he poisoned ours,' it snarled. 'He tricked us, said all those things would help us. Tricked everybody, and Lathos said- he said we'd get him. Said we'd make him pay if it had to be the last thing we did. Tear out his soul, tear out his soul and eat his heart!'

'It's Kheron,' Aleera spoke up. Cassidy turned sharply to her. 'He's talking about Kheron.' Of course. Of course this would all lead back to him.

And again, they'd have to help him, because they were supposed to try and be "good" people. "Good" people who were about to carry out a hit for Kheron.

'Tonight,' the wraith spluttered, 'they drag him down tonight. Find him, kill him, eat his heart, eat his soul for what he did to ours!'

'How many?' Cassidy demanded. 'How many of them?'

The wraith looked up. It snarled, turning into a snicker of wicked delight. 'How many?' Cassidy roared, 'how many, you bastard?'

'Twelve,' the wraith wheezed, 'twelve in all.'

Aleera felt the shiver spread through the soldiers. Only twelve of them. Twenty-three deaths in a week, and it had been only twelve of them.

Cassidy stepped back. 'Get him back to headquarters, slap some cuffs on him and don't talk to me until we know where Kheron is,' he ordered to the room.

Behind him, the wraith stirred. With a burst of spraying sewage, it leapt up.

'*No!*' it screamed with the madness of death, 'no! We kill him tonight! We kill him for what he did!' it struck Cassidy, pushing him down into the water, scraping at his helmet and pushing it down under the water.

Now, that thing in Aleera's heart screamed, now! Kill it! Even Cassidy would have to thank her. Kill the wraith, humiliate Cassidy, and do it now! Kill something and be a damn heroine for it! Do it!

There was a sick, wet tearing noise. The wraith coughed, its eyes blank. It hunched forward, its arms stiff but still slipping off the helmet as Cassidy, with a gasp, rose from the sewage.

With another tear and a trail of thick, blackened blood, he pulled the end of the spear back out, chunks of dead flesh and brittle bone falling as the wraith collapsed into the dark, foul water. He paused, hands still tight around the staff as Aleera sensed what was going through his mind.

'Find out where Kheron is tonight,' he ordered. 'Now.'

They moved silently. No going back now. Nothing more after this. No going back. Nothing to go back to. So they would find him. He had taken their lives, and so they would take this.

He led them. It would be dark soon. Time to hunt. Time to feed.

28

Ah, now that buzz was there. It passed from one soldier to another in a ripple effect that soon flooded the entire headquarters with hushed whispers and nervous twitches. Even if it brought excitement for Aleera, for all others it carried apprehension and a stream of mounting dread.

Oh, but for her, for *her*, there was that rush. That promise of satisfaction, vengeance and vindication. They'd torn out her soul, and soon enough they'd have to rest of her to answer to. She could get her revenge, kill those things and be a heroine for it. Far too good to resist.

This was to be it, then: the final showdown, as it were. Whether they saved Kheron tonight or not, it would be the end of it.

Which, of course, led to the inevitable question of why, if the wraiths wouldn't have much left in them anyway, were they going to save Kheron?

Aleera had arrived at that question back in the sewers, and had been considering possible answers for a couple of hours. So far no acceptable answers had stood up to be accounted for. There were a couple that made sense, and were probably true, but none that were really good reasons. No reason Aleera could think of, essentially, not to just leave the bastard to it; as far as she was concerned, he deserved anything the wraiths could dish out.

Of course, she knew what he was going to feel. Oh, yes. She'd felt it herself. She idly traced the scars on her neck. Soon, she told herself, very soon, Kheron would feel what she'd felt, feel his life being sucked out of him as he was submerged in all of his worst horrors.

But would he? Would the Guild allow that, when, she reminded herself in disgust, half of them probably had his money in their pockets? Kheron, along with his influence, was everywhere, spreading like some lying, murdering cancer, and they were going to do nothing about it. They were going to stop it, and why?

Because with him gone, New York City would be a free-for-all. Because even if he went down, a dozen more would take his place. Because if he went down, he'd take half the supernatural dignitaries in the country with him.

And that was the real reason. It finally, really sank in, how Kheron had managed to carve out such a dark and far-reaching sphere of influence when at the top: because being at the top was all that was needed. If there was nothing to stop all the others from scrambling for the top, what you had was a tower of madness.

It hadn't just been planning the occasional heist that got him where he was; it was long-term planning. Understanding. Cunning. Politics. He'd arranged everything in the city so meticulously that, whatever he did, bringing him down would only mean trouble.

And that was what made him as dangerous as Guild and wraiths. They might be smart, they might be clever, but Kheron was *cunning*.

That twisted part of her couldn't help but admire that just a little bit. Most of her, on the other hand, just wished that she could rip Kheron's eyes out.

But none of that was the real reason. Maybe once upon a time, but since then it had evolved, mutated, changed. She knew the real reason as well as every one of them.

She'd spent the time since returning to headquarters arbitrarily visiting the staff canteen, remembering that she hadn't eaten since breakfast, and it seemed that the day was indeed one on which it would pay to keep her strength up. On the way out, she bumped into, surprisingly enough, one of the few people she tended to trust with any kind of moral quandary.

(Also, part of her noted, somewhere in the background, the irony of someone like her giving such consideration to morals).

'You doing Ok?' Jake asked.

'Not too bad,' Aleera said. 'Have we found Kheron?' It was probably best to introduce this particular topic with some diplomacy.

'His penthouse,' confirmed, 'at least, he'll be back there for about six, and it won't be dark by then.'

'And are we going to be there?'

'Looks like it,' Jake said. There was something deeply unhappy about his voice.

'So we're helping Kheron,' Aleera said. In all fairness, she was more summarising the conversation thus far than being confrontational.

'Yes,' Jake replied bleakly. 'I know.'

'Why?'

Jake shook his head. 'I don't think anybody around here's happy about it,' he said, 'but every rule that gets followed in this city comes crashing down like a pack of cards if Kheron gets taken out of the equation, and we just plain can't afford that.'

'I still don't see why we need to be there,' Aleera said bluntly. 'Kheron's got bodyguards. Hitmen. Assassins. Whatever he wants to call them.'

'He could get every gun on his payroll, and at least one of those wraiths could get through,' Jake said, 'they're determined. They've got nothing to loose.'

Aleera nodded in quiet understanding. She knew that feeling well enough. She'd been there before, as she recalled. The memory of hunting down Azrael came back to her, the feeling that she had nothing left to lose. With that came a feeling that there was no reason to hold back, or to let anything get in her way.

For the wraiths, it would likely be even worse. And there were eleven of them.

'Besides,' Jake said in open contempt for his surroundings, 'the High Council's been following this one from the start. If a cabal of wraiths tears down the only stabilising force in this city as big as us and we stand by, they'll come down like an atom bomb. The division's hanging by a thread as it is.'

Aleera gave no form of reply. She still knew the real reason, she thought bitterly.

'Jake,' Katya called, poking her head around the corner at the end of the hallway, 'Hartwell says "my office. Now".' Jake nodded and walked over. Aleera noticed that he was folding that old coin over his fingers.

'By the way,' she asked after him, 'what about Khazahn?' Jake had said, had he not, that the Eighth Division was hanging by a thread. Would he bring it crashing down over a personal vendetta?

Maybe. Jake knew right, he knew wrong, and he seemed to have something on his shoulder that never let him forget which was which. Khazahn hadn't just bent the rules this time; he hadn't just lied to him. This time, he'd done something truly terrible. Jake wouldn't let that go unpunished.

'I decided,' Jake answered as he walked away.

'And?'

Jake paused. For a moment he seemed to hesitate. He looked torn, as if trying to turn in three directions at once.

Khazahn had betrayed him before. Lied to him. That was something Jake didn't do. He didn't betray. When the Guild and the High Council had pressured and bullied him to betray Aleera, he hadn't betrayed her.

Loyalty. In the Jake Connolly English Dictionary, it was Page One. The Gospel virtue.

And here was that loyalty, and another loyalty, and the betrayal of that first loyalty.

'I decided "one crisis at a time",' he finally said, and with that, he walked away as Aleera stood in the middle of the corridor.

And that was that. One at a time.

First, she knew, would come the wraiths. That was the emergency at hand.

First, she reminded herself, they helped Kheron. They would actually have to help him.

And why?

Because someone did run the supernatural side of New York City, and it wasn't the Guild. The city was Kheron's, as was everything in it.

Because the sick truth was that Kheron, that lying, murdering, corrupting scum held sway over them all, because he was what they all were. Because what he'd told her had been absolutely right.

When the chips were down, they threw away their rules in a heartbeat, because when it was all boiled down to it, all that remained was the bad part.

'Evening soon.'

Kheron idly sipped at a glass of brandy as the turntable carried on its rendition of the Who's *Baba O'Riley*. He reclined in his favourite seat as Leo jumped onto his lap and curled up.

Kheron muttered something to himself and gave the cat a slow scratch behind the ears. It gave a sharp hiss, its fur standing on end.

'There, there,' Kheron said calmly, 'we'll be perfectly fine, isn't that right, gents?'

One of the men besides the door nodded. He was at least seven feet tall, as well-dressed as any of Kheron's most directly involved employees and distinguishable mainly by the thick, ropy scar that ran down one side of his face.

Sighing dully to himself, Kheron stood up, holding Leo under one arm, and strolled over to the window. The thick, smoggy, glistening city stretched away forever.

Just look at it, he thought to himself. And here he was, right on top of it. And even after tonight, he would be. Everything to ensure that was already in motion.

Still, that last little nagging doubt continued to encroach upon the edges of his reasoning. Everything was indeed going to hinge on tonight, and as gambits went, this would be the big one.

He turned away from the window and strolled over to the turntable. It played quietly through the rest of the song before he reached down and unplugged it. Then he set Leo down gently and carefully picked the machine up with both hands.

'I'll be in the saferoom,' he said to the guard at the side of the room. 'See that everything's dealt with.'

They moved as one. He led them. No turning back. No stopping them now.

Time to go. Time to hunt. Time to kill.

Khazahn seated himself behind his desk, shaking slightly as another coughing fit passed. Sighing and wheezing, he poured another glass of scotch.

This was it, then. No going back.

Still, he thought as he wrapped his fingers around his Guild staff, he wouldn't need to before long.

The intercom crackled to life. This was it.

Aleera navigated herself through the last in a series of barriers comprised of Guild soldiers, and found that the front of the briefing room was, at long last, in view.

Oddly enough, it wasn't quite like the last one she'd been in that very same day. That anticipation was still there, as was the anxiety that had accompanied it before, but there was something else there to mar it.

None of them, she realised, wanted to be there. Of course they didn't. No honest Guild soldier- provided, of course, that there were more than five- wanted to do a damn thing on behalf of Kheron.

And yet, they were about to. They would do it without objection, however much they might chide themselves for it. In the morning, they might tell themselves that it would make them better than Kheron, or that it was the right thing to do, or that they'd done it for the sake of the city.

And they'd keep on going through the motions, keeping up that façade of goodness.

So why, the question was thusly begged, was Aleera there? Discounting, of course, the fact that she didn't have much choice other than following orders if she wanted to have half a chance of getting out of there. She'd never exactly pretended to be good.

It was a chance to slice the wraiths to bits, she reminded herself. That dark hate inside her purred at the idea. Beneath her armour, the scars on her neck bristled.

But ultimately, she knew that she was there because she had to be there. The choice to be there or not be there was hers no longer.

The bastards, she thought to herself, they'd march her to her death if they had half a chance…

Stop it, she snapped at herself. Just get through this. Get through it, maybe slice a couple of wraiths to pieces, and then go home.

But why be here? She'd feel nothing for Kheron.

She had not felt, it dawned on her, anything for the others either. For the twenty-three people lying on mortuary slabs, their faces frozen in sick screams forever.

It was part of the job now, she reasoned. What would be the point in dwelling on it? It would make her less effective, if anything.

She didn't feel for any of the ones Azrael killed either, though, and she wasn't working for the Guild then.

She felt nothing for the wraiths she'd sliced open, whoever they had once been. She hadn't even thought about any of that, or about Rick Lawson.

She felt empty. She felt sick. She felt wrong.

And the dark thing inside sat in her heart and rumbled in glee, and made her want to cry and scream and…

Then the room fell silent as Hartwell, Khazahn and Jake stepped up to the front, and Aleera forced her insides to stop gnawing at her. At least then they didn't get mixed up into the rush that started to build inside her chest.

'People,' Khazahn started, stepping forward. It was easy to miss, but Aleera noticed it; the wavering in his voice, the tension on his face. 'We've had two weeks of this. For the last fortnight, we have been in the middle of a war that should have nothing to do with us. We've had our people attacked and killed. We've had bodies in the streets.'

He stepped further forward. 'Now it's time,' he announced, 'to stand up and say "enough is enough". They think that they can drag us down into the gutter with them. They think they can get the Guild of

Guardians mixed up in their own petty feuds. And this has gone on for too long.'

He began to walk slowly from side to side in front of the assembled soldiers. The collective gaze of the room turned to follow him, almost as if expecting that something in the path might change.

'This has been a bad case,' Khazahn announced gravely. 'We were blindsided by this.'

Blindsided, Aleera thought, or blindfolded?

'Some of you,' Khazahn went on, 'may have your doubts about what we're going to have to do tonight. But this is the job. This is what we have to do. The greater good. That's what we all committed ourselves to when we signed that dotted line.'

If they signed it by choice, Aleera thought darkly.

'And this is what makes us better than the things that have been out there for the past two weeks, murdering people in our city. Tonight, we do the right thing.'

"The right thing". So much to be inferred from that, so little time.

Helping Kheron, then, was meant to be the right thing? Because the good guys show mercy? Because killing is wrong?

In all fairness, though, she did have to give Khazahn credit. He'd never actually managed to sound like an after-school special before. But she knew, as much as Khazahn and Jake and anyone else, this wasn't the brave and noble hero turning around to save the villain from the fire so he would see the error of his ways. This was nothing but the gophers covering their own backsides, trying and failing to keep their own sense of authority and self-satisfaction afloat.

Nothing but dogs defending their master.

'Tonight,' Khazahn continued with, admittedly, a certain grandeur that Aleera couldn't quite recall seeing in him before, 'we draw the line. Tonight, we end this.'

It started slowly, rippling away through the mass of soldiers. Then the clapping swelled, becoming a thick, roaring applause that spread through the ranks.

Aleera's hands remained still, and she fixed her dark eyes on Khazahn.

He took a slow step back and wiped his brow. He wasn't even anxious anymore, she realised. There was no nervous twitchiness, so crushing apprehension. His face was vacant, stoic, like a convict being led to the noose. A man resigned to his fate.

A pretty speech, her detached little persona allowed her to note, motivating the ranks in preparation to carry out the criminal's dirty work. And they'd do it, and justify it to themselves, and then the day after that they'd be back to treating her like the sick little monster she was.

'Now,' Khazahn said as the wave of applause subsided, 'this is what we're going to do.'

The night became still. Thick banks of fog filled the sky and stretched over the city, blocking out everything except thin, faded shafts of moonlight.

The guard shook his head in dismay and lit up another cigarette, wishing he was at home. Damn and hell, he'd never agreed to this. He didn't agree to standing in some stinking back alley to square the debt.

One more week, Kheron had said, and they'd be square. The gambling debt would be off, and Kelly would never have to know how close he'd come to having to sell the ring. Just one more week, he told himself.

Then, a week away, he was standing in the cold, stinking air and shitting bricks because Kheron got off the phone with someone at the Guild and told them that those thing were coming.

Damn. He'd been in Pentagram when those things showed up. Been lucky enough to get out. He'd never agreed to this. Not to wraiths. Any time but this, nobody could pay him enough to be in the same room with something like that.

He'd seen those things, those damn bastard things. He'd seen what they did to people.

Something moved.

He turned and tightened his hand around the gun. The pile of garbage rustled again.

Something moved inside.

The stray dog sniffed its way out, then turned and trotted off up the alley. He and the other four guards in the alley looked nervously at each other with awkward laughs.

Christ, they were shitting themselves at every little thing that moved. This couldn't be over soon enough for-

It descended on him hard and fast, crushing him into the ground with a mad scream. He thrashed, punching and kicking as the thing forced him to the ground.

Somewhere, unregistered on the edge of his vision, the others fell, one screaming and begging and scraping at the ground as it was dragged towards the rotten flesh and scraggly clothes.

Then the hand clamped around his throat, and he screamed.

The scream went on for a long, loud time, mingling with the others into one fusing, nightmare chorus. When it ended, the stiff, frozen corpses fell without resistance, fingers still bent and mouths still wide open in mid-scream.

Loud screams. Loud noise. They'd have heard.

No matter, he thought. Let them hear. Let him know they were coming for him.

It was time now. No going back.

Time to kill.

29

Bang.

The guard felt his heart stop for a second. The insides of his chest jumped. There were nine more in the room, all armed to the teeth and more than capable enough in basic magic to know what they were doing.

And those dumbass bastard wraiths were just pounding on the front door. Idiots. They'd come through the door like cows into a slaughterhouse. All they'd have to do was put those sick freaks out of their misery.

One hand tightened around the silenced USP. The tips of the other's fingers danced with sparks of magic.

Bang.

The door shook this time.

It would be easy. Gun them down on the way through. They'd never even know what hit them.

So why this rotten feeling?

Bang.

Why did he still have that aching doubt in his gut? Those sickening nerves? Why did something feel so very not right?

Bang.

The door shook again. Dust fell from its hinges. Every pair of eyes in the room focused on that shaken, weakening barrier of wood that suddenly seemed so weak.

That feeling was still there. That fear.

What was it? What was this feeling creeping its way up his spine? What was wrong?

Bang.

And everything went dark.

His heart leapt up through his throat.

'Jesus- Oh, Mother of-'

Relax. Nothing to worry about. No big deal. Probably just a power cut. Yeah, that was it. A power cut at best. One of those things getting smart at worst.

No big deal. They were dead either way.

That feeling was still there.

Bang.

He heard a hinge fall from the door, hitting the floor with a "clang". The screws fell from the hinge and rolled slowly across the floor.

Bang.

The door fell.

Then there was the explosion of glass from the side, a great, smashing crescendo mixed with mad, howling scream.

The guards turned as one, shouting and screaming as the door burst inward in a shower of splinters and sawdust and howling, screaming monsters.

The room descended into mad, roaring screams as guns blazed, bullets and spells firing randomly in the midst of shots and shouts. Volleys of metal and coloured light sailed into the air, some hitting their targets, some vanishing, all ultimately useless.

The guards fell. Those who weren't ploughed into the ground kept firing. One wraith fell, black blood erupting from the side of its head. The few guards still standing were tackled to the ground, cold dead hands clamping onto their flesh.

The room was flooded with screams.

'Hold position.'

'For God's sake, they're-'

'Hound-One, hold position,' Khazahn's voice barked over the radio. 'Is that understood?'

Makian turned his eyes away from the windows. 'Understood.'

He didn't want to sit there and watch, Aleera noted. She honestly couldn't help but sympathise, albeit probably for different reasons.

She hazarded that Makian, unlike herself, didn't want to see such a waste of human (approximately) life. One of the advantages, or disadvantages depending on how one chose to examine it, of being considerably detached was that she didn't have to have sympathy getting in the way of more practical decisions. The men in that room, as far as she was concerned, had made their choice, and their presence during what was about to happen in there would only exacerbate matters. The whole thing would be much quicker and simpler with only one set of targets to worry about.

Besides, the third-eye spell had confirmed to her that at least one of the wraiths had been shot dead. They'd been softened up, so to speak, for them.

So why, then, did she have this rotten feeling gnawing away at her insides? This feeling that she shouldn't just be sitting here watching them die? Not a conscience, surely. She'd never even been entirely sure that she even had one, so she found it rather doubtful that it should choose this particular time to plague her so.

The Guild was willing to watch, she noted. They, the "good guys", were perfectly fine with the idea of sitting back, kicking off their shoes and watching the show, letting lives go needlessly for their own agenda, however just and noble they might think it to be.

At least she didn't claim to be good. That was the real kicker. They did things like letting those men die, like dragging her from her own life, and still claimed that they acted only for the greater good of all instead of just to cover their own backsides. Honestly, in some twisted way she could even somehow think she wasn't that much worse than them. Maybe even better. Her, better than them? A month ago, she might have thought the idea laughable.

The flashes of gunfire and flailing, desperate spells died down, the last of the fireworks in the inky darkness. Another window smashed, jagged sheets of glass falling and breaking apart in the air.

All became silent.

Everything stopped. The last shards fell in slow motion. Aleera felt her heart pound away against her ribs.

The third-eye made their forms clear. Ten shapes remaining, moving fluidly through the rooms. Separating. Searching. Hunting. And now, the Guild's prey had presented itself, split apart, made itself vulnerable.

Time to hunt.

No holding back now, she told herself. No restraint. No rigid Aleera code to be kept to. Back to the kill or be killed. And as much as it sickened her, she couldn't wait.

'Hunt to Hounds-One, Two,' Khazahn's fizzing voice said, 'move in.'

The order was followed quickly, efficiently, almost robotically. Those with the grappling guns fired, a whine of released gas the only sound to be heard before the ends attached themselves, thick metal claws holding the adhesive pads in place. Twelve attached, twelve to move over on them, and any with wings to clear the distance independently.

Aleera had honestly not been at all surprised to learn which group she was to be in.

Those to use the wires positioned their hands, as instructed, on the handle attached to the line. Aleera felt her wings slip out, folding neatly behind her. With it, of course, came the unpleasant sensation of foreign eyes fixing on her.

'Take a picture,' she told Cassidy. After checking that she could still feel the invisibility spell that was to keep the group hidden, she perched herself on the edge of the rooftop, and with a kick of her feet and a rush of air, launched herself toward the penthouse.

As she heard the static-afflicted message regarding the other group's progress from the penthouse's rooftop, it dawned on her that this flight had none of its usual freedom.

And... here... we... go.

The five wraiths left in the immediate area turned and snarled, moving as one to this new source of prey and being met with gleaming bolts of force from the remaining forces on the opposite rooftop. The cover fire proved effective as the wraiths ducked, screeching and snarling.

Now.

The nearest wraith lunged at her, biting and screaming. She spun to one side, letting the claws tear out and, just this once, she reminded herself, acceding to their cries for blood.

Here. Amuse yourselves.

The wraith's flesh tore before the flailing claws, its screams of pain bringing music to her ears. No calmness. No restraint. Kill it, or it would tear off the helmet and kill her. She brought the claws over in an arc, stabbing them into the wraith's head as it screamed, twisting them as the old, dried bone broke apart.

The door exploded inward, another black wave of soldiers pouring in through shouts and hurled spells. A wraith turned down through the air, and, with a cry of *'Blaish,'* struck of wall of solid air, bouncing off and rolling across the floor.

Right towards her.

Aleera didn't pause to think. Maybe she'd reason it to herself later that she didn't have time. She just thrust the claws downward through eye socket, nose and brain, then pulled them back out in strings of gore.

Oh God, the blood, blood, beautiful blood everywhere!

A wraith sailed over the swarm of soldiers, two more besides it, and then Aleera realised the mistake.

Oh, those *idiots!*

Overkill, pure and simple. There were only eleven wraiths left, but they were sending in thirty damned soldiers. Nobody clearly, had bothered to think that this might be too much.

The whole room was a mass of swirling, flailing black and randomly hurled spells. It was confusion. Chaos. Delirium. Far too many soldiers to possibly coordinate themselves.

The wraiths tore through the confused crowd, ripping off helmets before their owners even found out where they were coming from, the screams mingling with the wraiths' desperate howls.

One rose, screaming. There was a shout of '*FwaiyalShliahsh*' and a myriad of burning slashes formed on its body, sparks dancing as its skin was sliced open by a hundred red-hot blades of air.

The wraith fell. Daniel Cassidy's hand returned to his side as another soldier made the always-deadly mistake of giving him a pat on the back in the middle of a fight.

Everything was happening in slow motion for a second. The next wraith collided with Cassidy from behind, carrying him across the floor and bowling a clear path through the falling soldiers. Even as Cassidy thrashed and punched, the wraith, so desperate at the smell of fresh meat, tore off the helmet and reached down for his face.

The dead, decaying hands clamped onto exposed, living skin.

Aleera fixed her blood-red eyes on the wraith. Oh, Cassidy would hate her for this.

'*ThuraiShiahl!*' The wave erupted forward, a mass of solid, glowing air striking the wraith from one side, sending it falling in a shower of smashing bones.

Cassidy pushed himself up on one arm, silent and glaring something that Aleera, for all her detached reasoning, couldn't quite grasp.

And then it was back to the screaming chaos of the fight, and yet another wraith falling in a shower of its own blood. Four left in the room; four wraiths that sailed up on high, screaming for blood.

And somewhere, over the shouts and frantic spell-casting of the room, Jake Connolly said 'Right, This Has Gone On Long Enough.'

Jake thrust both palms towards the wraiths, holding them together, unarmoured and, frankly, of a presence that was much to the room's collective surprise. He said nothing. No incantation. But the stream of writhing colourless light that erupted from his hands spoke for itself. The column was easily a foot wide, with only the middle of its starting point in Jake's hands, and surrounding by snaking, wrist-thick bolts of light. It struck the first wraith, ploughing it back into the wall and a crater of bent wood and plaster. Than Jake turned and shouted what at least sounded like 'Duck.' Every soldier near the beam did so immediately, black cloaks falling as one as the beam turned, catching the next wraith and similarly blasting it away. Then Jake turned it up as a third monster descended upon him, the beam catching the howling thing and slamming it up and away into the ceiling. Finally, the fourth and last wraith in the room was struck, cutting a deep, jagged trench across the floor.

Then the beam shrank away into nothing, and the penthouse was left dark and thoroughly emaciated. The walls, ceiling and most of the floor was replaced with jagged, splintering piles of wood and the corpses of what looked like the entire wraith cabal. The last remnants of the spell flickered away in concentric rings around Jake's hands.

The room went silent. The only sound was the groaning of weakened wood and tinkling glass from a window that had, at some point, crossed the path of the beam.

'That,' Katya gushed, breaking the silence, 'was *fucking awesome!*'

Jake exhaled, leaning forward with his hands on his knees. Whatever he'd just done, it was some phenomenal magic. 'Haven't done that in a while,' he breathed. 'That all of them?'

Aleera thought. While she was impressed, that healthy detachment helped her see that she could still let the being-impressed part of her brain operate while the thinking side of her brain considered the reply. There'd been eleven wraiths, so: one dead before they got in, she'd killed two, Cassidy one, she'd blasted one off of him and was fairly sure the nearest soldier had dispatched it, and another had been shot out of the air at one point, so that was six before Jake's trick, add in the four he'd taken out, and... ten.

Ten out of eleven.

Then her eyes were drawn upwards, and she saw the flicker of movement at the top of the staircase. There it was. All alone. Blood to be spilled.

She shouldn't go. She'd killed two, she'd gotten what she wanted, so now...

Oh, to hell with it.

She spread her wings, launched herself towards the stairs and tore up, even as Jake shouted after her. By the time she reached the upstairs corridor, he was shouting something at her over the radio. She turned it off.

There. To her right. She tore in through the bathroom door, and...

And the wraith leapt at her, screaming and tearing and howling, grabbing only thick, padded armour. Aleera pulled back her head in mock surprise and brought the hard metal of the helmet smashing into its weakened face. As it fell back, the thing caught the mask, prying it off and falling back.

It looked up.

'*Nnnnnaaaaaoooo!*' It howled madly, 'you! You, you... you...'

Yes. Her. And it.

'It was you,' Aleera said levelly. She felt her blood begin to boil. Oh, here it was, here was the damned thing that...

The door burst open behind her. She didn't bother to turn around; she knew who it would be, and that he would have told all others to stay back in case things got out of hand.

Which, considering the feeling mounting in Aleera's chest, was entirely possible.

'You did it,' Aleera breathed, pulling down the edge of her collar and exposing the white marks on her neck. '*You!*'

'I didn't,' the wraith said, and Aleera realised that it was sobbing. It was... it was *scared*? 'You...' the wraith sobbed, 'so strong, so dark, so... what are you?' it wailed, 'What are you? *What will you be?*'

Kill it.

She could.

Look what it had done to her.

So kill it!

Yes!

Kill it! Strangle it! Burn it! Choke it! Kill it!

Then Jake's hand was on her shoulder, and all that melted away.

'Aleera,' Jake said gently, 'come on. It's over.'

'Not over,' the wraith sobbed, 'they're still there. Still not dead, still... after what they did...'

'Kheron,' Jake said. 'Is that right?'

The wraith wheezed, pulling itself up on the side of the bath. 'We thought,' it hacked, 'it was supposed to be simple. We were supposed to be doing the right thing. We bring Kheron down, we plant the goods and inform the Guild. Then... then he caught on,' it shook, snarling now, 'then he knew what we were doing!'

'What Khazahn was doing,' Aleera realised. 'It's you, isn't it?'

The wraith, on its knees, looked at her, empty hopelessness in its eyes. Aleera knelt down in front of it, claws down but still tense, just to be sure. 'Lathos,' she whispered, 'that's your name, isn't it?'

'We tried... tried to use the dark magic against him,' Lathos wheezed, 'tried to leave it with him, call in the Guild, take him down. Last chance, he said, last chance to do it. Not to tell anyone. The other one, the kid, he got out, Rick got out, but me- too late. He knew, and he made us use it. Not what we gave him, the real stuff, the strong stuff...'

'Kheron knew what Khazahn was up to,' Jake breathed, 'and that's what he did? Just got them consumed by it?'

'He tore out our souls,' the wraith shook, sobbing, 'so we said we'd tear out his. We'd tear down him and everything he had.' He took a long, ragged breath. 'Over now,' he wheezed, 'all over. All lost. Just left like this now...' he let himself fall back to the floor. 'Want it to go away,' he whimpered, and managed to point one already-dead finger to her claws. 'Please?'

Please? *Please?*

Aleera looked up at Jake. Her eyes were brown again.

It had said please.

Jake nodded slowly. 'Do it,' he said.

Aleera pushed herself up on her knees. She held one hand out, the claws pointing down, with another hand on top of it.

Something shone in Lathos' eyes.

Aleera brought the claws down. She felt them rupture its heart. She felt it stop instantly.

Lathos turned one empty eye up to her, and in a faint, breathless sigh, he said, 'thank you.'

Aleera pulled the claws out. Lathos lurched and shuddered. She knelt back down. There was no satisfaction to be found in it.

She stayed there in front of Lathos, and remained there as he died.

30

Everything seemed to slow down when Jake and Aleera returned to the front room. The rows of soldiers turned sharply to them.

'It's done,' Jake said before anyone could ask a single question. 'Get forensics down here, do a sweep and move the bodies out, and…' his voice trailed off as he turned and looked around the room. 'Where the hell is Kheron?'

The soldiers shifted uncomfortably. Nobody appeared to be all that excited to speak up. Jake's face quickly fell into one of urgent despair.

'There's a panic room upstairs,' Makian finally said from among the ranks, as clearly only someone who knew him would risk the anger of someone who'd just wiped out four wraiths with a single spell. 'The door's not locked, and Kheron isn't in it.'

Jake looked around the room. All he could do was slap his arms against his sides in a moment of frustration.

He wasn't there. He never had been. He'd figured out where the wraiths were and just left them the apartment as a red herring.

He'd let his own men get killed for nothing, Aleera thought, and then she saw the number of stretchers being carried into the room. 'How many people did we lose?' she asked.

'Four,' Makian said quietly. 'Four of us.'

For Guild soldiers dead, and for what? So that Kheron should sit there and give himself a pat on the back for being so creative? That filthy, stinking son of a bitch!

'So where is he?' Jake demanded. Again, nobody offered anything.

Think, Aleera told herself, where would he be?

Well, there was one place she could think of where he was likely to be found.

'Pentagram,' she thought out loud. 'Definitely.' And it was indeed definite: what better place could there be for him? He knew it like the back of his hand, he had an escape route ready, and it was an ideal place to wait while, if all went to plan, the wraiths were wiped out.

And, Aleera reminded herself disgustedly, all had indeed gone according to plan. They'd played right into his hands. Again.

And of course, they wouldn't arrest him, not even after all this. There would be no evidence to be found; the last possible shred of proof was now dead on the floor. His lawyer would point out that there was no warrant and he'd be off without a hitch.

And all of them, the wraiths, the many, many people who'd died by their hands, Rick Lawson and Lathos, they'd have died for nothing. And Khazahn would just grow ever more desperate, and…

Khazahn.

She gently nudged Jake in the side. 'What about Khazahn?' she hissed.

Jake's face froze in a moment of cold, realising shock. He pulled a cell phone from his pocket and dialled. No answer. He tuned his helmet radio and attempted to contact 'Hound-One?' Nothing but static.

Desperate, not long to live, and now with the one possible dividend of the entire sordid thing up in smoke.

'Jake?' Katya asked anxiously.

'We have to get to Pentagram,' Jake said hurriedly.

'I'm coming,' Aleera declared.

'No.'

'Jake, I'm coming,' Aleera said, more fiercely this time. No doubt about it, she would be there. Because, she remembered, Jake didn't know, and there was no time to tell him before he'd use the teleportation spell and be outside Pentagram in a heartbeat. Jake was one of the few people for whom she might feel some small semblance of sentiment, and it stood to reason that, if possible, she should at least try and mediate things.

'We don't have time for this,' Jake said.

'I'm coming, and that's it,' Aleera announced.

'Same,' Katya said, stepping up to him, 'and you don't have time to argue.'

Jake looked in frustration to each of them, and, knowing he'd lost, moved a hand down and shouted '*Appiras*!'

The air spun with that sick, lurching feeling, twisting and twirling as the world shot by in a blurred tornado. Then it stopped just as suddenly, everything falling and rising and twisting and turning over inside and outside itself, and it stopped with the force of a car crash.

Aleera felt herself strike the ground, everything still spinning in a mindless, random cacophony. Finally, it settled, and she picked herself up off the floor. Not Jake's best re-entry, but as she looked round, she saw that they were indeed there.

'Jake,' Katya gasped, kneeling down next to him as he winced and pushed himself up.

'I'm fine,' Jake said quickly, 'where's…'

'FwaiyalSheahm!'

There was the thick, heavy sound of a body hitting the floor. The world slowed down.

The doorman collapsed to the ground, the red-and-black pit in his chest gushing thick streams of red smoke as a trickle of blood leaked sideways out of his mouth.

Khazahn's hand, still smoking, moved back to his side. 'Jake,' he said off-guard, 'what are you doing here?' Then he looked down, his face white, at the body. 'This-' he said quickly, 'this isn't-'

Jake pulled the envelope out of his jacket pocket and held it in front of him. Khazahn turned even paler.

'I know,' he said. His voice, uncharacteristically quiet, filled the alley. 'And I know why you're here.'

For a long, slow moment, Khazahn stared at him. 'Don't,' he said, his voiced hushed to a whisper, 'please. Don't.'

'Khazahn,' Jake said levelly, 'what have you done?'

Khazahn held something in. 'What I had to,' he finally said. 'Just- just leave it, Jake. Forget this happened.'

'Did you kill Rick Lawson?' Jake asked.

Khazahn didn't look at him. 'You don't understand-'

'Did you kill him?' Jake shouted. The question echoed off the walls.

'I didn't want to,' Khazahn said quietly. 'But- he'd have talked. I know how that sounds, but he- I couldn't risk it. Not then. Not so close.'

'To what?' Jake demanded. 'It was to do with the wraiths, wasn't it? Dark magic smuggling.' Khazahn didn't answer. 'Is that it? Where the wraiths came from? Because that's what Lathos told us.'

Khazahn appeared to shiver.

'Yeah,' Jake said. 'He was one of them. Now he's dead, just like the others. They're dead. So are four soldiers.'

'This wasn't supposed to happen!' Khazahn barked. 'It was- it was supposed to be simple, is that what you wanted to hear? Or do you just want me to come right out and say that I failed? Completely?' Every word seemed to have its own echo. Now he was roaring at the very top of his lungs. 'We plant the goods on Kheron and call in the Guild. He goes down. Finally,' he bellowed, 'finally, after everything that sick, twisted bastard has done, he goes down!'

That was it, then, Aleera thought. Confession. Soon time for her part.

At least he'd admitted it, she couldn't quite help thinking. He at least admitted everything she'd heard from Kheron. He had his code, he had his morals, and then, as soon as they constrained him from something, he'd dropped them. The very moment he got desperate, the pantomime morality went out the window.

'Then it went wrong,' Khazahn said, quieter now, 'Kheron found out. So he took his retribution. Did what he did best,' he snarled, 'took what we did and turned it on its head.' He stared at the floor. 'He got Lathos and the rest of them consumed by that stuff.'

'The soldiers?'

Khazahn shook his head. 'Lathos and Lawson were the only ones involved,' he said. 'I told Lathos I'd help out his mother- she's in hospital. And Lawson… we took care of a demon kid who'd been harassing his girlfriend. All off the records. Then Lawson got scared,' he said, 'after what happened to Lathos, he said that he'd tell someone. Go to the High Council if he had to. I couldn't afford that,' he finally said.

'Why?' Jake asked darkly. 'Why'd you do it?'

'Last chance,' Khazahn said emptily, 'last chance to bring Kheron down.'

'"Last chance"?' Jake repeated. 'What "last chance"?'

'My last chance to make this right!' Khazahn shouted. 'We- we're supposed to be decent men! The good ones! And we just sit there, and let Kheron keep his penthouse and his club and his god-damned empire, and us? What the hell do we get out of doing what's right, compared to what he gets out of lying and stealing and killing?'

'And why now?' Jake shouted back, 'why now?'

Khazahn was about to reply, and then looked at Aleera. 'You haven't told him,' he said.

Well, here it was.

Jake turned to Aleera. 'Tell me what?'

'You didn't,' Khazahn said. 'I should've known,' he chuckled emptily.

'Tell me what?' Jake shouted.

'Six months,' Khazahn said hollowly. 'Cancer. Six months to go.'

Jake's face turned into something Aleera couldn't read. But what she could see in it was pain and confusion and hurt and the very, very deepest betrayal.

'What?' he asked emptily.

'I have six months at the outside,' Khazahn said hollowly, 'inoperable. Six months, and I'm supposed to go to the grave with Kheron still running my damn city, and just end things that way. Or six months to turn things around after all that time, and finally get him out.'

'And now?' Jake asked. 'What are you going to do now?'

'Now, I'm ending it,' Khazahn growled, 'I'm putting an end to it for good. To this. To him. If that means I go down, fine. I'd be dead a few months into the sentence anyway.'

'You thought you'd get away with this?' Jake demanded. 'This isn't like before, Khazahn! Before, you were scared or trapped or whatever, but this…'

'I was *desperate!*' Khazahn roared. 'Desperate! Are you happy now?' His voice quietened. 'What are you going to do now, Jake? Arrest me? Turn me in?'

'As opposed to what?' Jake asked.

'Let me go,' Khazahn said. 'I'm down to my last days as it is. No sense spending them in a cell. Let me go,' he said desperately, pleadingly, 'let me live out the last of it in peace.'

Jake breathed deep. He tensed.

'I can't do that,' he said.

'Yes you can,' Khazahn pleaded, 'Jake, just think of everything we've done. All the scum we've taken off the streets. How many of them have we taken down over the years? After everything we've been through together, can you really do it?'

'*Stop talking!*'

Jake stood still, shaking, his mind working over a hundred different outcomes, all in their own way unacceptable.

Khazahn fell silent. He looked down, then back up at Jake. 'Alright,' he finally said. Then he raised his hand, its end buzzing with sparks of magic. Jake reacted immediately, his own hand dancing bright red.

'Don't do this, Khazahn,' Jake warned, 'you know who'll win. It's over.'

'Can you really do it?' Khazahn asked, 'can you really turn me in? After everything? Can you do it?'

Jake looked at him. He gritted his teeth and, with deep, torn pain in his eyes, looked away. His hand moved down.

It wasn't Jake who said 'I can.'

Daniel Cassidy moved forward, thrust a hand forward and yelled *'ThuraiShiahl!'* Khazahn, in the very same second, ducked, rolled to one side and yelled *'Blaish!'* Cassidy's attack burst into shimmering particles against the shield, and Khazahn, quick as ever, thrust a hand forward and yelled *' 'FwaiyalSheahm!'* The burning, sparking bolt struck Cassidy's shoulder with a fizzing burn, a shower of sparks and a howl of pain, and the Sergeant fell to his knees.

Jake's reaction was immediate. He turned, thrust both hands down and yelled *'ThuraiShiahl!'* Pure, glimmering force struck Khazahn from the side; he keeled backwards over himself and hit the ground with a dull, final thud.

Jake moved his hand back to his side and closed his fist.

'You bastard,' Cassidy snarled, rising and moved achingly forward to Khazahn's prone body, 'you dirty son of a bitch…'

'Cassidy, that's enough!' Jake snapped. 'It's over.'

'What is this?' Cassidy demanded, 'what the fuck is going on around here?'

'It's over,' Jake said blankly. 'Take him in.' He walked away, glancing sideways at Khazahn's prone body.

'I'm sorry, Khazahn.'

31

If there was one thing Aleera had learned in her life, and would perhaps have done well to remember during the last few weeks, it was that actions had consequences. People made decisions, they acted on them, and then it was down to them, and only them, to deal with the consequences of those decisions and those actions. Nobody else was there to answer for them, no outward worldly balance of right and wrong, just the people who made choices, dealing with them and making the choice as right as they could.

Everything that had happened, had had consequences. The war had its consequences. What had happened to her, losing her friends to a madman those months ago now, had its consequences. And this, now, would have its consequences.

There were the immediate ramifications: the very fact that thirty-seven people had died. This one, even Khazahn had known, was inexcusable. Thirty-seven families had lost someone in those two weeks. It had been the absolute worst case the Guild had dealt with since the Secret War itself.

Aleera still felt fairly sure that Khazahn felt it the most. He genuinely didn't look the same man when he was escorted into the courtroom.

Of course, as surely as things had their consequences, such things as this could never simply end and be done with. Khazahn knew that, too, Aleera suspected, as he sat down and heard the list of charges. That had been the first surprise: the murder of Rick Lawson and the Pentagram doorman were the only charges left out.

Jake hadn't told them.

But Khazahn knew the consequences. He'd known them from the very beginning. He'd sat and listened calmly as the charges were read, and then he'd stood up and pleaded guilty. The trial, of course, was little more than a formality. It was a foregone conclusion, and the High Chancellor herself had rendered the verdict. Just as curiously as the small list of charges, Khazahn's condition had also somehow been leaked to the High Council, and in light of that and a not-inconsiderable number of years spent in loyal service, Khazahn was sentenced to only three years imprisonment, even if it was still technically a life sentence.

And so, there Khazahn sat, in the middle of the visiting hall. The guard had told him, rather surprisingly, that he had two visitors.

He arrived at the table and found a chessboard sitting in the middle.

'Remember back in college?' his visitor asked, 'you always were a challenge.'

Khazahn looked up. He'd have had to fight the urge to strangle him if not for the handcuffs.

'What do you want?' he asked venomously.

'Just a game,' Kheron smiled, sitting down oppositely, 'for old time's sake.' He gestured towards the board. 'Whites move first.'

Khazahn moved a piece. 'So how's business?' he asked bitingly.

'Slower than before,' Kheron replied as he made his own move, 'but I'm an optimist. I'm sure things will pick up, however much a bite was taken out of it. Just a bad time. We all have them.'

Khazahn moved a piece. 'I take it the Guild found no evidence to link you to anything.'

'Nothing that was still breathing,' Kheron said, moving a piece and then pausing as a thought crossed his mind. '*Do* wraiths breathe?'

'I'm not sure,' Khazahn said honestly. Another move.

'Still,' Kheron said. 'I do owe you great thanks. Splendid job you did with that problem.' He gleefully watched Khazahn's eyes darken. 'Come on,' he whispered, 'you've got to admire it. Just a little bit? I mean, just look at it,' he broke into a childish giggle, 'all your people, all those wraiths, and who comes out on top?' he grinned from ear to ear, 'and you know what the real kicker is? I didn't have to lift a damn finger!'

Khazahn glared at him. He said nothing in reply.

For the next few minutes, the only sound between them was that of the chess pieces moving and clicking against the chequered surface of the board. Click, click, click, click, click…

The time ticked by. The rows of taken pieces mounted on both sides.

'You know,' Kheron said as the game was nearing its end, 'I really am very sorry. The way this all turned out.'

'I doubt that,' Khazahn said flatly.

'No, really. You, old man, you always were…' Kheron made a move, 'my best enemy. And I suppose that's why I'm sitting here now,' he said, watching Khazahn move a piece, 'you were a worthy opponent, Khazahn. Very dedicated to the job, I have to say; never married, no kids. Still, a worthy opponent, without a word a lie. Know that.' Another move. 'That's why it was such a shame, really, when you broke the rules,' he sighed as Khazahn moved a piece.

The move Khazahn had just made was a gamble. His king was wide open.

'Just a shame you had to go and overstep things.' He moved his knight into position. Khazahn, right after, moved a Rook that had somehow evaded Kheron's attention.

'Of course, you realise,' Khazahn said, 'it's only a matter of time before Jake catches up with you.'

Kheron looked down and saw that his king was in check. He went to move it, only to find that the only option was to move into the path of a knight.

'Checkmate,' Khazahn said.

Kheron nodded slowly. Yes, there'd be no stopping Jake Connolly now. 'Good game,' he said, standing up and shaking Khazahn's hand.

There was nothing more to be said. Kheron stood up, turned and walked slowly away.

Khazahn sighed and leaned back in the chair. Having a feeling about who his next guess would be, he began rearranging the pieces.

'I thought it'd be you,' he said.

'Had to stop putting it off eventually,' Jake said as he took the adjacent seat. 'How are you?'

'As you might expect,' Khazahn replied. 'Chemotherapy starts next week. Everything's prepared,' he said without enthusiasm, 'even wrote letters to the families of those people.' Clearly he didn't intend to elaborate on the matter. 'How's Cassidy?'

'He's fine,' Jake said, 'although it'll be a few weeks before he's back from suspension.'

'He went too far,' Khazahn said quietly. 'I know the feeling.'

Jake folded the old coin over in his hands. 'People do that sometimes,' he said. 'When they do, all they can do is do their best to make it right. Face the consequences and do what they can.'

Aleera stepped out of Jake's office, which she'd been allowed to use for what she had learned was indeed among the most mind-numbing of tasks. Magic or no magic, being involved in an incident like the one two weeks ago incurred a considerable amount of paperwork. Still, it made a pleasant change from wraiths.

It was odd, really, the way she'd felt at the time of cutting those wraiths open, and not just Lathos. Less satisfying than she'd thought. Who was to tell, maybe there was a tiny bit of life left in the dark little hole that was Aleera's soul.

The day had been at least calmer; an oddly-tranquil Saturday a little over two weeks after the whole debacle. The High Council was apparently still up in arms, and the consequences of the entire thing were likely to be felt for some time to come. From the sound of things, the Eighth Division's future was more in doubt than ever.

Anyway, she was off-duty as of now, which left her the afternoon free. She had, after all, something to do that wasn't going to wait any longer. The choice was made.

Then, on the way out, the really strange thing happened. A young soldier, evidently in something of a hurry, jostled her on his way past. Just a knock by the elbow, nothing serious.

But then the familiar voice barked 'Lieutenant!'

Aleera looked round, even though the voice's owner clearly wasn't talking to her. The man who'd just so physically passed her, however, was identified as such by his shoulder plate.

'Sir?' The lieutenant asked.

Daniel Cassidy, of all people, stepped towards him. 'You just struck a fellow soldier, lieutenant,' he said. The soldier looked at him, quite obviously unsure of this particular piece of social protocol.

'Sir?' he asked dumbly.

'I believe you owe Private Maheste an apology,' Cassidy barked.

'Oh- oh,' the soldier stuttered, turning awkwardly to Aleera. 'Um, sorry. Uh, miss.'

'...That's fine,' Aleera said awkwardly. The soldier swallowed a particularly large lump in his throat, then moved along.

Cassidy nodded curtly to Aleera, then turned and walked off.

Hmm. Maybe some things do change.

'Gets hard sometimes,' Khazahn said. 'Doing the right thing.'

'Tell me about it,' Jake said. 'I guess we just need encouragement now and then. Maybe sometimes,' he said as he helped Khazahn finish setting up the chess pieces, 'people need to have their faith rewarded.'

'Hey,' Jasmine said as she opened the door to Aleera. 'What brings you here?'

'I was wondering if you were busy?' Aleera said.

'We did finish the project,' Jasmine said. That was true. It had even turned out to be an "A", about which Jasmine was ecstatic.

'I know,' Aleera said, 'like I said, if you're doing anything…'

'No,' Jasmine said, 'kinda bored, really. You?'

'Same,' Aleera replied, 'so I was thinking; maybe you'd feel like going to the movies?'

'You mean, like friends?' Jasmine asked.

'Well,' Aleera said, hands behind her back. She found herself fidgeting like a schoolgirl. Well, fair enough, she was one, but still. 'Unless…'

Jasmine seemed to try and stop herself from smiling. 'What movie?'

'Who cares?' Aleera smiled, 'they're all terrible.'

Jasmine's smile was the most beautiful she'd ever seen.

It was a little over a half-hour before Jake and Khazahn finished their chess game. Jake, pleading lateness for another engagement, had said he'd needed to leave. Among the conversation they'd dropped was the titbit that Hartwell, apparently, would be transferred to the position of Head of the Eighth Division.

'Jake,' Khazahn said as he was leaving, 'what about Kheron?'

'We'll get him,' Jake said with a half-smile.

'You really think so?'

'Guy can't run forever,' Jake replied. 'Trust me. It gets old before long.' His smile faltered.

'One more thing,' Khazahn said. 'What about… I mean… well, you might as well tell me. Who am I going to tell?'

Jake nodded in understanding. He slipped the old coin into his pocket.

'How long do you have?' he asked.

'Five and a half months.'

Jake blinked slowly. 'I'll tell you then,' he said.

'And in the meantime?'

'In the meantime,' Jake said simply, 'I think it's time I had a word with a friend about some plans.'

The walk out of the visiting hall seemed to be a lot longer than normal. The only thing that sped it up was that Katya was waiting on a bench outside.

'How is he?' she asked, standing up and following him.

Jake shook his head slowly. 'Dying,' he said simply. Katya sighed distantly and followed him out to the car park: big, empty and letting every word echo. She could find nothing to say on the way out. She even stopped herself from retching when, with Jake's half-hearted casting of *'Appiras'*, they were standing back in the apartment, the air settling around them.

'So,' Katya finally asked, 'we going out tonight?'

'Could do,' Jake said simply. He walked round, sat down on the sofa and picked up his Guild pass from the pile of clutter on the table, turning it over in his hand. He stood back up again, if only as a way to vent something.

'Jake,' Katya said quietly, 'this isn't your fault.'

Jake pocketed the coin. 'Did I do the right thing?' he asked rhetorically. 'Honestly? He-' he paced round the room in frustration, his knuckles white around the pass, 'he was my friend, and he was dying. *Dying!* And what did I do? I knocked him out and let them- *DAMN IT!!!*' he hurled the pass across the room, leaning on the back of the sofa and nearly crushing it as the projectile smashed through the front of the T.V. screen. Then he sank to the floor, his back against it, and rested his forehead in an open palm.

Katya walked round, sat next to him and put an arm round him.

'You know something, kitkat?' he said distantly, 'I'm five hundred years old, and right now...' he shook his head, 'I feel tired.'

And so, here she was, two weeks on, with only the faint marks on her neck to remember the experience by. The consequences would roll on, maybe there would be investigations, maybe arrests. Problems, perhaps. Insurmountable, hopefully not.

Still, here and now couldn't quite help feeling like a nice reprieve. Even for a Monday morning, it had been a good one. Aleera, of course, knew exactly why. It was nice, this whole "solid relationship" idea. She could easily see herself getting used to it. People still stared sometimes, and they got the odd dirty look, but the opinions of humans still never engrossed Aleera that much. Even if they both had the same sex organs, the little differences really did become a moot point when you were of a different mindset *and* species.

And work was better. After her first month, she'd received what actually turned out to be a passable pay check. Hard to complain on those grounds. She didn't even have an awful lot to do; she was still assigned to, essentially, follow Jake around.

Then her first real surprise came a week later when she found a note pinned to her locker before a class. Inside was a piece of paper covered in the epileptic-spider handwriting that could only belong to Jake Connolly.

Usual place. Lunch. –Jake

Of course, from the moment she read it, there was that apprehension mixed with sheer, wall-punching frustration. It had been a wise man that once said "no rest for the wicked", and apparently she still qualified.

Jake was under the stands in his usual place, passing the time by fiddling with that old coin.

'I didn't expect to see you here,' she said as she navigated her way through. 'Business?'

'Not really,' Jake said. He flipped the old coin over, caught it in one hand and pocketed it. 'How's the neck?'

'Fine,' Aleera said. The scar was quite faded already; now it was just another for her collection. 'So what brings you here?' At least he'd already said that it wasn't work.

'Kheron,' Jake said. The word, admittedly, caught her somewhat off-guard. 'I figured it was about time we did something about him.'

'Anything in particular?' Aleera asked. It wasn't a conversation she'd been expecting to have on such an outwardly normal day.

'Take him down,' Jake said. 'Legally, by the book, give him nothing he can use. I think it's been about long enough.'

True enough, but 'why the sudden whirlwind of activity?'

'It's been a thought-provoker,' Jake said, 'the last couple of weeks. So I'm telling you this, now, because I trust you. And that's also why I'm here to ask you something.'

'Ask me what?' Aleera asked.

'Well, the Guild seems to have made the decision anyway,' Jake shrugged, 'thought we'd make it official.'

'Make what official?' Even all Aleera's logic found it somewhat awkward to keep abreast of the matter without knowing what the matter was.

'Aleera,' Jake said, slowly and clearly and extending a hand, 'I'm asking if you will be,' he searched for the right word for a moment, 'my second. My protégé. I'll keep training you, you can still help out, and we just might get rid of Kheron for good.'

Aleera smiled. An offer she couldn't refuse. 'Deal.' She took the offered hand and shook it.

Kheron poured himself a glass of brandy, sat down, gave Leo a scratch behind the ears and listened to the record humming away in the background.

There was no denying that it really had been one hell of a fortnight. Things would pick up, as they always did, and he still maintained the disposition that the entire affair would be considerably more damaging to the Guild than to himself.

Of course, he would miss his old sparring partner. Those had been the halcyon days of their subtle conflict, their well-played game. And then, just as he'd had him backed into a corner, his worthy opponent had brought out one piece he should always have been prepared for, and now it would take something particularly clever to keep himself out of checkmate.

Oh, his best enemy had risked all, and it had been the ultimate sacrifice play, but it was still gratifying to know that there were schemes in the old dog yet.

So, Jake Connolly now. And with him, of course, would come Kudra's little pride and joy. Aleera would be a problem; no denying that. She was clever, though; maybe more so than Jake. And of course, unlike many others, she'd sent a wraith packing.

Yes, she would bear watching.

Kheron turned and looked out at the vast, shifting mass of New York, rolling, inky black dotted with twinkling lights, and raised a glass. 'To Khazahn,' he said, and took a drink.

That poor, foolish, clever old bastard.

The record carried on playing and eventually faded into silence.

DRACONIC TRANSLATIONS

A list of translations of the examples of the now-unspoken Draconic language used in this novel.

Draconic	English
Appiras	**Teleport**
Blaish	**Shell**
FwaiyalSheahm	**Burning Arrow**
FwaiyalShliahsh	**Burning Cut**
Hthwail-Yiens	**Third Eye**
PhoaLiah	**Pull Magic**
Sola	**Light**
Sheahm	**Arrow**
ThuraiShiahl	**Wave of Force (basic offensive spell)**
Whoahn	**Away**
WhualLiah	**Suppress Magic**
Yhiehl	**Unlock**

Aleera will return in

The Burning Kingdom

Book 3 of the *Aleera* series

Lightning Source UK Ltd.
Milton Keynes UK
10 September 2010

159700UK00001B/81/P